Frances Fyfield has spent much of her professional life practising as a criminal lawyer, work which has informed her highly acclaimed crime novels. She has been the recipient of both the Gold and Silver Crime Writers' Association Daggers. She is also a regular broadcaster on Radio 4, most recently as the presenter of the series 'Tales from the Stave'. She lives in London and in Deal, overlooking the sea which is her passion.

By Frances Fyfield

Helen West series
A Question of Guilt
Trial by Fire
Deep Sleep
Shadow Play
A Clear Conscience
Without Consent

Sarah Fortune series
Shadows on the Mirror
Perfectly Pure and Good
Staring at the Light
Looking Down
Safer Than Houses

Diana Porteous series
Gold Digger
Casting the First Stone
A Painted Smile

Other Fiction
The Playroom
Half Light
Let's Dance
Blind Date
Undercurrents
The Nature of the Beast
Seeking Sanctuary
The Art of Drowning
Blood From Stone
Cold to the Touch

THE ART OF DROWNING

FRANCES FYFIELD

sphere

SPHERE

First published in Great Britain in 2006 by Little, Brown
Paperback published in 2007 by Sphere
This reissue published in 2018 by Sphere

1 3 5 7 9 10 8 6 4 2

All characters and events in this publication, other than those clearly in the public domain, are fictitious and any resemblance to real persons, living or dead, is purely coincidental.

A CIP catalogue record for this book
is available from the British Library.

ISBN 978-0-7515-7371-8

Typeset in Plantin by M Rules
Printed and bound in Great Britain by
Clays Ltd, Elcograf S.p.A.

Papers used by Sphere are from well-managed forests
and other responsible sources.

Sphere
An imprint of
Little, Brown Book Group
Carmelite House
50 Victoria Embankment
London EC4Y 0DZ

An Hachette UK Company
www.hachette.co.uk

www.littlebrown.co.uk

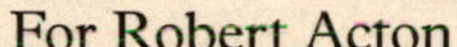

For Robert Acton

With thanks to Ken, for showing me a farm quite different from the one of my childhood, and the one in this book. All mistakes are my own.

Prologue

Someone wants to kill me.

It was the first time he had got this far, and he toyed with it in a thoughtful way, because he had reached this conclusion logically. Carl was always thoughtful. He only wrote something down when it was true. *SOMEONE WANTS TO KILL ME.*

He looked at the words he had typed on the screen, typed instead, *SOMEONE WISHES I WAS DEAD.* This did not have the same impact. *Wish* was different to *want.* Wishes were easier to misplace; they could be substituted by instance, by another wish, like saying to a child, you cannot have that sweet, but you can have this piece of chocolate instead. The more assertive words still sounded louder in the silence of his room. He made a correction.

SOMEBODY wants to kill me.

He shivered, typed in, *How do you know?* And then his own answer, *Perfectly obvious.* Then, *Why?* He sat back.

Because he could feel it. Because someone had invaded his

sacrosanct office space two miles from the safety of here, accessed his computer to send him the image which sat on his desk now in printed form. A black-and-white drawing of a hanged man on a gibbet, suspended over water with his feet kicking and his hands clawing at the rope round his neck, embellished with a crudely written caption, *Even the judge is judged.*

He knew someone wished him dead, because of that, because of the car and the rubbish. Because of the violence which was out there all the time, the formless desire to kill. None of that, not even the image, was nearly enough to threaten the composure of someone who lived as he did in an apartment overlooking the Thames at Canary Wharf. It defied logic to be afraid. He did not have enough money to attract pointless murder, or a sufficiently great profile to woo his own terrorist, no known affiliations to any cause or religion which excited extremes, nor enough power to excite envy. He was no more or less than an Englishman of mixed heritage who had done rather well. Not popular, yes, but that went with his territory. The weekly threats of the present and the recent past were all merely verbal and spontaneous, as harmless as shaking a fist at a passing train.

Somebody wants to kill me

He looked at the image of the hanged man, questioned it as if it could speak. Why do you want me dead, since there is nothing to survive me which is of any use to you? I have nothing to treasure except the son who does not resemble me, and once he is older, he will be free. Someone will profit from my premature death, but no one who would do this, and surely him least of all. Who wants me to feel this malice, creeping up from the river like a mist? I am not worth kidnap, let alone murder.

Who am I? he typed in, along with his own answer, *It doesn't matter.* And alongside that, *So, it's only a feeling that someone wishes you were dead? Only a feeling?*

Feelings are ephemeral. There are only passions. No one tried to push you under the train; it was crowded; we all pushed one another. There are thousands of blonde women in this city. You did not see her. Someone is playing jokes on you and your boy. You are maudlin and overimaginative because today is the tenth anniversary of your disgrace, and you are dreaming of what she would be like now.

Anniversaries have that effect.

So that was that, then. The past was past, the future what it would be, and the screen was full of the gobbledegook of legal text. He closed it down, and found the photographs long since scanned into the memory of the machine, etched into his own. He needed to dwell on them to gain perspective, to honour the dead, consult his conscience and be made humble. Mourn.

Ten years ago, and it felt like yesterday. Vivid snapshots, glowing with summer. The first one showed an aerial overview of the landscape, crisscrossed with narrow roads leading to distant huddles of buildings, which looked insignificant against the rest. There was one such huddle in the foreground, nearest to the pale patch which was the lake. The buildings seemed small and colourless against the vast expanse of gold-and-green fields, and the broad, dark bands of trees which littered the scene into the distance, the real landmarks. The lake was shrouded by trees on one side. A track led into these woods. The view encompassed miles, to where the land petered out into a blue line of sea at the top of the picture.

He went on to the next. This featured the lake itself, looking larger once in focus, the vehicles parked by the edge like tiny toys. A large piece of still water, reflecting the sun from a slate-grey surface, showing a spit of brown land protruding into the grey and another track leading away from it. The next shot was earthbound, taken from the edge of the lake, as if the camera had closed in. A lyrical picture of a hot summer day, with the trees on the far side reflecting vivid greens into the mirror of the water, through which four majestic swans – two adults followed by two cygnets – swam in a military line, leaving an elegant ripple in their combined wake. Grey summer willows encroached in the water, and a paler object drifted beneath, attached to the bank, blurred by sunlight and reflection.

The camera changed tack for the next shot, taken from behind the posse of men standing around the object, but leaving a clear view of the white body, sprawled on the bank, feet still in the water. Then a shot of the head and neck of a yellow-haired girl, beautiful in sleep, half-profile, with sandy eyebrows and soft down on her cheek, the calm loveliness of her marred only by the livid patches of red on her chin, the watery blood which had seeped from her nose into her mouth, staining her lips a deeper red, and the mark on her neck. Death by drowning had not otherwise disfigured her. She was still his daughter, before the brutality of a post-mortem changed her.

He had wanted to see how that was done, indeed, had wanted at the time to supervise it. He had wanted no one to touch his daughter's body but himself. If she was to be brutalised by the scalpel of some forensic surgeon, he wanted to be there, guiding his hand, making sure they did not play her false. But there is no property in a body; it belongs to no one.

He had no rights, and in the end he was glad he had not seen. Better not to know what was done. They had mended her nicely for her cremation and arranged her golden hair to hide the missing portion of skin they had excised from her neck. He had asked for this to be returned to him. Reluctantly, they had done so. He never told anyone about that. He kept it, like others keep a relic, a small piece of skin desiccated into hard brown leather, in a box, somewhere.

Carl played back the photographs to the beginning, pausing at the one of the swans in their regal progress, ignoring the body they sailed past. They were all dead now. Ten years ago he had been a good shot, even with such an old rifle. He turned away from the screen and wiped his eyes.

Then had nothing to do with *now* and anyone wanting him dead *now*, except to inflame his imagination and make him worry about the boy. The death of his ten-year-old daughter had been nothing but a freakish accident. The lake was not deep; she could move like an eel; the water had been her natural element as soon as she had learned to swim in the sea with her mother. Water babes, both of them. The problem had been that Cassie loved the water so much she would not come out, and her father could not make her obey orders from the bank. Nor could he have fetched her out, or even threatened it, because, to his deep and abiding chagrin, he could not swim.

The thought of this ridiculous omission in his otherwise comprehensive education made him ashamed, even now. Athletic on land, unable to swim, like any child of his striving back-street background, where any such knowledge was redundant. He had learned only to study, plus the other skills acquired on those summer days, such as the handling of a gun and the making of hay. There was something self-indulgent about immersing the body in water without any particular purpose. No one passed exams that way. But in the end it was this knack with the water and the love of it which gave them the power. It was the one thing she could do which he could not, and she flaunted it.

He looked out of the window, thinking what a terrible irony it was that he lived with this urban view of the water, and wondered why he had done it. Because it was desirable, good for the boy and therefore valuable. If someone wants me dead, all they would have to do is push me into deep water. I would sink like a stone and die. Maybe Cassie would want to watch me drown, as I watched her, poor brave child. Maybe it would be better to believe she had not died, but simply turned into another creature instead. That was what her mother believed.

The tyres of his car had been deflated whilst it had been parked in the underground car park overnight. Nothing stolen. There were empty, grubby envelopes bearing his address in his post box; the beggar outside in the street stuck out his dirty foot to trip him as he passed; he had been jostled by an old woman who glared at him as he pushed his way into the Tube; someone had searched through his rubbish and spread it on the floor. City life, that was all, not enough to amount to this sense of menace. Someone had yelled in his courtroom, 'You're dead, mate,' and he had merely smiled, because it was true. Death was an ongoing process, part of him dying with his first child, needing to live for the other.

And yet it was true. Somebody wanted him dead, or if not dead, suffering. His bones ached; that was how he knew. He could feel the eyes on him all the time, and that was how he knew. He could feel the knife in his chest, in his back, and the water closing over his head. That was how he knew.

There was a timid knock at the door of his apartment. He moved towards it without hurry, pausing to comb back his hair with his fingers. Then stopped abruptly. There was no reason to knock; there was a video screen to reveal any legitimate visitor, provided they pressed the bell, alienating security that he detested. Who the hell . . . The cleaner, the caretaker, the man about the car? There was a spyhole in the door; he was not going to stoop to looking through spyholes, so he opened the door, yelling '*Yes!*'

There was a pitter-patter of distant footsteps along the laminate floor of Level Five. The footsteps were light as mice and then grew silent.

A dead rat lay on the floor, so freshly dead there was bright blood in its nostrils.

He laughed with sheer relief.

He was not squeamish. He picked it up, as it was, shut the door behind him, marched across the floor, flung open the balcony door and hurled the rat overarm into the river beyond.

Judge not, he told himself, that you may not be judged.

He would have to do something, for the sake of his son, but the relief was enormous. He knew now who it was *not*.

Ivy would never, ever go anywhere near a rat.

His name was Joe, aged twenty-six. Worked in IT.

He had not really wanted to go for a drive to the sea, and had not even imagined the prospect of a swim in the dark after an evening in the pub, but the whole project was infectious. He was, after all, well and truly chilled out, buoyed up by night after night of good, loud company, and still illuminated by the entirely novel experience of five days in a farmhouse. Yup, that was him, city slicker living on a fucking *farm* for a week; wait till he told *them* at work. You bastards go snorkelling and deep-sea diving, he would tell them. I had a ball. Before this, he could scarcely manage a short cut across a park. Now he could walk for ever. The whole experience had worked better than he could ever have imagined. It had healed one of the rifts in his broken heart, and the ongoing welcome, the seductive sense of belonging, culminated in the last night. He really felt as if he belonged in that house, in the front room of this pub, with that family, and the girl who had walked out on him, cancelling the holiday for which this had been a last-minute substitution, would be jealous of that. Nothing like country air, and nothing as good as a real country pub. For a start, it was the men who ruled it. You could squeeze a girl's tit and put your hand up her skirt, no one minded and everyone laughed.

Joe's bags were packed, ready for the early start home in the morning. He was like that, considered a trifle anal about his clothes and personal possessions, always prepared, but for now he was no longer a man who merely read magazines about how to spend money, but an amusing devil, sitting in a pub with his new friends, drinking another, sneaking a spliff, and then someone suggested they drive to the sea for a swim. The sea was two horizons away, even if it was only a matter of miles. It had not featured in this glorious valley, and suddenly it seemed a great idea to include it. One last experience, hey? Another first, appropriate for this freakishly hot, humid early summer evening, a suddenly good adventure to cap all the others. The simplest things were best. He could not remember which of the group had made the suggestion, only that the word went round faster than a virus. Yeah, yeah, yeah, great: only take fifteen minutes on deserted back roads. And while he had been a wimp when confronted with horses and cows this week, as well as a bit of a weakling over a ten-mile walk, he knew he was a good swimmer, and this might be his chance to excel. He could do forty lengths in the pool near the office. All nannyish thoughts about swimming when pissed got shoved to the back of his mind. They'd helped him home before, these lads, earlier in the week, and anyway, he wasn't drunk, he was intoxicated on atmosphere, with the cosy, hot pub room and the pressure of that arm alongside his on the table and the smoky air full of other perfumes and laughter. He had walked the ten miles and his blisters had healed; he had ridden a horse and the ache of that humiliation had faded. The one thing he had not done was swim. The one thing he was any good at.

It seemed like a real crowd in the bar, full of sweaty armpits. Hot. Shiny, smiling faces. *Horses sweat, men perspire and ladies glow,* someone said. It was him who said it, and it made them laugh. Over the week he had certainly developed a talent to amuse. They didn't laugh at him; no way, only with him. He had been mothered and brothered and loved.

So, whoopee, transformed from an ordinary computer nerd into an amusing flirt and Action Man by the simple fact of a holiday, he found himself in a car, bumping down a track, with his companion giggling beside him and driving the thing at the same time. Never been skinny-dipping, my lovely, well, there's nothing like it. You said you were a good swimmer, didn't you? That I have to see. Yes, I could probably do a mile. And fast. All those things he used to do, and would do again, after this. Joe could see the headlights of the car behind theirs, good that the mob were tagging along, feeling utterly safe with this crowd. Yokels he would call them when he got back to London. He would poke fun at their thick, Kentish accents when he returned home and told the tales. The person at the wheel had strong brown arms, with light hair, tanned by the sun.

The bay was as promised, lit by moonlight, calmer than the lake he had merely glimpsed, and far more inviting. The warmth of the night and the calm of the sea were ripped by banshee yelling as the posse alighted and ran down on to the sand. He was not sure it was actually sand; it felt harsher than that, like ground shingle, but sweetly cool on the feet.

First one to the Point! See that bunch of rocks? Race you. See what kind of swimmer you are. Last one buys the drinks. First one gets a shag, later. You waiting for something, or do you want to give me a start?

He was waiting. He was suddenly scared, focusing on the rocks, spot-lit by the moon, listening to the smooth hiss of little waves, nibbling. A final shuffling-off of clothes, the lithe form next to him naked, the yelling of support, and all doubts vanished. He was going to be at the rocks first, he would, he would, he *would*. Someone overtook him on the way across the beach and crashed into the water first. Joe ran, following the track of foam-kicking heels. He would show them.

It was shockingly cold, until after a few strokes the memory of the first exhilaration of learning to swim came back with a force of delirious warmth and wonderful weightlessness. He was plump, but in here he was slim and forceful. He spat out the first, involuntary gulp of water, developed his best crawl stroke, deviated to the side of those teasing heels, revelling in the bracing salt, and swam furiously. It was not long before he had overtaken the first swimmer; in his mind's eye he could hear the amazement of all who followed that he had gone so far, so fast. Forty strokes crawl, forty breaststroke, forty on the side, keep the rocks in sight, he would win, and when he came back they would all know he was the winner.

When he looked up, the rocks had moved. Everyone else was far behind.

The lone figure moving out of the gentle waves, back on the sand, paused for a little while to view his progress. Then picked up Joe's clothes and went back to the car. The only car.

Oh Lord, look at him now, still ploughing out to those rocks. Only the current will have really and truly got him now, because it isn't a bay, it's a treacherous piece of coast, and you can swim for the Olympics and not have a chance of beating that, and the cold gets you sooner when you're pissed, and you were waiting for me to catch up. Only I didn't, having more sense than to go out of my depth here. So I'm going to drive your car back, with your bags already inside it, and tomorrow or the next day, since you told me so much about yourself, I reckon I've got time to put it outside your house in London.

You were a gift, Joe, an absolute gift. A sad git who was never going to be happy. A waste of space.

Murder by persuasion. You were the perfect practice, but I need more.

Rachel Doe's personal file, kept in her pocket organiser

I look back at myself and the person I was and I can't believe it. I was a vacuum, and nature abhors such a thing. I don't know how I evolved like that. Perhaps I'd had a slight breakdown, I just don't know. I don't know, either, how I evolved into what I was. I had tunnel vision, you see. If I succeeded in a conventional way, by which I mean being someone with a status in life approved of by the majority of the population; if I became, in other words, a professional woman of whom it could be said, 'She's done well,' and provided I achieved that through work, rather than cheating, I thought I would be proud of myself, and others of me. But it's all compromise. I never believed I could have it all; only those with a sense of entitlement can have that. To anyone else, the prospect is simply too bewildering. So it never occurred to me that I could have love and contentment as well as hard graft, to say nothing of fun. I was a drone from fifteen to thirty-one. I was my father's Thatcherite baby.

I had a partner of course, in my twenties, de rigueur. I fell in with him, and he with me, same ambitious attitudes, same ambitious firm, and we locked ourselves away together, he with his mortgage and me with mine, never quite trusting one another, never committing, too busy, just needing to keep the rest of you at bay. Couples don't need friends; couples don't necessarily know one another either. I never noticed how much he criticised me (I was used to that), or how prudish and shy he considered me, but I did notice when he upped the ante of his ambitions and started to steal. I blew the whistle on him, and then it was as if a bomb went off, and the fall-out came down like a nuclear cloud. At the end of that, I realised I was hardly anyone's most popular person, and also as ignorant of any world outside my own as if I had never glimpsed it; a philistine, a number-cruncher, living on an island of my own making. A stranger to real cruelty, suffering, privation or even lack of self-control. A person without a talent or inclination for self-analysis, a very shallow creature who had avoided all the lows, as well as the highs. A two-dimensional creature. Even my hormones had never bothered me. I knew my rights, and had always been granted them; I had never wanted for anything, since I had never really considered what I might want because I was too busy doing it. I had never looked sideways, or shied away from decisions which were clearly *right,* contemptuous of time-wasters, and now I had to look up, or down into an abyss. I had to learn to *look.* Timid and obstinate, he said. A bitch. Only one of these descriptions is true.

All my life I've been chivvied and criticised. I have a Pavlovian attitude to it, and, as I found, a completely over-the-top reaction of unutterable delight and gasping gratitude to its opposite. Protection and criticism were my parents' way of making me do better; criticism was my partner's way of making me look better and my employer's cultural method of making me achieve more. It was only as far as I was useful that I deserved to exist. No one had ever been curious about what else I might be good at, least of all myself, apart from doing sums and earning a living. I had no other skills to offer, no talents, and worst of all, in comparison to others, all my tragedies were pathetically small. More than anything, I was ashamed of that. I was never, ever going to betray anyone ever again. All my life I have knocked on the door of belonging, and found it locked.

I was unlocked by praise. I was knocked sideways by acceptance. I wanted to be passionate about the suffering of others, to understand it, to grow.

Wait a minute, I'm telling lies. I was naïve for my years; I wanted mother, sister, friend to fill the gap. I needed to *give.* I needed a mission to be not useful, but indispensable. I wanted to make life better for somebody. I wanted to be loved and trusted, and when I found it, it went straight to my head.

Love, the universal need, the most selfish ingredient in the mix. If only it had been lust, so much less complicated. At least with lust you think you know what you want. It's a poor imitation of the real, grateful thing.

I was wide, wide open. They could have spread my legs in the air and tickled my tummy, raped me alive or dead, and I still would have loved them.

Still do.

Chapter One

'It's lovely to be here,' Rachel said, sounding lame and rather overpolite to her own ears. It was a feature of herself, among many others, which she did not like. Her social awkwardness, which she reminded herself was hardly surprising in the circumstances, and she should not make it worse by dwelling on it. Or on any of her so-called faults for that matter. There was nothing wrong with her, except desperately wanting to make a good impression.

'It's so marvellous that you could come,' Grace Wiseman said. 'The pleasure's all ours. And you brought the fine weather with you. We're well and truly blessed.'

It was a formal welcome speech, but delivered at such breakneck speed and with such warmth that the sincerity was obvious. It occurred to Rachel to wonder what she should call Ivy's mother. Surely not Mrs Wiseman? Grace? Definitely Grace. Grace addressed most people as 'darling' and meant it. Grace was a name which suited her. Warm and gracious.

Grace Wiseman had been outrageously pleased to see them both, actually quivering with excitement and pleasure, beaming with joy and holding out her arms. Hugging Rachel into an embrace which smelled of baking and lavender, soap and polish, overlaid with pipe smoke, somehow exactly the mix of aromas belonging to a comfortable farmer's wife straight out of the pages of fiction. She was not apple-cheeked; she was as brown as a plump, sun-dried raisin. The embrace was strong; Grace looked far younger than her sixty-five years, possessed the strength of a man of fifty. She had grannyish spectacles parked on her head and a vigorous amount of bulk. There was precious little resemblance to her daughter, who seemed, when they stood together, a whole foot taller, cool and willowy, even in her trademark T-shirt, jeans and trainers. The smell of Grace, the scent of a provider, nurturer, cook and cleaner, went with the confident physique. She could just as easily have smelled of diesel fuel and emerged in dungarees with a spanner in one hand. Her bare brown arms were both soft and muscled. Then there were the other surprises, adding another dimension. Her cotton shift was brilliant green, her abundant hair was a startling shade of purple, and her wrists rattled with bracelets.

'She's every inch the farmer's wife and landlady,' Ivy had explained on the way from London. 'Only she never quite got over the hippy stage. Probably peaked in the 1960s just before I was born, and I wouldn't put it past her to dance naked in the moonlight, even now, but you'd certainly know if she did. If you want my mother, follow the noise.'

Rachel loved her. She thought she would have killed to have a mother like this. A housewife who baked bread and biscuits, washed and ironed, thrilled to visitors and the drudgery of cooking, and in the meantime tended a garden of flowers, vegetables and herbs whilst oozing sympathy and wisdom. Watch out for homilies and homemade wine, Ivy warned. They're her specialities.

'They have to augment the farm income,' she said. 'Ma thought of that long before anyone else. Long before Common Agricultural Policies, BSE and foot and mouth. She said, if you've got a big house, use it. Bed and breakfast, with ambience. Only she can change the ambience at a whim. It's been an artists' retreat, writers' retreat, partygoers' paradise. Actually, it's all her. She has to turn them away.'

'Won't I be taking a room that someone might have paid for?' Rachel asked.

'Don't be daft. Rooms are something we have, and she does insist on having weeks off, even in the height of summer.'

Hers was a pretty room under the eaves, adjacent to Ivy's and separated by a shared bathroom. It had a mellow wooden floor, a white rug for feet getting out of the warmth of the high bed, which was covered with a blue-and-white patchwork quilt. Fresh white towels on the iron frame of the bed, flowers in a vase and a jug of water on a folding table next to the bed.

'She's got the knack,' Ivy had said. 'She loves it.'

'And your father?' Rachel had asked anxiously.

'Couldn't give a shit. As long as he doesn't have to part with his animals or his privacy, he's as happy as one of his pigs. Turn right at the next junction.'

Ivy had chattered like a sparrow throughout the journey, surprising Rachel with the knowledge that she was actually nervous on both their accounts, anxious that Rachel should like what she would find at the other end, and that she, in turn, would make a good impression. As if Rachel's opinion was vital. It touched her. As the car lurched down the narrow track towards the farm, Rachel ceased to listen and lost herself in the novelty, finding it all as beautiful as it was mysterious. Hawthorne branches flicked against the windows, making her flinch; it was like going into a tunnel marking the boundary between one country and another, but then she had felt like this in the months of utter loneliness, last year, living in a dark tunnel, bursting into sunlight only after she had met Ivy, and now this glorious fuss and juvenile excitement of being *wanted.* No wonder she did not quite know how to behave. It was all too much, like a surfeit of love and caring.

Grace hugged her again, those big brown arms like delicate pillows. Rachel looked towards the attic window and the blur of sunshine and wanted to turn her head from the light.

'It's all too much, isn't it?' Grace said. 'We're all too much. I'm so sorry. You mustn't let us overwhelm you. But Ivy's talked about you so much, I really was, literally, dying to meet you. You've done her so much good. You're so welcome, you've no idea.'

Rachel stood, smiling idiotically.

Grace scrutinised the room and then made for the door. 'Come down for tea or whatever, whenever you're ready. I'd better get my big flat feet out of here and leave you to it. You can orientate yourself from this window, not like the paying guests. They never get beyond ground level.'

She came back and tweaked the curtain. 'Ivy'll be having her scout round the territory, like she will later as well, I expect. She's like a cat. She does that whenever she comes home, even if it's only for a couple of days. We can sometimes pin her down for a week at a time in the summer, when she stays on to help. She always has to check that things are the same. Fortunately, or unfortunately, they usually are. Right, I'm off to brew tea. Whenever you need me, just listen out. I'll be somewhere around, you'll always be able to hear where I am.'

She paused at the door and grinned. 'Do you know, there's one thing Ivy failed to mention about you, although she's told us an awful lot. Can't stop talking about you when she phones. She never said quite how beautiful you are. Sorry, that's rude of me, people must tell you that all the time.'

Then she was gone, in a jangle of bracelets.

Rachel could feel the lump in her throat. It was so *nice* to be here. An understated description of a feeling of intense pleasure to which she hoped she would never become accustomed. Exhausting. She tried to control it by analysing why she felt as high as a kite. You are so suspicious of happiness, John used to say. You even treat contentment with contempt. Like someone with a healthy flowering plant who keeps digging it up to see if the roots are still OK. What's wrong with you? You can't accept the good things in life. You don't even think they exist. She had believed everything he said, and it was only much later that she realised how little he had ever wanted to know her at all, and how small a person he had made her. And no, he had never told her she was beautiful to look at. He had simply implied there was good enough raw material to justify a makeover, and she must not blame him. It was she herself who made life so small.

It was *nice* to be here, she analysed, because it was a good place to be in which she would learn a little of a way of life so different from her own she may as well have travelled to Mars for the experience; and also, and more importantly, because no one had been so wonderfully pleased to see her since the second time she had met Ivy on her own, by prearrangement, outside of the classroom. On that occasion Ivy's face had lit with such pleasure and relief that Rachel had felt as if her own mere presence was a miracle. Oh, you've got here, Ivy had announced, with a sigh of rapturous relief. I can't tell you how good it is to see you. I was worried about you. I've been thinking about you.

Worried about me? Thinking about ME? No one had done that in a long time. It had been like music to the ears, as well as ironic. She was not the sort of person people worried about. Capable thirty-two-year-old accountants did not excite worry; if anyone in her civilised city world deserved worrying about, it was footloose, scatty, penniless, unstable and riotous Ivy, who was way too old at thirty-nine to live the squalid way she did. The other *nice* thing about being here, from Rachel's point of view, was to see that her anxious concern for Ivy might have been misguided. It was a little as if she had discovered that a seemingly poor friend was really rich. Ivy might have lived like a hobo in London, but she had to be as stable as a rock, because this was her parents' home, and she was rooted here.

In this house it was if the roots had risen to the surface and extended themselves, haphazardly, to form a shelter. The kitchen, once Rachel found it again, was a joy. A film-set kitchen, with an Aga, a huge, well-scrubbed pine table, flowers on one window ledge, an orderly row of herbs in pots on the other and a real ham hanging on a hook. All it lacked for theatrical perfection was an old dog to greet strangers with a wagging tail, and a cat curled in a basket by the stove. The heartbeat of the house, on a second look not quite so old-world conventional. There was plenty of stainless steel, too, and the walls, which might have been whitewashed, were tinted bright yellow. Homely, yet vivid also, like Grace herself.

'The thing is,' Grace was explaining while pouring tea from a surprisingly elegant china pot, 'the buildings on this so-called farm are the only blasted things about it which are really organic. It was all based round the needs of the animals, you see. Human beings took second place. So the first permanent things were animal shelters. The house comes second. First a house, then bits added to a house. I think we've redressed the balance towards human priorities, but I'm never quite sure. I doubt if the paying guests realise they live in the old pigsties.'

Rachel realised it would take her a while to get the measure of it, and then thought it didn't really matter if she did or she didn't. She must stop trying to control her environment by pinning it down into a map in her head. She just wanted to *be*. Happy. Ivy's descriptions had always concentrated on the land, rather than the house. Rachel felt it a disgrace in herself that she had never set foot on a real farm, except once to ask directions to somewhere else. Farming and the countryside was the stuff of myths and politics. It revealed her ignorance and innocence. She was secretly rather afraid of animals larger than a cat.

'Will you look at yourself, Ivy!' Grace bellowed as Ivy came ambling in through the open door. 'You're five minutes out of doors and you've already got mud on your shoes. Don't know how you find it. It hasn't rained in days.' She turned to Rachel. 'She was always like that, you know.'

Ivy grinned and bent to unlace her undoubtedly muddy shoes. Rachel could not remember ever seeing her wear anything else other than a variation on jeans and T-shirts, except for the first time they had met, when Ivy was wearing nothing at all. Even then her bare feet had been black with dust.

Ivy nudged the soiled training shoes away from the door and into an alcove next to it, containing a washing machine of industrial size and other footwear on the floor.

'Everything goes in there,' Grace mourned. 'Shoes, the lot. My darling husband thinks the washer's omnipotent, reckons it can clean boots too. He puts his in there, next to it, in hope. Where is he, by the way, Ivy? Did you find him?'

'With the piggies,' Ivy said. 'Says he's too shy to come in while he smells. And doesn't want me giving Rachel the tour of his fiefdom. He wants to do it himself, when all's clear and fresh in the morning, he says. What a spoilsport. He says it's his privilege.'

They are vying for my attention, Rachel thought. I like it. Grace pushed a plate of biscuits towards her. Somehow she had expected scones, but these were small and delicate almond wafers, perfect with strong tea. The bubble of happiness remained intact.

'So that's where you throw your clothes,' Grace said, nodding in the direction of the alcove. 'Some of the paying guests have such a strange notion of what people wear in the country. They bring the whole caboodle of waxed coats and things and don't seem to realise that all you need is a lot of old rags and a washing machine, since everything's dirty or wet most of the time. Ivy, love, if your dad's earmarked the livestock tour, why don't you show Rachel the rest while the sun's still out? Supper'll be a couple of hours. You could take a bottle of wine to the lake.

'Sure. It's mad to stay indoors.'

'What lake?'

'It's a pond, really,' Grace said.

A look passed between mother and daughter which Rachel could not decipher. She looked down at her own feet, and noted with satisfaction that her old, worn sandals had certainly not been bought for the occasion.

'You just want us out of the way,' Ivy said.

'I just want you out of the kitchen,' Grace said. 'It's far too soon for Rachel to see what goes into the food.'

'You didn't tell me about a lake,' Rachel said, as they walked down the hill. 'Can you swim in it?'

'Ah, yes. Your exercise of choice.'

It had seemed like an endless day, which was always on the point of beginning a new episode.

'Here, hold this, would you? Thanks.'

Ivy handed over the bottle of wine with cork perched precariously on the rim of the neck, making it look as if it was already tipsy itself, a creature with an undersized head held at an angle. She rummaged in her canvas bag for her cigarettes, lit one and then took back command of the bottle, with another, murmured thanks. It was what they both did, Rachel realised, Ivy and Grace. Never a demand, always a request. Would you? Could you possibly? And then, thanks: a recognition that whatever you had done was not taken for granted. The charm of that was infectious.

Ivy stopped at the curve of the track, and took a deep breath. She had her carpet bag of many colours over her shoulder, the bottle of homemade wine held between two fingers of her left hand, and was using her right to puff on the cigarette.

'I don't usually come down here,' she said. 'Grace must have wanted you to see. She's so manipulative. She hates things to be hidden.'

She had walked ahead by then, round the turn of the track, which seemed to Rachel to lead to nothing but trees, and then, on another turn, the water stretched below them, gleaming in the evening sun, a great, even stretch of lake, the shore they were approaching littered with shrubs, the far side flanked by dense woods. It shimmered calmly with reflected colour, the foliage mirrored in the water in shades of gold to olive to dense, hungry green against the further bank. It took Rachel's breath away. She simply followed Ivy's expert steps down the side of the overgrown track, right to the edge of the water. They were not entirely alone. Two skinny kids were stuffing towels into a bag, shivering as they left on foot. A swimming place should have attracted far more than these on a hot evening, but they were all.

'It's usually deserted,' Ivy said. 'There's no road to it, only a path.'

Rachel sat down suddenly. It felt like her own decision, but Ivy had sat first. Big bunches of hay grass, natural resting places close to the edge.

'Oh, Ivy,' Rachel whispered. 'Why would you keep quiet about this? This is heaven. I'd have come for this alone. Water magics me. Even a bath.'

'Like I said, I don't come here so much myself,' Ivy said.

She pulled out the cork from the bottle, produced the two glasses which had clinked together in her bag all the way here, balanced them on the tufty ground and poured. It was elderflower, described earlier by Grace as a thin thing with a mean punch, delicious if you wanted to drink the flavour of hay. Rachel sipped. From the woodland side of the lake four swans appeared, as if they had been waiting: two portentous adults, followed by two cygnets, sauntering across the lake, mirrored in it, in a regal procession.

'According to Irish legend, there was a king whose second wife was so jealous of his daughters that she used her powers to turn the girls into swans,' Ivy said. 'The spell was incomplete, as all spells are, so they were left with the ability to sing, and sing they did. The song enticed suitors and friends, and in the end the stepmother was killed, for her sins. I like that story. Only fucking swans don't sing. Not ever.'

She pulled on another cigarette, pointed again.

'See that one, over there? That's my girl. The most beautiful of the tribe. She can sing if she wants, I bet. I don't believe much, but I do believe that a girl can be turned into a swan. Like the daughters of Lir. I always wanted to be turned into a swan when I was a child. Shame it never happened.'

'There's nothing I wouldn't believe in a place like this,' Rachel said. She shuffled to sit close to Ivy. Their thighs touched, companionably. Shared warmth. From doubtful beginnings the wine grew better by the mouthful. The grass tickled her calves. Rachel felt as if she was floating free, suspended between the water and the sky.

'I suppose you shouldn't believe in myths and legends, except when tempted,' Ivy said. 'And you know me and temptation. Always give in.'

'Is that why you don't come here first when you come home? In case you succumb to the lure of legend? Big old bruiser like you?'

Ivy shook her head, violently. She had tough blonde hair which looked as if it had been hacked with scissors rather than styled. Hair which had been bleached and tinted, permed and ignored, and finally left to grow into a thatch.

'No. I don't avoid that. I leave it until last, because . . .'

'Because what?'

Rachel watched the white swans fading into the darkness of shadow. Ivy lit another of the hand-rolled cigarettes she kept in a battered tin.

'Because this was where my daughter drowned.'

The sun was sinking lower in the sky; the outline of the woods was blurred. Nothing was as silent as it seemed. There was a myriad of noises, the sound of water, the calling of birds over the trees, the slight, audible movement of the long grass. Rachel did not know if it was the beauty of the place, the sounds or the announcement which made her want to cry. She felt an absurd sense of disappointment, and hated herself for her own selfishness. Ivy plucked a grass and chewed the end.

'Sorry for springing that one on you. I know I told you about it. Child, *children,* marriage, death and breakdown. I just didn't tell you where it happened.'

'I thought she drowned in the sea.'

Ivy shook her head. 'No. Here. Yards from home. Don't let it poison the lake for you. You must come here and swim whenever you want. It's wonderfully safe now.' She touched Rachel's hand. 'I didn't tell you the details,' she went on, lightly, 'because, first of all, it's a lot to burden anyone with, and I thought I'd burdened you with enough.'

'You don't burden me,' Rachel said, equally lightly. 'You've brought colour and meaning into my otherwise monochrome existence and I want to know everything about you. I've told you everything about me. Knowing stuff isn't a burden, it's a privilege.'

'Do people ever tell one another everything?' Ivy said. '*Especially* if they love one another.'

Then, suddenly, she was laughing. 'There, I've said it. I love you. What an utterly scandalous state of affairs. What a fucking admission. Two straight women, crazy about one another. But seriously, dear, I didn't tell you all about Cassie, and how and where she died, because I can't trust myself to tell you the truth. I no longer know it, you see. So, if you really want to know, ask my mother.'

Rachel nodded.

'And then you can ask my father about the lake. There's quite a history. He'd love to tell it. They both love to talk. But for serious swimming, dearest, we get in your car and go to the sea.'

The swans disappeared into the deep shadow of the woods. Rachel wanted them to come back.

'They were so different, my two kids,' Ivy said. 'Cassie loved it here. My son hated it, probably in self-defence, but then he hated everything except his father, poor mite.'

'Was he here too? How did he react, oh, poor boy . . .'

'React? With the indifference of childhood, I hope. I really don't know for sure. I was absolutely out of it. Incapable of motherhood. Post-heroin fucked up for years, and then it was all too late.'

Her tone was still light. The air was still warm.

'All for the best, probably,' Ivy said, without rancour. 'He was better off without me. I don't much like men, especially young ones. Shall we amble home? I could eat a horse.'

She was always hungry. Rachel was torn between two tempting prospects, moving towards food with a belly so empty it wanted to crawl, and staying where they were. Hearing more, not wanting to ask, waiting to be led.

'Do we have to?'

Ivy was smiling. 'How many times do I have to tell you, Rachel Doe? You have to learn to do whatever you like and not hesitate about it. But I must warn you, my father likes to talk and can be a bit of a bore.'

'Wait,' Rachel said, 'until you meet mine.'

Chapter Two

Ernest Wiseman should have been a teacher. A long, lean, stooped but nimble old man, waiting to start his lecture. Younger than Grace, but looking older, in his owlish way, with his half-glasses perched on his nose. There was something about those two which made Rachel think they were still lovers. The way they touched, perhaps, or more aptly, the way Grace touched him in passing behind his back to the stove, quickly pressing his shoulder as if to let him know he was never forgotten, making him smile in acknowledgement. Maybe it was merely a code, an affectionate giving of signals, or just an expression of some sort of delight in one another. Maybe it was just the joy of the feeder and the being fed. The food, should Rachel have noticed it, was casually excellent. The outside light seemed to die, leaving them sweetly marooned around the anchor of the candlelit wooden table, full and contented, too lazy to move. It was quite appropriate for Farmer Wiseman to be called Ernest. He was, rather. There were just the three of them sitting round the table at the end of the meal, completely at ease. Ivy had gone to the pub: the invitation had been extended, but nobody else wanted to go.

'Ah, the lake,' Ernest said, squinting at Rachel with his sweet smile. 'You wanted to know about the lake. Well, when you and Ivy find a hilltop and look down, you'll see a landscape which looks as old as time. But it isn't that old. What you see is only what's emerged in this decade, never mind this century. Much further back than that, you'd have seen an estate, this farm and the next farm all serving a big house, with a river landscaped into a series of lakes as part of the grounds. No more house, only one farm, and a single lake in limbo. Recent history, too. My lifetime, anyway. It was the war changed it more than anything else, far more than the decay of a dynasty. There are half the trees there were.'

He crumbled a piece of cheese, picked up the crumbs with his forefinger and swallowed delicately. The cheese lay, waiting to be picked at, an invitation to linger where they were. It was a part of their hospitality, Rachel thought, not to rush food away from the table, but always to leave something there to nibble.

'Towards the end of the war,' Ernest said, 'there were more Germans here than English. Prisoners, you see. A camp built round the big house, which had been used as an army billet and came to serve as HQ for a prison settlement. You wouldn't have recognised the landscape then. Nissen huts and wire, although they hardly needed that. Where were they to go, poor sods? Not that people round here thought of them with pity. I was told when I was five that they were better fed than we were, and what with rationing, I could believe it. But then my father, who farmed this farm, got to like them. One or two, anyway, because they worked the land. We got more free labour then than ever since. And that was when you realised that while they weren't actually starving, they were always hungry. Well, the ones who worked here were.'

Grace coughed, and touched his arm. 'Rachel was asking about the lake.'

His hand hovered over the cheese, and took an apple instead. 'Oh, yes. Not much choice then. At the start of the war, before the family in the house gave it over to the army, or were forced to, the lake was a place for swans. All swans were once registered to the Crown you know. Preserved for beauty and for eating, latterly only for decoration. Fat chance of that in wartime. People roasted crows, for God's sake. So the swans went, German prisoners always suspect, but they didn't have guns, so it probably wasn't them. So the lake was empty, got fouled up and polluted. You need birds to keep a pond clean. Birds and fish. Both dead. And the water level rose.'

'Rose?' Rachel asked.

'Soldiers. Soldiers and guards, going into town – well, not much of a town, and only a village without a shop now, but a town with three pubs and *girls* then. As well as the sea for swimming. On the way back they'd pinch every bicycle in sight and dump it in the pond. A car, once, and God bless us, even a tractor, and both of those things like gold dust, as well as petrol. The river silted up. The thing became a stagnant pond.'

He bit into the apple.

'My father told me that farmers like him came to reckon they were better off with German prisoners of war than bloody soldiers. They did a deal less damage. And some of them really felt for the land. My dad said we were lucky to have them. Well, we were lucky with Carl, and he reckoned he was lucky with us.'

'Humph,' Grace snorted.

He touched her hand. 'That was later, sweetheart,' he said. 'That was Carl the younger. We weren't so lucky with him. Where was I? Oh, yes.'

He seemed to tire suddenly, then brightened. Rachel loved the way Grace listened to him so intently, when she must have heard this dozens of times before. This family had the habit of listening. Ivy listened as if every word counted; Rachel listened now.

'Carl was a German, from Berlin. It took a while after peace broke out before all these Germans could be got back, and Carl, who seemed old to me – I was only ten, but he was scarce more than twenty – found out that his whole family had died in the bombing. He was at home with us, billeted in the outhouse. We needed him; he stayed. And he made a start on the pond. He loved to work, that one.'

He finished the apple, including the core.

'I found him there one day, dragging a bike out. We made that lake a project, him and I. My dad used to say, fancy him caring, but he did. Said he wanted to see swans on it again. So there's the history of the lake. We owe its survival to a prisoner of war who left when he finished, fifty-five years ago. Shows you can honour what you don't own.'

'Did he ever come back? This . . . Carl?'

Grace stiffened. Then she moved and began to clear the table, surreptitiously. The place where Ivy had sat was comfortably empty, her absence as natural as her presence. They were well-mannered, without strict rules. Each evening would vary. Rachel hugged the thought that there would be more evenings like this, this time and the next. She knew there would be a next time.

'Oh yes, he came back. I don't think he ever wanted to go.

I know I didn't want him to: he was a sort of big brother to me, but I don't suppose there was any money or future for him here. He went to London, worked his balls off, married, had a son, and came back, in the summer usually, year after year. Haymaking, he loved making hay. Then he brought his son. We were his family, you see, or as close as it got. Summer holidays . . . it was always hot, wasn't it Grace?'

'When we were first married,' Grace said, 'child bride that I was, sharing a house with my in-laws, I used to resent this big, silent bloke and his son pitching up for two weeks at a time, and every other weekend. Especially the little boy. I resented the fact that my husband adored him, and they spoke a language all of their own. One does, at that age.'

'He wanted his son to know about things other than smog,' Ernest said. 'He wanted him to know about the land.'

'God knows what they wanted,' Grace said sharply.

She had been moving deftly between sink, stove and fridge, putting away, wiping down and organising with an almost deferential quietness. Rachel realised that she was not always noisy. Even with the bracelets, she could be as quiet as a fox. Ernest's head drooped.

Grace stood behind him, kneading his shoulders. 'To be continued,' she said, kissing the top of his head. 'Tomorrow is *always* another day.'

'Boring you, am I?' Ernest asked.

'No, no, quite the opposite,' Rachel said, truthfully.

'He doesn't need much encouragement really,' Grace said. 'You'll have much more of it in the morning. Time for bed, I think.'

He nodded agreement, rose, flexed his knees before leaving the room, his mellow voice drifting back. 'Good night, sleep tight . . . a good night.'

There was a comfortable silence after he left. Grace took his seat and sighed happily. 'Bugger me,' she said. 'There's a bit of wine left. That won't do, will it? We can't go to bed sober in case Ivy comes home pissed. Here . . .'

Bottles had appeared, wine had been drunk. Rachel did not know how much; she felt mellow. It crossed her mind to wonder if she was being nicely manipulated. No, that was the wrong word: manoeuvred, so that she was left without Ivy in the company of Ivy's parents together, and then her mother alone. If there had been an element of calculation about it, she certainly didn't mind. She was utterly charmed by both of them; she wanted to listen for hours. She was being trusted, that was all. Ivy really wanted her to know them, and it was a very flattering thought. It felt like midnight and was only half past ten. She wanted to be here on the longest day of the year and every day before it. She was excited by the thought of the morning.

'Well,' Grace said. 'This is nice. Not that I don't like the pub, but I'd rather have a person to myself. Must be my age. A little bit of deafness. I can only hear one person at a time. Ernest says it's deliberate. He says I must have deafened myself.'

In this light, she was pink and flushed. Definitely apple-cheeked in the way of a russet apple. Her strong fingers stroked the stem of her glass affectionately. A bottle a day keeps the doctor away, she had said earlier. Plus an apple.

'Do you talk to the paying guests?' Rachel asked impulsively. She thought it was a rude question. It sounded possessive, jealous, as if wanting to know if others were as welcome and as trusted as she felt herself.

'Oh yes, if they want. We only have one or two at a time. Some of them love to talk. Some of them want company, book dinner every night. Some of them are lonely and silly, and . . . oh, never mind. Some need introducing to the pub. Some want mothering. Talking at them makes them relax. It's the only way to get them to talk. If they don't like it, they can always run away. You can too, you know.'

Another question hung in the air, like a light shadow of the first. It said, are you a true friend of my wayward daughter? Can I trust you?

Rachel laughed. 'I love people who talk,' she said. 'And anyway, you don't fool me. You talk to make people talk. You got the whole story of my life out of me while we were making the salad. Ivy's the same. She could get blood out of a clam, and she talks nineteen to the dozen without ever missing a single thing anyone else says. I suppose it's an inherited talent.'

Grace grinned. 'You've rumbled us. Nope. It's entirely accidental. The result of curiosity. I'm not clever enough for anything else. I'm not like you. Not educated, apart from reading. Ivy'll mislead you. She blows my trumpet for me. She thinks I had commercial foresight to do what I did with this house and the old pigsties. It was nothing like that. I just wanted Ernest to go on doing what he does, and to have a home for Ivy.'

Rachel pushed away her wine. She wanted a clear head for the morning, but she did not want to move, either.

'Tell me about Carl the younger. And how Cassie drowned in the lake.'

'Whoah,' Grace said. 'Did Ivy give permission for this?'

'Yes. She's told me some of it.'

Grace lit a cigarette from the burning stump of a candle. The multicoloured wax clinging to the sides of the old Chianti bottle which held it bore tribute to the dozens of candles this one had supplanted. Grace breathed smoke through her nostrils like a dragon. Rachel was absolutely sure this was not what she talked about to the paying guests.

'Of course she must have told you. Carl the younger, son of Carl the pond-maker, was the man Ivy married. At seventeen, I ask you. He and his father came here first when he was a mite, and Ivy not even a twinkle in the eye. And then, in another twinkle of the eye, he was a teenage boy, and she was a little girl who adored him. And then, in another fucking twinkle of an eye he was a man a decade older than her, the bastard, coming back to lay claim. I wanted so much for her. She was destined for art school.'

'She got there in the end,' Rachel said.

Grace sat back, letting out an indignant whoomph. Then sat forward, bracelets jangling, noisy again.

'I wanted a wild child who wanted to experiment, like I did. You know, go native, take to art and everything. Not get bogged down far sooner than me, even. Not a pregnant teenager, with a child begotten behind a haystack by a man ten years older, and just as much of a control freak as his fucking father. I ask you. You still had to get married in those days. There's a hell of a difference between then and now. Anyway, he wanted it. That was what it was all about. It was part of his master plan. He was always clear about what he wanted. Establish a career; get a wife, in that order. Preferably one with a lineage he could prove. That's the German in him.'

She was holding the stem of her glass as if she wanted to crush it.

'And then they came back, with *their* children. He wanting for them what he had had as a child, and Ivy a mother of two before she was even twenty. Unbearable. But lovely for me, as well.'

Grace put out her cigarette in the spluttering wax, and looked at it critically.

'The boy and the girl, fifteen months apart. Chalk and cheese as they grew. Ivy, always wanting to bring them back, because she never really left. She wasn't grown up enough to leave. Never settled there. They fought like cat and dog, Ivy and Carl, over everything. Cassie was part of the game. Every inch her mother's wayward child. Ivy threw her in the sea when she was four. She simply started swimming.'

'She's certainly a city person now,' Rachel said.

Grace released the stem of her glass and waved her hand at the smoke.

'Oh, you are a lovely creature, for wanting to know.'

'She told me to ask you. I do want to know.'

'Tomorrow, if you still want. My sweet child, you're dead on your feet. We won't wait up for Ivy. You know what she's like.'

'Yes, I do. Night-owl Ivy. Works and plays all hours. Has to be independent and not questioned. Free agent. Blithe spirit.'

'Can you cope with that when she moves into your flat? All those jobs, all those funny hours?'

'No problem. I'll love it. We aren't in each other's pockets. She's taken some persuading, though.'

'You are the most wonderful girl,' Grace said. 'The most beautiful thing on the planet.'

She really wants them to know me, and me to know them, Rachel thought wonderingly as she splashed water on her face. I've never been treated like this. She would not have let her own contemporaries near her father. Tucked into her high bed, she thought of her London flat, as she might have done of some distant, grubby planet, to be congratulated for being so far away. I shall tell *them,* she told herself, thinking of the office where she worked, that I slept beneath the eaves and below the stars, and they will not believe me. I am mended by knowing Ivy and her kind.

Now, it really was silent. There was the selective deafness created by food and wine and then there was her own, delightful exhaustion from the doing of nothing much really, other than driving, being loved and cared for and the lake, and listening, and everything. And then a deafening sound from the tiny bathroom which was between her room and Ivy's room on the top floor. Water, gurgling away with a sound, in that silence, like the end of the world. *Whirrrup, bang shcush, gargle gargle spit.*

She got out of bed, lifted the latch on her bedroom door, and moved sideways over the half-landing. The door to the shared bathroom was open. Ivy was there, as Rachel had first seen her, naked as stone, bent from her slender waist over the basin. The taps gushed, noisily. The pipes gurgled, without rhythm. The room was whiter than white, the tiles white, the paint white, the bath white, white white, and the water flowing into the basin from Ivy's big, capable hands ran pink as she washed. The tufty blonde hair stood up in spikes. The face in the mirror was deathly pale. Ivy had seen her, gave a fleeting smile.

'Oh Christ. I forgot what a noise the plumbing makes. Sorry I'm so late. You been OK with Mother?'

'Your hands. You're bleeding.'

Ivy looked at her hands, then stretched towards the also white towels and began to wipe them dry, shaking her head.

'Me?' she said. 'No, it's not me. I'm not bleeding, just a bit bloody. Some car on the road hit a bird, and left it thrashing. Had to finish it off.'

She finished drying her hands. The towel remained white.

'Country life, honey. Road kill. Mercy killing. Had to be done. Sorry I woke you. Go back to bed.'

Rachel did as she was told, sleepy and reassured, leaving the door ajar. The latch was cold to the touch. She did not know how much later it was when she woke again into shivering consciousness. Footsteps on the stairs, the abrupt ending of screams, which dwindled away into muffled noises. Almost silence. Rachel did not know from where it had come, outside or inside, animal or human, only knew city sounds, stood by the door of her room, shivering and indecisive, listening to noises now minimal and human. She slipped round the open door and stood on the landing.

Light streamed from the room which was Ivy's. Through the half-open door, Rachel could see the shape of Grace, with her back turned, leaning over the bed in which Ivy was huddled and mumbling. Grace made hushing, soothing sounds with skilful ease. It was something they had done before.

'Only road kill, darling. You mustn't let it upset you.'

'No, Mummy, no. Mustn't.'

'There, there.'

'Can't do it. We've got to get him here. *Here*.'

'Yes, darling, yes, yes. Shhh.'

'Gotta get him here. So he can see. He's got to come here.'

'Bogey man dead, bang, bang,' Grace's voice teased softly. 'There, there.'

Rachel withdrew, as quietly as she could. The instinct for diplomatic self-effacement was always there. Eavesdropping was contemptible, her own father had told her. She was half in love with them all, and she wanted to belong; she knew nothing and wanted to know what it was like to be them. Silence fell, as if there had never been noise. All Rachel knew was that Ivy should not live alone.

You are coming to share my empty space, Ivy. I don't want to be your keeper. I just want to give you a base. I want to make things better for somebody, the way I never have.

Grace would like that. They were already allies.

The boy stood looking at the London river before going indoors. He was either a boy or a man, depending on the eye of the beholder. So what if the wing of the other car got smashed when he parked downstairs? The wall had come up and hit it; underground car parks confused him; it was a crap car. Not his; his father's. Everything was his father's. The damage to the other car would not be noticed for days – the owner rarely used it – but his father would notice because his father always did, and would, if necessary, own up on his behalf, like the bloody bully he was.

There were rats in the car park. He would say he was distracted by a rat. They came out at night, he would say, to and from the river at low tide.

He went back into the underground space, kicked some of the broken glass under the front wheel of the other car, then went up, via the steps, and stood by the door of home, feeling as if he was going back into prison. Sam. Nineteen. Scared of his dad, sneaking into his own home as if he was a thief. Well, that was how his dad made him feel. Own room, everything a student could want, DVD, mobile, laptop, so it made economic sense to live with Dad at Canary Wharf, even if it meant living with a tyrant. Key in the door, reminding himself to be up early enough to get to the post before his father, post never arrived now before ten, good, no problem, plenty of time to get rid of anything he didn't want him to see. The credit card bill, another of those whingeing letters . . . Why should he want to see her? She was the one who left.

Tiptoeing through the apartment to his own room, he could recall the last sodding lecture, word for word, *na na nanana* . . . Dad by the window, him by the door. *We're different generations, Sam, stands to reason we get on one another's nerves. Time you moved out, broke your own things and learned the value of them, instead of this ridiculously privileged and private way of life which exposes you to nothing.*

He mimicked himself in the bathroom mirror. There are rats in the underground garage, Dad, isn't that real enough? I'm not going anywhere, and *don't* give me that old lecture again. That old aren't-you-lucky theme. Brought up in peace and plenty, as if I'm supposed to do penance for that. Remember again that I can't take anything for granted, because you couldn't and your father couldn't. Why not, Dad? Why can't I take it for granted? Other people do. Isn't that progress? Why do I have to be so grateful all the time? For fuck's sake, you even expect me to be grateful for the generation I was born into. Well, I'm not. I didn't choose it, and I think it sucks. And I'm not moving out. Or do you just want me to go so you won't be blamed for something I've done? You want me to leave for my own safety? Get lost, that really is stupid.

He would turn his back so he could not see the expression on his father's face. The expression, or lack of it, anger, sadness or nothing, his best blank face, the face of an inscrutable judge, talking the way he talked in court, the old hypocrite. An echo of his dead grandfather's verdict, *Er ist richtiger Junge*. Or face him to hear him say, We all have issues, Sam. Don't you think it would help if you would . . .

No, he would say. No. Leave me alone. Why should I? Just all of you, leave me alone.

It's your fault I'm scared to go it alone. You've done too much.

Fuck you, Dad.

And then, getting into bed, Are you awake, Dad? I didn't mean it, Dad. I just go into one when I'm ashamed of myself – and scared.

We both need a bit of looking after sometimes, don't we, Dad?

Oh, and I heard this really good joke, I've got to tell you in the morning. Don't let me forget, you'll love it.

I wish you were awake.

I need to talk. You're not so bad when you laugh.

Chapter Three

Ivy Wiseman (her maiden name; Schneider when married) had three or four jobs on the go at any given time. She was also a very part-time student at the art college on a foundation course which had so far lasted five years. That's what saved me, she told Rachel. Going back to the beginning of something, that, and work. Who cares about the hours? There's still plenty left, and I don't want anyone else's money. I pay my own rent.

Somewhere in between a day shift, a modelling session and a night shift, Ivy arrived with her refugee bundle of belongings at Rachel's flat. She was not a stranger to it; she had stayed overnight, but this felt permanent. She had a single, but huge, bulging gingham bag of clothes and shoes, a folio case in pink plastic, a mobile phone, and that was all. Not much to show for my years, she laughed

On Tuesday evening Rachel faced her own father, who disapproved, as he would. He was a small, grey widower who came up once a month to check his daughter was all right.

Unless he could do something practical and useful, he liked to keep these visits brief, in case it looked as if he was interfering in her life. He was proud of his daughter, but constantly worried about her financial security, especially since she had changed her job. He suspected extravagance and held debt in horror. After two redundancies, prudence was his own personal God and anxiety his constant companion, which all served to make him awkward when sitting in her London flat, perched on the edge of the armchair as if afraid to sit back into it. Rachel's father never looked as if he belonged, and always seemed anxious to leave, as if the distance between himself and his own home, a mere commuter train ride away, was really a thousand miles and he needed to get back before his retreat into safety became impossible.

Rachel was still tingling from the sensations of the weekend before, anchored in her mind as being mainly sunshine, laughter, fascination and a longing to go back there as soon as possible, to somewhere which already felt like home. She had daydreamed through Monday, almost forgotten the meeting with her father and knew it showed. It was wrong to compare parents with other parents, but she could not avoid it. Ivy's were glamorous; her own was not.

'Everything all right, Dad?'

'Yes, yes, perfectly all right.'

'All right' was the height of his ambition. Anything better than 'OK' would alarm him. She could not admit to either happiness or sadness with him, nor he with her. Whenever Rachel met her father, she felt as if she was letting him down by failing to give him something to do. And failing to understand him. She loved him helplessly, worried for him, always expected it to be different, but it never was. He would never allow himself to be spoiled. Shall we go to a show, Dad? Eat Italian?

What for?

He would never ask for anything. He despised spongers, believed you should work yourself out of your own messes, never borrowing, lending or begging. His wife had been the centre of his universe, and their tiny house in Luton was a temple to the art of do-it-yourself, through which all love was expressed. The children of parents in love are often orphans. Rachel hated every brick of it.

They talked on parallel lines, the way they always did, with nothing much to say. She could hear Grace's full-bellied laughter echo in her mind, and wished that she and her father could hug one another like that.

'How are you really, Dad?'

'Mustn't complain.'

'What've you been doing?'

'Not a lot. What about you?'

The joys of London life left him cold; the wonders of Sky TV and shopping on eBay had a similar effect on her. Not much to say, really. At least, this time, she could tell him about the farm. That way they could postpone irritating each other, if it was not already too late. She looked at her watch. Time for class. He would respect that.

'I don't like you sharing this place,' he said. 'But I suppose it'll help with the mortgage. You don't want a freeloader.'

In his eyes, the world was full of freeloading thieves. People who promised security, and then took it away.

'No, Dad, it won't help with the mortgage. She's no money. Anyway, I was telling you about this brilliant weekend with her parents. They've got a farm, with a lake . . . well, the lake's not theirs, but it's there.'

'Oh good, they must be worth a bob or two then.'

Rachel gritted her teeth. 'Doesn't follow, Dad. Only if they sold it. Not otherwise.'

'Can't see you on a farm. Did they get you milking cows?'

'They get milked by machine.'

There was a glimmer of interest in that. He forgot to look at the time and finger the train timetable in his pocket along with his medications.

'Oh, do they now?'

'Yes. And it's all on computer. They each have a number round their neck. There was one that was blind, poor thing. They're probably going to have to get rid of that, because it won't calve. They all plod into this milking parlour, like they're on autopilot, and when you see how much milk they've got to get rid of, you can see why they're pleased to be there. The weight of it! Then they're plugged in. Three hours a time, it takes, every drop measured. Then they plod out, and go and eat more hay. Silage, mixed with stuff. Molasses. It smells wonderful. I couldn't believe how *technical* it is. The milking side of it, I mean. The rest is sweated labour. Moving tons of straw and food. They seem to eat their own weight, every day.'

Rachel did not mention that standing in the well of the milking parlour with the penned beasts surrounding her had almost made her sick. They stood level with her head, while Ernest demonstrated how the suckers he fixed to the teats of those enormous udders actually worked. They don't pull, or suck, see? They just exert a little pressure. He had made her put her finger into one; it squeezed, slightly. The atmosphere was thick with the smell of milk, shit and, most of all, the sweet, fetid breath of the beasts themselves as they looked at her with intense curiosity, and she tried not to shrink from their monstrous size.

They were huge, soft machines themselves, with sharp spines and helpless faces. They trod in their own faeces. They needed a barn as big as a church. They tried to ride each other when they were in heat. They were that stupid. And strangely, vulnerably lovely.

'I didn't see the pigs. I'll see them next time. I saw the fields. He grows grass for the cows, and he's giving up on growing wheat. Except it's useful if the hay runs out. He can cut the wheat when it's green, and add it to the silage.'

Too much information. Rachel's father adored technicalities; details of the construction of the barn and what it was made of would have kept him there, but enough was enough. He looked at his watch.

'I'd best be off. And you to your evening class, isn't it?'

'Oh, yes.'

'I've heard farms are dangerous places,' he said. 'You don't want to be going back.'

Don't rise to it. Rachel helped him into his coat. Always a coat, even in a heat wave. Always wearing too many clothes. The coat was the equivalent of a handbag, but he would never have carried a bag. His pockets jangled with his inhaler for chronic, controlled asthma, his tranquillisers, the acid stabilisers he took like sweets for his suspect ulcer; he had the illnesses of a worrier, the stoop of a labourer and a whole raft of prejudices. She looked round her flat as they left. What a colourless place it was. A good buy; he had approved of it. Her father turned at the door.

'You want to be careful about sharing this place, you know. It's difficult to get people out. You don't want to risk it.'

She felt an overwhelming rush of irritation then. Enough to make her want to shout at him. She wanted to scream because she could not make him happy, but all the same, like every other time, when she waved him goodbye and watched him descend into the bowels of the underground, she wanted to cry. He looked so small, so free of any enchantment.

I want to meet your friend, he said. You should have kept that man of yours, you need someone to look after you.

No, Rachel thought. It's the other way round. I am your child, a child of the Thatcher era, bred to succeed, to own property, to wed myself to a career and not look left or right. Exactly as my untrained, factory-working father, traumatised by two redundancies, wanted for me. The pride of prosperity, the solidity of a good, professional job, and the safety of a qualification. Master, not servant. And now he worries in case he got it all wrong. He's not the only one.

She was walking fast, aware that her step was light, and her face was turned to the sun. After the weekend at Midwinter Farm, she was always looking towards the sun, dreaming of it. The farm, and the promise of the farm, was only the last of a long line of gifts from Ivy.

London was sweaty inside, dry out. Looking out of the dusty window as the bus lumbered down Oxford Street, she reflected, not for the first time, that the London she inhabited was so very different from the one Ivy knew. Rachel's was high-rise, glass-fronted buildings, computer screens, takeover bids, carpeted floors, civilised meals out and microwaved meals indoors. She was highly focused, driven, the city just a place to work, admired from a taxi. Ivy's was sleazy bars for cheap booze, a series of more or less dirty jobs to fund survival and an art course which had run on for years, with her cash payments never quite enough, her homes a series of squats rising to the tiny basement room she had just relinquished, her employment status that of a reformed heroin addict, and her instincts those of the streetwise, homeless beggar she had also been. Ivy knew hostels for the dispossessed and the temperature of cold pavements. Washed up at thirty, that had been Ivy. Once upon a time, Rachel would have walked round her and left her there, if she had even noticed her.

Rachel walked into the Institute and nodded a greeting to the man on the door. She loved the contrast this place made with the tidiness of the rest of her existence. There were no uniforms, such as suits, no social code, no rules, no pretensions; you were whatever you wanted to be. No one noticed or cared; no one remembered your name or questioned why you were there, but simply accepted you were. She went down the corridor, through the swing doors which bore the scuff marks of a thousand kicking feet, into the alleyway, left past the lockers and into the studio where the life drawing class was held. Strange how quickly this anarchic place, so unlike a sanitised office, had become part of her life. It was gloriously scruffy, like her first, beloved primary school, and Rachel had always loved school. Perhaps that was why she breathed the musty air with pleasure and blinked in the bright, artificial light. It was hotter than a hospital ward, hotter than outside. Models without clothes needed heat. This was where Rachel had met Ivy.

'Hi. Warm in here, isn't it? Who do you think we'll get today?'

Somebody else was early, putting out chairs, teacher's pet. The only awkward student, the Plonker. Norman. The only one with a less than intellectual interest in the unclothed female form. You get them, Ivy said cheerfully. One weird man per dozen.

Rachel had gone to the life drawing class originally because it was available, because she had needed something radically different to do, and because she wanted to learn how to *look*. She had known she had been naïve; she wanted to learn how to observe. It was more than an attempt to fill a gap; it had a purpose. At the time she had been assiduous, organised, and utterly hollow. Her mother was three years dead, her lover of a decade had gone. She was an earmarked stranger in a new job where she was suspected, but no nervous breakdowns were allowed. You filled blank time and cried in private, that was what you did. You distracted your awful, inconvenient conscience by doing something which demanded total concentration, especially if it offered a warm room filled with other people on a cold winter night and the chance to learn something missing from a streamlined education. Besides, it was essentially pointless in career terms, and that, too, was deliberate. Every other course had *led* somewhere; this didn't and no one would judge her success or failure. It was a private process. She could justify the time by saying there were terrible gaps in her cultural knowledge; observation had never been a strong point. And then, after lesson three, she was hooked. Something about the science of drawing began to make sense. You had to learn with your eyes. The hand from wrist to fingertip is usually the same length as the face from chin to hairline. Only a small part of the head is the face, leave space for the rest. You must get the essentials on the page, otherwise you run out of space. LOOK. Measure, if you will. Feet are enormous, beautiful things, and hands are obscure; everything is curves and angles, nothing is straight. Her own hand began to move against her will. The models fascinated her, made her understand how much personality a human being could express without saying a word. How much we give away, express or withhold while simply staying still, without the disguise of clothes or speech.

The room was shrouded in a cloak of dust, with a paint-stained podium in the centre and a mess of plastic chairs and easels lying against the walls. The hum of bus traffic permeated through the frosted windows. The room bore the paint splashes and charcoal residues of countless experiments. There was a sink and a waste bin and a row of hooks, the accumulated rubbish of old work. The life model had a cubicle in the corner in which to change. From it, Ivy had emerged in all her glory. Week six, that was. Bolder than brass, fluid as water. Giving and grinning. A lined face, a thatch of hair, a long, lean body with pendulous breasts, giving off a great big heady cloud of life and the soles of her enormous feet already grey with dust from stepping across the room.

Four short poses, two long poses, and then there was an interval after an hour. Most models rested, sat in dressing gowns and chewed. Not Ivy. Ivy perambulated in a raggy T-shirt. Rachel was always anxious about the models. Were they warm enough? Were they treated with respect? Who would do this for a pittance an hour? It beats the shit out of waitressing, Ivy told her later, it helps pay for the course. It's not as good a rate as cleaning on the night shifts, though, but it's OK, it's fine.

Ivy used the interval time to swig tea and talk. So what do I look like, then? she said. You tell me, I don't know. She laughed with them, teased them, created chatter in a normally silent, serious group. Rachel had seen her out of the corner of her eye, pulling up alongside, stopping like a bus when someone has flagged it down. She had stood, and stared.

'Good God,' she said. 'I could be looking in a mirror. You've got me. You've really got me.'

I had, too, Rachel thought. I was having a good day and Ivy inspired me. I forgot my passion for detail, went for the broader strokes, made quick decisions. I was freed by *her*. Ivy had been standing in a classic pose half turned towards where Rachel sat, looking over her shoulder, one arm clasping her waist. Rachel had drawn a long, lithe animal, pausing before flight or fight. She had even sketched in the suggestion of a tail.

Ivy laughed, a gorgeous sound in the dusty room more used to murmurs and the forgotten hum of the road outside. Then she took Rachel's pencil and sketched in a pair of ears for herself.

'Could be a cat,' she said. 'Or a skunk. Anyway, it's me.' She bent towards Rachel, and whispered in her ear.

'Better than that idiot over there. Pity I was facing him. He goes to other classes too, and never gets further than my tits.'

Today, Rachel glanced across the room where the dust dazed and settled, and sharpened her pencils and thought of the moment when she had felt so flattered by a sense of achievement and Ivy's praise.

'I think you're the one person in the room who ought to persist,' Ivy said. 'You've really got me. No one else has. That means you've got a piece of me, for ever.'

At the end of the session Ivy waited, Rachel waited. They went out for a drink which turned into many. Laughed themselves sick. Arranged to meet again, and the rest was history. Rachel adjusted the sketchbook, propped it on the plastic easel, and opened it, turning the page back carefully. She could not resist being careful with paper, although in the intervening months she had become relatively careless with everything else. She was breaking the habits of a lifetime.

Waiting for the model to take the stand, Rachel found herself wondering what her father would have done if he had found himself with a daughter like Ivy. What it must have been like for Ivy's parents to stand by and watch while she drove her own life over a cliff, and then clawed her way back. They were proud of her. They had learned not to be overtly protective. They were right to be proud; Ivy had done braver things in her life than Rachel ever had. Dispelled demons Rachel had never had to acknowledge.

Emerged like sunshine on a rainy day. Generous and strong, still fighting.

'It was me who screwed up,' Ivy had said. 'And me who had to unscrew it. If I'd taken help, it wouldn't be the same. And I did have help. I always knew I could go home. Now I can. I'm thirty-nine. I'll get to the end of this blasted course, and then maybe even my son will want to know me.'

Five years on a foundation course which should have taken two. Ivy was an art school fixture, who haunted the place. Ivy was a cleaner. She cleaned offices and shops and theatres and clubs.

She did not look thirty-nine. She looked eighteen, apart from her older, wiser, watchful, mischievous face.

There would be no Ivy in this week's life drawing class, although she was a regular round several venues. The models varied in sex and age; they needed to see different bodies, different proportions in order to learn, but all the same, there had come to be a sense of communal disappointment when it was someone else's, because Ivy's spirit lifted them all. The man Rachel and Ivy called the Plonker, the one who attempted to confine his drawing to bosoms and genitals whenever the teacher was not watching, drew his chair nearer to Rachel's, so that she could almost smell his breath. There was always someone who wanted to be too close.

'I wish we could have Ivy all the time,' he whispered to her. 'She grows on you, you know. I do the Saturday class too. She followed me halfway home, you know. Think I'm in with a chance?'

Rachel ignored him and the peppermint smell of his breath, bent to the task. She was all fingers and thumbs today. Would Ivy be home later?

'We'll begin as usual with the quick poses. Three minutes only. Remember, get down the essentials.'

Today's model had coffee skin and a black scrotum, a yoga-honed body and a sense of mischief, using modelling as a form of exercise. Ivy could have trained him in attitude. You have to have a degree of confidence to do this, Ivy said. You have to *give* something. And you can play tricks when you're bored.

Slowly and deliberately, the model stood on his head, cradling his skull in his hands, everything pointing down, and held the position.

The class collapsed into giggles and then into howls of laughter.

I must tell Ivy, Rachel thought, Ivy would *love* this. Ivy would be home soon.

There were a fleet of them who descended on the building at eight o'clock. They gathered in the foyer, some arriving on foot, some waiting, some disgorged from a van with the supervisor who counted them in and counted them out and showed the newcomers where things were. All doors were open to them, all secrets revealed if they knew where to look. The aim was to be in and out as fast as possible and on to the next. There was the six-to-eight shift, the eight-to-ten, and the morning shifts. Most did either/or; some did all of them, committing themselves to a rolling timetable the week before. No show, no pay. There was an endless supply of them. There was the minimum opportunity for theft, and not much for camaraderie. Three people to each floor and a strict timetable. They advanced like tired foot soldiers. More like a herd of cattle, slow-footed and obedient.

The night cleaners had arrived.

They spread around the place like busy ants, fetching and carrying after the supervisor unlocked the cupboard doors. Machinery was released, rubber gloves donned. A large, grizzled black man joshed a bigger, broader Nigerian woman, under the gaze of an inscrutable Albanian. They were not a team, but they could behave as if they were. Jokes made the dirty business easier. A little revenge upon the inconsiderate was permitted, if not permissible. Curiosity about their environment was not a virtue and there was no time for it.

Most of them knew the building and went on to automatic pilot. They liked it for being relatively easy. Nothing old, nothing wooden, no areas which did not permit the ruthless application of short-cut chemicals, all done with a wipe. No hierarchy among them, no pecking order. Everyone had to do lavatories.

The woman with the scarf tied over her hair always hummed as she worked, inaudible over the whir of Hoovers and polishers. Polish on the shiny floors by the lifts could be an excuse for sabotage to anyone so inclined. Left half-done, someone might slip and break an ankle when he came out of the lift in the morning. Some of the people who worked here were no better than pigs. One of them littered the floor round his desk with the detritus of what he ate during the day. Chicken bones, soup, sticky crumbs, and his high-smelling spare shoes under the desk. Another left grubby gym kit over the back of his chair. The men who used the washrooms on this floor had very poor aim. Someone had wanked at his desk last week and dropped the tissues in the bin. Amazing what could be done in an open-plan office.

The floor spread, with its islands of desks, each accompanied by a pedestal drawer stand, easily shifted, for the tools of their trade and personal possessions. They could lock their little drawer in accordance with office policy, and they mostly did, but they could still leave traces of personality hanging like a cloud around their own little bit of space. The expression of a personality in its absence.

Here was a desk which deserved extra care. A nice tidy desk, with photos of children pinned to the barrier wall which separated it from the next, a well-watered flowering plant, and a box of sweets. No litter in the desk-side bin; a considerate desk. The cleaner cleaned the surfaces, and looked at the children. This woman had a top drawer full of household bills and divorce papers, poor cow.

The cleaner was on the wrong floor today. The next floor was off limits.

What did they do, all these punished people who worked in this silent place? A shelf of books at one end. Advertising, insurance, buying and selling, accounting, something, and who cared anyway? There was plenty of time for a quick worker to explore, but by eight thirty-five it was time to speed up. The supervisor was on his way upstairs, the lift whining, someone waiting to explain the bits they could not reach, the need for more equipment. Or things which needed special attention, such as a washroom flood. Not their problem.

The only problem on this floor was the man asleep at the last desk in the far corner, on the left. Out for the count. A big, fat, ugly brute, with a belly distending his shirt as he sprawled on a swivel chair, trousers mercifully zipped, head lolled into stillness, one arm resting on the desk, with his fingers next to a pint glass of water. Gone out for a drink or seven at five, slipped back into the building. Fallen asleep. His desk was sticky; he had fetched the water while he could stand, been sick in the bin, would wake with a raging thirst. All that was predictable.

The cleaner held the plastic container of clear bleach in one hand. It was the unnamed brand they used in the lavatories, more powerful than the milder antiseptic spray used for other surfaces. What they used on the stained porcelain was not available in the supermarket. Pure poison was quicker.

Pour out the water in the full glass, top it up with bleach, swirl it around a bit, and leave it for him. Easy. He was a loser. Revenge of a sort, could not be easier. Three minutes to go.

Then she saw that his cheeks, lined into grooves of exhaustion, were still wet with tears. Salt crusted his eyelids.

She drew back.

Not even for practice. No matter how miserable he was. It was too much like killing a dumb animal.

Do it anyway.

At eight thirty, the klaxon sounded in the Institute which housed the evening life class, and the model stepped down off the podium with relief. Reprimanded for the headstand joke, he had become subdued.

Unlike Norman, who sat next to Rachel. A sad-looking man, when she troubled to notice, always seeking attention. A fidget, when the model was male.

'Fancy a drink?' he asked her.

There were ten women and fifteen men in this class. Rachel reckoned the Plonker had probably asked the same question of all the women and certainly some of the models. He had the contagion of loneliness. She was sure her response was the same as all the others.

'No time, thanks. Got to rush.'

Then she was sorry for him. She knew about rejection. The sorrow had faded to anger by the time she reached the top of the road and waited to cross. It was still bright summer light, the evening crowds waning, settling in to their entertainments. She wanted to be home, and there he was behind, following her, waving. Then he was not pitiable; he was a nuisance. A lone figure in the playground of central London. Rachel began to run.

Her flat seemed ultra-quiet, as well as bland, when she reached it. On the bus she had longed for the sensation of going home and finding someone there. Once indoors, she went to the phone and called Ivy. Ivy wore her mobile in a pouch on a leather necklace at all times. Even when she stripped to model, it was the last thing she took off.

'Hi! Are you coming home?'

'In a while. Mopping up here. How was the class?'

'He stood on his head!'

'Good,' Ivy said, laughing with Grace's laugh. 'Good boy. Good, good, good. We're going to learn how to do that.'

Chapter Four

This was a complete waste of time, but never mind. No one knew quite what to do with him anyway. In his own view, the police service had always been excellent in the mismanagement of its human resources when it came to the proper use of age and experience. He was used to it and entirely resigned. It was years since he had wanted to be at the sharp end of anything, even a pin. Lost his bottle, see? Known for it, especially to himself. Detective Sergeant Donald Cousins, enthusiastic historian, was the perfect officer to manage paperwork rather than a riot. The pen-pushing man of non-action who liked a quiet life. He had the advantage of being unfazed by the officialdom which scared most of his contemporaries far more than a straight fight, and he was the ideal diplomatic candidate for something pointless going nowhere. Nursemaiding a judge, not even a quality judge elevated to the red robe and the trials of terrorists or murderers, simply a crown court judge who dealt with a daily diet of theft burglary and bodily harm. If the said Judge

Schneider thought he was going to qualify for protection, he had another think coming.

What irked Donald Cousins, albeit slightly, was the fact that if the judge had been anyone else, his nebulous complaints would receive no attention at all. It was simply not fair, but at least the judge did himself a favour by being embarrassed. The first thing he did was apologise.

'I'm sorry,' he was saying. 'I wouldn't have said anything on the basis of this kind of evidence, except that my son lives with me. Not an ideal state of affairs, but I worry about him. Do you have children, Mr Cousins?'

'Call me Donald, please, sir. Yes, two daughters. As grown up as they ever are. It does go on for a long time, my wife says.'

They both nodded, agreeing with each other. Parenthood was a great leveller.

'Not long enough, in my case,' the judge said.

Men could usually bond, or unbend a little, by mentioning their children, Donald thought, but there was no answering invitation from Judge Carl Schneider to use his Christian name. Cousins liked that: he did not mind what he was called, and preferred the anonymity of sir as a method of address to any member of the public, especially one who wore a wig. The term could easily be divorced from either endearment or respect.

'Sam's nineteen,' Judge Carl said. 'Not a particularly mature nineteen, I have to say. Public school since he was ten; now he's a student, living with me, and he doesn't know much about the real world. He's clever and lazy, and vulnerable. His mother left when he was small and I've overprotected him. Do we ever know if we're doing the right thing by our children? I don't.'

The judge was nervous, talking too much. Wanting to have

something in common. It established a working balance of power Donald liked. The man needed him and his approval, much more than the other way round.

'We do the best we know how at the time,' he said. 'That's all we can do. The awful thing is wanting to give them everything and not getting it right.'

Carl bent his head in acknowledgement. In the sunlight streaming through the window, Donald noticed how his hair was blond, laced with grey, in a cruelly selective process of ageing which made it look as if he had paid for streaks. Dark-haired, sallow-skinned himself, he found it slightly repellent. A woman would kill for hair like that.

There was no hurry to get on with the matter in hand; nor was this a bad place in which to waste time. They were in the judge's office, which surprised DS Cousins with its sheer, modern austerity. Minimalist. Where he would have expected old-fashioned tradition, plenty of old wood and leatherbound volumes, here were laminate floors and furniture contrived from pale wood and black metal. The reference library was behind the flat screen of the computer, rather than in venerable books. Cousins was disappointed by the lack of the wood-panelled tradition he had associated with the chambers of a barrister. There was no sense of history, or even comfort, a single framed photograph on the wall which looked as if it had been there for a long time, forgotten, rather than chosen. The man's home, from where he had collected him, was even worse. Not Cousins' taste, but then he knew, with his passion for history, that his own preferences were on the old-fashioned side. His daughters said so. His wife always teased him about it. The judge had caught his not so subtle examination of the scenery. It was a small room.

'I'm lucky to have this, since I went to the Bench. Space is at a premium. These days chambers have to be high tech. We look like any other office in the City. We could be peddling soap. Instead, we are merely people, peddling ourselves and our forensic skills. This room's my refuge, from court and home.'

'And the trouble started here?'

He tried to inject sympathy into his voice. So far he felt little.

'No. It was the slashed tyres at home, in the car park, which may have nothing to do with anything. The post going missing, the rubbish bags taken apart and examined. Perhaps I have it the wrong way round, now I come to think of it. There was some . . . interference here, which seems to have been confined to my room. I thought at first it was . . . internal. One of my colleagues, looking for something. Not theft, as such, simply interference; we don't lock doors. Someone wanting a bit of space. The use of a computer. Then I got the e-mails. A bit too erudite to ignore.'

Such a dry wit the judge had. He was drier than old bone, with his yellow-streaked hair. It was that and his expressionless face which made Cousins think not only of a hairdresser, but of someone who had been at the Botox, to redeem or improve his middle forties. As though he was so pampered with treatment, he could not afford to smile. The features of a sphinx, but then it would not do to have a judge who giggled. Maybe it was entirely natural: the youngest of Cousins' daughters, the beautician, would know more than he could guess. He himself knew only that in previous centuries the place in which he now was had been a stew of prostitutes who preserved their blonde locks by dyeing their hair in their own piss.

'I forwarded you the e-mails, didn't I?'

'Yes,' Cousins said. 'A mixed blessing, e-mails. I only know enough not to open any if I don't know who sent them, let alone open anything attached. You can't risk porn, viruses, that kind of thing. You surprise me. I would have thought . . .'

'But I *did* know who sent the first. The first was sent from *me* to *me*. As if to prove that whoever had done it could. I have this computer and the laptop at home, you see. Sometimes I work here after court; sometimes I work there. I e-mail unfinished business to myself. So I opened it.'

Cousins was appalled.

'But even supposing the sender of the first e-mail had got into your office here, how on earth could he log on to your computer? Don't you have passwords? Doesn't it turn itself off if you leave it at night? Surely there's a firewall?'

The judge looked shamefaced.

'Hmm, yes, there's *supposed* to be, but I'm not very good at that stuff. I forget the password and things, so I leave a note of it here,' he pointed to a worn Post-it, stuck to the desk, 'telling me how to do it. How to get in and out, my password, my e-mail address in case I don't remember.'

He seemed rather proud of the care he had taken.

'I see, *sir*,' Cousins said heavily. 'You leave yourself and anyone else a clear set of instructions which a child could understand, telling them how to access your confidential information and bypass the security system. Amazing. Isn't it a bit like leaving your house unlocked?'

He was enjoying a sense of superiority. Carl looked even more ashamed.

'It's simpler, you see,' he said. 'We lawyers aren't necessarily clever like that.'

You lawyers are stupid, Cousins thought, but didn't say.

Wait till he told them back in his own office what idiots barristers were. His supply of sympathy shrank even further, but telling others would be fun.

'What did the e-mail say, *sir*?'

'You know. *Please see attached.* The same as what I say to myself when I e-mail myself with, say, a judgment. It was a drawing, of a hanged man.' He swallowed. 'The next was of a man drowning. About to drown. He's tied up and being pushed over the side of a boat.'

'And the next?'

'A boy, drowning. And the next was a girl, chained by the neck, laid on a slab, overlaid with wooden planks and big stones. They were not from me, to me. I don't know where they came from.'

'Messages?'

'Nothing specific. *I want justice. You must die.* Then, *You* will *die.* Almost as if I had failed to co-operate. Or the sender was puzzled. Very crude drawings.'

Cousins coughed. 'You think so, sir? Do you know what they are?'

'Crude little drawings.'

Cousins did not know why he was suddenly so disappointed. Had the man, a judge, for God's sake, never studied the history of his own profession? Or looked at the illustrations of his forebears?

'I think you'll find, sir, that they are all illustrations of the Inquisition, I believe. Or maybe even trial by ordeal. The precursors of the modern trial. You can get such things out of a book or on a website. They were a matter of record, then, sir. This one,' he pointed to the third, 'is a woodcut, produced all over Europe.' He coughed politely. 'From Germany, I believe. A favourite method of the Inquisitors, in order to extract the truth, was to weight a body down with stones until it literally burst. Little, yes. Crude, no. They were the record of what the Inquisitors did, in secret. Protests. They regarded the confession as the last word in truth, however it was obtained. Some say the modern method of trial is no better.'

A hint of mutual dislike was percolating between them now; no way to know how far it would go, until the judge smiled.

'Tell me,' he said. 'My fascination with the law began with my father's fascination with Nuremberg. Didn't trial by ordeal pre-date the inquisitorial method? Even less reliable, but still avoiding the inconvenience of the jury, invented, or at least established I think, by the English?'

Donald noticed that the picture on the wall was of swans. An old, tired photograph. 'Someone is sending you old illustrations, sir. A well-wisher, perhaps.'

When he came to think of it, Carl looked more like a farmer than a scholar. A man who lived in a series of solid bubbles, moving from courtroom to chambers to apartment without his feet ever touching the ground. He would be very difficult to get at.

'I suppose, with the messages, it amounts to threats to kill, although they're usually more specific. I'm looking ahead, sir, to the matter of proof. Of intent. Have any of your colleagues received any of these?'

'I presume not. They would have complained if they had, and they haven't as far as I know.'

'And they stopped when you changed your e-mail address?'

'I didn't change it. It's far too much of a nuisance. Besides, I want to know what's being sent. I haven't received one for a week.'

Give me patience, Cousins sighed. 'Who do you think dislikes you enough to do this?'

'I don't know. Judges aren't popular people.'

'Anyone you're afraid of?'

Carl paused to straighten the framed photo on the wall, spoke in a judge's voice, which reminded Donald of a lecturing priest.

'Mr Cousins, we all have people we would prefer not to meet. People who dislike us for what we are, or for real or imagined injuries. Especially a judge in a court of law, and also, if I may suggest it, a policeman. In a court, some might imagine it is I who convict them, whereas it is not. It's the jury. Others might also blame the judge for the failure to convict, which leaves them without redress or revenge. I do know a little history, although not as much as you. I know, for instance, that the word *miasma* once referred to the vapour exuded by murderers, but which also attaches itself to the one who fails to avenge the death, and poisons his life for ever. It exists, today, that obligation, in cultures older than ours, and it certainly still exists with us. So I am quite sure I am blamed and disliked for appearing to fail to punish, for failing to be that instrument of revenge in the event of acquittal. The defendant who goes to prison from my court, on the other hand, is usually prepared and ready. Since I've never had the onerous privilege of sentencing anyone to death, I suspect the real anger comes from the first category.'

Donald forced himself back into pragmatic police mode. Abandon *miasma*, although he did like the word. Only investigate the obvious. He could not investigate the obscure, however long he wanted this job to last. So, those disgruntled by a negative result were an impossible line of enquiry, unless they had announced themselves first. What he could and would do was waste time going through the records to find any of the judge's old defendants who had made known their displeasure at their treatment and check them out. Isolating those still aggrieved, still aggressive, taking it personally, and who also had historical illustrations to hand as well as the means to send them, should keep the number small. Forget the slashed tyres. Look at the son, obfuscate the report to invite conspiracies, avoid the conclusion that the judge had colleagues who played tricks on him. He could make it last weeks. Good.

'What worries me,' the judge said, 'is the order of things. Someone invaded this room here, and thus found out where I live. This room is more important than home. I keep my private life here, albeit very carelessly, as you've pointed out.'

At least he admitted it. Donald wanted to say he was criminally careless, but refrained.

'Any personal enemies, sir? Family, perhaps?'

Carl shook his head. 'There are none of those left, Donald. Few enough to begin with. My parents were both orphans of war, no uncles or aunts. There's only my son, who studies economics, so he knows it's hardly in his interests to do me harm.'

Cold, but interesting. Give him the usual spiel. 'You should vary your route to work, sir. How do you usually go?'

The judge was surprised. 'I walk. How else do I see the world?'

Oh, shit. He was beginning to like the bloke. There were worse ways to waste time.

Must get a look at the son.

Ivy had the chance of weekend work. Good money. Well-paid life modelling on Saturday, followed by a theatre shift.

Look, I can't go home this weekend. Got to settle in, got sixteen hours' paid work, can't do it. Got to work, got to pay for myself, got to study. Go yourself. Mother will love it, Ivy said. Mother phoned, and Mother did. Rachel could not resist.

So there she was, proceeding down the dappled lane to the house she already loved better than the farm. There would be paying guests in the pigsties, she had been told, the private kind who stay in their rooms and go to the pub to eat. Dead easy. Walkers, twitchers. I'll have time. Ernest will have time to show you the pigs. How lovely to have you back, by yourself. We'll go shopping. We'll go to the sea.

It was ridiculous, Rachel thought, to be so happy with all three of them. I don't care if it doesn't last.

The air was musky. It was nine in the evening, still light at that time of the year when light seemed endless and summer was going to last for ever. Rachel shivered. She detoured up a side road, in pursuit of a view. This time last year she would never have detoured at all. She would have gone straight to her destination, criticising her own navigation. Following her instincts, she found Pointed Hill, a mile away from the farm, with a view of the flatter land. From the top, where the wind gusted warm and strong, she orientated herself and looked. There was the valley; there was the narrow road going through it, meandering to the village, which was nothing but a smattering of houses, a church and the pub; there was the other, shaded track which led to the farm, and there was the faint glimmer of the lake shrouded in trees. A bright red car chugged towards the village, as if seeking the company of other, parked cars. Instead of looking down, she looked across, and was surprised to spy, in the distance, separated by further dips and hollows and fields of wheat, the sea, stretched in a blue line. A full stop, where the land ran out. It only surprised her because, from the shelter of the valley, the land seemed endless and limitless. In the middle distance she could see a deserted air strip, unattached by any road, and closer to the edge of the valley, a site of low, derelict buildings, surrounded by green. How different this would have been, sixty years ago, populated by soldiers and strangers, bicycles and horses, rather than cars.

Grace was in saffron yellow, with endearing grey roots to her plum-coloured hair, bellowing welcome and rattling with different silver bracelets. 'They're all out! Isn't that marvellous! You must be starving.'

Rachel was.

It was cooler in that room she already thought of as her own. A breeze through the window, the next-door room and the shared bathroom vacant.

Cold chicken. Roasted potatoes with rosemary and a crust of salt. Earthy spinach. You don't think I grow all this, do you? Grace said. What on earth is the point of a supermarket if I did?

Darkness fell, and the kitchen exerted its charm.

'I've had an excellent week,' Grace said. 'A couple staying, been before. Walkers. Out all day, even when it rains. Don't want more than breakfast, and a meal midweek. Don't want conversation, either. They spend the evening in the pub and walk home singing. You might hear them later. Would you like to try this cheese?'

'No thanks. Tell me something: if the paying guests stay in the pigsties, where do the pigs live?'

'Oh, I forgot, you never got round to that last time. Pigs live in barns these days. Like cows, but not like cows. The pigsties, sorry guest rooms, were stables before. Once used for horses, then pigs. They make nice little single rooms, or two adjoining. Rather dark, of course. Ernest put windows in the back walls, long before you needed planning permission for that kind of thing, of course.'

'Were is he?'

'Milking. Cowman's day off, so he has to do both milkings. Which leaves us more wine. I do love this one you brought. It tastes expensive. The only time I get to drink good wine is when people bring it.'

'I'll remember that,' Rachel said.

The now familiar sloth was stealing across her, the same laziness which had turned the weekend before into little more than half a tour of the farm and a lot of sitting around in the garden while Grace fed them senseless. Without Ivy, she would behave more like a tourist, who explored and asked questions.

'I can't tell you how pleased I am that Ivy's moved in with you,' Grace said in a rush, anxious to say it, but postponing it until now. 'Pleased and grateful. What did she do to deserve you? What has she done to deserve someone who sweetly and sensitively trusts her to get used to her new abode in private? Aren't you worried she'll trash it?'

'No. She's the tidiest person I know. And it wouldn't matter if she did.'

Grace nibbled a breadstick.

'If I were your mother,' she announced, 'I'd go after that man who left you, and cut his balls off. He must have been out of his mind.'

'Oh, I think he was totally in command of his mind. I just wish he hadn't lasted so long. My mother would have said it was all my own fault, but I don't have a mother any more.'

'Yes you do,' Grace said airily. 'You've got me. Thirty-two

is way too young to be without one, and I've always needed more children, so count me in. I'll kill him for you.'

Rachel laced her fingers together on the warm wood of the table, looked down at them.

'Did you feel that way about Carl? Carl the younger?'

Grace touched her fingers. The touch was rougher than the wood. 'Do you really want to know?'

'Yes. If you're going to be my mother too, of course I really want to know.'

Grace plucked a daisy from the jug of flowers on the table. A tiny little blue jug, like the jug full of lavender Rachel had noticed in her room. Small enough to be significant.

'Kill him? Nothing as mild as that. Getting her pregnant was forgivable, I could see he was crazy about her. Marrying her, well, who wouldn't? You should have seen her then. I don't think anyone could have resisted her. The passion was mutual. It was after that. He wanted to tame her, make her a respectable wife and mother. Understandable, also. She longed for city lights, that kind of life; she wanted to be what he wanted her to be. And he wasn't bad, as husbands go. Let her enrol on the arts course, paid for it. Then, when she wanted to come back and give her children what she'd had, he didn't like that. I could see it was threatening. I tried to understand him. I never knew what a cold monster he was.'

She put the daisy back in the jug before she could damage it in her twisting fingers, selected a piece of fern.

'No, not then. I didn't know him then. Ivy wasn't going to tell me. As you'll notice, she has her pride. I only began to detest him for his refusal to admit things. Cassie's death was his fault. He was supposed to be looking after them both, down by the lake, on his own, for once. He always had more time for the boy. Sam was acting up, so Carl brought him home. He left her to drown. OK, an accident. It was what he did after, and has done ever since. Closed down and shut Ivy out, hugged the boy close to him for comfort. And when Ivy wailed and screamed, he hit her . . .'

'No,' Rachel said, sharply.

Grace shook her head.

'Oh, to be fair, she was impossible. Crazy with grief and guilt, sure, but she was already into the drugs. Living the sort of student life she'd missed, only worse, because he gave her money. Drink and drugs. Didn't go home to the nice town house to be hit again. She ran away from them. Came back. He locked the door on her. The worst thing he did was not tell us. Until she cracked and disappeared. Then he told me. I got used to tramping those London streets, I tell you. I found her in Centrepoint. It took a year. The worst year of my life.'

'I somehow can't see you in London, Grace.'

Grace laughed. 'Can't you now? I know it well. I used to go to every exhibition, but I know the less salubrious bits better. Hostels and hospitals. Of course she wouldn't co-operate. She was shacked up with some druggie. Panhandling for dope and food. Told me to fuck off. Then she got arrested for the last time, and got shoved on a rehabilitation scheme. That, or prison. The first one didn't work, the second did. She began to see the light. God, those people were patient, but then Ivy never lost her charm. She got better. Not a linear progress, I can tell you. And she did it all by herself. Got better. That's when Carl did his very worst.'

'Could he do worse?'

Grace nodded. 'Yes, he could. To her, and to us. Much worse. He kept her from seeing her son. And his son from seeing us. He still does. Which is why,' she added with a watery smile, 'I have such a dearth of children. Do you know, you're the first person Ivy has ever brought home?'

The kitchen door opened quietly. The sound of scraping. Grace turned towards it. 'Oh, Ernest love, you late-night stop-out, you. Do you want a cup of tea?'

Ernest Wiseman came in, and struggled with his boots. He kicked them into the washing machine alcove, came into the circle of light around the table, leaving the door open. His blue eyes widened and his face opened into a smile of guileless pleasure as he looked first at Grace, then at Rachel.

'Now here's a sight for sore eyes,' he said. 'Hope you've brought boots for tomorrow, girl. You're going to need them.'

From the open door they could hear singing, and the soft sound of rain. The paying guests were home.

Never was the early morning so wonderful as after rain. Ernest and Rachel, in her borrowed boots and socks, walked over the field to the cow barn. Next to it was a barren little office which housed desk, chair, filing cabinet, and the dirtiest computer screen she had ever seen. It was a civilised hour of the morning, post-breakfast, if only nine o'clock. Milking still in progress, half done. A long process, even for forty cows, with some of them back in the barn. Ernest walked her through them. They ranged free in the hugeness of the barn, and yet converged on her with wide eyes.

'Just curious,' Ernest said. 'All newcomers get that. Come here every day and there's never a flicker. Unless one's got a calf, and you were to come in here, newer than paint, with a dog. Then she might have a go at you. Not otherwise. They'd only ever knock you over by mistake. The pigs are over there. OK to walk?'

Despite the reassurance, Rachel did not think she could bring herself to trust the cows. Stupidity, weight, and the feelings she could not doubt they had unnerved her. It was better out in the field, away from the dirty backsides of the ten-ton beasts.

'Pigs are much cleaner,' Farmer Wiseman said. 'They won't lie in their own shit, they hate it, but all the same they smell worse, whatever we feed them. I shall have to phase out the cows, never the pigs. I love 'em. P'raps because they're not lovable at all, except sometimes.'

Certainly he loved the pigs, and gave her every detail. The pig barn was a one-storey unit with a pit beneath, with a raised wooden floor made of slats. The pigs seemed to demand little to lie on except these slats, through which faeces fell to the level beneath. Ernest explained all this. Rachel could only think of who would clear away what fell between the slats into the pit, grateful it was not her, worried that she might one day be asked to do it. In the barn there were fifteen stalls, the first two occupied by enormous sows-in-waiting. The next stalls were sows with newborn, suckling pigs; then sows with older piglets. She could see how they doubled their weight in a week. She hated them and shrank away from them, keeping to the middle of the central aisle which ran between the pens, not touching anything and hoping he would not notice.

'You can wean these in days,' Ernest said, pointing at a crop of almost shockingly pink piglets draining mummy dry. Mummy lay on her side, held in position by bars.

'But only if you give them the right food,' he added. 'Which is very expensive. So leaving them with mum is best. Greedy little buggers, aren't they? Don't worry, she can always roll on to her tummy and deny them. The bars only stop her rolling over and squashing them to death. I can open the pens from the outside when they go to market. Then they try and bash down the doors.'

The somnolent sows with their sniffling, squealing feeders raised heads and slumped back. Like the cows, it was the sheer enormity of them which disturbed her. In one stall, an undersized thing, as pink as a flamingo and the size of a small cat, crawled away from brethren three times its size and lurked in a corner.

'He won't last,' Ernest said.

The last pens were young pigs, squealing for food.

'They'll eat anything,' Ernest said with evident admiration. 'Problem is, we can't feed them it.'

'How do you clean them out?' Rachel asked, itching to get out.

'Sweep out the straw down the middle, let it drop through into the pit. Empty the pit every now and then. Grace won't let me in the house after I've done that, not until she's hosed me down. You don't like them, do you?'

'No, they scare me, to be honest.'

He laughed. 'I won't tell.'

He pushed a lever, which sent pellets of food into the dishes by every stall in a clatter of sound. Silence fell.

The smell: she knew the stench of them would scent her clothes. A feral, animal, acid smell which permeated everything. *Eau de Cochon*.

'I love them because they haven't any inhibitions. No manners either. When a boar mounts a sow, there's no pleasure like it, really. His eyes roll and his feet tap, and he makes noises like I never heard, while she vibrates like a violin. They know how to have fun. They take pleasure in everything.'

Rachel found the stench made her dizzy. She was

remembering a murder story, with a body fed to the pigs. They'd eat anything. Outside, she gulped for air. There were steps down from the door; Ernest stumbled and put his hand on her shoulder for support, briefly, then stood upright.

'I'm getting old,' he said. 'They're too much for me, really. Pigs and cows and fields to feed me. Makes nothing. There you go. Got a friend in Normandy makes a living out of fourteen cattle. Not here. Come on, love, I'll show you the hay barn where me and Carl used to hide.'

It was as if she was part of a story, and he assumed she knew the rest. Ivy was like that too, but Ivy had none of the occasional vagueness she noticed in Ernest, the long-term memory so much better than the short.

The barn was vaulted beauty, the beams as old and bent as time, the roof littered with holes.

'I've no duty to this,' he said, 'except to preserve it for ever. These days, I'm paid to preserve buildings and hedgerows, not to grow food. There's nothing for sons and grandsons. I still keep hoping he'll come back, though.'

She did not know what he meant. Didn't want to know.

'Last week,' she said, 'I saw the little blind cow who could not calve. Is she still here?'

'For a while,' he said. 'I can't kill her. I've got to call for the knacker. I can't just kill a beast unless she's running wild, then I get a man with a rifle to do it. No rifles on this farm; well, none anyone knows about except me. I kept Dad's hidden. We've only got handguns. A handgun does, from three feet away. I can't do it, myself, have to wait for Ivy or Grace. I'm not allowed to kill my own cattle and give them a decent burial, oh no. Not since BSE. You have to have your cattle killed for you. Different for pigs.'

She was relieved to be further away from the pigs. The

stench clung to her clothes. She was glad she would never have to clean out that pit. The mud of the yard squelched beneath her feet. She could see the virtue of rubber boots. Ernest looked at hers, and his own heavy suede boots.

'I get through a pair of these every six months,' he said. 'They rot. Then they can go in the incinerator. Here it is. Fired it up, especially for you. Too expensive for every day.'

They had walked away from the barn. In the yard on the other side, nearer the pigs, was a small bunker. It reminded her of an old pill box she had seen in the field, a war relic too heavy to shift. Nearer, the bunker hummed. Ernest fiddled with a thermostat on the side, and then opened the door on the front.

There was a blaze of heat and light from inside. A roar of flame. A cupboard of fire, the size of a large wardrobe. Propped at the back was the remnants of a smouldering form, and at the front the still identifiable forms of three piglets, surrounded by ash. It smelt clean. Ernest leant down, plucked something white from the front, and closed the door.

He handed it to her, beaming. 'There you are,' he said.

She took it gingerly. It was like a small piece of crumbling chalk.

'Just a bit of bone. Everything in there will be pure ash by tomorrow. Magic, isn't it?'

He looked at her pale face. 'Time for a cup of coffee, I think. Grace wants to take you to the sea. I think that's what she said.'

On the way back, downhill across the field, she felt she had been churlish, should have asked more questions. She pointed to a mound by the side of the path. A funny thing, looking like nothing, except for the huge manhole cover on top.

'What's that?'

'Oh, that's the pit. Goes down like a well shaft. Don't know who made it. That's where we used to put dead animals. They rot down nicely, except sheep. Can't use it now, in case it does something to the water table. Bollocks, it never did before. Locked shut. You should be allowed to kill your own, only way to show respect. You shouldn't be forced to send them away to die. Animals have souls. They should die at home.'

He swiped at the long grass by the side of the path with a filthy hand. 'I wish he'd come back. Then I could cope.'

Then he patted her shoulder.

'Sorry, lass. Shouldn't go on, should I? Especially when I've lost my place. Only we've got this grief, see? Such grief. All of us. We're just like those swans.'

Chapter Five

Rachel paused at the kitchen door, listening to the sound of it. The birds sang in the garden, and someone wept within. Ernest went in ahead of her, as if she did not exist. She waited on the threshold.

'Don't be silly,' he was saying. 'There, there, don't carry on so.'

'Another letter sent back! I can't bear it. He reads what I write, puts it back in the envelope and sends it back. Second-class post, I ask you. Insult on injury. Oh, the bastard.'

'You mustn't upset yourself.'

'Oh, mustn't I? Why the hell not? Why not, why not?' Her voice was rising. The bracelets on her wrists jangled. Then she saw Rachel at the door and stopped moving.

Rachel's eyes were blinded by sunlight, the kitchen was dark; there was an adjustment to be made. Grace was embarrassed. Rachel was glad she could scarcely see, until Grace began to wipe her face with a dishtowel. There was a slight smell of bacon, the residue of the paying guests' breakfast. The dishwasher hummed.

'Ernest, make the coffee, there's a darling. Sorry, Rachel dear. I'm being tragedy queen this morning. It's my turn.'

'For what? What happened?'

Again she caught the glance between them: Grace looking to Ernest for some sort of approval, not getting it. He had turned his back and stood nursing the kettle. Grace blew her nose on the dishtowel and sat up straight. She made a quick recovery. Then she crumpled again. It was unbearable to see her cry. Rachel put an arm round her shoulder, clumsily. She welcomed gestures of affection herself, but was slow to learn how to make them. She was always waiting for the other person to withdraw. Grace leaned against her. It was extraordinarily satisfying to give someone strength and have them take it.

'Can you tell me?'

'No,' Ernest said. 'Don't. It isn't fair.'

'Please,' Rachel said. 'I want to help.'

Grace had massive shoulders, but the flesh on her bare arms was damp and feverish.

'Ernest darling,' Grace said. 'Ivy's living in Rachel's home now. I think perhaps she ought to know. Even though it isn't fair she should.'

She turned towards Rachel with a tremulous smile which touched Rachel's heart. Grace and Ivy; Ivy and Grace: they were both in her bloodstream now. In months she had learned the necessity and privilege conferred by trust and she was going to honour it. She could feel the small piece of bone she had taken from Ernest beginning to crumble in the pocket of her shorts. Life was short. Now that her eyes had adjusted, Rachel could see the morning's post scattered over the table. A few unopened envelopes, which looked like bills, circulars, adverts, and a couple of sheets of hand-written paper.

'Why does he scrunch them up?' Grace said. 'I always write so carefully. Why mess up my writing, stuff it into an envelope and send it back? Why not reply? Or ignore me?'

Ernest left the room.

'It's that bastard Carl,' Grace said. 'Look, I don't know quite what Ivy's told you. About her son.'

Rachel hesitated.

'Very little. Except that she has no contact with him, and that's probably the best thing for them both.'

'Huh. So she might say. It simply isn't true. It's *torture* for her, and what about me? Once she got better, she wanted to see him. I'd always kept in touch with Carl. Ernest always kept in touch with Carl the elder, until he died. Not long after Cassie. He was the voice of reason, I tell you.'

'Hang on. Ivy told me she'd tried to establish contact with her husband in order to keep contact with her son, once she surfaced from the mire, but he – Carl, I mean – thought it was a bad idea. She only really resurfaced when Sam was in his teens. She agreed. She doesn't seem bitter about it. How old is he now? Eighteen? Nineteen?'

'What Ivy doesn't know,' Grace snapped, 'is that *I* have always kept in contact with Carl. I wanted to know what happened to my grandson, even when that bastard got an injunction taken out against her. Barring her from the house. He was good at first, I must admit. He sent me progress reports. He told me, not in so many words, of course, never specific, where he went to school, how he was doing, all that. Turning into a little public school prick of a product, probably. I told Carl that Sam should meet his mother. Then he wrote, after a whole fucking year, saying, sorry, Sam's doing exams, et cetera. I held off. Then I wrote again, and this is what happens. Five times now. Bastard.'

She dabbed at her eyes. 'And never mind *me*. What about Ernest? Carl the elder was the big brother he never had, Carl the younger was the son he never had, and he dreams of his grandson. Oh, shit.'

'Does Ivy know this?'

'No. Of course not,' Grace said, quickly. 'She was beyond receiving any information of any kind for years. And there was this injunction forbidding contact. Even I don't know where they live. The letters always go to his solicitor, who forwards them. That was the only way Carl would consent to keep in contact at all. I can't tell my daughter that I've been going behind her back, can I? And I know my child. I know she'll never be right until she sees her son. Whatever she says.'

For the first time, Rachel felt the burden of information. She did not want such secrets.

'Ivy doesn't know her arse from her elbow,' Ernest said, coming back into the room.

'Who are you talking to?' Grace yelled. 'She could shoot handguns when she was five, drive when she was ten, paint when she was fourteen, procreate at seventeen, and Rachel knows her better than you do. Get out of here. No, not you, petal. You need coffee. Come back, darling, please. Please.'

Ernest left, quietly. Rachel sat down again.

'Ah, fuck it,' Grace said. 'Men. Forget I spoke. He's right, I'm not being fair. Let's go to the sea. That's what we were going to do, wasn't it?'

Grace drove with the same verve with which she did everything. The car was the oldest Rachel had ever seen, so old she could hardly discern its make. A third-hand Volvo of ancient shape, built like a tank.

'Good for absolutely everything,' Grace yelled. 'Except when it comes to getting it out of a ditch. Did you bring your swimming things?'

'No.'

'No worries. There's some in the back. Not that you have to. You don't have to do anything. Oh God, what a glorious day.'

It was the height of a green, wet summer, before the rot set in. The car rattled down the lanes on to the main road, where the presence of other traffic seemed almost impertinent. They passed the pub at the crossroads and the hamlet surrounding it, charged downhill, then uphill, past fields of wheat, then on to the flat, where Grace surprised her by slowing down to a sedate pace in deference to bigger vehicles.

'That's better,' she said. 'Sometimes I just need to get out of there. A trip to the supermarket doesn't do it. Sometimes I feel trapped. There's that push–pull effect of loving things and hating them at the same time. Do you feel that way about work? Is it worse when it's high-powered and responsible?'

'Don't know about that,' Rachel shouted above the rattle of the engine. 'Sometimes I can't wait to get to work. Other times, I'd do anything not to go.'

She watched the road ahead, thought about what she was saying. 'But then, I work purely for money. It never occurred to me there could ever be any other motive. I check and balance other people's money. I sort out companies in danger from the tax man. I advise on due process. I'm a cog in a wheel. I never once imagined there might be a chance to do something enjoyable *and* be well paid for it. I'm not vocational. I definitely went for the money. And that's what I get.'

'It must be strange,' Grace said, slowing down for a junction, 'to do something where you never quite see the end result. Strikes me you're always sorting out cock-ups. No wonder you like drawing.'

The dark mood was gone and Rachel had reached a decision. Which was not to resist being dragged into the lives of this family. If they needed her, she was theirs, dark moods and all.

The first sight of the sea always made her want to clap her hands in applause. Any stretch of water had the same effect on her. Calm or stormy, it spoke of freedom. There had been dutiful, hygienic trips to the coast when she was a child, when she was allowed to paddle, before her feet were dried and put back into solid sandals, in case of glass, prickles, turds and germs. Later, there had been package holidays to Spain, full of complaints about the heat and the food, where, lathered in Factor 50, Rachel learned to swim in the safety of a small hotel pool, stinking of chlorine. She wished she had learned in the sea.

The place where Grace slewed the tank to a halt in a scrubby car park was not an idyllic piece of coastline. It was a flat, untidy shore, full of thistles and stones, but the sea and the sky were there.

'When I was a kid,' Grace said, 'all these beaches and bays would be crowded out in summer. Now they get in aeroplanes and go somewhere else, thank God. Be careful here, won't you? You're safe by the shore, but further out, the current's stronger.'

Rachel could see why this particular bay did not attract families. It had a clandestine air of neglect and the beach was littered with the detritus of bonfires and picnics, adult frolics, bottles and cans. Sea-lovers did not notice. None of that mattered, if it kept the others away and left them with a whole expanse of water to themselves. They stood by the boot of the car, stripped quickly and unselfconsciously. Rachel tugged on an old swimsuit which both covered her and hung off. They were both laughing like children. She had never done this with her own mother. Hand in hand, they tiptoed to the water. It was twinkling cold; they screamed. A few minutes splashing in the waves was enough. It was the act of immersion which gave the sense of triumph; distance and duration were unimportant. Rachel had always found the desire to be in water difficult to describe. Grace understood it instinctively. It simply made everything better.

'Is the lake warmer?' Rachel asked through curses and chattering teeth.

'Oh, yes. Much. Warm and shallow.'

Grace stood back and looked at her while she towelled her hair dry with a thin towel.

'Rachel, you've got to get yourself an itsy-bitsy teeny-weeny bikini,' she said. 'You're drop-dead gorgeous, you know. Even with blue skin. Clothes are bloody wasted on you.'

Rachel looked out to sea and laughed. It was the remark; it was Grace's own beauty, as she stood towel-clad, like a magnificent, gnarled tree trunk restored to strength by sacred immersion in cold water. Baptised, redeemed.

'That's exactly what I said to your daughter, madam. The day I met her. She threatened to test the point by leaving class without her clothes, but it was rather cold.'

'She would have done, you know. Never dare Ivy to do anything. It's as good as done,' Grace said, shivering. 'I first started to worry about her when she was twelve,' she went on. 'She had a school report which said, *This girl is a bad influence*. I congratulated her, of course. Maybe they were right. What was your mother telling you, at that age?'

They were huddled back into clothes before Rachel replied.

'That I'd better lose weight, work harder, stop eating so much, and stop complaining about the braces on my teeth. Otherwise she'd be stuck with me for ever. I paraphrase, but that's the gist. She was right, too. She always was. She wanted her ugly duckling to become a swan and sail away.'

'A swan?' Grace said, faintly.

'Anything that could fly,' Rachel said.

'Bit of a bum deal, being a swan. A bird that can't sing.'

Rachel laughed again, twisted her hair into a knot, and sat down on the shingle, tingling warm. Ivy was the one, the only one who had ever suggested she was good enough as she was. She felt disloyal talking about her own, strict mother, whose ambitions for her daughter were translated into constant criticism.

'She may have had in mind a beautiful creature mating for life, without singing or dancing either. The way she did with my father. She loved me, and she meant for the best, but the fact was that she loved my father more.'

Grace nodded, understanding. 'I think I know what you mean. There are parents like that. It's tough on a child when the parents stay in love. Send baby to bed or to study, so they can be alone.'

'I was very lucky,' Rachel said.

'So was your mother,' Grace said. 'Christ, look at the time. You ate scarcely any breakfast, you must be starving.'

'You're at it again.' Rachel laughed – it was natural to laugh with Grace – and the sea glittered. 'Do you ever *stop* being a mother?'

Grace shuddered. 'No,' she said fervently, 'never. There's always room for more. Should have had a brood. Shame it didn't happen. God knows, I tried hard enough.'

Seagulls wheeled overhead, joining in the chorus of laughter with their piteous, cunning cries. Talking in code to one another. Rachel loved that sound.

'I'm guessing,' she said, 'that you're the kind of parent a million miles from mine. The sort who believes the child can do no wrong.'

'Absolutely definitely. In Ivy's case, and now in yours, dear. You'll always be right. Fuck the rest, they're wrong. Anyway, in Ivy's case, she never did wrong. She had it done to her.'

'I don't think she thinks that.'

'Well,' Grace smiled, 'mothers know best. And it's only because I now love you both that I'll have to tell you a little more about husband Carl. So that you'll know what kind of a destructive freak she married. And I know it isn't fair, but she's living in your flat, and she still has nightmares. Better to know why. You both need space to grow. And, by the way, Ivy will be nesting in your house. She does that, but not like a cuckoo, I promise.'

It was lovely to be here. There was nothing better than being welcomed into a home, told to treat it as your own nest, even a corner of it.

Ivy was nesting in the small, second bedroom of Rachel's flat, wondering from time to time what her best friend and her mother were doing, but not thinking about it that much. There was no point in thinking about anything much. It interfered with the contentment of the day. Plans had to form in a vacuum, of their own accord.

She must pull her weight here, Grace said. It had to work. First she rearranged the room, and found a place to hide the portfolio of drawings. Rachel would want to see those; Rachel always wanted to see her work, but she couldn't. For this arrangement to work, it had to be equal. She would not be a taker. Love of whatever kind depended on each giving what the other needed. Rachel was giving her a home and a base: that was an awful lot. Ivy felt light in the balance and she was drawing up her own list of what had been given and received. She drew it on a sheet of paper in a series of scribbles and symbols which were her own shorthand, checked the time. She was the model in the second half of a one-day life drawing course, due in an hour. Better paid on Saturdays. Easy work.

What did Rachel need? Acceptance, praise, fun, less inhibition. She drew a mouse. Ivy had supplied plenty of that. Encouraged Rachel to let down that long blonde hair and reveal the beauty. Dress in colours. On a shallower level, taught her to drink without having a conscience, listen to music and look at paintings without feeling self-indulgent, nurture a talent, find new routes, eat heartily, be late for work, and occasionally answer back. Made her explore her own city. Ivy had even made her dance. Rachel could dance, a natural rhythm, deeply suppressed. What else had she given? She had given her own mother, gift-wrapped. The best therapist under the sun. A gift of love, both ways round, that is. Grace always needed another daughter as well as me. Yes, they were pegging equal, as if they were sisters.

Ivy looked in the mirror. There was, after all, a superficial resemblance. A pair of gorgeous blondes. Teutonic-looking, her ex-husband's type. She covered her thatch with a cap. She owned three. A hat and a naked body worked wonders in drawing class. Rachel was two inches shorter. Rachel should learn to wear heels.

Time to go. Life modelling for amateur students and beginners, Saturday afternoon four till eight at the Institute. Strictly clean work at weekends. No offices to polish. It would be so good to come back to a convenient flat, instead of trailing out to the boondocks on the grubby Central Line train.

She could do murals on the walls in this flat, here. Perhaps. Only if Rachel wanted, but a different colour scheme at least. What she could do before Rachel came home was fill it with flowers. It would be sparkling clean and full of bloom. Give her ideas.

She would take a hat to class, make them laugh, lower their inhibitions.

The phone rang. Not the mobile she wore round her neck on a leather thong, retrieved, warm from contact, from the inside of her bra. The other one. Rachel's landline. She had forgotten there were people left who still depended on these. She picked it up.

'Hallo.'

'Is that you, Rache? It's your dad. Look . . .'

'It's not Rachel. She's away.'

'She never goes away,' he said petulantly.

'She does now,' Ivy said cheerfully. 'She's staying with my mother at the minute. Getting a bit of fresh air. How are you, Mr Doe? I'm the new flatmate.'

'Oh.'

There was a full beat of silence, redolent with mistrust.

'We were hoping you might come up to town for supper one day next week, Mr Doe. I know you're worried about my existence, but I am paying rent and everything. Would love to meet you. Can you do it? Wednesday and Friday are best for us. I can cook.'

Another, longer beat of silence.

'Wednesday,' he said.

'Fine. Look forward. About six thirty? Rache says you like to eat early, so you can get back.'

'OK.'

She was only trying to do more to equal the balance and please Rachel, but he sounded suspicious and confused. Fine. She put the phone down, distastefully. Anything larger than a mobile felt like an intrusion in the hand. She scribbled the date on a piece of paper, thought of phoning them. Should I ring? No. She might be down by the lake with Grace, and anyway, it was time to go to work.

Norman, the Plonker, would be at the weekend class; he went to them all. The one with the blond hair, who had frightened her darling Rachel a few days ago. There was way too much of the wrong kind of love all round. Some of it a person could do without. If Norman asked her out for a drink this time, she would go, because she felt like it and Saturday night made her restless to prowl. She wanted to be out, to see what would happen. Maybe he would buy her something to eat. He would be the sort of company she could ignore, use, shed like a cloak, possibly an ally. She thought no further than that, and missed her other friends from the good old, bad old days, where someone might really know who she was.

She was dressed in neat dark blue jeans, matching top, almost official. She looked more like Rachel dressed for the office, before Rachel discovered colour, except for the cap. She could merge with the darkness, coming home. It would be light for hours yet. She could feel the energy of the street waiting for her.

Later. Sticky, hot Saturday night. There was a running fight in Leicester Square, where the last, paralysed spectators ebbed away with the first sirens and the arrival of police and ambulance. There had been a stabbing, there were blood and teeth on the ground, injuries, a flashpoint reached so quickly that no one rightly saw, even less knew why the carnage had happened. There was confusion for the paramedics and the shirt-sleeved uniforms, struggling to establish priorities. Who to chase, who to treat, who to question or rescue first.

A couple, still looking for an open bar, paused on the corner, not sure what to do. They needed to get across, to that side road over there, but waited, huddled in the doorway of the cinema. An ambulance was parked in the pedestrian zone, with the doors open. They had a view straight into the brightly lit interior, where a man lay on the gurney, mask on face, unattended. Two paramedics and the driver were twenty-five yards away, tending to another youth, who lay on the ground, screaming.

'Come away,' the man said nervously, pulling at his friend in the doorway of the cinema. 'Let's go. This is awful. Why did you want to come here?'

'*You* go. Go on, just go. That's the best way. Run down there, I'll follow. Quick. There'll be police around. We don't want to get caught up in it.'

He looked to the left and ran, skirting round the square. Stopped, uncertainly, looked back. No sign of his friend. The light from the ambulance illuminated the nearest piece of ground. The orange street lights threw shadows through the trees. He blinked. There were two figures in the island of white light which was the ambulance.

Two. The one on the gurney, and another one, standing over it.

A police car edged into the square.

He ran.

The second figure sprinted from the ambulance, running like a greyhound, something utterly gleeful and carefree in the stride.

The morning light was kind in the country. It seeped into the room, rather than intruding, as it did in London. It invited her out, rather than reminding her that she must get up. This Sunday, with the idea of departing already looming like a threat, Rachel joined the paying guests for breakfast. They were dressed for a day's serious walking, anxious to be off while eating whatever Grace served and looking out to the perfect morning seen through the open door. There were no leftovers for nonexistent pets. Midwinter Farm did not run to pets.

'Where were we?' Grace asked, after the guests departed in a chorus of thanks. 'Oh, that's where we were.'

She settled herself.

'In all fairness,' Grace said, 'Ivy wasn't fit to look after Sam after Cassie drowned. She was sedated with legal drugs and sedated herself with the other kind. Carl wouldn't let me take the boy, even for a while. Who could blame her? She blamed herself for not being there, for encouraging Cassie to fight with her father. And I think she blamed Sam for not going to the rescue. We all expect too much of men, even little ones. Carl had already brought him home.'

Grace snorted into her tea.

'Carl exaggerated, of course. He's such a convincing liar, believes his own lies. Said the boy was terrified of her, but really he was terrified of seeing his mother being beaten up. Better keep them apart, he said. She ricocheted between

London and here. To begin with, she was delusional. She convinced herself that Cassie wasn't really dead. She kept saying Cassie had been turned into a swan, not dead, simply transformed. It was the drugs talking, but she believed it. I let her. Anything for comfort. Then . . . something else happened. She went back home to London, but he locked her out, and then she disappeared.'

'Didn't he try to find her?'

'Not for long. He sent me money to do that. And divorce papers. All she had to do was sign.'

'But, rights of access, alimony, all that kind of thing. Grandparents' rights. There's law, isn't there? You've got rights.'

'You've got rights if you want to pursue them,' Grace said bitterly. 'You've got rights if you've got *money* to pursue them. You've got rights if you're not in the middle of nowhere with no idea of what to do. You've got rights if you've got qualifications, know someone who has. We didn't, we don't. We had to keep a farm going. We didn't have a bean, still don't. Not much sophistication, either. I wouldn't have a clue where to start exerting rights. Pay a detective? With what? What chance, anyway, against a lawyer? All he ever had to do was stay still, and hide. Tear up letters and send them back. He knows we're helpless. Ivy knows it too. I wouldn't even know how to begin to find him. Nor would she.'

'She could, couldn't she? She could look him up if she wanted.'

'Sweetheart, don't you realise Ivy can scarcely read the small print? She sees shapes rather than letters. Our fault, undiagnosed dyslexia. Carl despised her for that too, she told me. She hides it; she learns everything by practice, off by heart. He was ashamed of her. Doesn't do, does it, lawyer with semi-literate wife? How could she defend herself?'

Grace was crying again. Rachel wanted to cry too, out of shared frustration and rage, pity for what she had not known.

'And you know the worst thing about him? The one thing I do know, because I saw it in a newspaper someone left. You know what that bastard does for a living now? Why he would never want to know us? He's a judge. A fucking judge. Therefore untouchable.'

'Does Ivy know that?'

'Yes. That's all I told her.'

'Oh.'

There was so much Ivy omitted. Ivy despised pity, and therefore deserved it.

You might not be able to find him, Rachel thought. But I could.

Chapter Six

Donald Cousins waited at the back of the court of His Honour Judge Schneider on Tuesday morning, watching and only half listening while a witness blundered through evidence. It had been difficult to force himself inside, out of the sun, but in here the cool was welcome. Middlesex Crown Court, facing the Houses of Parliament, was once poetry in carved oak and Donald mourned it. Now, Court Five, where the judge sat, was a white-walled box full of power points and laptop screens, as anonymous as any other, although an incongruous throne-like chair had been preserved for the use of the judge. The shield and coat of arms above it, bearing the old legend *Honi soit qui mal y pense*: *Evil to him who evil thinks*, was painted in bright blues, reds and golds, and looked like a garish warning sign. The insecurities of the English, Donald thought. The language of the law was Latin, the courtroom mottos were ancient French, and in this case the judge had a Teutonic name. Schneider. Next door's court was presided over by a diminutive Goan, whose brown skin was peculiarly suited to his white wig. The witness in this court was a resident Scandinavian, who had seen a man savagely attacked by a group of other men, one of whom was in the dock. She was being cross-examined by African counsel. Donald Cousins felt his chest swell with pride in being English. Nowhere else was the law quite so colourful. He attempted to concentrate.

The trial in progress was rehearsing the story of an outdoor fight on a dark night, witnessed by strangers, six months before. A man had been disfigured for the simple crime of being in the wrong place at the wrong time. The witness currently on the stand was distressed by the reliving of it. He said something, yes; then he hit him, then the other one went to hit him back, and then they were fighting, then one went to the ground. Three of them kicked him.

Can you identify the man in the dock as one of those men?

Yes. He was the one who went on longest. The others stopped.

Yes, but can you identify my client?

To Donald Cousins, it was all no more than proof that fists, feet and knives still prevailed as the favourite inner-city weapons. On Saturday nights, high days and holidays, post-football, the west end of central London reverted to historic type. Strong drink was the recreation of choice long before Victoria ruled and gin was a penny a pint; brawling followed and still did. In the same central areas, on Saturday nights, a drunken swathe, lured by bright lights, music, cheap drink and each other, were left marooned with no means of getting home and no sense of direction either. Donald blamed the 1960s, for the kick-starting of a new wave of no inhibitions. Carnaby Street, all that. Silly clothes and drugs, new money. Protest marches sponsoring the right to violence. He had first really lost his nerve much later, in the vicious poll tax riots, buried it for good on future demos, and kissed it goodbye on a New Year's Eve celebration policing gig in Trafalgar Square. *Honi soit* . . . The love of life which went with New Year's Eve rapidly turned rancid in the early hours of the new year itself. There were endless opportunities for casual murder. Currently the action was in the environs of Leicester Square, haven of bars, cheap eats, cinemas, where pubs and clubs disgorged their fun-loving thousands after the night buses became scarce, leaving them to wander aimlessly, fight indiscriminately and abandon one another. Even a prime minister's son. And nothing united a celebratory or protesting mob better than the presence of the police, who rapidly became the common enemy. It was on these battle lines, these unpredictable Saturday nights, that a man in uniform, surrounded by historic monuments, learned to hate, fear and hold in contempt the pitiful, pitiless public. Sometimes that particular iron never left the soul.

He listened. The witness stuttered. Of course it was him. He was wearing a baseball cap. He had stripes on his shoes. He was kicking the man on the ground, long after he was still. It made me feel sick. He was the worst, he aimed for his head. It was as if he never wanted to stop.

How blind are you, Miss Gunstrom? Were you wearing your spectacles that night? I note you wear them now. You couldn't really see, could you?

Donald groaned. Cheap tricks from defence counsel, questioning the witness like that.

'Many of us wear spectacles, Mr Peal,' the judge said, adjusting his own. 'They don't nullify sight, and can, indeed, enhance it. That's what they're for. And you must not bully the witness. I think we should adjourn here. Back at two thirty.'

Judge Schneider wasn't bad at this, Donald conceded. He kept his interruptions minimal and took care of the witness. Cold and careful and surprisingly sensitive. He had recently begun to suppose that the same iron which entered a policeman's soul might also infect that of a judge, only later, rather than sooner, since the judge was better rewarded, never had to handle the bodies or touch the blood, regarded the evidence of carnage from a distance, at third hand. But the verbal and visual repetition of man's inhumanity to man would always be wearing in the end, however sanitised it became in the telling, especially when it was as pointless and stupidly wicked as this. As for punishment, the judge could never deliver an eye for an eye and a tooth for a tooth. He had no such privilege. He would sentence by formula, while the hungry eyes in the public gallery lusted for revenge.

It was an apposite case for this particular Tuesday morning, when the *Evening Standard* headlined a variation on Saturday-night brutality. A stabbed man had been left alone in an ambulance in Leicester Square, safe at last, until someone joined him there and finished off what wasn't even half done. Throttled him, like a chicken, with a wire garrotte, while a phalanx of preoccupied police officers stood yards away. Someone with plenty of malice aforethought, getting into an ambulance and killing an injured man. Donald did not know which shocked him more, the cruelty, or the nerve.

On the Monday he had spent hours with the judge's clerk, going through records, and realised during the process that Carl couldn't be all bad, because his twelve-stone, big-bosomed, no-nonsense Jamaican clerk, shared with three others, actually seemed to like him. She was very helpful with the facts, had a memory like Methuselah, and was interesting. He gets racial abuse all the time, she said, 'cos of his name. Only from thick whites, I ask you. I keep telling him to change it to Smith. If he calls himself Dolores Smith, I tell him, and puts on some jewels, then he'll get promoted. He's a nice warm man.

What about his personal life? Donald asked. She shook her head, and said if she knew she wouldn't tell him.

Nice? Warm?

He was like an iceberg when he came into the tiny retiring room, smiled so briefly it was like watching a light bulb turned on and then off, in the same second. He nodded towards Donald, acknowledging the appointment.

'Can we go out?' he said. 'If that's all right with you. I prefer to go out.'

'Certainly, sir.'

'You're the only one round here calls him sir,' the clerk chipped in. 'The rest of us call him God. Don't we, Carly baby?'

He smiled at her then, and the real smile was a revelation. He led the way down the labyrinth of corridors which led from the back rooms of the courts, and out of a side entrance. Once out in the street he took the lead, walking away from the building with what seemed to Cousins to be unnecessary speed.

'We can walk down the river to my chambers,' he said. 'Or sit in Parliament Square with Winston Churchill. That's what I tend to do on a day like this. Anything to avoid other lawyers.'

His yellow-grey hair was flattened by wearing the wig for a morning. It was a mystery to Donald why courtroom lawyers failed to rebel against that bizarre and unflattering piece of uniform. Anyone sane would resent wearing horsehair on their head on a day like this, but perhaps it made them concentrate and forget what they looked like. Wig, gown and white wing collar made all equally anonymous. Carl simply looked smaller without them.

To reach the square from the court, they had to sprint across the road, avoiding three lanes of traffic. The judge seemed used to it. The square was not the ideal place for conversation, because of the pigeons and the noise, but the traffic isolated it into an island which few people chose to risk, even for a better view of the Mother of Parliaments and the smiling face of Big Ben. Carl sat on the stone surround of a flowerbed facing the massive back of the statue of Winston Churchill, who was dressed in his old overcoat and glowering at the world. Donald had no option but to sit alongside. The stone was nicely cool. Donald could imagine the judge sitting here even when it was covered in ice. He did not seem a man who revelled in creature comforts. Carl patted the stone with a large, capable hand.

'Winston was my father's hero,' he said, as if explaining his choice. 'Since my father was a German prisoner of war, I never quite understood why. He said we needed to be vanquished.'

It was a remark which did not seem to demand a reply. Carl sat, expectantly, with his hands in his lap. Donald, who had looked up the judge's history for the scant detail available, simply nodded to indicate he knew about that, and then asked a question, because he wanted to know. They sat close together, the better to hear above the traffic which circled around them and became a neutral hum of sound.

'You were born in the late fifties, weren't you? Not so long after the war. How did your father being German affect you?'

'I'm honestly not sure. Maybe simply that I had a different childhood from other people, although it didn't seem so. If he was discriminated against, he didn't say. He was simply very pro-British. I was brought up to be grateful for being alive and to venerate all things British, with a certain Germanic discipline, of course. The difference was later.' He smiled apologetically. 'By the time I was a teenager, and my mother had died, it was puzzling to see my English contemporaries pouring scorn on tradition and hating the establishments I was taught to revere, as I still do, although perhaps a bit more selectively. I was always slightly at odds, I suppose. Ultra-conservative, with a small c. Nothing more than that. Do you have any news for me? Again, I'm so sorry to be such a nuisance.'

Donald cleared his throat. He was yearning for a nice warm pint. 'I've isolated a few possibles,' he said. 'The good news is that the list isn't long; the bad news is that they're difficult to trace. And I have no means of making any one of them answer questions when and if I do find them.'

'How on earth do you select?'

'By using a few basic principles, which even in themselves take a lot for granted. First, I've been looking for any person who has expressed a grievance against you, i.e, the widest category. There are plenty of those. Angry young men, mainly, customers who shout out threats as they go down to the cells en route to prison . . . Those who were free before.'

'I told you . . .' Carl interrupted.

'That they're usually prepared and resigned, yes,' Donald said impatiently. 'As people are, theoretically, for deaths and smaller tragedies which have been looming for a time. We may have been warned, but nothing prepares us for what we feel when it actually happens. We're still angered and insulted by it. As I said, the widest category of threateners are those who publicly blamed you for them going to prison. Hatred is so often the displacement of blame, especially blame of oneself.'

Carl was silent.

'So,' Donald continued. 'the widest category is the *I'll see you dead, you bastard* brigade. Those who actually shouted, because they were humiliated by the sentence. Especially those within that category who already had a propensity for violence. I mean, those you sentenced for violent crimes, as opposed to any other kind.'

'That's very scientific,' Carl said. 'But those people aren't the most cunning. Fraudsters are worse. They ruin lives without a shred of violence. They almost make thugs look admirable.'

This felt like an attempt to change the subject.

Donald went on. 'I've also ignored the other category you mentioned. Those who may loathe you for what, in their eyes, you *failed* to do. Such as not imposing a sufficiently vengeful sentence on someone who hurt their child. Or overseeing an acquittal which seemed unfair. Those deprived of a fitting revenge – the old *miasma*-ridden we were talking about – because of a technicality which got someone off. I can't possibly track down those, unless they expressed themselves publicly. I have to stick with the obvious, which is the violent, verbal ones who shouted, and I've broken down this little grouping into those with the necessary skills. And endurance.'

Carl leaned forward to rest his hands on his knees. He looked up towards the sky, enjoying the warmth on his face, like a cat reacting to the sun, stretching his neck. His profile was harmless, with a stubby nose, broad forehead and round, non-aggressive chin above a thick neck, but his hands were enormous, as if meant for toil. The hands of a surgeon were like that. Donald had the uncomfortable feeling that for all that the judge was older than himself, he would not like to be on the wrong side of him in a dark alley at night. His was a solid body.

'What exactly do you mean by endurance? Is this new police jargon?'

Donald had the feeling that the man was laughing at him; that he knew in advance that the investigation was useless and all this was playing with words. He raised his voice and slowed down.

'I mean the capability, and the willpower, to carry through. To go on wanting to do something. To harbour revenge, to plan it and hone the plan, to have an aim and sustain it, over months, years if necessary. I'm only looking at the last two years. I'm also only looking at men. Women don't do this stuff, and anyway, you've only ever sent a handful of the fairer sex to jail.'

'The jury convict,' Carl began. 'I don't.' He was being obtuse.

'Or fail to convict,' Donald said, suddenly furious. 'The stupid jury may convict, they carry the can, but it's you who actually send the bastards to jail, and it's you they'll remember, not the twelve grey people.'

'I never think the jury stupid,' Carl said. He *was* trying to change the subject. 'They've been bullied for centuries, first as hired witnesses, then dummies, ordered to do nothing but convict. No heat, food or water until they did. Then they rebelled with the trial of William Penn, the Quaker: 1670, wasn't it? Trumped-up charges about a prayer meeting. Not a million miles from here. The jury wouldn't convict. They were starved and imprisoned, and still they wouldn't. They resent it when the state creates bogeymen and expects them to hang them. The jury won, in the end. Penn took the jury trial system to America. Now look what they've done with it. What was it William Blackstone said? *The judgement of twelve men, indifferently chosen and superior to all suspicion . . .*'

'. . . *is the sacred bulwark of the nation's liberties*,' Donald finished.

The judge looked at his watch. 'That's all I have to preserve. The jury's right not to be bamboozled. So that *they* can judge. I do wish defendants could see that. I digress. You were saying?'

The crafty bastard, pretending he knew nothing of history, Donald thought. In other circumstances he might enjoy this man. He wanted to argue that the William Penn jury were hardly unbiased, since the leader was a diehard Quaker himself. And what about the fate of the poor deluded imbecile who was hanged for starting the Fire of London? That was a jury too. They could go on, he sensed, for a long time, and the judge was trying to distract him. He wondered why, and could only guess.

'The man who sends you threatening images, sir, and who maybe got into your room in chambers, is certainly dangerous, potentially at least, because he's calculating, and he has to have two qualifications. The last three images, by the way, came from two sources: one from a college with a bank of computers open to everyone in the place, two from an internet café. Maybe our man is capable of untraceable trespass, but he's got to be computer literate. Capable of accessing or scanning a picture, using a machine.'

'Isn't everyone, these days?' Carl said airily.

He did live in an ivory tower, after all.

'Not the unemployed riff-raff who pass through your court, yelling threats, unless, of course, they go to prison, where they may learn how. They do learn computers in prison.'

'I'd be glad if they learned anything,' Carl said, 'apart from a drug habit. So you think the person who is threatening me is an ex-con, still holding a grievance *after* he's free? Having learned the necessary skills?'

'A computer-literate ex-con, capable of breaking into your chambers. Multi-skilled, perhaps with a history of harassment and planning. I doubt if he cares if you live or die, but he does want you to be uncomfortable.'

'Anyone obvious on your little list?'

Donald sensed he was trying to keep the sarcasm out of his voice. He could risk being offended, because he was waiting to play his trump card. Produce the jack of spades which justified keeping him going on with this cushy number as long as he liked. Unless, of course, the murder of the man in the ambulance turned into a spate of murders. Then they would all be called in.

'Yes, there is, as it happens. Remember a man called Blaker? Recidivist, drop-out? Leniency because of age, even though he's spiteful? Convicted for robbery. He mugged women for handbags, sold on the credit cards, kept the cash. Then, just when they were beginning to recover, he contacted the women. Told them he knew where they lived, watch out. Scared them for no particular purpose except his own enjoyment. When he was arrested, which he was because he only had one patch and always went back to the same places – he can't operate or feel at home in any place other than Soho, that one – he had a fine old collection of keys. Hadn't tried to use them, but still, must have had it in mind. You've sentenced him twice, and he didn't like it either time. Released in April. Crazy but articulate.'

Carl sat up. He seemed to be enormously relieved.

'Ah, yes. Blaker. Unpleasant, to say the least. Yes. He did shout, didn't he? Said he was framed and I was part of an endless conspiracy against him. He should still be inside. Where is he now?'

Big Ben chimed two. The sonorous notes cut through all other noises and echoed around them. Donald waited for the sound to roll away.

'Don't know where he is,' he said. 'Early release, courtesy of the parole board. There's an address where he isn't, so I either walk the streets where I know he might be, or wait for him to call on his parole officer. In the meantime, I have to talk to your son. I've called his mobile, like you said. He doesn't get back to me.'

A stiffening of the judge's shoulders showed Donald he had been right, and that this was one of the subjects His Honour wanted to avoid. Carl seemed deafened by the chimes of the clock, shifted uncomfortably. Then he rallied, shook his head. 'I do apologise for his rudeness. I've had to tell him, of course. He says I'm paranoid.'

'When's the best time to catch him?'

Donald wanted to call him Carly baby, if only to provoke. Carl sighed, rose from the bench, and looked back at Winston, as if for inspiration.

'He's a student,' he said. 'Of economics, I think I told you. So it makes sound sense for him to live with his father and sleep all morning. That's where you'll find him in the early part of the day. I'll tell him to expect you, shall I? By now, on a day like this, he'll be sitting outside college holding court with his friends. He might conceivably be attending a lecture, but I doubt it. You've got the photo I gave you?'

'Yes.'

He had photos of both, as a matter of course. Donald wondered how anyone who had formed a grievance against the judge whilst he was wearing his wig would ever recognise him without it. Maybe that was what it was for.

'The photo of Sam may not be very helpful,' Carl said. 'They change very quickly at that age. My son in particular.'

'Funny, that. My wife says that about the daughters.'

They began to walk back towards the courthouse together. There was this strange moment when Donald did not want to leave him. Wanted, instead, to say, let's go for a pint and find out what you really know about history. Discuss the ignorance of children. How they know bugger-all about it. He was momentarily grateful to Carl. After all, the judge was facing the next few hours effectively locked up with scum-bags, lawyers and jurors, while he himself could roam free.

'Do you think your jury'll convict the bloke in the dock?' he asked, as they waited to cross the road back towards the court. The traffic seemed endless and angry, racing against time, as if wanting to be far away before the monstrous clock struck the time again.

'Oh yes. The evidence is all there, for once. It was like the witness said, *it was as if he couldn't stop.* He didn't stop kick-ing, our man in the dock, until he was hauled off, with blood on his striped shoes. A frenzy. I don't understand it, do you? Repeated kicks to the body and head, ruptured spleen. Where does that kind of hatred come from? They didn't even know each other.'

They were on the other side of the road, breathless.

'Does that make it better or worse, Carly baby?' Donald asked, panting.

Carl stopped in his tracks and considered. It was as if the question was all that mattered and all questions had to be answered. He spread his big hands, honestly bewildered. 'I just don't know. I wish I did. Only the victim could tell you that. It's violence without any purpose that I can't understand. I can understand planning it, for money, retribution, whatever you like, but not for *nothing*. I can understand running and hiding and lying. Sensible people take aim and fire once, don't they, Don? I can't understand the kind of anger which doesn't fizzle out.'

'Oh, I can,' Donald said, smiling. 'I can understand that. Did Your Honour ever learn to shoot? You have to go on until you stop missing.'

'Don't be hard on my son,' Carl said. 'He's very . . . young.'

He inclined his head, left him abruptly. Donald stood on the lonely pavement, with no priorities for the afternoon, except how he would later justify the time spent. A little creative reporting. He was lured by the thought of a walk by the river, any vain mission which involved staying out of doors, so he may as well try and track down the student. There was something satisfying about looking for needles in haystacks in a way that could be regarded as important, at least on paper. The rude little bastard who did not respond to phone calls could also be a prime suspect, and both he and the judge knew it.

He walked. Westminster to the Temple was not far along the side of the river. The son's college was uphill from the Embankment, not far from the Aldwych. Stone buildings were the order of the day everywhere after the Great Fire in 1666, all of them built and rebuilt beyond recognition, changed by wars, fashion, money. He was taking a bet that a spoiled student had no idea how lucky he was to be where he was, in an age of extraordinary peace and prosperity lasting longer than almost any in centuries. His own daughters were just the same.

It was hot. Eighty degrees, humid, London hot. He turned away from the river with regret, uphill to the Aldwych and the pale buildings of the London School of Economics. The kids sat outside in their dozens. The crowds, as he went uphill, seemed to move downhill, thicker as he moved. He hated not being able to walk in a straight line; it was like being inside a swarm of flies. He surveyed the milling groups of students with profound distaste, and turned back. Even with a photo of the boy, he would never find him here. Instead he found a pub and a place to sit outside with a pint, pulled out his time sheet and scribbled on it.

Mr Terry Blaker, loony tunes of no fixed abode except a hostel address, did exist, of course. The judge remembered him better than he was letting on. Blaker's valedictory message as he was led screaming from the dock was unusually biblical, according to the court notes. Judgement will be upon you, he had yelled. Your own sins will find you out. You murderer! It would be nice to know what all that was about. Donald began to be convinced by his own argument, his own categorisation of the various degrees of potential culprit for the heinous crime of giving the good judge sleepless nights. The more he thought about it, the more he convinced himself that Blaker could be good for this, because Blaker might consider himself vindicated by the parole board, an innocent, bent on revenge. Donald found to his surprise that it was all, also, beginning to matter, just a bit. He would rather it was Blaker than the judge's son, because he liked the judge. He liked his men served dry, when they knew about history. He liked it when they tried to protect their children. It did not follow that there was any urgency. He was perfectly sure that the judge was safer than most people who risked crossing the road, and that meant tomorrow would do.

It rained in the late afternoon of the Tuesday, overdue rain released in a rush after the muggy heat of the day. Rachel thought differently about rain these days. In the city it was simply a nuisance, even if it cleansed the air and brightened the trees, it did not have any obvious purpose. Now she thought of Farmer Wiseman and his hay. They needed rain, he had said, proper rain, not like the drizzle of Saturday. The more the better. A week's worth would be nice. She no longer resented the rain, except for the fact that it made people behave badly. A downpour after drought had the same effect as a snowfall in the city, creating bad temper and amazement, as if it had never happened before. It was an excuse to be late and for trains to stop. The model for the life drawing class failed to turn up. Everyone else did, and no one believed the excuse.

It happens, the teacher said. They aren't all reliable. Sorry, folks, we have to rely on ourselves. Regard it as an opportunity. Today we do heads. Our heads. Any volunteers? You? May as well start with a pretty one. Five minutes, please.

Rachel followed his instructions, sat on the dusty plastic chair on the podium in the middle of the room and made herself comfortable, as she had watched other models do, trying to find a position she could maintain. It was more difficult than she had imagined. There were precious few times in the day when anyone kept entirely still for any length of time, except when asleep, and not even then. She stared at the far wall, and immediately wanted to move. The room was silent apart from the swish of traffic in rain outside. It was a sound as soothing as the sea. She did not find the sensation of being scrutinised uncomfortable; keeping still, gazing in the same direction, she let her mind roam free. It was a great time for dreaming and planning, Ivy had told her.

'You rarely see a smiling portrait,' the teacher was saying. 'Not in pencil or charcoal, anyway. Not drawn straight from life. No one can keep up a smile for long. Not even a politician. Remember the way it seems fixed on their faces? It starts to hurt after a while. Solemnity's the natural repose for the face.'

What a short memory you have, Rachel thought. Ivy could keep up a smile for ten minutes. She had once done it here, but the teacher was right. It had been slightly disconcerting.

'Those of you who've only got a view of the back of the head,' the teacher said, 'don't worry. It's just as revealing as the front. Especially when you can see the angle of the neck. Necks are like stalks, always bending.'

Rachel's hair was severely knotted on the top of her head as usual. Lately, she was always longing to let it hang free. Now she felt she was being obliging.

'Thank you. Now you, Norman.'

A male head, by way of contrast. The one they called the Plonker took the hot seat. It reminded her of a medical examination in front of an audience. He was facing her, chose to stare at her beseechingly, rather than at the wall. Not a bad face, once she looked at it directly, gauging the distance between hairline and eyes, nose and mouth, the narrow chin. Nothing unkind about it. Any slight frisson of dislike and embarrassment he had caused disappeared completely. He was simply a face. No one else noticed that he was staring at her, willing her attention with his pleading eyes. He twitched; he was limited to three minutes. She decided that heads were less revealing than bodies. On his way back to his seat on the other side of the room, he paused by her easel.

'Listen,' he whispered urgently, taking advantage of the shuffling round as a new head took up position, pages turned to a fresh sheet of paper. 'Listen, I've got to talk to you. You flat-share with Ivy, don't you? I've got to tell you . . .'

'No you don't.'

'I was with her on Saturday night,' he said, his voice growing louder as the shuffling ceased.

'In your dreams,' Rachel muttered.

'Five minutes, please.'

He went back to his seat.

'When drawing the head,' the teacher intoned wearily, glaring at Norman, 'always remember to leave room for the brain.'

Rachel got out first at the end of the class, leaving someone else to stack her easel and chair. Ivy would be at home and her flat was full of flowers. It was still raining, and it was lovely to be going home.

In the pocket of her jacket she found the piece of bone Farmer Wiseman had handed to her out of the incinerator. A souvenir of another country. She and Ivy would go back there soon. This was the summer of her happiness, and her achievement.

She *could* find him. It was only a question of whether she should.

Chapter Seven

Rachel was proud of her flat. More aptly, she was proud of owning it. Owning anything was an achievement. Your own place, with your own door, that was the goal. It was the promised land, her father swore, the only honourable debt, the passport to safety, but then, the repossession of his own had been a nightmare never forgotten, not even when they struggled back into the gentler waters of being able to manage in a place improved within an inch of its life. They never thought it was a false dream to aspire to a lifetime of debt, or that there were others worth pursuing. Their daughter would do better. Their daughter did. Ivy didn't get it at all.

'I think he might be envious of me sometimes,' Rachel explained to Ivy. 'As well as terrified that someone will take it away. First flat at twenty-five? Beyond his dreams. His generation began with rationing, saved up to get married. Then he saved up to have me. Couldn't afford another.'

'What a pity,' Ivy said. 'There should have been more of

us. Mine tried and couldn't. I suppose I couldn't give a toss about owning anything because it was always *there*. Dad's farm was Dad's farm and his dad's farm; our house was our house, never a landlord's. It didn't make them free, because they're bound by it. They've had to fight tooth and nail to keep it, no question they could ever leave it. Dad's in debt to his ears, but he couldn't do anything else. There's never been a bean to spend and they could no more sell it than fly to the moon. It owns *them*.'

They were curled in armchairs, as comfortable as cats, barefoot and warm. The window was open to the sound of rain.

'Who's going to take over when they get too old?'

'No one.'

'You could.'

Ivy shook her head. 'No, I'd never be strong enough for that. It's not in my blood, and he couldn't bear it. It's just not the natural order of things, you see. It simply has to go to a man. He doesn't talk about it, but I know what he dreams of. A son to take over, or a grandson now. Or if not to take over, at least to admire, understand, appreciate. To *see*. To share, or mourn, something like. Poor man. I've let him down.'

Rachel focused on her glass. 'You never know. Maybe Sam's out there, yearning for real country life. Wanting a grandfather.'

Ivy laughed. 'Wouldn't that be nice? Carl would have to be dead before Sam would ever be allowed to go back there, even just to see.'

'You don't know that.'

Rachel was uncomfortable. It was the wrong time for the conversation. Ivy thought so too.

'Yes I do. Believe me, I do. He'd do anything to prevent it.

Where does this wine come from? It's a lovely piss-coloured yellow. I'd rather talk about that than talk about parents. Why do we always do it?'

'Because you invited my father to supper, and we were talking about him. Because we're attached to them by that blasted umbilical cord no one ever severs. They have their hypodermics into our veins. We want them happy; they want us happy. They're the only people who remain the subject of mutual fascination. Oh God, look at the time. Again. What time are you starting in the morning?'

'It is the morning. I start at five. I'll have plenty of time to go to Berwick Street after I've finished the shift. It's my old stomping ground. There's a bit of this lovely stuff left.'

'Wish you didn't work such crazy hours,' Rachel grumbled. 'Don't know how you do it. Three hours' sleep and you're raring to go.'

She was drowsy. Well past midnight. They could talk for hours; it was easier than breathing; they were pleasantly, indolently drunk. She had come home to home-cooked food: Ivy could cook like her mother. The flat was still full of flowers, smelled of herbs and perfume and coffee and home, like a lived-in lair. Ivy had that knack, without changing a thing. It was a strange talent for someone who also relished homelessness.

'I'll do better with the grub when you father comes. What time did you say that was?'

'Tomorrow. About six thirty. He won't have anything with garlic. How much did you use? Oh, I shall be sweet in the morning. Mustn't breathe on anyone.' Rachel burped, discreetly.

'Will he be safe to get home if we give him wine like this?' Ivy asked.

'Oh yes. He'll go like a homing pigeon, soon as he can. He's only sixty-eight. One stroke, plenty of anxiety, bit of arthritis, asthma, controlled as long as he's got his inhaler and his calming pills. He's short of breath and timid. Doesn't like the dark. Lonely and refuses to admit it. God know what he's inhaled from DIY. More than the forty fags a day which were mandatory in his youth, he says. Gave them up when they got pricey, mourned them ever since. I never know where real illness ends and hypochondria begins, he won't tell me. And he won't drink wine unless I tell him it's cheap. The cheaper the better.'

'Speaking as one weaned on the homemade variety,' Ivy said, 'I think anything else is wonderful.'

The flat was on the fringes of the City, where Gray's Inn Road met Theobald's Road in a welter of multipurpose streets. It had been bought for investment, rather than beauty. Rachel had not cared. She could walk or bus to work.

Not a thing of beauty in its own right, a series of four featureless rooms in an old house, with no hint of what it might have been. The advent of Ivy, the presence of the flowers and the contrast of Midwinter Farm made Rachel notice how bland her own home was. That was going to change too. There was a single wall in her bedroom she had begun to paint and never finished. She was going to be late for work tomorrow, again, and she didn't care.

'I swear there's an old fireplace behind that wall,' Ivy said, pointing vaguely. 'Should be, anyway. We could make this place really cool, you know. Don't ever ask Grace to visit. She'd rip the wall down as soon as look at it. Forgot to ask. How was the life class? Did you miss me?'

'We certainly did. Absentee model. We did heads. The Plonker was there, asking after you.'

'Was he now? He was at my Saturday class too. I reckon he goes to them all. It's me next week, I think. I'll certainly turn up.'

It was so easy, being with Ivy, having Ivy there and a bottle of wine between them. A full stomach. No need for the conversation to make much sense. No need to be clever, or witty, or even talk in a straight line. Nothing to prove.

'My father will ask you lots of questions,' Rachel said. 'He's like that. Critical and suspicious.'

''S only natural. Wants you safe and well with suitable friends, preferably male. No debts or debtors, get the picture. No probs. That's a parent for you. Oh God, we should be asleep. Honestly, what are we like? I'm bad for you.'

'No you aren't. You're good for me.'

Rachel stood up, uncertainly, sat down again. Surely there was no real urgency about going to bed. It was nicer here.

'Did you hear about that man who got murdered in the ambulance? They said it was done by garrotte. Who the hell goes round with a garrotte in his pocket?'

'Oh, I dunno,' Ivy said. 'People who sell cheese.'

It seemed, at the time, inordinately funny. The best thing about Ivy was the giggling.

The fourth image had been sent to the judge the evening before. He had e-mailed it on, as instructed. A printed copy was folded into Donald's pocket.

Another old woodcut, from a book maybe. It showed Eve being banished from the Garden of Eden. God stood by an apple tree, waving a sword, with his foot upon the head of a serpent, directing Eve from the safety of the wood towards a wilderness containing nothing but water. She covered her face with her hands, begging for mercy. Even with the large foot of God standing on its head, the conquered serpent he trod into the ground squirmed with delight at its own success. Donald thought it was amazing how many messages could be shown in a few lines.

It was embellished with the legend, *The worm has turned. You will die soon.*

Donald loved a good misty morning. Especially if it obscured traffic in the mean end of the city, round about City Road, Whitechapel, Commercial Road, where all was ugliness. He could concede the hinterland was rich in exotic markets, sweat shops, Asian and African endeavours, but all he could think of was the solid identity and history it had lost, and he could not love it. The high rise of the City, the gherkin tower and all the landmarks were behind, while in front was early-morning, heavy-duty traffic on the way to the Blackwall Tunnel, that sinister, curving, underground conduit which snuck under the river Thames and connected the east of London to the east of Kent on the other side, without ever affording a view of either. Slower by car than by water. It would have been better to take the monorail train which sailed above and over, and made the sweating developments and distinctly old-fashioned poverty beneath look glamorous in sunlight, even better in mist. You could live by the river on the south side and commute into the centre without your feet ever touching the ground, without ever seeing how all those who crowded on and off came to reach their point. It was the same, less picturesque, but equally removed experience by car. Eyes straight ahead, looking for the chance to overtake, avoiding the humiliating prospect of getting lost.

He found the complex, got rid of the car, and cursed the fact that he would, at some point, possibly sooner rather than later, have to come back and find it and do the route back all over again. Never mind, it clocked up the hours. No one ever could ever deny or disbelieve the amount of time it might take to get to anywhere in London.

The judge's apartment was part of a complex, where residents parked cars underground and visitors reported to a gate for instructions from a man in a booth, who looked as if he was rooted to the spot, in command of two syllables, yes and no. The man in the booth seemed to be dealing with another man, both of them debating methods of pest control. Twenty apartments here, all turned outwards, so nobody faced the hinterland, only the water. He found his way.

It was always a gamble to imagine a nineteen-year-old would keep an appointment, or return a phone call, but less of a one to calculate that a student would still be asleep at ten in the morning, even in his father's house. Donald kept his finger on the buzzer, and turned his harmless profile to the small screen which would show his face inside. Video entry. Localised to this flat. Appropriate for a judge, perhaps. Not, as far as he knew, for a student of the wider world.

He was right in his assumption, based on his own experience, that Sam would not have left the house; Donald's wife would have said the same, and both of them would be wrong in assuming he would be asleep. The boy who flung open the door, without giving himself time to look at the screen within, was wide awake, as if waiting to present himself and knowing he was a pleasure to behold, as if dressed in new clothes he wanted to show. His face fell, then he lifted his shoulders in exaggerated acceptance as he glanced at the ID card.

'Oh, shit. I thought you were the man about the rats. Or my friend.'

'I'm everyone's friend,' Donald said. 'Can I come in?'

Sam turned from the door, leaving Donald to close it behind him and follow him into the living room he recognised from before, with a balcony facing the river, easy seating, comfortable enough, unnaturally, office-like tidy and as much dominated by a desk as another kind of room would be by an overlarge piano. Donald was grateful to turn his back on the boy in order to compose his face for the second view. The judge was right: the photo of the teenage child did not help. This was a vision of loveliness, moving like a dancer interrupted in the middle of a rehearsal, midway between a change of scene and certainly a change of clothes, possibly awaiting a second opinion. The outfit for Scene Two included voluminous white trousers, spilling over bare brown feet, a sleeveless top of orange linen, a small row of delicate beads round a slender neck, and studs for ear and nose which, in the light of the room, flashed purple, discordant with the red streak in his short, dark, spiked hair.

'Do you like it?' he said, rubbing one hand through. 'It takes *ages*.'

'Prefer long hair on a bloke myself,' Donald said. 'Hate this short stuff. I love a good curly perm myself. Least you don't have a buzz cut, like all the gays. Is that you, by the way? Or are you just camp?'

Sam shrugged.

'Both,' he said. 'Been this way since twelve. Coffee or tea? You must be the copper dealing with Dad's bugbears, right? OK, OK. I'll own up. I did it. 'Twas I brought in the rat. On my coat tails. So to speak.'

'Oh? Why was that?'

'There's a woman lives downstairs, keeps her precious car in the basement. Afraid I scratched it, parking ours. I forgot to mention it. She might have left the rat as a message.

There's always a problem with rats. Tee hee hee. Terrible people live here.'

'Coffee, please,' Donald said.

The peacock son disappeared, with waggling hips. The trousers did not fit. Thinking as a father, Donald hoped they had not cost a lot of money. Not for the first time, he was grateful for the experience of being a parent, had a fleeting memory of trying to control his own sense of shock and outrage the first time one of his daughters had appeared with a belly button stud. If this father's son thought he had the capacity to shock with his peacock display, he had chosen the wrong type of person, although Donald did have to admit to surprise. A judge's son? Dressed like that and as camp as a tent? Why not? Look how judges had to dress, for God's sake. Red robes and ermine for special occasions. Maybe it was catching. From the sad vantage point of impending middle age, Donald wished he had once had the nerve to dress like that.

He followed the boy's flowing progress into the kitchen. The room was small and spotless, utterly functional, devoid of any decorative touch. There were no residual cooking smells. The kitchen was not the heart of the house in this place; it did not seem to have any heart. Framed by the window, the sun striking though the thin fabric of his shirt to reveal a thin body as he filled the kettle from the tap, Sam looked suddenly vulnerable. He was just another kid, with kid's problems and a hell of a lot more thrown in, poor sod. No wonder his father wanted to protect him. He had a lifetime of trouble ahead already. What a boy like that needed was a mother. Donald was more at home with a boy he could think of as a girl than he would have been with some sporty, macho, more typical public school youth. He perched himself on a high stool, next to the kitchen counter. There was another stool on the far side, which would leave a comfortable gap between them.

'Your dad tells me you're studying economics. Shouldn't it be fashion design?'

Sam spoke over his shoulder, spooning ground coffee into a cafetiere. No simple instant here.

'Politics *and* economics. No, I find it fascinating. Sometimes. Besides, it's a safer option, and whatever my father thinks, I do want to earn a living some day. Milk?'

'Please. Isn't it a bit restricting, living with your father? Wouldn't you be better off in digs or something?'

Especially if you crash cars and go out dressed like a tart.

'For the good of my soul, yes. For the good of my pocket, no. I don't study economics for nothing. He's always trying to get me to go, especially now. Says all this is too overprivileged for words, unsuitable for my age, blah blah blah, but why should I? Why should I rough it in some dump when I can smooth it here?'

His voice was shrill with almost childish indignation.

'He's always going on about it. How a generation of peace and prosperity has spoiled us. Why not? Isn't that progress? Why should I have to live in squalor and work every hour just because he did as his father did? Honestly. He wants me to go back to his ghastly roots. No way.'

'His German roots?'

'No, the other ones.'

Donald found all this slightly amusing and kept quiet until the coffee was poured. Sam sat across from him, challenging him to say something. Donald was wondering if the tan was fake, then sighed and shook himself. He found the young desperately fascinating, but there was the matter in hand.

'You know why I'm here. Someone's threatening your dad. It happens with judges. They aren't popular people.'

Sam snorted. 'I think it's all bollocks. I think he's exaggerating. He's trying to get me to leave . . .'

Think of him as a daughter. Make yourself at home. Risk having an argument.

'Oh, come on. You really think he'd tell lies, just to make you go? Draw attention to himself like this? He could just put your stuff in the street and change the locks, if that's what he wanted.'

He wants to protect you. I can quite see why.

Sam slumped. Then he shrugged and smiled. It was a great relief to find a kid without an in-built attitude problem to the filth. Maybe it was just his own face. Maybe the boy was lonely.

'No, to be honest. But he wouldn't actually throw me out either. He can't make things up, he's too literal. But he might want to make me feel sorry for him, so I'll do what he wants. You know, poor me, someone's after me, just do this little thing to please me, like, leave. He's always going on at me...'

Probably frightened of leaving. Donald sighed.

'Parents do that, Sam. That's what we're paid for. What I wanted to know from you was whether you had any idea of who might be doing it. Such as, was it yourself? Or might this little campaign have been aimed at you, rather than him?'

He waited for an explosion of offence at the very outrageous suggestion, but there was none. Sam seemed mildly amused, even flattered, fluttered his eyelashes and placed his hand over his heart.

'Me? What a thought. Some poor broken-hearted rejected, spiteful boyfriend of mine? Puleese! No, Mr Cousins sweetie, despite what I say, I'm quite fond of the old bugger, except when he nags me and bangs on about the past. I don't want to leave him alone, and I don't want him dead until I'm ready to inherit. He hasn't done too badly by me, really, and I haven't made it easy. At least he didn't drag me in front of a shrink when I showed all the signs and got expelled from the first school. But he isn't consistent. First he keeps me away from my mother, now he wants me to get in touch with her. He nags and nags.'

The self-absorption was fascinating, but children were irritating when they whined. How many times had he told his own it was the worst thing they could ever do, especially when they wanted their own way. Hysteria was more effective. Donald did not need family confidences; he simply wanted to be seen to be thorough. Of course he had to interview the son, but he did not really need adolescent angst, even if he was interested. It wasn't as if a missing mother/wife could come into this equation. She and the judge had parted years ago, amicably, the judge said. There was a daughter who had died in a drowning accident. The marriage never recovered; they went their separate ways, and he brought up the boy. Donald had not, so far, investigated mummy at all, except to see, from her sheet, that she was a bit of a raver. He wished the records would show who had paid her fines, but they didn't. Odd that she wanted no contact with her boy, but then maybe he wasn't her type. Not everyone would cherish a son like this. What he really needed to ask was had sonny boy seen anyone hanging around, in a real or metaphorical sense? Did Carly baby have a jealous girlfriend, was there another, obvious suspect?

He had already put aside the notion that Sammy was either the target or the perpetrator. He was far too ineffectual for that, and there was something about the boy which shrieked of virginity. Not literally, perhaps, no one ever knew about that, but he did seem to have an innocence of subterfuge. Too innocent by far, too self-absorbed for any criminal enterprise, way too concerned about what had been done to *him*. There was always the circuitous route to information, such as let them blather on and pick up a clue. Make them think they were witty and wise beyond their years. Really, he had learned more about interviewing technique from being a father than he had from any other training course. His wife said so.

'I expect your mother's worried about you,' he said. 'They never stop, you know. Worrying.'

The result of these remarks was dramatic, as if he had placed a syringe into a major vein, or given the kid an electric shock. Sam picked up the empty cafetiere and flung it against the wall of stainless steel units to his left. It thumped, intact, fell to the floor, and smashed into pieces. The result was a mess of coffee on the pristine floor, and a shower of black liquid over Donald's trousers, below knee level. They were dark blue jeans; he didn't care and stayed still, aware the boy was watching him.

'My mother,' Sam said dramatically, 'did not give a shit about me. OK, so she was fucked up when my sister died. I can get that. She was *awful*. She pinched me, she tormented me, she was fucking *dangerous*, and then she went. When I was a kid, I was dragged to this farm, chucked in the sea, dunked in a pond, because that's what my sister wanted. I hated that stuff. My mother hated me because I hated that stuff. *I hate her*. So when my grandmother writes, I get to the letters first and send them back. Dad doesn't know. Why the hell should I ever have to go back to that awful place? Why should I *ever* see her? *He* thinks I should. Oh, fuck.'

He got up, and with scrupulous, speedy care wiped up the mess with a wodge of paper towels, using a fistful to clutch at the glass remnants. He ignored the impact on Donald's ankles, blue denim not worth preserving. Donald stayed fairly still, merely extending his ankle to survey the damage. It would look as if he had been wading in liquid shit. In pursuit of rats on a riverbank. Never mind.

'Go through many of those, do you? Like, one a day, or what?'

There was a rattle from the area round a corner as Sam tipped the rubbish into a bin. He came back, visibly refreshed; sat on the opposite stool.

'Only when you mention my mother. You won't tell Dad about the letters? I mean, they're written to him, from my grandmother, but I see them first 'cos I'm always here when the post comes. Then I send them back. And it would be nice if he were to know about the rat from someone else. I can't tell him.'

'When I was a boy,' Donald said, 'you got a man with a ferret in to deal with rats.'

'So did they, on the farm,' Sam said dreamily. 'My father is always reminding me that his father was a farm labourer. He thinks that's part of my heritage, and he thinks I ought to rediscover it. They want to drag me back there. Into that lake. My mother would drown me. She tried hard enough. Why should I want to know her?'

This really was getting off the point. Or maybe not. The lad smelt clean, no dope, just kind of volatile. Donald cleared his throat.

'We might have found someone with the right kind of grudge against your father,' he said. 'Someone he sent to prison. Can you think of anyone else who might hate him? After all, you know him best.'

Sam was making more coffee. Donald reflected that it was his own, desperate ordinariness which was the talent most overlooked by his employers. People told him things because he was indistinguishable from the man who came to read the gas meter. And because, after all, he looked like everyone's dad. Not everyone's dad, to be fair. Sam continued the process of making the coffee.

'Know him? I doubt if anyone does. He's a hard bastard who drives himself hard and thinks everyone else should do the same. Work, work, work. He doesn't need anyone threatening to kill him to make him miserable. He can't even get himself a woman. Wish he would.'

There was a quick grin in Donald's direction.

'He moans at me, you know? Like you all do, right? Other days, I tell you, he's a laugh a minute, a fucking gem. He needs a bit of teasing, know what I mean? It's just sometimes I wish I wasn't the only one loves the silly sod. He deserves better than me, really. A real woman. Have you ever seen him laugh? It's a treat, I tell you.'

No.

'Has he ever done anything he's ashamed of? As far as you know?'

Sam shook his head, then reconsidered.

'No. I very much doubt it. Unless you include shooting the swans.'

There were great advantages to a big, blank face.

'Oh, he can shoot, can he?'

Sam poured water into the new jug, releasing the coffee smell to which Donald remained addicted, even when he shook with caffeine shock.

Sam's hands were steady. Donald admired anyone who could move from temper tantrum to calm as if cleansed by it.

'My father can bring in the harvest, pick apples, climb trees and shoot,' Sam said proudly, counting off these talents by clapping his hands together in slow applause. 'Which gifts he would like me to share. But . . .' He moved across to the countertop, depositing the coffee before going back to wash his hands beneath the tap. No way this boy ever handled a dead rat. 'That was a long time ago. He was taught by his father, *liebling*, and his father was a soldier. So, copper, don't go looking for guns around here. All that was down on that bloody farm. Where Mummy came from. I can hardly blame my father for learning about murder. Animal farming's all about killing things. And shooting the swans was a terrible thing, because his father had done the same. Blah, blah, blah.'

'Do you think,' Donald said, 'we could go back to the beginning?'

Grace took the gun in both hands and shot into the wall. The sound always surprised her. The blind cow which was never going to have a calf skittered at the sound of the shot, but without spirit. They were in the far barn, away from the others. The cow, which was smaller than the rest, was tethered to the wall with a rope halter, and it was not the rope which steadied her. She knew. Grace was talking to her. Your daddy bought you without a passport, silly sod, because he thought he could see promise in you. Do you wonder no one ever gave him the money to buy a racehorse? And you have to go, because the others shun you. They know you're never going to come on heat. You are causing ripples of discontent. Cows have feelings; they are capable of bearing grudges, fearing for the future, knowing one of them is under a death sentence and wanting it to be over.

There was something horribly moving about an unseeing head, swaying, ears twitching away flies, tongue working, digestion rumbling, all of that muscle supporting that flesh and mammoth quantity of weight, even her shrivelled udders. This one was so small, she was no bigger than three large men welded together. She allowed herself to be led. She would not eat, she would not grow, she would not reproduce. Her infertility rendered her undesirable even to those dumb females, herded together, mounting the one in heat in order to satisfy some primeval itch, mimicking the bull. No heat, no insemination, no pregnancy, no calf, no milk. That was that. If only she did not look so ashamed. She reeked of the sweet, bad breath of unproductivity. At least she was blind.

Grace raised the gun, steadied it. The shot made less sound than the practice shot which had hit the wall. Guns like these were only useful at close range, about three feet. Better this way, darling, than being herded on to the lorry with everyone else. So much more distinctive, and quick.

Grace was angry with Ernest. Ernest should be doing this. Ernest had agonised about the beast, as Ernest did, and she was sick of it. Ernest could not kill anything. He had bought the animal out of sentiment, and he could not even kill her. They could buy cattle and raise them, but not kill them, unless they had slipped the bureaucratic net, as she had. They could nurture but they could not kill humanely; they must pinion a bovine beast in terror and make it wait its turn for transport and ignominy. They could not kill, or bury decently, their own stock, raised on their own hay, on their own land. Piglets, yes, cattle, no.

The cow had buckled, gracefully, like a performer taking a drunken bow, collapsing on stage with a little elegance and scarcely a tremor. Grace eyed the size of her. Too big for the incinerator. Too much for the freezer.

She wandered off for a minute, smoked a cigarette; leave it a minute or two, let the blood settle. Tried not to get cross with Ernest for leaving her to do this. It was always her, or Ivy. Woman's work. Ernest could use the guns to scare rooks from trees, was all. He could use his knife to slit the twine on bales. Grace stubbed out her cigarette, grinding the stub into the mud.

She found the axe and swung it down. If she could take off that great big head, and sever the legs at the knees, the torso would fit, although it would take a long time to burn the bone. Hack it and make it manageable. He could do the rest. He was the butcher. Once a thing was dead, Ernest ceased to mourn. He could not kill, but he could pick up pieces. He was still as strong as the ox he would refuse to slaughter, with the memory of the elephants he had never seen in reality. If ever he watched TV, it was wildlife programmes.

She had stood to one side to sever the head with the long-handled axe, and still got splattered. It took practice. You could not kill things without practice; it was a skill, slow in the learning.

She put the head inside the incinerator, temperature at max, left the rest for him, and took the tether she had rescued first back to the house.

They knew: the cattle knew, the Polish herdsman knew what she had done. Beasts and humans. They were all in there, straight after milking. Looking at her as she went into the barn under the scrutiny of all those bovine eyes. Huge eyes, above slow-moving, chewing mandibles, staring as if fixated with accusation. Instead of ignoring her, letting her walk through, they turned on her and moved towards her, as they did with someone new, frightening in their fresh, accusatory curiosity. A hundred tons of flesh and bone, barring her path. She shouted at them: they stood back a step, and then came forward. Grace ignored them.

She peeled off the oversized, splattered overall outside the kitchen door, carried it in with her at arm's length and stuffed it into the washing machine in the alcove. Licence to kill meant licence to wash. Kill, wash, kill, wash. She hummed over the preparation of the late breakfast. Omelettes today; toast; cereal. No bacon, although, as she thought, she had never had the least sentiment about pigs. She hummed as she worked.

My young love said to me, your mother won't mind.
And my father won't mind you for your lack of kind,
And she stepped away from me, and this did she say,
It will not be long, love, till our wedding day . . .

Ernest came in, shyly.

'You've got to cut her up,' Grace said gently. 'You should have cleaned the gun. Oh darling, what are we going to do?'

'Wait for Ivy,' he said, then corrected himself, in the face of her stare.

'Wait for him?'

His eyes were still the same, pellucid, far-seeing blue. Paler now.

The guests trooped in for breakfast.

Ernest told them about the lake. He had told them about the lake yesterday.

They looked around for the cat and the dog they considered mandatory in a farmhouse kitchen.

Grace missed them too. And the chickens they had had when Ivy was small.

Chapter Eight

Pets were an indulgence, Grace explained. They did not need a dog to round up sheep, since there were no sheep. They did not need a cat to catch mice; chemical poisons did the trick.

What about rats? one of them said. You must get rats, on a farm. Grace opened her mouth to deny it. After harvest or haymaking, surely? the guest asked, with the wise look of one who knows such things from years of walking across other people's fields. She guessed he must have seen one: the next step would be to ask for a reduction in the bill. There was often a method behind the most artless of questions.

Ernest shook his head. For those you get in the rat man, he said. With his ferret. That's his job. Have you seen any ferrets? There's lots around here. You only see them at night. Beautiful things. Now that's what I'd call a worthwhile pet.

She had been aware of the rat in the house for the last three days. Their appearance was a mystery at certain times of year, although she was sure there was a logical explanation. *I can't stand the rats,* Ivy would say. Can't kill them either. She missed her daughter with a sudden, sharp pain.

As they scraped back their chairs, thanking her for omelettes and toast and fruit compote, an extra figure loomed in the doorway. Ed did not deserve the sobriquet of village policeman, although he looked as though he could audition for the role because he was fat, wore an unseasonal uniform and played the part of a weary paterfamilias. He usually arrived to check licences or the occasional stolen car left abandoned in a field, and Grace regarded him as simply another lazy bureaucrat with an alien accent. He smiled at the paying guests like a time-worn uncle, wished them a nice day, and wasn't it a good one.

It was, if she had time to notice. Bright and warm, but not too warm, just right for walking about in shirtsleeves. A good day, following rain, with more rain promised in the afternoon. Obliging weather for the hay.

'Make it quick, Ed,' she said, handing him a mug of coffee and banging about behind his back. 'Because I've got a lot to do. Like go out for a walk with my husband. You can't have come to check gun licences. You know we haven't had a rifle here for years.'

Ed sat down heavily, with the right ponderous manner for a serious errand.

'Not even an old one, I'll bet. No, Mrs Wiseman. It's about one of your B and B people. Do you recall a bloke who stayed here for a week, earlier on? Middle of May or thereabouts? Young man from London? He came on his own. They remember him in the pub.'

'I remember them all, but none of them in particular. Why?'

'Only it seems he went missing, back in London, or so they thought. Took a couple of weeks after he left here for anyone to notice. Then this body turned up, off the coast, six miles down from Wethering. Taken them all this time to put the two together.'

Grace was clearing the table. Ernest sat quietly.

'What's that got to do with us?' she said.

'Don't rightly know, but it looks like his last night staying with you was the last time anyone saw him. There was a party at the pub.'

'There's always a party at the pub, if someone's willing to buy the drinks,' Grace said crossly.

'He was in the pub most nights, they say.'

Her face cleared, she nodded and sat down.

'Oh yes, *that* one. I do remember him. Jack something. Jack the lad . . . No, it was Joe. Having a holiday because he'd split up from a girl or something. Remember him, Ernest? He was the only one I've ever had who wanted a quiet, healthy week in the country for the express purpose of getting drunk every night. Poor soul. What happened?'

'Don't know. He drove back to London, for sure. Put his suitcase inside his house, and that's all he did. They say in the pub that Ivy was in that last night.'

Grace nodded, trying to remember. 'So? Yes. I've got it now. She was home that week, wasn't she, Ernest? We were *both* in the pub that night. I'm allowed out sometimes, you know. They give me free drinks, for all the people I send there. We're good for trade.'

'That's nice.'

'He was a bit obnoxious, to be honest,' Grace said. 'My God, he was even flirting with *me*. I'd mothered him a bit. Now I remember. It was that little heat wave we had, like we sometimes do in May. I got him back here, he went to bed. He was packed and ready, wanted to go early in the morning, to miss the traffic. And he did. Not so much as a thank-you. I thought that was funny, since he'd really enjoyed himself. Made friends, he said.'

Ed got up. 'Is that all? You've no idea why he might have come back to the coast?'

'You want to ask them in the pub. They'd have known him best. We've no idea. He said he'd definitely book for next year. I don't know, I just don't know.'

They all bowed heads in silent sympathy.

'Ah well,' Ed said. 'I was asked to ask. I'll let you get out for your walk. Lucky for some. How are you keeping, Mr Wiseman?' he shouted, as if Ernest was deaf, the way he did with anyone old.

'Fine.'

It was not true.

It was an old habit, walking round the farm, or further afield. The courtship of Ernest and Grace had taken the form of walking, getting away from scrutinising eyes. What could not be done in a house could be done in a field or a copse. He could buy her a drink in a pub, once borrowed his dad's car for a drive somewhere else. The permissive, expensive hedonism of the 1960s had simply not applied here, only the same old rituals. The first time he had ever seen her semi-naked was by the lake. Grace in a swimsuit had taken his breath away; Grace being the better swimmer had alarmed him. She had been born by the sea a few miles away; she loved the sea. He had offered her the lake of which he was so proud, as if he had created it for her pleasure, presented it to her as a substitute for the sea. I made this with Carl, he told her. Carl was with me.

Ivy swam here, every summer day, only after Grace taught her first in the sea. It was easier to learn in the buoyant salt water. Even after the enormous expanse of the sea, the lake seemed romantically large to a child, from a child's height. In reality it was a hundred yards long at most, dwindling to the point where it became river, then stream, with a narrow breadth between the bank and the woods on the far side, where the swans nested. A swimmer could treat it as a pool and do laps. It was safe and sheltered, and semi-secret, because it was so far from a road, there was no official footpath, and people were lazy. Locals knew; kids with bikes knew, but it never featured on a map. It was supposed to have died. There was no toilet, no coffee shop, and no games to play except sitting and eating picnics. There were occasional campers, who asked at the house first. There was no easy access to the water, which was muddy near the edge, and the place had a reputation for contamination and danger. The Wiseman family did not own the water, although everyone assumed they did because it was Ernest who picked up the litter. But it was his. It was their starting point and their nemesis.

Grace had fallen in love with the idea of a pond on the doorstep far sooner than she had fallen in love with Ernest. Carl was always there, then and now.

The habit was to walk, and sit, anywhere, including here, to talk about what was important, or not. Sometimes the point was not to talk at all, and then whatever it was which was festing cured itself and could be dealt with later. Or never, because it had ceased to matter. The presence of the lake was indeed his gift to her. Grace had sat in the field above, paused at the curve in the track, sat on the bank, swum herself into exhaustion, and chewed the cud here, and in the process had submerged all her greatest resentments without actually burying them. The fact that it had turned against her, and that the place itself, as well as its reigning swans, had delivered up to her the corpse of her grandchild, was a temporary aberration, a defection and betrayal held deep, but usually forgiven. The impact of that event went far beyond. She wondered now, as they sat on the bank in high summer, if Ernest saw what she saw, or if she could see what he did through his dark glass, and how long ago it was since they had lost the knack of telling one another the truth, or at what point she had decided he could not stand it, any more than she could. Or quite when it was he had begun to fade. All she knew was that when they looked at the lake, he had memories longer than hers, different visions of happiness and horror. And that he had never once had an ounce of her cunning or her acumen, or her passion, for which she thanked what passed for God, and loved him more, because he was still beautiful and he could always surprise her. As long as he would do as he was told.

'Why did you lie?' he said to her, absently, as they lounged in the grass.

'About what?'

'About who brought who back from the pub. That poor, silly boy. What a pain in the neck he was.'

'I didn't lie. That's what I remembered.'

'You lie all the time, lovely. Thank you for dealing with the cow. You were singing in the kitchen. Can you do it again? You might bring them out.'

Grace hummed.

She stepped away from me, and she moved through the fair.
And fondly I watched her move here and move there,
And she made her way homeward with one star awake,
As the swan in the evening moves over the lake.

'There they go,' he said. 'Not waiting for evening.'

The swans came into view on the wooded side of the lake, the cygnets, two months old, big enough to fend for themselves, preening each other. The bulky nest was hidden away. Ernest knew what went into the nest, every single ingredient; he followed its progress. Grace never had. The nest was built in March and April, favouring an isolated shoreline. Made of vegetation, rushes, short-stemmed grasses, hidden but clumsy. Defended aggressively. They moulted on nesting, to feather the heap, could not fly away for seven weeks after and could only defend their citadel from the water. The babies were downy brown, half adult weight, but without their dignified serenity.

'Took them a while, didn't it?' he said. 'I mean, they're getting on, aren't they? They can start nesting at three, and these buggers were that old when I got 'em. How long ago was that, Grace? Five years? I know they can go on doing it, and it takes 'em a while to settle, and they'll maybe live until a swan song at twenty-one years, but isn't it great? They're eight years apiece, that mother and father, and aren't they proud? I am. It changes the view.'

She knew what he was seeing. He was not talking about *these* swans; he was talking about the other swans which had swum here a decade ago. The May swans, with their babies, blasted over the lake. May blossom from the hawthorn scattering the surface. Greasy blood on the rippling water, like an oil slick, white feathers dancing in the draught of a breeze, the reverberation of rifle shots, echoing. The real death. He could see it now, and Grace knew he could see it. He could see it behind the relatively new swans; he could see the old carnage. Ernest remembered a succession of swans, some more than others, Nina and Hans most of all.

'Oh Lord, how I hated him,' Ernest said. 'Old Carl and I, we got those swans, can't remember how. That pair we had ten years ago, we called them Nina and Hans, after his own siblings. They were already old, six if they were a day. I'd given up hope of them ever doing it. They built nests for three years, but it was only going through the motions, poor sods. No cygnets until that year, and then, hey presto, there they were. The darlings, they did it. No wonder Hans was so stroppy. It was probably his last chance. No one should swim here in May. And then he shot them all, even the cygnets. I hated him then.'

'So does our daughter.'

He did not seem to hear. She knew what he could see, and if she had not loved him for what he was, she would have hated him for the nature of his regret. Always Carl and the swans. It was as if he cared more about the death of the swans than the death of a child, as if the memory of the swans was superimposed on the image of that other, less interesting, less damaged, almost bloodless corpse.

'He came back in the evening. He got the rifle and blasted them out of the water.'

'I don't hate him for killing the swans,' Grace said. 'That's the one thing I could understand. I might have done it myself.'

'And I don't hate him any more, Carl the younger. Why should we? Nina and Hans came back. I want *him* to come back. And bring his son, like old Carl did.'

There were pockets of fluffy clouds moving across the blue sky, casting shadows on the water, turning it dull, then bright as they moved away. The swans were bright white one moment, dull white the next, with the orange beaks of the cob and his mate glowing as they appeared to confer. She could remember the other scene, the May assassination, when the feathers scattered over the water were confused with drifting blossom; saw the birds rearing out of the water, too late. There had been no swan song.

Grace could feel the old, familiar jealousy. The way she had felt when Carl the elder appeared with his baby son, when she was still childless, watching them embrace each other as brothers and loving friends, and watching Ernest fuss that child, because he was a *boy*.

'It was a mistake, wasn't it, not to tell Ivy at once. About how it had happened. To let her have dreams of Cassie being turned into a swan.'

'I'm glad you remember that much,' Grace said caustically.

'I heard you with her. I suppose it helped to get her to sleep.'

May heat waves. A sudden spurt of August-like warmth which made them all want to peel off winter clothes. There could be snow in April, heat fever in May, but never for long. *Hottest bank holiday on record since 1899*. They always said that.

'It wasn't Carl's fault,' Ernest said. 'I wish he'd come back.'

He always missed the point, Grace thought, curling her fist around a clump of grass. Of course it had been Carl's fault. She remembered him coming into the house, clutching that bawling, abominable boy, as if he could not walk, throwing him towards his mother, who was having a well-earned rest at the kitchen table, sharing motherly moans over tea. All *he* had had to do was supervise them down by the lake. He couldn't even do that. The boy got fractious, so he brought him back. OK to leave Cassie. Actually, it did seem OK to leave Cassie; they all thought so. She could swim like a fish; the lake was shallow; she could run home in her bare feet in three minutes. Only she didn't. She hadn't. Grace could never understand how Ernest did not hate Carl the younger for the casual, wilful destruction of his wife, Ernest's daughter, which followed.

'She must have been on her back, with her neck extended, for the cob to bite her like that,' Ernest said. 'And make that mark. She must have swum too close to the nest.'

As if she did not know. As if it hadn't been gone over again and again.

The lake was calm and dark under the fitful cloud. It was hardly a lake, more a pond. It was difficult to imagine the water churning, the swan's beak around that tiny neck, pulling her under, making her panic, drowning her noise. Such a noisy, determined, talkative thing.

'He shouldn't have left her,' Grace said stubbornly.

'I'm hungry,' Ernest said. 'Is there anything for lunch?'

He was like that now. A narrow concentration span, skittering away and taking refuge in the dreams she would love to fulfil for him. She put out her hand, took his and hauled him to his feet, feeling the weight of his bones. He still saw so much more than he ever shared. Sometimes she thought she scarcely knew him at all. The path back to the house seemed long. He would have to deal with the cow after lunch, even it meant there were more flies. Otherwise, he would not eat.

'Ivy's all right now,' he announced.

Her belief in his insight faded again. He had heard her that once, ten years ago, telling Ivy that Cassie had merely turned into a swan. He had never heard Ivy screaming in the night, never gone to hunt for her in the meaner streets of London, never known what ailed her, or the only way it could be cured. Revenge. He did not understand the coldness of anger, only the brief heat.

'I like that Rachel,' he said. 'Lovely girl. I don't like Ivy going to live with her, though. It isn't really fair on her, is it? You're using her, both of you.'

Yes, he did understand. She should never underestimate him.

'We must give her a better time when she comes back. Take her to the pub instead of talking her to death,' Grace said. 'No, on second thoughts, not the pub.'

He sighed, ignoring her again.

'Just as well he sends back the letters, really. The boy will come when he's ready. He'll find his own way. Just as well we don't know where young Carl lives any more. Just as well we don't have any way of finding out, nor Ivy either. We don't have the right, you know.'

'No,' Grace said, meekly. 'We can't find out where he is. Not without spending money we haven't got.'

'He said he would look after us,' Ernest complained. 'He *promised*.'

'That was when he married Ivy.'

He lived on another planet. The computer was only for the cows and his records, and he did that with difficulty and resentment. Of course they could find out where a man whom she knew had become a judge *worked*, if not where he lived. If they knew how to access internet directories, libraries, had the courage. Of course there were ways, but she did not know them. Nor could she leave him for long enough to find out. Ivy neither. Ivy had given up, hadn't she? That was what she told Ernest.

Rachel could. It would be easy for Rachel, belonging to the same world. Rachel could find him, flash a card, demand to see him, and they would let her in. Rachel had all the qualifications. Rachel could.

Yes, Rachel could. She knew Rachel would.

Ernest stumbled and took her arm, smiled his sweet smile at her, as if there was all the time in the world to get home, to deal with the cow and the future and the collapse of dreams. As if there was time, with his fading mind and Ivy needing to be made whole again. Wanting to be restored to her former self, and always wanting to please him, for not being a boy. There was precious little time.

'Such a clever little thing,' he said. Grace did not know if he was referring to one of the cygnets, to Cassie, to Ivy. He was probably referring to Carl's son, Carl. The boy. He looked at her; she wished her misjudgements of him were not as frequent as the times when she guessed his thoughts exactly right.

'I mean Ivy, sweetheart. I was hard on her, wasn't I? Expected her to do so much. Clever isn't the right word. She took everything to heart and learned it. She knew she had to practise and learn and memorise, and she did.'

'Yes, she did. She does.'

She put the thought of the drowned guest firmly from her mind.

Rachel opened the personal file on her private organiser. *Dear Diary* . . . She wrote to herself most days, usually in the office. *Do you know, there was never a more opportune time for a clandestine affair in a crowded place? Except for finding somewhere to lie down. In the middle of an open-plan office like this, where everyone is isolated with their own screen, the lovers can e-mail in code, or pick up the mobile and text, without noise. Never has so much been done and misunderstood without speech.*

I went into her room this morning, after she'd gone to clean offices. I wish she wouldn't. I didn't linger, promise. I just wanted to see if there was anything she needed which she wouldn't ask for, like a better bedside light, because she sometimes draws in there and looks at her books. Why was I so slow to realise she can scarcely read? How will she ever get a degree? She's so generous, and so proud. She's made it into a nest, pinned up a couple of drawings. I shouldn't look. It's her private space. I won't do it again.

Grace phones at eleven-ish, most days. Here. Otherwise, in the middle of the afternoon. Her fallow times, and mine too, I suppose. We don't discuss Ivy, we talk about me. Which I like. She's very tactful. She doesn't want Ivy to be a nuisance, as if Ivy was a child and still her responsibility. She didn't ask me to find out where that bastard Schneider lives or works, but I have, it's easy. He's in the Law Directory. I've already phoned up from here, said who I was and how I'd got a personal delivery for his home address, can they give it, and bless them, they did. I'd have got him off the electoral roll, anyway. I can't picture where he lives. What he's got to hide . . . I KNOW what he's got to hide. Cruelty and desertion. I just want to know a little bit more, then I'll find him.

We've got Dad for supper tonight. Sound like we're going to eat him, ha, ha. I've just got this awful feeling about it. Hers are so colourful, mine are so plain. Grace keeps telling me I'm beautiful: she makes me feel it. I can't wait to go back and tell her I've found him. No, I won't, I'll go and meet him. The bastard. The cruel bastard. I'll go to his office, chambers, whatever. Someone, some man, like that should be exposed. He's a judge!

It must be easy to divorce a person who cannot read. I went to the divorce registry yesterday, looked it up. On the grounds of adultery, I ask you.

She was wearing new clothes today. Her head ached; she wanted the sea and the lake, and she wanted justice.

OK to tramp the streets, though Donald did want to be home. It was not a day to be catching sight of himself in shop windows, especially in Soho, unless what was on the other side of the window was food. One of his favourite areas. It had always had people like Blaker. Soho changed its spots, but not its disposition. Sex and food, food and sex. Having lost interest in both, he was less than charmed. Sometimes he wondered if everyone had done as he did, i.e. short-circuited the whole process of judging human nature and come straight to the conclusion that everyone was vile. The effort of proving otherwise was scarcely worth it.

He saw her flitting round the stalls in Berwick Street, and knew he had seen her before. Tall, slightly gaunt, handsome, buying in vegetables and garlic, arguing the price. A tart if ever there was one, but a tart who cooked.

Donald really did not want to know about daughters and sons and wives. He was looking for Blaker. This was his patch, as it always had been. Blaker was a gentle mugger, only hit them when necessary, i.e. when they noticed they were being robbed. A daylight man who only ever got them when they were shopping. Favoured the good handbags, carelessly worn with the mind of the owner concentrated on shopping, that was his favourite modus operandi. He watched them first here on the stalls, and then in the silk shops. Theatrical types and curtain-makers went in there, foodies stayed outside. On the outside stalls of Berwick Street they had metal bowls with exotic fruit and veg at one pound a time. There was ginger and mangoes, one stall avocados only, another purely for pink apples, and the shops on the far side of the caffs sold silks, satins, videos and cheap, flashy jewellery, where the stallholders could stand outside, play cards and swear.

This was as far as the tarts from the other side of the river got in the 1870s. Over Waterloo Bridge, away from the drovers and market men worth a shilling a time, up into Covent Garden where the prices were higher. The unlucky ones went back in despair, some of them preferring to drown themselves in the river rather than return empty-handed. They called Waterloo the bridge of sighs.

The woman buying vegetables was streetwise. Her bag was strapped across her body and tucked into a belt, leaving hands free. No one would part her from her money without a fight. She tested the vegetables, disturbed the display, and no one argued back. She was a sight for sore eyes, if you liked them Amazonian. Donald had come here looking for Blaker. It was still a better bet than handling all that stuff about missing wives and old grievances. He could clock up the hours, looking for Blaker in the confident hope he would not find him in a hurry.

The woman stepped away from the stall, all negotiation done. Cash was king here, credit cards a no-no. This stall faced one of the few caffs down this stretch, ranging from bistro snacks to burgers. She waved towards the window. Donald looked in the direction of the wave.

Fuck this for a game of monkeys. The man in the window, being waved at, looked like Blaker.

Such a small world, and way too soon. Couldn't be right. He wanted this job to last.

Chapter Nine

The bad thing about being stuck in a rut, and the last thing she had noticed, was the habit of taking the same route to work in the morning and never varying it. How could you ever do that in London? Ivy had said. There's so much to discover if you go a different way. The habit of extending the route and thinking of more than simply getting there had begun ever since Rachel started the first drawing classes, because she found herself wanting the opportunity to look at faces and bodies with a new, almost prurient fascination. She wanted to linger, checking human proportions, the elegance and the lack of it in all of them, wanted to notice how each one sat differently on Tube or bus, walked at a different angle, how some would relax with a newspaper in a queue, others could not, stood twisted. How some were stiller than models, others in constant movement. Rachel no longer kept her head down, varied the route to and fro to make it longer, and looked, boldly.

Keeping her head down in all senses had become a way of

life; she was accustomed to it. She was still isolated in her relatively new job in the offices of Stirland and Co., because everyone knew she had been a whistle-blower in the job before. The smart, sanctimonious bitch who had revealed a major scam and could not be loved for it; the one who refused to ratify a company's accounts because they were as false as they had been for years, and refused to keep quiet about the fact that a senior consultant had been bribed to maintain a deceit. Management had been ostensibly grateful for the information, received in time to prevent a scandal and to turn what was corruption into a mere mistake, but they had lost money in the process, which was not easily forgiven. And everyone there, and thus everyone here, knew that she had got her lover the sack. She had not been particularly popular before: a beautiful, numerate girl who worked harder and quicker than anyone else, was socially timid but deadly obstinate, with ambition worn on her sleeve. The fact that she had championed the cause of the unqualified females groped and bullied by the overfed male of the species did not make her top favourite with either. She was bred uncomfortably honest; she hated bullies and arrogance, nothing could change it. It was simple conviction. The partners did not like to be reminded that they were only well-paid servants, oiling the legal and financial wheels of larger corporations, and that while vital to the life of the client, they were not as important as the rules they were paid to uphold. Not a good thing to be right all the time. Rachel Doe was too reserved for the men, too severely good-looking for the women, and she had to live with her reputation going before her. It was better at Stirland and Co. since she had lightened up and wore her hair down sometimes. She was more approachable. The firm had a high turnover of staff. Some of them had forgotten she had the makings of a traitor.

''Lo, Rache, can you help me with this?'

She had always wanted to make partnership; it was no longer important and it showed. She thought she was easier to get on with than she had been, that the mark of shame on her forehead had faded, but she did not really know what they thought, and while she had once cared so much she had shrunk into herself more and more, she now cared less and less, even though she was exasperated by the corporate refusal to see that long-term profit meant *never* doing anything underhand. She was still her father's daughter. It was her weakness and her strength.

A small hangover today. Rachel wished she had been a lawyer, rather than the number-cruncher she was. They were more important. She did not want attention, but would have liked influence. The lift took her straight to her floor, the fifth of ten. The other floors were different capsules, like decks in a ship. From her window she could see the street below, saw people spilling out from the station opposite, near and far, wondering if she would actually recognise anyone from this safe distance. She thought she would, and never had. These days she watched before getting down to work.

It was early. She sat at her desk and considered the personal file on her organiser, labelled DIARY. The débâcle with the dishonest consultant who was also her lover was what had made her keep this in the first place. She, who would never again trust any incriminating or confidential information to an office computer system, had recorded his, printed it out; and when he would not admit it, had called her a silly, treacherous bitch, she had shown *them* in logical sequence what he had done. The habit of keeping her personal file remained.

The diary file was thinking time. As for work, there seemed nothing which could not wait. They all exaggerated their own importance and the need for urgency. It was time to do something else which could not be postponed.

She wrote down all the things she knew Judge Schneider had done. She was enraged by the fact that he was a *judge*. The more the simple internet research told her about him via the chambers website, the more she was angered. C*alled to the Bar in 1973. Specialised in family law/criminal law/human rights issues. Judge: 2000.*

She knew enough about the system to know that Schneider was not at the top of his tree. He had avoided the brinksmanship of commercial law, as well as the high earnings. Might have taken a judgeship for easier hours and a pension. Not an ambitious high-flyer, so occupied the moral high ground of family law and crime instead. Opted for the anonymous, virtuous role of judge because he had something to hide.

This was what he had REALLY done.

Seduces young girl/wife.

Neglects child; lets her drown.

Shuns wife, shuts her out. Beats her up. Lets her drown too, in a manner of speaking.

Fixes a divorce.

Neglects grandparents. Denies rights of access.

Prevents son from maintaining/making contact.

Is cruel.

Shame on him.

Tomorrow, she vowed, tomorrow I shall try and find him. Phone? Yes, but why would he speak to me? Now wait a minute. I know Grace wants me to do this, she doesn't ask, but I know anyway, and I also know she doesn't want me to alienate him, just get him to . . . What? Grace really does know Ivy best. She knows Ivy will never be whole until her son sees her for what she is outside the ghastly picture his father has painted of her . . . Rachel worked on her rage. How dare he do this?

Still she prevaricated. And what would Ivy think? Ivy must want to see her son; Ivy cried in her sleep. There were sketches, pinned to the walls, of a boy child, a boy, the young man he might have become. And what of him? What of the son, what did he want, which no one else knew?

She told herself that all she wanted to do was find the judge and explain, but before all that there was her father, and Ivy, this evening, to which she was not looking forward. It was always like that with her father: she was proud of him, and his ridiculous standards. It made her ache.

As the others filtered in to work, she greeted them cheerfully. The hangover headache was secretly supplanted by a certain joy in being alive, which did not quite stop her noticing that the waste-paper bins had not been emptied since yesterday and the desk and floor bore the traces of yesterday's dust. Things often went wrong with the contract cleaners who came in at night. It made her wonder, with a smile, what Ivy was doing. Ivy would do better than that.

This was simply not fair. Blaker, the leading joker in a not very convincing pack, was not supposed to be so easy to find. It was meant to take days. Donald put the lid on his frustration. For a start, he did not know what to say to the man, since nothing was remotely rehearsed yet, and he could not think of anything he could do to set the ball rolling. Such as, look here, Terry, there's a bloke threatening the last judge who sent you down, is it you, by any chance? I don't really think so, but it makes a good theory, and I've got to find someone and it might as well be you, so would you kindly oblige with a confession, and would you mind leaving it until next week? Or at least give me an alibi which takes ages to establish and comes back solid? No offence, mate. OK, do you have access to a computer, knowledge of medieval images, can you draw? There's a good man.

Donald watched the woman walk away. Not a good handbag, cheap and cheerful. He stood still, watching with conspicuous uncertainty, and then went in the door by the window where the man who was a dead ringer for Blaker sat. He had to do that, at least, to make sure; maybe he was wrong and, hope against hope, it wasn't Blaker after all. Identification via mug shot photograph was not the last word in reliability, even if blown up on a screen to show the skin pores and the sullen mouth. No one smiled for a mug shot.

The setting made it clearer that it was indeed Blaker, or at least it did to a suspicious mind with an in-depth knowledge of Blaker's repertoire. This was an upmarket, no-smoking patisserie, redolent with good smells of fresh coffee substances, sweet pastry, anxiety to please, clearly favoured by the better-off of the consumers who used Berwick Street, in preference to the other caff, with its solid sausage rolls and bacon sandwiches, which was the haunt of the stallholders in the cold. The stall men were up with the lark; they were always hungry. No point trying to rob them; they would see you coming out of the back of their heads. This, on the other hand, was the perfect place for Blaker to sit and survey those who had, or were about to spend, money. The ones on the way to buy silk or ginger, pausing to check the list and speak into tiny, shiny mobiles. A stressed-out, multitasking female, juggling the luggage of shopping, job, self-consciousness, ambition; that would be his chosen type. Judged first by clothes and attitude, good handbag next, with cash in it, because that was the coinage here. From this vantage point, a thief like Blaker could seek the quarry, watch them shop, watch them pause with their espressos, and, if he was working, follow. All the short way to Shaftesbury Avenue, Theatreland, which was his other stalking ground, even if he always began here. They would be waving for a taxi, waiting for a bus, when he struck. And, blow me, if it wasn't an internet café, also. It had to be him. It was.

Donald sat with his coffee in the seat level with the window, with his back to Blaker and a sideways view of his reflection in the glass. The pavement outside was slippery underfoot as the rubbish increased.

The tall woman came back. There was a parcel of asparagus she had forgotten. Not so efficient then. This time she did not wave. Donald could allow staring at her to be his alibi. It was her height and strength which was interesting, rather than any hint of glamour. Amongst the discarded rubbish of the busy market stalls, she seemed conspicuously clean, like a polished apple. He could not have guessed her age. Ever since his own daughters grew into adults, he had lost his knack for gauging the ages of women. They came in swathes of the eighteen-to-thirty, thirty-to-over-forty, when they all looked the same. He told himself he could still tell something about their lives, from the faces and the hunch of the shoulders, the way his wife had taught him, what they shopped for and what they wore, but never how old they were. The coffee was good. He would settle for that for now. He could smell the man behind him, made the mistake of checking the reflection to see if he was still there, almost jumped out of his skin.

'She's a piece of work, isn't she?' Blaker said. 'I wouldn't try, if I was you.' He turned sideways in his chair, presenting a broken-nosed profile and a waft of dirty hair. 'She's a model, you know.'

Donald turned his own, harmless face with its fine, clean hair, glasses, combed moustache and caught a glimpse of brown teeth. It was a mistake to imagine that a con of Blaker's experience could smell a copper from forty paces, because they simply couldn't. Or if they could, which was as likely in Blaker's case, they simply didn't care, because they had nothing to fear. Or they were the sort who got on fine with those who hunted them so ineffectually, most of the time. They were simply two men, caught in the act of staring at the same woman.

'I thought she must be,' Donald said. 'Figure like that. I wouldn't mind bumping into it, slowly, if you see what I mean, but I'd be too scared she'd eat me alive. Model, is she? Since when do they do their own shopping?'

Blaker sniggered. 'She's not like that,' he said. 'She's the down-to-earth kind. She's come up in the world. You wouldn't want to know what she did before that. We were an item once. Still friends. She bought me this coffee. Buys me a drink now and then.'

There was a lingering note of pride in his voice. He tapped long, horny nails on the table.

In your dreams, Donald thought. Why would that shining woman with the figure of stone buy anything for an odorous loser like Blaker, but then there was such a thing as simple kindness. Donald scratched his head, adjusted his glasses, grinned. He knew it wasn't his open face. The man was lonely and bored; he would talk to anyone. He needed to protest that he was better than he looked; nothing to boast about and therefore needing to boast.

'I never get to meet women like that, not in my line of work,' Donald said. 'How come you get so lucky?'

Blaker sniggered again. He tapped his coffee spoon on the table. He smelt musty and his thin thighs were pressed round the leg of the table as if somehow restraining it from moving away.

'I tried to rob her once, matter of fact. Not slowly, either. I was good then.' He smiled sadly. 'But she saw me coming, belted me round the head. Then she gave me some money. She said, if you need it enough to do this, you'd better have it. Turned out she'd even less of it than me. We got to be mates. I used to read the newspaper for her. Those were the days.'

The clock on the wall said eleven thirty. Between the stalls, Donald could see the stallholders' pub on the other side of the road.

'How about a drink?' he asked. Oh God, it was so clichéd, it was a giveaway.

Blaker smiled, showing more of the teeth. 'If you want information on our lady friend, copper, it'll cost you more than that.'

Donald sighed. It was so galling to be wrong, and so nice to be given an opportunity, even when you did not want it. Always take the sideways option. They could talk about his lady friend, someone, something else, work backwards to him.

'Such as what?'

'A really good fuck up the arse,' Blaker said, and roared with laughter. They both did, as if it was really witty. Blaker wiped his eyes with a grubby fist. The dirt was ingrained. Donald could not see those fingers tapping on a computer keyboard. Blaker leaned forward.

'If you're looking to bump into that one slowly, don't even think of it,' he whispered. 'She's a judge's wife. A fucking judge, I ask you. We get all sorts here.'

Donald felt his world begin to spin.

'I've got fuck-all to do,' he said. 'Let me buy you that drink.'

He was the man.

Rachel's father arrived at six, resentfully early, out of place and feeling outmanoeuvred by the invitation in the first place, slightly sullen and anxious to get it over with. He carried his worry like a sack on his shoulders, looked like someone who had never gazed up at the stars and waited instead for them to fall on his head. Ivy bore his coat away to her room out of the way; he seemed to miss it. She towered over him. Dislike settled on his features. He said he was not feeling well. The preponderance of flowers in the small living room made him sneeze. He had bought a plant. He stared at Ivy, dwarfed by her, then stared at her again, as if she was a specimen.

The occasion was less disastrous than uncomfortable at first. They ate roast chicken, new potatoes, and asparagus which he did not like because he knew it was expensive, and he stared at Ivy.

'I'm sure I've seen you somewhere before,' he said.

'Must have been my starring TV role,' she answered.

She was making an effortless-looking effort; she could have charmed blood out of a stone with the way she fussed over him. He forgot to ask questions. Mid-meal, he put down his knife and fork, turned to Rachel.

'I bought my stuff so I can fix that tap in the bathroom. It was leaking last time.'

'Oh, Ivy fixed it.'

'And that dicky cupboard in the kitchen, the one with the hinge . . .'

'It's OK, Dad, it's been fixed. Ivy . . .'

Silence fell. There was the scraping of cutlery on plates.

'Place could do with a coat of paint,' he said at last. 'I expect Ivy could do that too.'

They removed from the dining table to the living end of the room, with coffee and chocolate. His temper had gone.

'She needs a man about the place,' Rachel's father said to Ivy, still staring. 'Only she can never get them to stop still. She puts them off. And now she's living with a lesbian,' he said, choking on his words, talking about Rachel as if she was not in the room. He was bitter with hurt. 'That's not how me and her mother brought her up. I know where I've seen you before. At Euston, wasn't it, a few years since? Begging. Not many tall, blonde beggars. I never forget a face. I try not to look at beggars, never give them anything, but I noticed you. I thought, she's young, she looks fit, why doesn't that girl get a job?'

'Dad . . .'

'I think it might have been King's Cross,' Ivy said smoothly. 'And I'm ever so respectable now. On my way out to work, as a matter of fact. Can I get you more coffee before I go?'

He seemed surprised by his own outburst, shocked by his anger but unable to stop it.

'At least you work,' he said. 'That's something. At least you're not living on handouts. Unless you're sponging off my daughter. What is it you do again?'

'Clean floors and lavatories, mainly, wait on tables, and strip,' Ivy said.

'You what?'

Ivy got up and cleared the table. They could hear her in the kitchen beyond, then her footsteps going towards her room, scarcely audible in her rubber-soled shoes.

Rachel sat, stunned by her father. He was like a small child, shrill with temper. She was so angry she could not speak. He turned to her, moved by feelings he could neither understand nor control.

'You fool. You silly fool. You always were a fool. You don't know good from bad. You're green as grass, you. She's a bad 'un. A sponger.'

She left him sitting, and moved the few paces to Ivy's room, where she knocked at the half-open door. Such simple rules of privacy had been easily established without discussion: knock before entering. This was the room where Ivy confined herself. Apart from the little improvements, the fixing of the tap, the cupboard hinge, and the influx of flowers, her presence was difficult to detect in the rest of the flat. An untidy nest in here, everything left tidy elsewhere, her own space deliberately small. Ivy was sitting on her bed, looking at the timetable she made each week to remind herself of which job to go to next, all written out in messy block capitals. She was crying. Rachel's father's unnecessary coat lay on the bed where Ivy had carried it when he first arrived. The first action of a hostess: take the coat, make him comfortable without it.

'I'm sorry,' Rachel said. 'I'm really sorry. I don't know what's got into him.'

Ivy dashed tears from her cheek with her fist, attempted to smile. The room was tidier than it had been that morning, Rachel noticed guiltily. Ivy was up at five, while she herself slept, out again to work at nine forty-five tonight, shopping and cooking in between, only to be insulted. She had taken her sketches off the wall, replaced them with a poster of Matisse's *Leda and the Swan*.

'Don't worry,' Ivy said. 'Please don't. It's not such a bad thing to be reminded of a past life. Any right-minded person would be suspicious of me.'

'I could kill him,' Rachel said.

'Enough,' Ivy said. ' He's maybe just a bit jealous.'

'Jealous of what?'

'You're all he's got, Rache. Try and understand. Don't be hard on him on my account. He's nice. At least he says what he thinks. He's not very well. I'd better go.'

She slung her bag across her body and began to whistle, stuffed the timetable into the bag and left the room. Rachel followed slowly, returning to the living room to see her father cowering, as if waiting to be hit, hating him for that too.

'Don't get up,' Ivy was saying gaily, bending to touch his shoulder. 'It was nice to meet you, Jack, honest it was. Don't mind me, will you? I look worse than I am.'

'I'm sorry,' he muttered. 'Sorry.'

Rachel was dumbfounded. She had never known him say sorry before. About anything, ever. The door closed behind Ivy, leaving them alone. He looked small, hunched and miserable and he was not going to say sorry again.

'Well, Dad. You were on good form. Are you all right to get home?'

'Course I am. What time is it?'

There was no losing face in front of a daughter. He looking distressingly pale. No point discussing it. She fetched the coat and walked him to the Underground station in silence, watching dark fall around them. Wishing it was different, annoyed, wanting to run after him as he moved out of sight. He was so stupid and so small.

The theatre at the north end of Shaftesbury Avenue was showing a musical, with a *Pop Idol* guest star whose name was on the lips of everyone under twenty. The small cleaning team for backstage had arrived on foot, their arrival timed for shortly after the audience and the last of the cast were gone. They stood around smoking fags, waiting for everyone to disappear so they could get in. The show had overrun; it was the last night; there was a crowd of autograph-hunters and semi-frantic fans crowding round the stage door, jostling and chanting one of the songs, half hysterical with anticipation. Fuck them, one of the cleaners murmured under his breath, moving forward. If we can't get in, we'll still be here after the last train. Come on, shove through. The fans did not like it. They, too, were kept waiting.

The cleaners were undistinguishable from the other, larger crowd at first sight, which was why there was trouble. There were the same hoodies and hat-wearers. Closer up, the working group were generally older, scruffier, and free of the adrenaline rush that follows watching a performance. They were not as lightly dressed; no music beat in their ears. The chanters could not see why anyone else should be allowed inside as they waited. Their number was swelled by others drawn by the sound and the spectacle of a crowd. The night had not yet started.

They had to get in; they had a timetable; they would not be paid for being kept late. The cleaners were jostled and abused. One man in particular, shielding a half-clad girl who bellowed out the last song of the show, pushed forward. Where the fuck do you think you're going? It was hot.

Aided by the stage-door staff, the group slipped through, jostled as they went, the man pulling at clothes. Only as the last of the six disappeared into the lighted doorway, and the loud girl began bellowing louder, and the Idol appeared, and the noise turned into hush and then into applause, did she notice her bloke, saying again, what the fuck, slipping to the ground and staying there as they surged forward and lost him in the roar of welcome.

Tomorrow's headline. *Man stabbed to death by rival fan.*

Rachel went back into Ivy's room. Looked around its smallness. It was not fair. It wasn't bloody fair. Too many people had spat upon Ivy. Her father's reaction was the same as many. It was not fair. Ivy deserved better.

Rachel's father felt bad. What the hell had got into him, except a feeling of being made redundant all over again? At his age? It would have been the garlic in the chicken; he could have sworn there was something in it. She was a bad lot. He felt ill.

One train cancelled, a crowd on the next. It was later than he liked it to be. The crowd in his carriage were carefree and singing. The windows were stuck shut. He was sick and old and tired and ashamed, and horribly breathless, overheating in the coat. He fumbled in the pockets for the inhaler, then for the pills.

There was nothing there.

CHAPTER TEN

Friday. Do it now.

Hello, my name is Rachel Doe. I'm a friend of Ivy. I need to see him.

No, that was not going to do. Appeal to self-interest.

Hello, my name is Rachel Doe of Stirland and Co. I need to set up a conference with Judge Schneider in his chambers, if that's convenient.

Can I ask which case? He doesn't do cases any more. He tries them.

Yes, of course, I should have said. It's an old matter in which he was involved several years ago. It's now the subject of a compensation claim between victims, and we wondered if we could trouble him for a few details of the criminal case which we seem to have missed. We need his memory. We will pay for his time, of course.

That won't bother him, honey. What was the name of the case?

Wiseman v. The Ivy League. R. v. Wiseman originally, I think. I'm sure he'll remember. To whom am I speaking?

I'll check and get back. Give me your e-mail and mobile. Judge Schneider's busy right now.

How the hell did anyone get anything right? What if he answered and what if he didn't?

Easy to find the court, easy to find the way in if you spoke with a degree of authority. Not so easy to cope with no reply.

It flashed up on her e-mail, two hours later.

He says, of course. Temple. Paper Buildings, name on the door. Four thirty this afternoon would be fine. He's in court until then. Please confirm.

If the judge had something to hide, or wanted to hide, he was bad at it, or else whatever method he had used to hide himself from his wife and his wife's family was only effective because they did not know how to look up a directory. Did not have the right voices, the right technology, the means, or even a telephone directory. The huge divide between the lives of the Wisemans and her own was humbling. They did not have the tools.

Rachel sat back and wondered how easy it was to fool some of the people some of the time.

Ivy was modelling this evening, out until late. There would be no opportunity to explain on her return. What did she want to achieve?

I wanted, she wrote in the personal file marked DIARY, *to know. I want them to resolve it. I want Ivy to have respect. Her rights.*

Every day had a regime. She and Ivy were going to the farm, early tomorrow. Something had to be achieved by then. She phoned her father. Peace could be established by pretending nothing had happened. There was no reply. He would take days to come round. He would not be saying sorry again.

She had been careful about her clothes, mainly Ivy's choices from shopping with her. Ivy positively enjoyed the process of pointing out things she could not afford but wanted to see on someone else; she enjoyed being a style consultant. No one does power-dressing any more, Ivy said. I clean more offices than you ever see, so I know what they like. They wear their training shoes all day and leave their high heels stuffed inside their desk drawers. Rachel was informal with attitude today. Linen trousers with loafers, pale, unstructured linen jacket, her hair long and loose. She was not going to wear black simply because she had the chance of meeting a pitiless judge. Tomorrow they would get in her car and go to the farm, early. Kick off shoes, run around barefoot.

Once the meeting was set, far more easily and immediately than she had thought possible, Rachel found the morning stretched like elastic, minutes taking hours. It was moving towards the holiday time of year, the place half empty while those with young families queued at airports. She did not envy them. By one o'clock she could not bear it any longer, tidied up carefully and left. Someone had complained about the cleaners; their efforts had been redoubled. Her computer printed off the right section of the map on a clean page. Middlesex Crown Court was right in the heart of London, and she was becoming a specialised form of tourist.

Since justice must be seen to be done, she knew that there was public access to all trials and most courtrooms, except where security was paramount, and even then, as far as space allowed. The few visitors to the public galleries of Middlesex Crown Court were directed through X-ray pergolas, as if at an airport, and once through could wander at will. After a morning's worth of justice procedure, the public waiting areas outside each court were lightly littered with dead paper cups, a Coca-Cola can under a plastic seat, waste-paper bins overflowing. A posse of people were standing outside, smoking; the smell had drifted in with them. Rachel found her way with confidence; she knew she had the right to watch. Court Five had a small public gallery at the back, reached by a separate entrance and a flight of stairs; once there, Rachel looked down. There were three other people, watching listlessly, apparently unconnected with the slow theatre played out below. They looked as if they had come in simply for something to do. Rachel wanted to watch the judge at work, and sneer at him. She wanted everything she knew about him to be confirmed, and she wanted to know what he looked and acted like before she met him at four thirty.

There was no jury. There was no on-going case. The usher informed her that it was an afternoon devoted to passing sentence on those already convicted, those who had pleaded guilty or been found so, cases adjourned for social enquiry reports into background circumstances, recommendations as to sentence and the preparation of speeches in mitigation, appealing to His Honour's discretion for leniency. They could all go to prison, or not.

The first defendant shambled into the dock without assistance, with the air of one sick of waiting, feigning nonchalance. It was only as he gripped the rail of the dock firmly enough to break it that she could see how frightened he was. A persistent daytime burglar, unsuccessful by definition. When he was asked to confirm his name, he could merely nod. She could sense a desire to be sick, to run, to escape. As someone spoke for him, facelessly, from behind a wig, about how he had turned a corner, about how he no longer felt driven to steal, how well he had responded to his drugs treatment, she could feel the stirrings of cynicism. Yeah, yeah, yeah. He'd stolen since boyhood; he would do it again. Prison was right. Tick the box, she heard herself saying, waiting for him to be dismissed. As the speech ended, the man began to shake. The judge spoke to him directly.

'You haven't had much luck, have you?' he asked.

A nod.

'Well, maybe it's time you did.'

It surprised her, the soft, brief pity of it, the lack of judgement and lecturing. The next was different, the approach the same. Bailed for reports as to why he should not be imprisoned for three counts of actual bodily harm, all done in drink. Off the street, alone in the dock, stripped of everything, his defiance pathetic, he shook with dangerous nervousness. Someone spoke briefly and condescendingly on his behalf, going through the motions, patently weary of him and his kind. Tension snapped; the defendant yelled that he had had enough of this, pushed his way out of the dock. Then he seemed to hesitate, as if knowing that this would seal his fate, half turned back, and in that split second, Rachel could have wept for him. It was so futile and so foolish, made everything worse.

'Going so soon?' the judge said. 'Aren't you even going to say goodbye? Please come back. We'll miss you.'

As if he had a choice. There was a brief underswell of laughter, but it was the judge who absorbed the ridicule and looked a little precious.

The same with the next, a fat recidivist benefit fraudster. His Honour invited her to sit. Tell me, he said, what I ought to do with you. It all flowed like silk in that hateful, barren room. One after another, prisoners and lawyers, whatever their sentences, however bad their speeches, left with their dignity. It was quietly impressive. It was not what she expected. Everyone here got a hearing.

Rachel shivered on her way out in the sun, hurrying down to the Embankment for the ten-minute walk to the Temple, passing Big Ben as it struck four, telling herself that surely it was easy to be magnanimous and even pleasant as a judge, when you had the support of all that regalia, a throne upon which to sit, a wig and gown beneath which to hide and someone to guard you if anyone produced a gun or a knife which had not been discovered by the X-ray at the door. She was trying to argue herself into feeling critical. A judge did not do his duty by being lenient and kind. He had to weigh the need of society to be protected against the hope of the individual to be spared, and it wasn't the individual who was paying him. What struck her most was how ordinary and diminished those people in the dock were, in relation to the damage they could do. Who lost most? Who won, who gained? The other abiding impression was how lonely the judge looked on his pinnacle, below the sign, *Evil to him who evil thinks*. Did he dream of them, these flotsam and jetsam who floated before his throne? Maybe it was they who had made him human. Maybe his red sash of office had given him a heart.

She had hardened her own heart by the time she turned into Middle Temple Lane and entered the quaint tranquillity of the Inns of Court, a series of cobbled lanes and squares, moving uphill away from the river, as if meandering without purpose. Ancient stone buildings bent towards one another at the beginning, opening out into shaded squares, then into colonnaded walkways, then into another lane and then into the openness of Temple Gardens, reached by steps descending to a lawn, shrubs and trees, so surprising in its secret, spacious loveliness and dizzying show of flowers, she stopped to breathe. Busy footsteps on paving stones seemed impertinent here. The larger buildings spoke of grandeur, the smaller warrens of cosiness and secrecy; she had forgotten how beautiful it was.

Rachel paused to remember the last time she had been here, remembering a wintry landscape, with the hidden gardens clad in a rare blanket of snow. Ah yes, Ivy had brought her here. It had been part of her winter education. One of those many city places which do not look open to the populace, but really are. No one was going to invite you, but all you had to do was walk in.

It was Ivy who made her look at a building and want to turn it inside out, as if it was a doll's house, the front of which could be removed to reveal the complexities, eccentricities and practicalities which lay within. Like taking up a curtain on a stage. Paper Buildings was pure Dickens. The rooms at the front would overlook the trees and the river; the entrance at the back with the hand-painted names of the occupants inscribed in order of importance, in glossy, old-fashioned red-and-black script, exactly as they would have been in Dickens' time, some looking as old, led on to stone steps, curling upwards and out of sight, with a black iron banister, knobbled from a dozen coats of rust-disguising paint and cold to touch. Even in August, the steps were slightly damp, bringing back the smell of winter. There was no room for a lift to the fifth floor, no such luxury. The walls were cold. She reached the top, passing separate nests of rooms on each floor, where stone gave way to carpet and the same script said Knock and Enter. Another world.

He was waiting for her inside the door. Behind him she could sense the familiar hum and smell of a twenty-first-century office, hear the sound of a fax machine, the ringing of phones, the burr of a printer and voices arguing.

'Miss Doe?' he said, extending his hand. 'Wiseman and Ivy League? I'm so sorry. We're very short of space here. There simply isn't any room. Do you mind if we sit outside?'

She could not shake his hand; she simply could not. The hand that had struck Ivy, shut the door against her, NO. They went back down; she knew she was being outmanoeuvred somehow, and all she could do was lead the way until the gloom gave way to light again and they were sitting on a shady bench, facing the gardens, him taking the lead. The first sight of him without the wig shocked her. His hair was flat against his head, and glinted in the sun. His presence in this outdoor space was twice as potent as it had been in the courtroom.

'I watched you in court this afternoon,' she said.

'Yes,' he said. 'I know. I saw you. It's unusual to have a single woman in the public gallery, unless it's a mother, crying. Or anyone beautiful, for that matter. I wish more people came.'

'I thought you were very . . . fair.'

He turned a pleasantly surprised face, smiled. The effect was paralysing.

'A pushover, you mean? Fairness is the least they deserve. Most of them have had a rotten deal in life.'

He did not ask, *Why?* Nor did he say, *What are you here for?* Of course the name of that fictitious case, *Wiseman*, was a clue. He was not defensive, or obviously curious, none of that. He simply sat and waited. She was trying to summon up the anger and found it difficult, wanting him to start, getting more flustered as he refused to oblige.

'We've had the best of the year,' he said finally, waving an arm in the direction of the garden. 'Maybe not yet, though. If there's nothing to say, perhaps I'd better go and let you enjoy the view. But you have to start, you know. I've absolutely no idea what you want, and it isn't *fair* to put words into other people's mouths.'

She stared at a vibrant fuchsia plant, thought, yes, the best of this summer is beginning to be over, and began slowly. The carefulness of his speech was infectious, like the protocol of the court procedure she had watched. The script she had rehearsed was already abandoned. There was nothing to do but be honest. He wasn't a judge; he didn't deserve to be a judge. He was just another dishonest man. She reminded herself of that.

'Your wife, your ex-wife, is Ivy Wiseman, right? You divorced her two years after your daughter, Cassie, died, ten years ago in May?'

He inclined his bright head. He did not wince at the mention of their names.

'We divorced each other,' he said. 'As one does.'

That was her trigger.

'It's hardly mutual if it's done on paper and one of you can scarcely read.'

He inclined his head again. It was neither negative nor affirmative, simply an indication that he was listening.

'And your son, Sam, nineteen now, has had no contact with her, or with his grandparents, Grace and Ernest Wiseman, since just after Cassie's death?'

This time a bloodless nod. The shadows were longer over the gardens. It seemed so unfair that there were tracts of lawn and roses and shade which no one used on a sunny afternoon. He looked as if he was nodding acquaintance towards the flowers rather than anything else, listening intently to another voice.

'Because you prevented it,' Rachel went on. 'As you still do. Breaking all their hearts, especially Grace's. Perhaps her husband's even more. It isn't right.'

'Whose heart?' he asked, as if coming back from a distance. '*Ivy's* heart?'

'Yes, Ivy's heart, and I do know. I'm her friend. She shares my flat. She's my friend. She befriended me, we befriended each other . . . Oh, shit. And her parents.'

He turned right round towards her, regarding her carefully, as if memorising every detail.

'Are you her only friend?' he asked.

'Yes . . . I . . . No, of course not.'

'Perhaps you should ask yourself why. Why it is you're the only one. And tell me what you want.'

What did she want? She was completely out of her depth. She faced the fact that she had expected someone demonic and Germanic. A guttural Nazi in sheep's clothing. Yes, she was prejudiced.

'Do you love her?' he asked gently.

'Not . . . like that. As a friend, yes. Very much.'

'I didn't mean *like that.* I meant as a friend. Highly underrated, isn't it, asexual love? Just as powerful as any other. Puts sisterhood and brotherhood to shame.'

That sounded pompous and got her back on track. She resumed with a machine-gun blast of questions and accusations which had been reverberating round her head ever since the last weekend.

'It was your fault Cassie drowned. No, I'm sorry, I

shouldn't have said that. But you drove Ivy away, you locked her out when she was vulnerable. Look, no one's responsible for someone else losing their mind, no one says you fed her drugs, but you left her. And she went over the brink and dragged herself back, and I bet you don't know what that takes, and she's fine and . . . and . . . It's just that I know she'll never be entirely fine, I can't imagine she will, anyway, until she can, sort of, have it out with you. And explain it to her son. She wants him to be proud of her, not ashamed. She can't initiate it; she daren't, but Grace tries, with all those letters she sends to your solicitor and you crumple up and send back. Now that really is despicable of you.'

The last, jumbled sentence startled him.

'Recently?'

'Of course recently. Over the last year, dammit.'

'Oh. Those.'

The carelessness of the response infuriated her.

'*YOU* kept them apart. You keep them dangling. You prevent any resolution. Grace can't live with it.'

'Do you mean closure?' he said. 'Dreadful word.'

'Not closure,' she said angrily. 'An opening. The chance to make amends. The chance to see things for what they are, oh, I don't know. Ivy blames herself, for everything. She wants forgiveness. She's done absolutely marvellously.'

He was nodding again, as if he entirely understood. A good trick. He probably did it with witnesses, to get them on side, make them think he was with them somehow, stuck right in the middle of their point of view.

'You aren't a lawyer, Miss Doe, although your firm . . .'

'You looked me up?'

'I didn't, my clerk did. That aside, have you ever heard of the hearsay rule?'

'Even accountants know a little law.'

'There's a rule which says that reported conversations between third parties are not admissible as evidence in a criminal court, because they themselves do not prove the truth of their own content. Just because one person says to another, so-and-so dyed their hair black yesterday, that cannot be evidence that they actually did. So we don't let it in. I often think it's a rule applicable in real life.'

'You condescending sod,' Rachel said. She was suddenly as angry as her father had been; indiscretion came upon her just as quickly. 'You just don't want Ivy to appear in any way, shape or form, in case your hypocrisy comes out with it.'

Neither moved, sitting on the bench, staring ahead, like lovers having an argument, with the difference that he still seemed at ease. The truth was that there were several reasons why she could not look at him. She was embarrassed because she had flunked this self-imposed test of sangfroid, because he was so composed and unashamed, because she was waiting for him to laugh at her, almost wished he would. And because she could feel this great gravitational pull towards him, a horrible desire to impress him with her own honesty, somehow, to be able to say to herself, later, that she had walked away intact, like one of his defendants. He made *her* feel guilty.

It had been a lousy idea to see him in court, discover in advance something of that ingredient which might have made Ivy fall for him hook, line and sinker in the first place. The stinking, cruel, cunning, bully-boy hypocritical bastard, the worst kind, honed into charm by sheer bloody practice. The shit. Dead right. The obverse of a talent for putting people at ease and granting them dignity was the subtle ability to humiliate. She wanted to snarl and grind her teeth, snap at his ankles, and above all, make him smile at her.

'If you don't mind my saying so,' he said in his quiet voice, which was surely honed, and practised too, to carry such resonance at so low a pitch, 'I do think you're very brave, doing this. I mean, it takes some doing. It's not everyone who can wade in and interfere in the name of friendship, duty, love or anything, and confront someone else's tragedy for them. Try and fix it, instead of doing that very English thing of *nothing*. To act as a friend as only a parent does for a child. It's brave. It's unusual. So are you. What I meant to say is it deserves hearing. Do you think we could start again? And before we do that, I should say I quite understand how and why anyone would love Ivy in whatever fashion they do. You'd have to be out of your mind to resist it. Such a capacity for giving love. Hatred, equally. Am I going on?'

She felt suddenly tearful, a child admonished and forgiven, bent her head in a kind of 'yes'. Let's start again, please. Please like me.

A series of people had passed in front of their chosen bench during the time they sat. The to-ing and fro-ing of the Inns, coming back from court, hell-bent on the work which preceded the next day or week, more time inside a court than out, always. She let herself relax, ever so slowly and unsurely, fraction by fraction; she was going to be let go without looking a fool. Footsteps came quickly towards them, from behind.

'There you are, Mr Schneider, sir. They said inside you'd be here. Sorry. Can I have a word, sir?'

He was like the setting, a relic of Dickens, with a droopy moustache, so harmless and sedulous he was almost laughable. Padding along in this sultry heat, as if there was any rush, trying to make a virtue out of a hurry.

'We could have dinner and go from there,' the judge said, peeling a card from his pocket and placing it, adroitly, inside the rim of her handbag. She had given him hers, with all the numbers, dammit. 'Or if that's too loaded, a drink whenever you please. Do give my best to Grace. It isn't me who crumples up the letters. Hello, Donald! Do sit down. Please, don't go,' he added, turning back to her with the smile she had not realised she craved.

He waved at the intruder. 'This,' Carl said, 'is Detective Sergeant Cousins, known as the Don. And this,' he nodded in Rachel's direction, 'is Miss Rachel Doe, of Strickland and Co., a great friend of my ex-wife's.'

Donald sat heavily, recovered his breath.

'Oh, that's helpful, ever so helpful,' he said, pulling out a handkerchief and mopping his brow. She had a feeling they were acting out a scene, as he might have done in court. Donald settled back into the bench, downwind of the judge. A breeze had developed, wafting over the gardens, funnelling in the direction of the Inns' narrow exits. There was absolutely no need for him to have run, or to perspire as he did. He could have stood and cooled.

'Just what I needed,' Donald wheezed. 'That'll save time. Bit of a development, sir. Might be a good idea if I had a word with your ex-wife. You've always said you don't know where she is, but perhaps this lady could help us? If she's a friend, that is. Save a lot of time.'

Rachel loathed him on sight, and felt caught in a trap, as if she were squeezed between them. She turned to Carl.

'Why do you want to find her? You never did, and you always could, so why the hell now?' she asked him. 'What is this?'

'It's nothing really, sir,' Donald said, looking to the judge first and then to her. 'Only it looks like she might be involved in our business, sir, simply because she may know someone who is, and it may just be useful to . . . to . . . have a word. Eliminate from enquiries, so to speak.'

He looked as if he could nod and wink at the same time, like a dozy donkey invested with cunning, pretending to shake his head to get rid of the flies. Oh my, what a good double act.

'So where is she?' Donald said, leaning across Rachel, looking as if he might be about to pat her knee. She recoiled, felt oddly exposed, sitting on this bench in the early evening sun, as if she had been placed there deliberately, for a purpose she had not understood. Placed here like a target, because as soon as the names Wiseman and Ivy had been mentioned on the phone to his clerk, Carl would have guessed she would at least know Ivy's whereabouts.

'Why does a policeman suddenly want to know where Ivy is?' she asked him, ignoring Donald. 'All he has to do is ask you. You could always find her. You always could have contacted her, either directly or through Grace.'

'Ah yes,' Carl replied smoothly. 'But as you've just pointed out, I haven't been looking. I haven't made the effort, therefore I don't know.'

Ivy was going to be blamed for something again. Rachel could feel the closing of a trap.

'Is this a set-up?' she asked him. His eyes were fathomless blue, locked in a brief gaze with her own, saying I don't know. She did not believe him; rose and brushed imaginary crumbs off her trousers, listening all the same. Carl turned to Donald.

'My wife's friend was only saying just now,' he said, in a chatty tone she automatically mistrusted, 'that although she's a friend, she hasn't the faintest idea where Ivy is. Isn't that right, Rachel?'

She nodded. It was true in a manner of speaking. She had no idea what he was playing at.

'There's no urgency,' Donald said, sensing something on the wind, addressing her with a winning, repellent grin. 'Only that I came across someone who used to know her. Or she used to know him. She just might be able to tell me something useful about him, that's all.'

The lameness was embarrassing. She adjusted her handbag, stepped backwards, as if she had just realised the time and had to go, now.

'I must . . .' she said.

'Go.' Carl said. 'But we're meeting next week anyway, aren't we? I'll phone the office. Tuesdays are good for me.'

She was about to say yes, and then, startling in its irrelevancy, there came into her mind the comforting vision of the life drawing class. The weekly commitment, never to be missed, the start of all this. The last class of term.

'Not Tuesday. Or . . . it would have to be late.'

'We'll speak, shall we?'

'Yes.'

She walked away, and once round the corner found herself running. Once she was out of the Inns and hit the roar of Fleet Street at the top end, she paused for breath and went into the nearest bar. Her face in the mirror blushed red. She had bloody well said yes.

Rachel drank the indifferent glass of wine she had ordered as if it was water, sat in a crowded corner as though waiting for someone. No one ever quite mastered the art of being alone in a bar.

On the table in front of her, someone had abandoned

the *Evening Standard*, flourishing a dramatic headline.

Yob culture hits the middle classes! Man stabbed in Theatreland! Young fans run amok. Is nothing safe?

She ignored it. She felt she was conspiring with the enemy.

Chapter Eleven

Quick, quick, get going. She was being shaken awake. Come on, Rachel, there's a love. It's a gorgeous day. Let's go, if we're going to go, before we get stuck in traffic. If we go now, we can get to the sea first. Sorry, were you dreaming?

Rachel had been asleep when Ivy got home, whenever that was. There was a mug of steaming tea in front of her eyes, and Ivy, imploring her to move, like an impatient child waiting to be taken on holiday. Ivy, who coasted on four hours' sleep and ten hours' work, brimming with infectious energy, because life was good, life was rich and you had to enjoy every minute. That was her gift. She could give away some of that energy even at six in the morning. She was nobody's victim in the mornings and took no prisoners.

Rachel had been dreaming of the farm again. Imagining the figure of Grace and being hugged by her in the kind of embrace which said, nothing else matters, you're safe here. Carl, hugging Grace.

Once on the road, it was singing all the way. Whizzing through the deserted streets of London as if they owned it and everything had been cleared and cleaned for their benefit, and even the traffic lights deferred to them, the skies lifting as they hit the motorway stretch and left it all behind. The first hour was nothing. The radio blared and they sang to that.

The lane going towards the house; the joy of it. Bluebells in May, Ivy said, blossom in June, every shade of green in July. August is for yellows. Snowdrops in February. *Ivy said, Ivy said, Ivy said.*

Grace was tending the tubs of lavender and herbs outside the kitchen door, but really waiting. The purple hair complemented the shocking red of her pelargoniums and the pink of her cotton shift, which looked as if she had sewn it the night before. She was barefoot and jangling with multicoloured beads. Follow the noise. The shriek of welcome could have woken the dead, and it was Rachel she hugged first, Ivy next, then both together. You made it, she kept saying, you made it, as if it was a miracle. I've been reading the newspapers, she said. I've been so worried about you. All those terrible things happening in London. It isn't safe. You can't queue for an autograph, or get in an ambulance, awful.

'I had a plan,' Ivy said, interrupting the flow.

'To go to the sea,' Grace finished. 'I've been craving it all week.'

'That's why we're early,' Rachel added.

'Party time for Mother,' Ivy said. 'The sea and the pub today. We've all been working too hard. Dad can make hay while the sun shines. We're going to bring Rachel's dad to keep him company next time.'

That had been discussed in the car. Ivy had suggested it.

'Just to warn you, darling,' Grace said to Ivy, as they bundled back into the car, Rachel relieved that she was designated driver, 'I mustn't be out too long. We have a slight problem at the moment. Because of the hay, they always arrive when he cuts the hay. Not to worry. The man's coming sometime, with the dog.'

'Is this code?' Rachel asked. 'Or can anyone know?'

'We've got a rat in the house,' Grace shouted from the back seat, yelling as loudly as she would in her own, deafening Volvo. 'Ivy's never liked them much. Oh look, we're nearly there. This bloody thing goes so much faster than mine.'

'I can't go into the house if there's a rat,' Ivy said. 'I can't.'

Rachel paused at the mention of a rat. Such a nasty word. She was not going to tell anyone, not about yesterday, or anything, not yet, and it felt like being a rat, all dispelled by responding to the instructions they yelled at her to take a different route, no, right, I mean left, did I mean left? No, I meant that way, to a different stretch of the coast which was over there, the five miles separating it from the farm and the fields like crossing the Gobi Desert, the same difference as the City and here. Another secret place they knew, reached by a series of back doubles, hidden under cliffs, with a railway line snaking above their heads into a tunnel. The City was another country, and the railway, hugging the coast, was only a reminder that there were people unfortunate enough to be going somewhere else. A tiny cove, hidden beneath a mysterious cliff, which hung above it more like a guardian than a threat. Mid-morning, empty, and still the same old glorious sea. This was the precise point where I learned to swim, Grace was saying, but then again, I'm not sure. We knew every scrap of this coast, Grace said, when we were kids. We cycled for miles. We were shoved out in the morning with jam sandwiches wrapped in greaseproof, and told to come back when we were tired. I thought we might try it. The sandwiches, I mean. There is really nothing quite as disgusting as a jam sandwich made with margarine and red pulp with woodchips in it.

'Golden syrup on toast,' Ivy said. 'Treacle sandwiches. Butter and sugar on fresh white bread.'

'Go on,' Grace said. 'You were way too young for that.'

'I know, Mum,' Ivy said. 'But old habits die hard. That's what you fed me.'

There were no waves like before, simply a breeze which ruffled the surface of the water so that it mimicked a smooth lake. It was like approaching a different, friendlier animal, which would embrace softly, rather than a rough, challenging hug. It was markedly warmer than the week before, a different stage of summer. There was the same rushed changing into swimwear, although Grace and Ivy had no shame. Grace simply stripped naked, hauled on the baggy swimsuit; Ivy did not bother with changing and reached the shoreline first, clad in her bra and knickers, ran straight in with a noisy splash. Rachel followed, wading gingerly to waist height, testing the ground for the way back, automatically looking on the way for jellyfish and monsters, laughing at herself for doing it, while Grace squealed and flopped and decided it was best to go in backwards, tripping and splashing, yelling, watch out, it's fucking freezing, Oh bloody hell fire. They were there to play, Ivy to swim. She outranked everyone as a swimmer; she moved away from them with natural speed in a graceful crawl into the distance, and only turned back to shore when Rachel and

Grace were sitting in the warmer shallows, feeling virtuous, kissing the last week goodbye.

Grace did it again as they were towelling dry, dropped a small stone of conversation into the flurry of movement, as if tossing it into the sea and getting rid of it. It was directed at Ivy.

'You remember that paying guest, Joe his name was, the one in May who got drunk all the time when you were here that week? Well, he died. PC Plod had to bestir himself and come and tell us.'

'Oh, what a pity,' Ivy said with careless politeness, wrapping her head in a towel, then balancing to pull on her jeans over bare skin with the ease of practice.

'One of your guests?' Rachel asked. 'How awful. Wasn't your food, was it?'

'Don't think so,' Grace said. 'Though he ate enough of it. No, he went and drowned somewhere after he'd left. Remember him, Ivy love? He wanted to swim in the lake and we told him he couldn't. Because of the swans still nesting.'

'Yes, that's right. Anyway, he preferred the pub. He was bloody rude to you. He was always trying to do things he couldn't do, wasn't he? Probably took up sailing next. He never could see the need to practise. Like that lot.'

She pointed to the horizon, where a small flotilla of yachting dinghies with yellow and pink spinnakers tacked about like waterborne butterflies, chasing each other. Grace shielded her eyes with her hand, and sighed.

'I wish I could do that,' she said. 'But perhaps not. I'd rather be in it than on it. God, I feel better for that. It's like taking the cure. What time were you up? You must be bloody starving.'

No unpleasant news was going to disturb this day; that had been decided. No paying guest stayed long enough to form himself into a ghost.

'Poor Jack the Lad.' Ivy finished it, picking up towels and bra. 'You know who he reminded me of, Rache? That Plonker in the life drawing class. They could've been twins. He's one of Rachel's fans,' she explained to Grace. Rachel laughed.

'One of yours, you mean.'

Grace threw her hands into the air. 'And what about me? Where are mine? Any left over for a woman in her prime? I don't care if they're stupid.'

'She can still pull them, you know,' Ivy said, 'The ones who want mothers. And she can swim better then me when she tries.'

'Here she is,' Ernest said to Rachel when they got back. The salt had dried on their skin from the air blowing through the open windows of the car. 'Here's my favourite girl. Are you coming out to make hay with me this afternoon?'

'Food,' Grace said. 'Food first. Followed by no decisions at all.'

There was smoked ham, a salad of herbs, raspberries with yellow cream, eaten in the garden. Ivy would not go into the house.

'The lake's murky today,' Ernest said, with a mouth full of food. 'You were better off with the sea. When's the rat man coming, love?'

'You never know with him,' Grace said. 'We may as well all sit in the sun. You never know how long it's going to last. You see to him, will you? I hate it. Ivy hates it.'

'My little phobia,' Ivy said. 'Bloody rats.'

Rachel and Ivy lay on blankets on the unmowed lawn, listening to the humming of insects, and Rachel drifted into sleep. The sea did that. There seemed to be all the time in the world for everything; it was an excuse for saying nothing and she was pleasantly tired. Before she slept, listening to the buzz of the semi-silent life which went on all around her at ground level, regardless of human beings, she was thinking, solutions find themselves for insects, why not for us? The solutions to dilemmas were often so much simpler than the problems themselves. The bees and the flies went on fine without much obvious thought. It was wonderful here. All she needed to do, surely, was to get Judge Carl Schneider. Get him to come back here. Him first, then the son . . . Yes, that would work. She felt a twinge of excitement. Get him to come to this place, be charmed by the goodness he had forgotten, and then everything would follow. He had loved them all once. He and his children and his father . . .

She woke, warm and heavy, the sun still hot on her back, her chin level with the long grass, her mouth dry and the salt on her skin itching. Something crawled on her calf; she twisted round to slap it. Ernest was sitting beside her, slumped in a very old striped deckchair. Half asleep, she noticed that the visible stripes of the cloth around his head were as faded as the wood of the chair, bleached into the colour of a pale mushroom, and he was wearing a vest, and he and the chair suited one another. *Old man in deckchair, wearing vest and knotted handkerchief*, like a postcard from the 1950s, still dressed the same, better in sepia. The weeks of sun, however intermittent and easy to ignore in the City, had turned his face, neck and forearms deep brown, with a sharp demarcation point above his elbows and below his chin, showing the precise point to which his shirt sleeves had been rolled up and his collar left open when he was out and about. Farmers did not care about nice even tans. Rachel thought of the builders seen from her high office window, stripped to the waist with evenly brown backs and builders' bums, a perk of the job, and then, looking at Ernest's milky-white shoulders, had a stark image of her father on holiday. She should have tried to phone him again; she tried to remember where she had left her mobile.

Ivy's blanket was empty. The lawn was small but seemed vast.

'Oh, hello,' Ernest said. 'You're awake then. I was sitting out here waiting for him to do his business. They had to go, Ivy and her mother. They can't stand it. Don't know why, when they're so good at killing things. Maybe they don't like to defer. But the rat man's indoors. I thought you might be interested. Shall we go and see?'

He began to haul himself out of the deckchair, the seat of which sagged ominously, and then gave up the attempt. The bottom half of him was still clad in his baggy canvas trousers, without boots or socks, showing feet the same milky white as his shoulders. He retrieved his shirt; the demarcation lines of white and brown disappeared. Rachel thought of a model in the life class. Saw through the wrapping to the way he might have appeared, stripped of his clothes and his role, emerging as a gnarled old tree trunk, already struck by lightning, discoloured by fungus, growing weaker.

'He's a very clever beast, Vernon. If he were half as sharp as the ferret, they'd have made a mint.'

She had been disconcerted to be found asleep in her shorts and cropped top, beneath Ernest's innocent gaze. She sensed that he had been willing her awake, simply because he wanted company, and she was slightly hurt to have been abandoned by Ivy and Grace, her chosen companions for the afternoon, and then she could hear them saying, she's sleeping, poor lamb, leave her, and thought, yes, that would be the reason.

'No rush,' he said. 'It's not the best time of day for it.'

'For what?' she asked, still fuggy.

'Flushing out the rat.'

'Why's Ivy so scared of them?'

'Got locked in the cellar with them once. Don't have a cellar any more. It spooked her.'

Rachel sat up, reached for her bottle of water and drank, resisting the urge to pour it over her head. Then she put on her hat and felt as if she had rejoined the world and looked around from a new angle. The garden was more like a meadow, left to run wild, apart from the lavender and flowers by the back door, and the obtrusive row of rubbish bins. It had resisted any kind of makeover. The back of the house was creeper-covered, mellow red brick. It seemed timeless.

'Tell me what it was like here, oh, twenty years ago,' she said.

'That's not long,' he said finally. 'I remember much further than that. Not much changes, only the way we use things. The way it was. All those people, all that company. That's what I miss. Used to be everyone in on it when we harvested hay. A gang of us, always a gang. Grace was feeding the whole lot. That's the difference. The company. Three of us for the pigs, four for the milking, ten for the hay. Now it takes me and a machine to make hay, all by myself. A farm gets run by one man and a Polish cowhand who can't speak English. It's lonely, that's the difference. Now most days are the same and always will be. Unless Carl comes back.'

He began to struggle out of the deckchair again. Deckchairs like these were traps for the unwary, lessons in indignity; his efforts were almost comical. He was not used to sitting anywhere for long except on the upright chairs of the kitchen, or perhaps in the comfortable armchairs in the living room which Grace told her only really came into its own in winter, when on wet days Ernest would watch wildlife programmes on the TV.

'Come on,' he said. 'Let's see how he's doing.'

Still mystified, she followed him back through the ever-open kitchen door, through that room, down the corridor which bisected the house. The living room faced the front of the house, next to the front door no one seemed to use. It was as if the kitchen entrance was the mouth of the house, through which everything and everyone passed, where everything was prepared and digested, debated and decided until it was time for bed. The living room door was closed. Ernest knocked very softly, entered on tiptoe, ushered her in behind him and closed the door, nodding to the man who sat at his ease by the dead fireplace with a dog at his feet.

'That's Vernon,' Ernest whispered, pointing at the dog. No one else required an introduction. They sat on a sofa, in silence. The room was cool; she shivered. It was odd to be sitting still and silent with two men and a dog on a glorious day; it made her want to giggle. The dog raised its head and cocked its ears. The strange man in the chair played with a soft leather pouch, squeezing it between his hands like a man with worry beads, keeping his fingers occupied. It was all rather peaceful.

It was then that she began to hear the sounds, at first from above her head, then from one corner of the room, then another, then almost under her feet. Scrabbling, scratching sounds, the pitter-patter of ghostly feet, a series of minute thuds, the sound of running, which made her turn her head to try and follow, detect the weird, unseen source. Then more silence; then the sounds resumed, *scritter, scratter*, running, bumping, something twisting and growing behind the skirting boards or under the wooden floor. She was struck dumb by the sounds.

Ernest leaned towards her and whispered, 'He's got him on the run.'

'Who's *he*?'

'The ferret. Look at old Vernon.'

The dog sprang to its feet and stood, quivering. The sounds grew louder, echoing into the room, a race coming closer and closer until it was focused on the furthest corner, where the old skirting board failed to meet the floor. It was a crooked room, she remembered, full of gaps and draughts, warped into its own shape, the dark side of the house.

She imagined something screaming, saw a brown shape squeeze through the hole and catapult into the room, a live creature running. Until the dog sprang, snatched it up mid-flight, shook it and tossed it twice, let it drop broken-necked, then picked it up and carried the trophy to his master's chair with the sedate, brisk movements of a well-rewarded servant. The dead rat was deposited with dignified indifference. The man patted the dog. The efficient brutality of the death took her breath away.

Again they waited. She followed the direction of Ernest's gaze to the same corner of the room where the rat had emerged. A sinuous, slinky animal, almost ash blond, emerged into the light and began to wash itself. The man crossed the room in his stockinged feet and picked it up with one enormous hand around its neck, so that its head protruded from his fist and its legs dangled. The man came back towards them, proffered the ferret in his fist for Rachel's admiration.

'You can stroke him if you like,' he said. 'Just the back of him, like. Not his head. He bites.'

She touched the spine of the thing gingerly, with a single finger, feeling shiny silk.

'He likes a good hunt, this one,' Ernest said admiringly.

He picked up the dead rat by its tail, moved out of the room, down the corridor into the kitchen. She watched him fling it into the ever-burning fire of the Rayburn, without ceremony.

'It's a lot more humane than making the poor bugger eat poison and die in agony. At least he gets a fair fight. Anyway, that's what happens to rats in this house. Doesn't work quite so well in the barns.'

There was no ceremony in the brief exchange of a note, taken from Ernest's pocket, palmed by the man and tucked into his own. He grinned a toothless grin, whistled for his dog and went out of the back door. She could think of nothing but a character from a film, utterly believable at the time of watching, but better never seen in real life. The strong smell of animal remained behind him. There was an insignificant sound from the Rayburn, as if it had belched. Ernest ambled around from sink to stove, filling and placing a kettle for tea, chatting as he went.

'Don't take it unkindly that Grace and Ivy upped and left you asleep,' he said. 'Grace said you looked so sweet it was a shame to wake you, and Ivy can't be around the rat man. They've only gone to the farmers' market. Not that they needed anything, just to get out the way. But I took the liberty of waking you because I know you like to know how things work.'

She began to relax a little, realising that she had been wound up by the shift from the sun in the Garden of Eden to the relatively dark, animal-smelling area of the silent living room, with its gap-filled skirting boards and the hollow floors and walls with conduits to all parts of the house. A rat could come and go and hide as it pleased in a house like this. Her father would have stopped up those cracks, those holes, years ago. No rat would ever be allowed in. He would have covered every board with carpet, fitted every hole and crack with plaster and wood cement, made everything smooth. The making of tea reminded her of all those things for which she felt gratitude. Maybe it would not be such a good idea to bring him here, as Ivy had suggested, after all, although he would revel in a certain kind of superiority which he might enjoy. At least his humdrum little house was hermetically sealed against draughts and pests, down to the smallest fly, and he did not have to take in paying guests in order to finance his pigs and cows. Grace would charm him, Ernest would reassure. It would be fine.

Ernest made the tea, handing her a mug already laced with milk and sugar, and it seemed churlish to ask for another without it. Nice to have sweetness, once in a while. She found her voice at last, heard it sounding clipped in this quiet, ticking, humming room, which was always warm, never hot, even with the Rayburn always about its business of heating the water, the oven, the whole house. The sunshine outside no longer appealed. How lovely it would be in winter. She was already thinking of the pleasures of winter.

'Well, fancy Grace and Ivy being scared of the rat man and

the ferret. I thought those two weren't frightened of anything.'

Ernest grinned and scratched his head. 'Reckon it's pride. They could neither of them kill a rat. They're too quick. Target's too small, however you practise. Me, I can't kill anything. So them two had to learn, but they never could manage a rat. That's why they scare them. You can only get it right with practice. Like that ferret. No finesse, my girls.'

'Wouldn't a cat be better?' she said.

He shook his head. 'Maybe. We don't have cats or a dog any more. Can't risk it. That's where Ivy got her first practice.'

'Got her *what*?'

'Practice, I said. What did I say?' He shrugged and drank his tea, forgetting where he was, drifting away and coming back.

'Not that there's any choice, you know. There never is. If the beast's got to go, it's got to go. Like road kill. Kinder to everyone in the end. He shouldn't have killed the swans and made such a mess. Would you like some more tea? What time is it? They said they'd buy a leg of lamb for supper, that'll be nice. Crazy that we can't eat our own cows.'

There was the sound of the car, heard from a distance, stopping noisily outside. Slamming doors, laughter, a flurry of footsteps over the gravel, the omnipresence of Ivy and Grace laden with bags, coming in with a chorus of apologies, chirping like the sparrows which had started their own early evening chorus in the creeper round the door. They exploded into the kitchen, bringing in colour and warmth and noise. Trailing behind them, as if uncertain whether they should, were two blond young men with knapsacks. Paying guests.

'Oh Lord,' Grace said. 'We thought we'd only be an hour, and the pair of you would still be asleep. Sorry. The rat man's gone, hurrah! Saw him on the road. Just as well we're late, because we picked up these two in the lane. They came in late last night, and they've been walking since dawn and they're shagged out. They're German, by the way,' she added.

Ernest beamed at them.

'Guten Tag. Ich hoffe Sie hatten einen schönen Tag. Aus welchem Teil Deutschlands stammen Sie?' he said slowly.

'I got some organic wine,' Ivy said, flourishing a bottle. 'Therefore entirely harmless. Anyone?'

'Do you have beer?' the blondest of the two asked. 'We are from Berlin.'

Ernest clapped his hands, looking delighted.

'*Berlin ist eine sehr schone Stadt*,' he said.

'Do we have beer?' Grace said. 'Do pigs have wings?'

'What . . .?'

'Never mind,' she said. 'Sit down, sit down.'

'Berlin people are very nice,' Ernest said.

A party atmosphere was prevailing, as if the departure of the man and his dog was an excuse. Not that Grace or Ivy ever needed an excuse to celebrate. Ernest needed company and they had brought it home. He was lit with smiles. Rachel wanted to join in, wanted to please. One of the paying guests was looking at her shorts with frank appreciation, and it was that and the remembered smell of the ferret which made her murmur she must have a shower before a drink. She went upstairs to her room, washed in the tiny bathroom, and found a clean shirt in the bag she had dumped on the bed. Her mobile phone lay accusingly beneath it, reminding her that she must check on her father.

Two messages. The surprise was that the first was from her father. He hated leaving messages, hated mobile phones and refused to have one. The sound of his stuttering voice alarmed her as much as the fact of the message itself.

Been a bit poorly, his voice said. Someone picked my pocket on the train. I had a turn, had to go to hospital. I was there all night, or was it two? Can't remember. I'll be all right. Just wanted to let you know before anyone else does. 'Bye.

He never told her when he was ill. Rachel checked the number. Number not available. She pressed out his home number: no reply. He was not at home; where the hell was he? She was furious with him. Typical to leave a message to worry her sick, without giving her any opportunity to do anything about it. Maybe he was at his neighbour's; he had one good neighbour; they went shopping on ebay for fun. They would shop for a bag of nails. She did not have the neighbour's number. It was in a book, in the flat in London. Damn, damn, damn. Maybe the second message would explain, but the second message was not from him. It was from Carl Schneider.

Any evening next week would suit him fine, for dinner or drinks or whatever she wanted. Please.

Rachel sat on the bed with the phone in her hand, hearing sounds of laughter through the open window, wishing she had not touched the thing, wanting to go back downstairs and join in and knowing she could not. She found herself shoving the phone out of sight. Ivy stood in the doorway, proffering a glass of wine.

'What's the matter, love? We're missing you down there. Dad's embarrassing everyone with his little bit of German. He's probably going to give them his version of the war. We thought we might take a stroll to the lake, but it'd be pointless without you.'

'It's my father. Left me a message. He's ill, or he wouldn't leave a message at all.'

Part of Rachel wanted to ignore it. Then she remembered how he had looked when last she saw him. Old and grey. She had forgotten everything else. He was her father.

'What exactly did he say?'

'Something stupid. He said someone picked his pocket on the train. He must mean the other night, going home from us. Says he went to hospital.'

Ivy slumped against the door, then came and sat down beside Rachel.

'On the *train*? Oh, poor thing,' she said. 'Are you sure he said the *train*? He didn't say anything else?'

'No.'

'But he's all right? He must be, surely, to phone at all.'

'He probably is. It's just that I can't get the number he called from. I'll have to go back and find out where he is. He's not at home, probably at the neighbour's and I don't have the neighbour's number with me. If he's in hospital I don't know which hospital. If I go now I'll be back at the flat by nine. Sorry, sounds like I'm missing a party.'

Ivy handed her the wine. Rachel shook her head.

'Wait until the morning and I'll come with you,' Ivy said.

'Shit, I forgot that. How will you get back tomorrow without the car?'

Ivy put her arm around her. She felt hot from the sun and there was the dry sweetness of wine on her breath.

'Same as I always do without you. Lift to the station, train. Are you sure he said he was pickpocketed on the train?'

'Yes.'

'The bastards. The fucking parasites,' Ivy said, sounding somehow relieved, and then hesitated. 'I could come with you now, if you like.'

Rachel felt grateful for that, but shook her head. She had heard the hesitation and that was enough.

Your father is yours, and mine is mine.

Chapter Twelve

It turned out Blaker had been a country boy, once. Came from somewhere up north, territory unknown to Donald, who was London born and bred, although he could understand why someone might want to live anywhere else, the way it was now. He wasn't a bad chap really, by which Donald meant he was interesting, he could talk, he was educated enough to have a nodding acquaintance with history, so therefore he passed. It did not make Donald approve of him, which was another matter, but in general he found thieves easier to understand than their more moral, less articulate counterparts.

All he had established that first time was that Blaker had the skill to threaten the judge in the way the judge had been threatened, and that by some weird coincidence he was enamoured of the judge's ex-wife. The coincidence wasn't so great when he considered the territory. The West End of London was still the uncomfortable but manageable refuge for runaways, thieves, opportunists, drug addicts, homeless drop-outs of all types and ages slipping through the social net. There was the official Centrepoint refuge in Tottenham Court Road, dumping ground for the displaced youth of several boroughs, there were the favourite places of shelter all around Charing Cross, with the warm underpasses for sleeping; there was the endless opportunity of casual, cash-paid labour; there were doorways and nearby hospitals and above all, millions of consumers. A person could live on what was dropped and left and a person could be paid to pick it up. Get to London, like Dick Whittington, because the pavements were paved with gold, flee inland from the coast, downhill from anywhere, get lost or found, and survive, for a while. Huddle together with kindred spirits, make friends and allies, or shun them. Celebrate a fresh misery or a win. Keep the cold out.

'I reckon some of us blag our way out of the homeless shit out of sheer boredom,' Blaker said. 'Either that, or you lie down and die. I've known Ivy a long time. She was always going to rise, like a cork floating on the muck, because she had the will, and she never quite dropped out of the system. She had support. She chose the street. She shared stuff, though most of us don't. I'd just got out of prison for the third time, back here like one of those bloody pigeons. Either here or down Embankment Gardens if the weather's nice or I want a change. Ivy's the same, but she has other places too. I saw her again when I was on bail for the last lot. Told her I'd come up in front of a German judge – is that what we fought the fucking war for? – but at least he gave me bail before the trial, and she said, You what? What was his name again? Then she laughed and laughed. Oh, he's a judge now is he, now isn't that rich? He wasn't one of them when I was married to him. A fucking judge. You could have knocked me down with a feather and I laughed back at her, didn't believe a word of it. Ivy doesn't like being laughed at. Nor being pushed about, or touched. You've got to be careful about that. You have to give it to her. She worked her way out of it. Said it was the only way. She said if you don't earn the money, someone's going to take it away; if it's nicked, they nick it back. I wish I'd listened, but work and me, we never got on. Now I've got no fucking choice, because I've lost my bottle for the other. She got me a job on a night shift.'

'What sort of shift?'

Blaker looked at him scornfully.

'There's all sorts of shifts. Honestly, you people don't know you're born. There's shifts for loading and unloading, shifts for cinemas, theatres, lavatories . . . when do you think they clean the shops? Pubs, clubs, shifts for packing sandwiches and scrubbing decks, gettit? A lot of them are sewn up, but they'll always take Ivy. Pity she couldn't have got me a job as a model, too. That'd be a treat for them.'

He sniggered with laughter at his own joke. Donald did the clichéd thing and got up and fetched another pint. They had not moved far from where they had first met. He was still smarting from his attempt to tell the judge his big discovery about the Blaker connection, storming up to his chambers at the right time of day, finding him out there on that bench. But the judge had been in a state at first, then cool and dismissive, listened and said, that's fine, but don't you need to know a little more? Has he admitted anything? I'm sure lots of people knew my wife. He had not liked his tête-à-tête with the girl on the bench interrupted. They had looked close; Carl had kept his eyes on her as she walked away, as if following a dream and wanting to run after her.

On second thoughts, he might have been right about

Donald not knowing enough and getting overexcited about finding a connection which could be nothing. Yes, Blaker had said he would do anything for this Ivy woman, but so what? That was as far as he'd got, apart from establishing that Blaker was lonely enough to be up for a longer chat any time and seemed to have nothing but regret on his conscience. Thus, today, Donald was doing his policeman's thing of buying pints for an old con and enjoying it. Saturday counted as overtime; Saturdays and Sundays were bad days for Blaker because there was less to watch. The pub in this street could have done with a spring-clean. They were like ladies, meeting for lunch, and Donald was resenting the money. Blaker could run just as well on coffee, not that the price was so different.

'Don't mind my asking,' Donald began, 'but you know after you mugged those girls, why did you phone them up? Why keep the keys? They'd have changed the locks. You were never going to go stalking, were you?'

Blaker shook his head.

'It was something to do. I was bored. Made sense at the time. I liked the idea of the silly bitches being frightened. Remembering me when no one else would. Silly. And the keys were just an insurance against some time when I might have nowhere else to go. Gave me a kick, having keys and addresses, rainy-day insurance. And anyway, they wouldn't all have changed the locks. It's expensive. Ivy said she probably wouldn't have bothered when she was married with a house of her own. It might have been worth a try sometime. Silly; it got me a bigger sentence from that bastard. I couldn't believe it was him sending me down. Fucking Kraut. Because I knew all about him by then. How dare that fucker sit in judgement on *me*?'

Donald wanted to seize his thin shoulders and rattle him for information; instead he moved his feet on the sticky carpet and imagined rats in the cellar. The beer was warm, the heat outside stultifying. There was no point in hurrying anything.

'Like I said, how dare he? All I'd ever done was steal from silly bitches who could easily afford it and it's them gets the sympathy. Losing your fucking handbag won't make a jot of difference the day after. What about the poor sod who's got no other choice but to take it? Once you start, you've got to go on. Not like him, a fucking Hun judge, been given everything, with nothing taken away. Just like the Germans after the war, innit? They got everything, we got nothing, and who got rich? Them. Aside from all that, I couldn't believe him being a bleeding judge, after what he'd done to her. He's a fucking murderer, for God's sake. I bloody told him what he was. Him sending *me* to prison? The cunt.'

Ah. That explained that.

'Bit extreme, isn't it?' Donald suggested chattily. 'Calling him a murderer. I mean, judges can't actually hang you any more, even if they might like the idea. There's probably some of them gagging for the chance to give out a death penalty, but they're not allowed. Not since the sixties.'

He was recalling the irrelevant fact that the last public hanging was in 1868, abandoned after that for the avoidance of litter, public unrest, and the awkward dispersal of the thousands who gathered to watch. He wondered if they would now. Probably. Blaker had calmed down again. You could never make anyone tell you a story in chronological order. History was not like that either. The only consistent thing was that the most civilised of men remained savages, and women could be worse, and that Blaker personified an individual episode in the Industrial Revolution where men drifted into cities because there was no longer work on the land. *Plus ça change.*

'Like I said,' Blaker went on, 'I didn't believe her when she said she'd been married to the judge, even if he wasn't one then. She told me all about her bastard old man. Never thought I'd meet him. Killed the kid and locked her out, he did. I thought she was making it up, but then we used to talk about lots of other stuff, like home. I worked on a farm, see, when I was a kid, would be now if there'd been a job; no, I lie, I wouldn't, but I know how to bale straw and make silage and what pigs eat, all that shit, and so did Ivy. She wasn't kidding, she knew what she was on about there, so I got to believe the rest of what she said about the marriage and *him*. I used to say to her, why don't you just go home, and she'd say, why don't you, and I'd say, there was nothing there to do when I left, why should there be now? And she said she'd never go back until she could hold her head up. But she did, because she could. She's been good to me, Ivy.'

He sipped at the pint with great delicacy, making it last. Another thing about him Donald quite liked. He wasn't greedy or demanding, except for someone to listen.

'When I was on bail, the last time, all that shit about phone calls and keys coming down on my head, oh, when was that, three years ago now, I said to her, wouldn't it be odd if it's your old man in the judging seat again. There's not that many to choose from, you can't choose, it's always the same bloody court you end up in. She was on the way up then, got a room; mind, Ivy always had a room if she wanted, and jobs and a modelling job, and said she was a student, but still she'd find me, somewhere near here, or down in the Gardens with the others. Not often, often enough to give me money if she had it. I don't know when she told me that her old man had killed her daughter, and that's why she hit rock bottom and got chucked out, that was long before. Couldn't be seen wedded to a crackhead, could he, wanting to be a judge and all? Drowned her and killed her.'

'Both?' Donald said faintly.

'That's what she said. And chucked his wife out on the streets, I ask you. Makes her go mad, so no one will know what he's done. The bastard. Hypocritical cunt. I was so fucking angry when he sent me down, I screamed at him. People should know.'

'I don't know how you can drown someone *and* kill them,' Donald said.

'Drowned her and shot her ghost, she said. Let's go out, Don, whatever your name is. I need a view. I know all you coppers think drink's the thing, but I need a view.'

They moved into the light and Blaker, totally unaffected by three pints, led the way. Donald followed him on to the hot pavement outside and felt disorientated by his own pint of gassy ale and the afternoon itself, found himself seeking the shady side of the street and dreaming of trees. Blaker led the way, Donald wondering if there was any greenery within a mile of here, or any place not thronged with people. They did not go far. Blaker was not seeking a rural view and was suddenly tired of him. He pointed to a café with tables outside in Wardour Street.

'They used to let us sit outside here for hours when they were Italians,' he said. 'All day if we wanted. Now it's fucking Starbucks, so I reckon it'll be ten minutes max before they move us on. Want to bet?'

Donald did not even want to know about the sensation of

being moved on. He left Blaker on the seat with a view of the newsagent's on the other side of the road, a place famous for selling every newspaper under the sun, and came back with two bottles of overpriced water. Blaker ignored the offering and belched noisily.

'We used to sit here and read the newspapers people left, still do, occasionally. Or at least, I'd read it and she'd ask me what I was reading. Ivy's as clever as all get out, but she can scarce read, you know. Knew everything by heart, though, a real learner.'

He adjusted himself on the metal seat and stretched his legs, challenging anyone who passed by on the narrow, ungolden pavement to manoeuvre round him. Donald curled his own legs beneath the chair, adopting the habit of the non-confrontational.

'Ivy'd changed by the time I came out last time,' Blaker said. 'Cleaned up altogether, not that she wasn't well on the way when I went in. Only person in my life I've ever worried about, or worried about me, for that matter. But you know what? It was always as if the more she cleaned up, the more she worked, the more she realised what had been done to her, and nothing was ever really going to cure it. Nothing could give her back those years. Couldn't give me back either, not after he'd sent me to prison. Two years! For nicking handbags! I couldn't be there for her then. She wanted to make him pay, she said, for what he'd done to both of us. And her mum and dad, and everyone else.'

'Revenge, you mean?'

Blaker nodded. 'Something like that. She said it would make her complete. Get her soul back. An eye for an eye. She said it would fix everything if he were dead. She hates him. It's only natural, isn't it?'

'If you say so.'

Blaker was angry at that. He moved from voluble passivity to rage and back again in seconds, his voice rising to a shrill whine.

'What's *natural* to you, you daft bugger? How do you know? I bet you've never even seen grass grow, let alone anything edible.'

'Sorry.'

The thread of narrative was running out; Donald could feel it slipping through his fingers and knew that if he pressed him now, he would only invent, as perhaps he was already. Giving him water had been tantamount to an insult; Donald knew he had no more bargaining power, no influence, nothing he could offer apart from company, no threat he could make.

'Death to all lawyers,' he said.

'Too right,' Blaker said. 'Too bloody right.'

'My wife says I'm a patronising git,' Donald said. 'But I think if she chucked me out, I might want to kill her.'

Blaker nodded sympathetically.

'Used to think that myself, about the bloke I ran away from home for, but shit, I would have gone anyway, and they all leave in the end. You're only going to get caught, so why bother? Since when was a fuck worth a lifetime in jail, and who'd get the sympathy vote? Him.'

The afternoon stretched before them. Like ladies who lunched, neither had better things to do, and the curiosity and mutual need which blossomed between them into mutual tolerance made Donald want to go as well as to stay, extend it or finish it, he was not quite sure which, but it was worth the gamble. He was wondering what his wife would think, and what she might have done if he had ever tried to part her from his daughters, yes, she would have killed him . . . Love was a many-splendoured thing. It was the gut ache he had now.

'If you want to know how come I got out of prison so early, you could always ask,' Blaker said.

'I was curious. None of my business.'

'I'm HIV positive, see? They don't really like us hanging around. You might like to think of it before you give me a hug. Ivy doesn't.'

Donald tried not to react.

'Fancy a walk?' he said. 'I know I know fuck-all about the way the world works compared to you, but I do know another garden where you can sit for free. Supposed to be private, but it isn't, not really. It'd take an hour at least before anyone moved you on.'

'How come you're not busy, copper? All those fucking murders I read about. That poor bastard in the ambulance, the other one outside the theatre . . . Shocking. What's the world coming to?'

'Rumour has it,' Donald said, 'that it's better than it was.'

What a waste of time. She was more than halfway back when her father answered the mobile calls she made every ten minutes, and just as she neared London, they spoke. Yes, he was at his neighbour's and very nice it was too, thank you. What was the problem? She was at the end of the motorway, mounting a three-lane slope which took her past the high-rise places where she would have hated to live, thinking, how do they do this, wanting to be by the lake, but not wanting, not capable of anything until she had heard his voice. She almost took the car off the road. The summer night had given way to near darkness, a sky beautiful and streaked with colours, magenta, blue, grey, purple, misled by artificial lights into a backdrop of marvels, the stage set for Act One of the night. Ten thirty, all at once in reach of home, and no reason to be there. He was fine, he said. No, he didn't want her coming to see him right now. He'd had an attack on the train, had a day and a night in the hospital, which was more than anyone got these days. Should have gone home sooner. It was because of the crowds on the train, someone picking his pocket, taking the Ventolin and the pills, and it was hot and scary. He kept repeating that, like a litany. Oh yes, all right, if she was free she could come tomorrow, but there was really no need. He'd rather not. Yes, he had thought he was going to die, but he hadn't, had he? He wanted to look better. Get back on the rails. Please. She thought of the crowds jostling that small man, the panic as he felt for his inhaler and the pills, and the humiliation, the hating of help, and she wanted to cry.

Bathos and pathos hit like a blow. Her car was parked with hazard lights flashing on the hard shoulder of a spaghetti junction of converging roads, ready to be hit and bounced over the crash barrier, and she did not care, as long as he was all right. The relief of hearing his voice was overpowering, however petulant he sounded. He was alive and that was all that mattered. The sound of a car horn brought her back to the present. One and a half hour's drive from Paradise; she found the gears and carried on.

Why had he not phoned her when he was first ill? Why was she the last point of contact when he was in need, rather than the first? What had happened? Who would pick the pocket of an old man in a train, hardly rich pickings. What was the exchange value of an inhaler? The thought of him wheezing and falling, scrabbling for breath in an overcrowded carriage had haunted her all the way. She should have gone with him; she should not have let him leave, she should not have upset him. She should not . . .

Inside the flat, it was dusty with trapped heat. She was tired and fretful, went round opening every window, tidying as she went, straightening a chair already straight, washing the already clean mugs in the kitchen, feeling as if she had been away for a week instead of a matter of hours. It was a way of maintaining control. Had he meant to sabotage the weekend? Didn't he know she would rush back in his direction as soon as he sounded the alarm? Did he have any idea how much she loved him, the cantankerous, miserable old bastard, with all his prejudices? Did he know she only wanted him to be happy? Which was, she reflected, all he had ever wanted for her. He just thought that contentment was dependent on status and success and the right kind of friends, all of which had evaded him. She looked at the shelves he had made in her kitchen, and wanted to weep again.

Dad had liked her lover. Dad thought Rachel's man was the best she could get, and he only wanted the best. Or maybe he wanted her safe. But the lover had been a thief, and Rachel had betrayed him. She had never told him that; she could hardly complain if he told her so little, the way they protected each other from the reality of one another. Maybe parents did not know their children and children never really knew their parents until after they were dead and they watched themselves turn into them. That was the dread of her life. But her father had liked her lover, and detested Ivy on sight; he had no judgement. Yes he had: he was a shrewd, if oversuspicious judge of character, and after all, the lover had been good, once, and she had loved him for years. His judgement was only as flawed as her own; how did anyone ever know? She had a memory of her father cross-examining her teachers at a school evening, not letting them get away with anything, and smiled at the image. He was small but he could make them cower; she had been embarrassed and proud at the same time. The house on Saturdays had been full of the sound of his hammer, fixing things, trying to make things better.

He did not *seem* to need her. He knew she hated his small life and his little house. At the moment she disliked this one too and felt that, modest-sized though it was, she was rattling round in it like a pebble in a can, and her skin was still sticky with salt. She had never had the shower at the farm, and she had missed a party, no harm in that, although she wondered what they were doing now. The flat without the presence of Ivy in it seemed horribly empty. Ivy had only been there for a couple of weeks and she was out most of the time; it was not as if they were inseparable, indoors or out, or that Ivy had colonised the place in any noticeable way, it was simply that Rachel knew she would always be coming back, sometimes late but always before the night was over, and that if anyone else unlocked the door, it would be her. They had come to spend the bulk of Sundays together long before Ivy took her to the farm. It would be strange to have that long day to herself, go back to the endless Sundays which had preceded the advent of Ivy and her unqualified friendship and her mountains of ideas of what to do and see for next to nothing. Back to the loneliness which had driven her to the life class.

She found her sketchbook and got it out, looked at last week's work critically, and put it away. She could draw all day tomorrow; she could take the book and show her father, and he would say, Why? She could regard the otherwise empty day as an opportunity. Rachel found her mobile and listened to the second message again. The one from Carl.

Ivy needed her. The Wiseman family needed her. Ivy would not be back until late tomorrow. She was no use to her own father, but she could be of use otherwise. It would be so much easier to meet the judge when Ivy was not around, rather than an evening in the week when she would be coming home and there would be the temptation, the obligation even, to tell her all about it, and instinct told Rachel this would be a bad idea, however awkward it would be keeping silent. She had no idea how Ivy would react to what she had already done: gratitude in the end, perhaps, if it all worked, but not immediately. She would have to work it out; she might have to tell Grace first, oh what the hell, do it. Think later, that's what Ivy would do. Make something out of disaster, use the time.

Eleven thirty, Saturday night. Was that too late to call? She dialled, quickly, knowing that if she hesitated she might not do it all, wanting him to be out.

It was as if he was waiting, picking up on the first ring, unflustered.

'Hello, Carl here.' Not too late, not asleep. Courteous and welcoming in two words.

'Oh, er, hello. It's Rachel Doe. Look, I'm sorry it's so late, but . . .'

'Not at all.' Waiting for her to continue.

'Do you have any time tomorrow? Could we meet then, do you think?'

'Yes, of course. I should like that very much.'

Later, when the conversation was over and arrangements were made and she was bathed and scrubbed and trying to sleep, she realised the source of her confusion. *I should like that very much.*

Yes, she would. Whatever the circumstances had been, whatever he was, she wanted to see him again. Very much.

Chapter Thirteen

Where we met before, he said. I can always come to you. The bottom gate, from the Embankment, is always open, even on Sundays. I'll bring the car, pick you up. Easy on Sunday. Then we can go wherever you'd like. We could lunch, we could walk, I could drop you at home.

Proprietorial, organised.

Do not ever get into cars with strange men. No. Certainly not to be brought home. That would mean he would know where Ivy lived. Wasn't that the whole idea?

No. What was she thinking of? He could always have found out where Ivy lived or had lived, if he wanted. Grace would have told him, if he had not been avoiding Grace. Maybe he did want to know where Ivy was.

In the long reaches of the night, when she woke from the dream of the rat being pursued across her own room, she tried to think it through logically.

Carl had long since abandoned his wife. He did not want to know her family. He might have remarried, repartnered.

He was doing all he could to prevent his son from seeing any of them. It would be better for him all round if Ivy and her kind did not exist. Maybe Rachel was acting the role of the ferret, flushing him out of his hole. Maybe she was the decoy, the deliverer of prey. Maybe she was not helping Ivy or Grace at all. Maybe she was simply exposing all of them.

She had put out of her mind the memory of the panting policeman who had interrupted them on the bench, the one who wanted a word with the judge's wife. Did they intend to frame her for something? Why would a policeman want a word with Ivy? Was he the judge's pet poodle?

Had Rachel disturbed a hornets' nest? She remembered with shame the careless way she had revealed to Carl that Ivy shared her flat, and the deft way Carl had sidestepped the policeman to deny she had any knowledge of where Ivy was. It had been smooth; it had somehow felt kind, at the time, as if he was sparing her something, and yet it was only proof that he lied with ease, whatever the purpose. Still, she treasured that memory, alongside that of his courtesy in court.

By the time she arrived at the Embankment gate to the Temple, she could no longer admire the view of the river behind her and the narrow cobbled road which led into the labyrinth of courtyards before her. She was wishing she was not there, uncertain of why she was there, feeling guilty, suspicious, nervous, impertinent, and yet, through it all, she did want to see him again.

As he pulled into the entrance and jumped out of the driving seat, neither his car nor his clothes was designed to impress. An old Ford, with a conspicuous dent in the rear left wing. He was dressed for the sticky, humid weather carelessly, in the clothes of a man who wore a daily uniform and did not otherwise care. A half-pressed check shirt, creased cotton trousers, shoes, no socks, no obvious thought behind what he wore. The clothes were clean and solid, like himself. They fitted his bulk. He smiled that radiant smile of his, the one which so discommoded the defendant in the dock, even when it came from behind that ridiculous wig. It was a grin which said, I know what you mean, and she hated herself for responding to it. She had a painless flashback to the last time she had got into a car with a man. Her lover would have selected every item of his expensive apparel with care, concentrating on the overall effect. The car would have to be a BMW, at least. He had liked money too much.

'I didn't bring the Porsche,' Carl said, 'in case it got wet later.'

A joke, she realised. He looked better suited to a tractor than a Porsche. 'My son is so ashamed of this car,' Carl said, opening the door for her, 'that he almost refuses to borrow it. Almost.'

They could have been a man and a woman interested in one another, going out for a drive and a meal, like thousands of others across the city and beyond. Simply seeking entertainment. Could have: it was a nice illusion. She was trying to guess his age. Mid-forties, minimum, the kind who improves with age, except she could not imagine there had ever been anything callow about him.

'Was it him or you who backed this heap into a wall?' she asked.

He manoeuvred the car back into the slow Sunday traffic, across three lanes, turning back at the next junction to go in the opposite direction, entirely certain of his route.

'It was him this time,' Carl said. 'But for the sake of good neighbourly relations, it's always better to be me. I thought we might find somewhere near the river. The Tate? A view of the water always helps.'

She was not being given a choice, and since she was so confused about the nature of the occasion, she was glad to have decisions made for her, simply nodded, fine.

'What freed you up for today?' he asked. 'Nothing unpleasant, I hope. Nothing disastrous.'

Rachel had decided on sight of him that any kind of subterfuge or messing around was beyond her today, especially since she did not know what game she was playing. She had never been good at games.

'I was at Midwinter Farm, with Ivy and her parents. My father was ill and I had to come back last night.'

'Oh,' he said, slowing down almost to a standstill. 'I'm so sorry. Where does he live? Shall I take you there? Is he all right? I could take you, that's what cars are for.'

It was so disingenuous, she laughed out loud.

'He lives in Luton, and he doesn't want me there today. An asthma attack. Nothing terminal. He just wanted me to know.'

'You're sure? My son was asthmatic; luckily he grew out of it. It's terrifying. Are you really sure? Doesn't matter where it is. I can take you.'

'Yes. I'm sure. Or at least I'm sure he's sure. If we're going to Pimlico, it's the next turning on the right, there.'

She was glad to be able to give directions, relieved that he had almost gone the wrong way. It made him fallible. In profile he looked so much like the photo of his father in the Wisemans' underused living room. Carl the younger, the image of his dad.

'What's your father like?' he asked as if guessing her thoughts.

She was surprised into replying.

'Mine? Oh, stiff-necked, proud of it. High standards, low prejudices. Finds it difficult to relax. Has to be busy.'

'Sounds a little like mine was. I wonder if we all make life difficult for our children. It's the only reason I dread being old.'

The car was parked; they walked towards the river, another section of it with a different view. He was saying how he was never quite able to get away from the river, and wondered why. He hated getting wet, but there was nothing quite so wonderful as the spectacle of light on water, and had she ever been to the Tate at St Ives? Yes, she said, she had. She had been everywhere and seen nothing; the knowledge surprised her. Years before, she had gone. Maybe the drawing class had not been such a random choice. Even before Ivy she had always been attracted to shape rather than nature. The interest in drawing had always been there, or maybe she meant an interest in lines. She told Carl where she had met Ivy. I would kill to be able to draw, he said; my father thought any such thing frivolous. Mine too, she said. If he knew, even now, that I went to a life drawing class, he would think I was crazy. He'd say, what for?

'Mine,' Carl said, 'would have said, *for what?* He took English as his second language very seriously. He learned how. Never put the preposition at the end, nor split an infinitive. I grew up speaking like a grammar lesson. Composing sentences in my head in advance. *You must get it right. Don't speak as I do, people will know.* He never did get it right. If he were here now he would say, at which place lunch are we having? Let's be sitting, shall we?'

'Mine would say,' Rachel said, laughing at his mimicry and the speed of his speech, 'I don't care where we go, because I'm not going to like it.'

'Well,' he said, 'I hope the same thing doesn't apply to you.'

They were under a blue awning on a balcony, the colour casting shade on their faces, before she remembered he was the enemy and that an ease of manner, masquerading as charm, was part of his profession. No, that was not true; she knew many an ill-mannered lawyer. It seemed a shame not to enjoy it: she wanted to postpone the shattering of the temporary illusion and the going back to the knowledge of what a shit he was, the picture of Grace weeping over the crumpled letter in the kitchen and Ivy working so hard so that she might be fit to see her own son. It would be nice to be out on a summer's day with a man whose face she liked, and who, it seemed, liked hers, talking about fathers in the shade, with nothing to do but eat and fill in the blank spaces of each other's histories, which in his case, right here and now, she would have liked to forget. She looked round at the place he had chosen, and remembered that Ivy would have to work two long night shifts to pay for a meal in a place like this.

'Shall we get down to business?' she asked more shyly than assertively as the waiter went away with an order. Just a drink for now, thanks.

He became businesslike.

'My pedantic father would have said business always involves money. Everything else is personal. On second thoughts, maybe it *is* about money. Is that what Ivy wants?'

'No. *No.*'

Rachel was immediately defensive. The pleasantness had been too good to last.

'It was a question,' he said, 'that's all. A question. An entirely pragmatic question. *You* aren't on trial. It's me who's on trial. I never thought of you as an emissary with instructions, and I have thought about you, incessantly. Maybe because you're beautiful and I liked you on sight. As I said, you're brave.'

'Oh.'

Crisp white wine under a shaded sky. Praise, of a sort. Rachel steeled herself. Praise instead of criticism; being listened to, waited for. The preposition was in the wrong place. She knew her weaknesses, rallied to attack.

'There's nothing brave about it. It's . . . necessary. And no, it's not about money. It's about dreams. I love them, you see. Ernest and Grace and Ivy, Ivy first.'

'And I,' he said, 'have loved them longer. Since I was a boy, and my father before me.'

'You've a fine way of showing it.'

'When you have children, you might, just might think differently. You have to have priorities. Them first and always. If there's conflict, something has to go. The child is always first. You must keep their innocence as long as you can, I think. Even if you have to sacrifice someone else.'

Now she was really angry, inhibited because she didn't really know, had no experience to quote, except her own. She felt ignorant; the selfish, childless one who only dreamed of having children.

'When I married Ivy,' he said, 'it was the most natural thing in the world. Shotguns weren't necessary, although the gun had been jumped, if you see what I mean. I wanted Cassie. My father wanted Cassie. I wanted lots and lots of Cassies, boys and girls. I'm an only child of an orphaned child. Boys for my father, boys for Farmer Wiseman, girls for me. *Success* for me, so that I could keep them all. I don't know how much you know about all of this, but . . .'

'Quite a lot. From Grace. Just tell me the story.'

She was reasserting some semblance of control. He looked away. The sky beyond their blue canopy darkened.

'Ivy was eighteen, I was twenty-seven, when Cassie was born. Ridiculous. She was the most beautiful thing, *they* were the most beautiful things. I wasn't a good father, not with babies. I didn't know any more about shared responsibility than Adam and Eve. Old-fashioned, work-obsessed. I didn't understand why Ivy still wanted to kick over the traces. Go out, behave like eighteen, as if motherhood changed all that, instead of imprisonment, stretching away, for ever. I don't know, I wish I did. Sam was born the next year. I really had put her in prison. We were a big old battleground. Cassie clung to her, Sam to me. We fought.'

Like cat and dog, she finished. Something came into her mind. Ivy practised on the cat and the dog. Can't risk having pets.

It had become warm and muggy. Maybe Ivy and Grace would have gone back to the sea. Or down to the lake. She must swim in that lake. She wanted to dive into the dangerous river Thames, get cool. It was pre-thunderstorm, oppressive heat.

'All I want,' she said, 'is for you to meet Grace and Ernest. That's it. That's all I have to do, all I want to achieve.'

'All? And for what purpose?'

She had thought about this, scaled down the ambition of whatever it was she had wanted.

'Ernest is getting old and uncertain. He dreams of you, or your father, coming back. I've done the sums, unofficially, on the farm. It loses money. Grace has a bed-and-breakfast business which just about keeps it afloat, but not for much longer. It might . . . reconcile him, them, one way or another.'

'It might enrage him. He might ask me for money, in advance.'

Money, again. She knew what judges earned. Not bad, but not mega-riches either. She could not help but be interested in the money aspect of everything. It was her job. It was natural to be preoccupied with money.

'What do you mean, in advance?'

'Ernest has always known that if I die, prematurely or otherwise, half of what I own will go to them. My money, such as it is, is never mine. Unfortunately, everyone has to wait until I die, and I'm only forty-five. Ancient, I know. That was a provision in the will I made when I married and I haven't altered it. Prudent people make wills when they marry, as you know.'

Yes, prudent accountants always advised it.

'I made that provision because of my father. He wanted me to look after them. He said we owed our start in life to the Wisemans. It was his home, you see. But I can't help them yet. What I earn is earmarked for Sam.'

'Carl the elder,' she said.

'I see you know the history. Or some of it. Why are we talking about money?'

'It's always . . . relevant. But not the point here. Ernest has to work out what to do, and dreams get in the way, perhaps. As for darling Grace, I think if she clapped eyes on you, all would be forgiven. If she could get to see her grandson, *once,* all would be forgiven. There would be an ending and a beginning, and from there you could all work out how to get Ivy and Sam together.'

It sounded depressingly optimistic and naïve, even as she said it.

'And Ivy would have no part in this initial meeting?'

Rachel shook her head, sure that that was right.

'No. She wouldn't know. It would be a . . . strategic meeting. Tell her afterwards. Let Grace tell her.'

He poured more wine into her glass, scarcely touching his own. He did not fidget. She noticed the way he applied his full concentration to everything she said, and everything he said himself. Not a man for the ill-considered remark. Rachel was trying to remember his cruelty. Beyond the awning, the sky darkened.

'All right, I'll do it, on those terms.'

'What?'

'I said, I'll do it. Or at least I'll consider it, as long as you do too, because there's something you have to understand. Wisemans don't do forgiveness, at least not the female of the species. I don't think Ernest would ever forgive me either; God knows, I've a lot to be forgiven for. And Ivy herself may never forgive you at all for your part in it. The result could be as hurtful as the hurt it intends to avoid. Especially if I have to explain that Sam is so absolutely adamant that he does not want to meet his mother, or his grandparents, that he resorts to deceit to avoid it.'

She did not believe him. How could anyone not want to know Ivy and Grace? How could anyone not be better for knowing them? This was the man who had virtually killed his own child by neglect, left her to drown, blaming his other child for not wanting to make amends.

'It's always useful to have someone to blame,' she said.

'You could,' he said, 'apply that to Ivy as well as to me. Are you sure she would like this to happen?'

All of a sudden, she wasn't. She fell back on it being, feeling, the *right* thing to do. It was all too easy. He was too damn straightforward, too *likeable*. The images simply didn't fit with that of a man who had thrust his wife out into the cold because she was mad with grief. But then she herself had loved a man corrupted by greed, and that had not shown either.

'Look,' he said, 'will you come home with me? I've got better wine than this, and if you really do want to remain involved, there's a couple of things I'd like to explain. You might meet my son, although I doubt it on Sunday. Alternatively, you can back out now and we never had this meeting. Ivy need never know.'

She did not want to go to his home with him, and yet she did. It seemed an insane, risky thing to do, but the curiosity was stronger. So was the challenge. She had wanted to be involved, and that meant being willing to be involved up to the neck. What kind of friend backed out now? And there was that inconvenient visceral thing. She did not want to leave him yet, not for a long time. He smiled that smile which had surely duped dozens of people into thinking he cared about them. She hesitated. Going back alone to the house of a man with a record of violence was a stupid thing to do, and she shouldn't even think of doing it. Better stay on neutral territory. Then she thought, sod the risk, don't flatter yourself, and besides, he's already conceded a lot, so why not? She thought of all the things Ivy would risk for her without counting the odds. Ivy would jump into a pit of rattlesnakes for her. Besides, she dearly wanted the explanations, whatever they were. She wanted to give him a chance. He saw the hesitation.

'Don't worry,' he said. 'As a judge, I have a reputation to keep. I shan't do anything nasty. Not to a successful professional woman who would report me anyway.'

But you would to a woman with no qualifications or status. Like a wife.

The thought was ironic but reassuring. She was protected by a certain status; shameful that Ivy never had been. He had too much to risk. She made up her mind. The whole scenario was bizarre; let it be more so. She was helped by the conviction that this simply was not planned.

'By all means phone someone and tell them where you'll be, if it makes you feel safer.'

She shook her head.

'Where do you live?'

'The other end of the river, by the water. Not far, on a Sunday.'

It began to rain. He took her arm as they ran back to the dented car, and she shivered.

Back through the centre in the pouring rain, keeping to the river, then into the hinterland she had never known, all of it obscured by the rain on the windscreen. Diving into the half-empty streets of the banking district, which she knew, out the other side towards the east. The territory of old markets, tide upon tide of immigrants who stayed and colonised, laid waste, rebuilt, moved on. She had never quite understood the romance of the East End and the old Docklands, apart from it being a route somewhere, and looking at it through the rain, she could understand why it impelled each new generation to get out.

'This was where I grew up,' Carl said. 'At a time when no one was quite sure what nationality they were, or wanted to be. The main division was white and black. There were two many races for anyone to be racist. It was a good beginning. My father was a cleaner. Rose to supervisor.'

That jolted her. The judge had come a long way.

'Did your father ever go home?'

'He had no home. He never wanted to go back to see the

ruin of what had been his. Berlin was razed to the ground. He thought it would make him feel angry, and he couldn't afford that. Something he taught me. Keep your anger dry, boy. Otherwise it rots you.'

She forgot the route, and once the decision had been made and caution put to the back of her mind, she felt oddly comfortable in the passenger seat, being taken somewhere she did not know, like a patient, curious passenger on a coach trip. Nothing to do except say, Oooh, look at that, and wait to arrive. The destination, any destination became desirable as the rain increased into a torrent, beating against the car. There was a moment of anxiety when they entered an underground garage which looked like a prison, reassuring to find it light. She followed him up endless stairs into his flat, stifling the recurrence of unease, thinking how clever he was. This would be hard to find. It felt like entering a fortress.

A comfortable fortress, with attractive minimalism, the bare necessities of furnishings, wooden floors and rugs, enough clutter to show signs of life, and the luxury of silence. It was both domesticated and orderly and made her feel better. She scarcely noticed the details except for the cool clarity of it all, the balcony and the mesmeric presence of the water beyond that big window. That did it. Assessing it simply as a place, Rachel could have gone home, packed up her bags and come to live here tomorrow. She almost said so.

He came back from the kitchen with wine, olives, roughly cut cubes of bread and cheese, the work of minutes. Better than lunch, a mere relaxing ritual. The eating of something made her feel better. So did the realisation of knowing that it was he who was nervous and anxious to please, and what he provided was leftovers. Kind, but hardly part of a grand master plan. This was not quite what he had expected to happen. He was not used to entertaining at home. No rings on his fingers. The bathroom she had used was notably free of feminine smells. The wine had gone to her head. Stop it, she told herself. Listen. Remember who he is. He is trusting you. Now you know how *he* lives, it makes us more equal.

Why is he being so nice to me?

Carl wiped his hands on a napkin.

'What I wanted to explain is something you may not know, but it is the clue to rather a lot more. Ivy is . . .'

'If you're going to badmouth Ivy to me, forget it. I won't hear it.'

He drew breath patiently.

'I was going to say Ivy's complicated. I've never criticised my wife, least of all to another woman. I've had to point out certain features of her, but that's not the same thing. I don't criticise her to my boy, or to anyone else. I tell people she had her reasons, as she still has. You'll know better than me about that. But I do want to point out her *unreason*. If Ivy ever worshipped any god, it would be the great god Pan. Or some marvellous creature of a mythological world, Thor, or Diana the Huntress. A vengeful god at any rate, one with the power over life and death, although I suppose all gods have that. What I mean is that hers is a primitive soul, with all the sophistications that follow. Conventional morality simply does not matter.'

Rachel tried to stop him.

'That doesn't prevent her from being the kindest, most generous person alive,' he went on. 'But her head is full of images you and I might not be able to guess at. And a binary set of rules. She loves you or hates you. White or black, no shades of grey. Perhaps because she's never mastered more than rudimentary reading – and no, I could not make her do that – she has less chance of analysis. There's nothing to mitigate a fixation. She was reared on fairy stories. Love, death, revenge. Unless you read, you don't shift the imprint of what you've, literally, learned by heart. You don't change your own maxims. Practice makes perfect was one of hers. I can see why now.'

'There are other ways of learning and analysing. Like drawing and listening.'

'Yes, sure.'

'You're saying Ivy's thick and irrational.'

'No, I'm not. I'm saying she has a very literal mind, even if it isn't literate. She'll choose a single track and stick to it. She's had to fight her way to what she knows. She sticks with what she's good at. You're right. Of course I don't know what she's like now, and I'm only saying anything at all because I don't want you to risk Ivy's hatred. It's awesomely determined, especially when turned on herself. Oh, hell. That isn't what I wanted to explain, though, even if it might be part of it.'

He moved across to the desk which dominated the room and came back with a folder of photographs, selecting a couple as he moved.

'I wouldn't wish these on anyone,' he said. 'They aren't exactly holiday snaps, but if you really want to stay involved – and you can stop, whenever you like – then you must know how my daughter, Cassie, died. It's the only way to get a grip on who has to forgive whom, and for what.'

He sat beside her. Her skin tingled. She felt as if the sea salt lingered from yesterday.

'Police photos. Only the setting is aesthetic. You know the lake. You didn't know Cassie.'

A pale, dead face in close-up, turned to one side, blood in

the nostrils, red-blonde hair, and a triangular mark on the neck. Rachel wanted to turn away, and disliked him for being able to hold the photograph with a steady hand. He withdrew the last picture and turned it face down on the table beside the remnants of the food, watching her reaction with concern.

'I'm sorry, I've looked at these so often, and judges see photographs of injuries all the time, I forget other people aren't used to it. One more.'

A photo of a piece of excised skin, pinned and stretched on to a grey surface, the same mark, stained brown. Revulsion was at war with curiosity. He pointed at the mark.

'Exhibit A. A section of skin, taken from the neck. No one could understand why Cassie drowned. All right, she was left alone. I was in charge, impatient father that I was, half asleep, time for tea. She wouldn't get out of the water. Sam was furious with her: she was ruining his afternoon and he was hungry. He went down to the edge and threw stones at her. Pebbles, really, pathetic aim, no chance he would hit her, but she swam further out. I caught him and spanked him, yelled at her to do what she damn well liked and carted him back home, yowling all the way. I didn't worry about leaving Cassie. She would come out as soon as she wanted; she was like an eel and the lake was her playground. Not usually so early in the year, because it would have been too cold, but it was a May heat wave. I didn't know about the swans. Ivy's father's precious swans, the descendants of those which Ernest and my father had reintroduced to replace the ones Carl and his hungry mates had killed to eat, years before. Another story that was always on his conscience.'

Carl the younger was speaking faster and faster, as if to minimise it without omitting anything and get it over.

'There were no injuries to Cassie, no third parties. Only that mark on her neck. Ernest pointed the police in the direction of the swans. It was too early in the year . . . she went too close to the nest. They trapped the adult swans, made beak imprints. One of them matched. Daddy Swan had done for her. It took quite a while to establish that.'

He took a deep breath and steadied himself. There was a slight sheen of perspiration on his brow. Rachel wanted to wipe it away. He put the photos back into the folder.

'Ivy stayed with her mother, who tried to calm her. It simply wasn't possible. Sam wanted to be with her. He cried in her lap and told her about throwing stones at Cassie in the water. She went ballistic. I took Sam back to London with me. My father was dying, then. I was trying to comfort them both in my ham-fisted way, and trying to keep myself under wraps. I had to stay in control at all costs. Then, a fortnight later, when I finally heard from the police that Cassie's drowning was caused by the swans, something in me snapped. I drove down overnight, got Ernest's rifle – he had a licence for one then, never used it, someone else always had to do the killings; my father had taught me, like Ernest taught Ivy. Anyway, I'd lost my mind. I bribed the swans with crumbs, and blasted away like a madman. I shot them all.'

He stopped abruptly. Pushed the folder away and gave a short, mirthless bark of laughter.

'I don't know quite why I'm telling you this. It makes me a helluva lot more primitive than Ivy. As stupid and wicked as a seventeenth-century judge, presiding over the trial and execution of an animal, as they did. Sanctioning the hanging of a pig for harming a baby, the ritual slaughter of a goat for damaging property. I've never been more ashamed of anything.

More ashamed than I was of leaving Cassie. I hated them and I shot them.'

Rachel was silent. She wanted to touch him. He turned to her, as if imploring her to understand. She thought she did. She wanted to take hold of his hand, and didn't. The silence seemed to relieve him.

'*That's* what I wanted to explain, because I never have. And also to put your very kind master plan into perspective. Ernest took the blame. The police sympathised and did nothing except take away his licence for a rifle. Only handguns left with a three-foot range, I expect. I think of it every day when I sit on the bench. It's not so difficult to forgive people really, not when you're me. I not only let my beautiful daughter die in terror, I killed her ghost as well as Ernest's swans . . .'

'They've come back,' she said. He was not listening.

'So you see, there's rather a lot to reconcile, more than possible, I think. And if you should ever meet my son for long enough, don't ever mention he threw pebbles into the water at his sister. He's a nice boy, he doesn't deserve to remember that. It had nothing to do with anything in the end.'

He turned back into the considerate judge, clicking his tongue, tut-tutting at himself, agonised with apologies.

'I am *so* sorry. I've burdened you with more than enough. You look pale. It isn't fair. Look at the time. I'll take you home. Public transport on a Sunday's a bugger from here. I shouldn't have invited you here. I'm amazed you accepted, amazed you listened. I don't want you to regret it.'

She wanted to say, yes, I'm amazed at myself, and I've got no problem with anything you've said. I'm just gobsmacked that you trusted me with it and I don't doubt a word of it. I'm lost. And I'm also thinking, I've got no issues with that piece of history, only with what you did next. Did you apply all that leftover anger to Ivy? Is that why she had to go? Is your son frightened of you? I would be. Ivy was.

There was the sound of a door slamming, a noisy entrance into the place, whistling, the banging down of something. Someone wanted to be noticed. The door to the main room of the flat burst open in response to a kick and he shambled in. He was, she thought later, a rather beautiful sight. Better than any view of the river. He was long and rangy with an elegant slouch, brilliant blue eyes, black jeans and vest.

His own view took in the scenery, from the rainswept balcony to the half-eaten olives and empty bottle of wine, to Rachel's face, figure and clothes, right down to her feet. The boy and the man gave each other a look of quizzical affection. Sam winked at him.

'Cool, Dad,' Sam said. 'Is this your new squeeze? About bloody time.'

He went over to his father and hugged him briefly. Then turned to Rachel, smiling.

'I wish,' Carl said. 'Sam, this is Rachel, Rachel, Sam. She's only my accountant, unfortunately. Recently demoted to being my confessor, poor woman.'

Sam shrugged his shoulder in mock despair.

'Shame,' he said to Rachel. 'It's been *years*. I have my hopes, but he never delivers. You're very welcome. Are you sure you don't like him? Even a little bit?'

Rachel found herself laughing. He was entirely infectious. He had his mother's ranginess, and Grace's outrageous smile.

'Mustn't keep you,' Sam said. 'I'll get out of the way, just in case anything develops. Can I borrow the car?'

'Not if you've been drinking.'

'You joke. On the Sabbath? I mean, not yet.'

'Depends on where you're going.'

'Up west.'

'Fine. Provided you take Rachel home.'

Sam looked at her steadily and grinned. She could not help but grin back.

'Cool,' he said.

She turned to Carl, still grinning.

'I promise I won't reveal *all* your financial affairs en route.'

'Feel free,' Sam said. 'I love gossip.'

'Hope not. We'll talk in the week about the meeting, when you've thought about it, if you like.'

'Fine,' she said. 'Fine.'

He *trusts* me.

Chapter Fourteen

Sam drove the dented Ford as if it was a taxi, complaining about the fact that it did nothing for his street cred. He knew every back double between the Isle of Dogs and the West End, and every road-checking camera. It was not simply the speed of it, before they reached the City outskirts, which made Rachel feel old; it was the confidence. He chattered like the dawn sparrows at Midwinter Farm; he seemed to have a talent for confiding which reminded her of both Grace and Ivy, as if it had never occurred to him that anyone would disapprove, and everyone he met was a potential friend who would like him as much as he liked them. Self-absorbed, yes – who was not, at nineteen? – but likeable and beguiling and artlessly funny. He had a beautiful profile. A strange thought arrived unbidden, namely that she was at risk of being at least half in love with the whole damn family.

'Pity you're Dad's accountant. On a Sunday! Just get him to up my allowance, will you? He's really tight. Wants me to discover financial necessity before it's too late and I'm totally corrupted. Wants me to move out, for the sake of worldly knowledge. Preaches a lot. I want to stay 'cos I don't want him to be alone. Are you sure you wouldn't like to move in? Pity. So how much is he worth, then? No, don't answer that. Don't Sundays go on and on? A day for the movies. At least you can park. Not near Leicester Square, though. Did you read about that bloke killed in the ambulance? And the one behind the theatre. Awful. We don't need terrorists, do we, got them already. I suppose there's a difference between one at a time and fifty all at once. Where do you live again? Cool, that's a really cool place to live.'

Rachel remembered that she had not read a newspaper for weeks, and felt vaguely ashamed of the loss of an old habit, but she was concentrating on the opportunity she was being given. She adored the chatter, but wasn't going to give up a chance. Surely Carl knew he was either misguided or overtrusting to leave her with his gloriously garrulous son. Perhaps he intended it; perhaps it was planned: either way, it was fun and she did not care.

As they bowled across London Bridge, she said, 'I know your father's divorced. Do you ever see your mother?'

Sam slowed down for the red light on the far side of the bridge. Beyond that, she could see the inevitable queue of traffic, scaffolding and building works narrowing the road into a funnel. Good. People of all ages talked in cars. It was turning into a lovely evening, with the vehicles ahead still shining wet after the rain. She wished she had not left that balcony with its view of the river.

'No,' he said. Then laughed. 'You want to know about my mother? Cool. Could this mean you're interested in my old man after all? Isn't that the way? Scout the scene? See if there's any opposition lying around? Old or new?'

'You're a very impertinent young man,' she said, mimicking a pompous voice, and laughing at the same time, because Sam made her laugh. Like his grandmother, like his mother.

He punched the steering wheel, veered to the left and up through the City. Confident and sure and just in control. He would worry me to death if he was mine, she thought. I would worry about him getting cold. The traffic remained stalled.

'Well, you're in with a chance,' Sam said with his infectious grin. His hair glinted chestnut. His skin was sallow. He would tan easily, like his granny. ''Cos there's no one on Dad's scene. The ex least of all. *We* haven't seen her for years. He likes clever women, see, preferably blonde. Short supply. Can't bear junkies. And all I remember about my mother is her trying to kill me. And telling me how she was going to kill Dad one day. She grew up on a farm. She knows how to kill things. She's really, really good at it. Made me learn to swim. She was barking bloody mad. She stuck pins in me. She hit me. I hit her back. I had asthma. I could pack a punch when I was nine. Do you know we're three-quarters grown at nine? Couldn't do it now, though. Don't like to think about it.'

He hit his fist against his forehead in a dramatic gesture which neutralised any hint of self-pity and made it all seem contrived for amusement.

'I was a *tortured* child. Does it show?'

'Not that you'd notice, no.'

'Shame. You might feel sorry for me. That's a great linen jacket, where did you get it?'

'Camden Market,' she said, nearly adding, with your mother. Your mother knows where to find things. Didn't say it. Not all of Sam's remarks were in the best of taste. He exaggerated, fancied himself as a comic clown. She bit her tongue. Sam looked at his watch.

'Film showing at six. I'm going on holiday next week, courtesy of Dad. Have you been to Crete? I've got the end-of-term high. I'll miss that when I have to go to work. Don't you love Sundays?'

'I certainly liked this one.'

'Good,' he said, pulling out of the traffic and down a side street. 'Goody good. So he's *really* in with a chance, is he? Don't worry about my mother, she's long gone. Hope it stays that way. He's got the police on the case anyway.'

You rotten little lying hound, she said to herself, without quite the fervour she meant, and without, quite, being able to lose the instinct to like him. That profile, so unlike his father. Life drawing class, creating new tiers of judgement and appreciation. Too much information today. The traffic unsnarled and they raced through the city like a bullet. As they drew closer to Clerkenwell, with Sam chattering about which film to see, what did she think, Rachel thought, why don't I ask him in to the flat, maybe Ivy will be back, and I'll say, Ivy, this is Sam, Sam, this is Ivy, and maybe they'll fall into each other's arms and he'll see she's not what he thinks. Or what he might have persuaded himself to think, in order to dramatise himself. It'll be love at second sight. Instead, Sam found her street without further directions, as if he had a map of everything in his head. He knew it, he said, because there were some really cool bars nearby, did she ever go? She didn't, but she would now, she said. He bowed her out of the decrepit car with a flourish and roared away, tooting the horn, leaving her on the pavement, smiling.

The rain was in abeyance, replaced by the muggy, damp warmth which signalled more, and the flat was as empty as a plundered grave. Rachel checked the messages on the landline. Ivy knew she preferred it. None from her father. One from Ivy, warm and concerned. How's your father? Don't forget we can bring him here next weekend, or the week after. I've got to help Dad this afternoon, coming home on early train tomorrow, straight to work, see you. Phone if you need. Love you.'

Rachel was dizzy with impressions. She did not quite know what to do with herself. The curse of Sundays descended. Confusion, dread, the ordinary desire to push the next week back, clear up, prepare, a reluctance, a horror of facing the dead space for thinking which yawned now. The flat seemed subtly different, as if a breeze had blown through it. She could not find anything, looked for something to occupy her hands, and where had she put the mobile phone? Safely in her room, instead of leaving it lying around, why?

Thinking time. Dangerous. Tough day, Monday, meetings wall to wall. He had said, *Let's discuss meeting after we've thought.* She just wanted to see him. She was a stupid, credulous idiot, bearing the impression of the last person who had sat next to her, with a history of being duped by men. She *liked* him, that was all. And they were *wrong,* so wrong, about Ivy. That boy said shocking things. She was beginning to feel suspicious and wanted to put that somewhere else too. She wrote a list for the week in her clear, strong handwriting.

Monday, Tuesday, full to bursting. Wednesday evening, last life drawing class. Shit. Her sketchbook was full. Meant to buy another. Drawing was therapy. The pencils she had used were down to stumps, too small to sharpen. She did what she often did, hauled out the sketchbooks and examined what she had done these last evenings in class. She could see her own progress, her own increasing freedom. Looking at what she had done over the last term cheered her. There was the Plonker, there was Ivy, there was all the in-between. She wanted to draw; she did not want to listen. She had run out of paper. She wanted to draw *him*. Drawing soothed her. She had first wanted to do the drawing because of endless Sundays. It used up her brain and cleansed it.

The landline phone rang. She answered. Dad, Carl, Ivy, Grace, anyone please.

'Hello. Is that Mrs Schneider?'

'Mrs Who?'

She was late in recognising the name. There was no Mrs Schneider here. There was Ivy, Ms Wiseman, and herself. Get the names right. Mrs Schneider? Ivy was that person once, not any more, he meant Wiseman. She spoke without thinking, Ivy always on her mind.

'Nope. Sorry, she's out at the moment.'

Then she put her hand over her mouth. It was as good as announcing Ivy lived here.

'Oh, sorry. Is that Miss Rachel Doe? It's DS Donald Cousins here,' he said. There were the sounds of a TV in the background, the sonorous voice of someone talking to camera about live things in jungles. 'We met the other day.'

'Did we?'

She remembered him, with fleeting dislike. There was an uncomfortable pause. The TV sound droned on. She looked round wildly, imagining it was hers. The blank screen looked back.

'Well, if she's not there, that's that. If she should happen to come back, would you tell her that her friend Mr Blaker is asking after her?'

'Her *friend*? Mr Who?'

She has no friends. Her hands felt slippery wet on the phone she held. She was suddenly angry.

'I'm not a message service,' she said. 'Get lost.'

She put the phone down. She was furious. She had been set up again. Bastard.

The swine, the *shit.* That bloody judge, using her and her emotions, all that trust-me, shite. Treating her sweetly, leading her on, food, wine, fucking *trust,* and then he goes and gives out her number to a wet, sedulous policeman with a moustache, who wants to find Ivy for some miserable purpose of his own, how *dare* he? Somehow it followed that neither Carl nor his son was capable of saying anything which was true; every single bloody thing was all contrived and engineered, for WHAT? She found herself shredding the last piece of useful drawing paper out of the sketchbook, tearing it up into ever smaller pieces. Thinking of Carl warning her against Ivy's hatred, the *shit,* Sam speaking casually of maternal violence for something attention-seeking to do at a traffic light, and she, silly child-free ignoramus, had listened and swallowed as if she was being paid for a blow-job. What they wanted was for Ivy to be abandoned and given up, like before, for something she had not done, like before. As if they could not stomach the sheer fact that Ivy had emerged from her chrysalis as good and strong as she was, and that she had a *friend.* They wanted her to buried all over again, and they could fuck off, because it was not going to happen. It was not going to work because *she* knew what she knew and she was not going to be deflected from what she knew. Which was what was right and just, what Ivy deserved, what Grace wanted.

When Cassie drowned, Carl had lost a child. Ivy had lost everything.

Rachel prowled. She wanted to talk to somebody, but there was nobody. She wanted to pick up the phone and shout at Carl. Instead, she dialled 1471 and wrote down Donald Cousins' number. Then she sat with the full sketchbook on her lap, turned over the pages. She had drawn Ivy several times in the last term; she would do it again, this week. She had an overpowering desire to scribble, she felt the urge to etch graffiti on the walls, make herself concentrate on something in order to clear her mind. The very act of drawing anything had that effect of release, whether she did it well or badly. She wanted to draw what was in her mind. Sinuous shapes, slithery ferrets, rats, swans. There was nothing better to do, but she had torn up the last sheet of paper and the pencils were stumps.

Ivy always had pencils and paper. She never used a pen, only a pencil. Ivy was always willing to share what little she had. She would give you her last penny. Rachel went into Ivy's nest, looking for the pencils and paper she knew Ivy kept in her pink folio.

The room was tidier than when she had seen it last. There were traces of Blu-Tack from where Ivy had detached the sketches she had used to decorate the walls, replaced with the poster of *Leda and the Swan*. The folio case stuck out from under the unmade bed. Rachel moved to straighten the duvet, an automatic reaction which was the same as the one which made her pick up anything which had fallen to the floor, an instinct for tidying up as she went along for which Ivy had teased her. Ivy would leave the dropped object where it was until she needed it. Rachel stopped herself. How Ivy left her room and her bed was entirely up to her. Rachel had given her this room for her own. She pulled out the folio case, opened it and searched inside for pencils and paper.

That was all she wanted. She would always resist the urge to look at the rest. It would be like reading someone else's post. In the middle of this slow activity, she had a mental image of Sam crumpling up the letters from Grace which might have been addressed to his father, posting them back. She could see him doing that.

There were no pencils in the untidy mess of the folio case. Rachel sat down on the bed, suddenly weary beyond belief. There was a lump under the duvet, a sound of crackling plastic. She got up and pulled the duvet back, concerned that she had sat on something breakable, found a polythene bag bearing the legend of a shop she did not know. She opened it to see what she might have broken. Inside she found an inhaler, and two small brown bottles of pills, folded into a handkerchief. She held one of the bottles up to the light. Prescribed pills, with a white label almost worn away from contact with the material of his coat, and her father's name still legible.

The room began to spin around her. She put the bag back.

Donald Cousins was thinking to himself that maybe the phone call to Rachel Doe had not been so very clever, and he was still trying to work out why he had done it. Perhaps because there was no one at home on a Sunday evening, the whole lot of them round at his mother-in-law's, and he was bored, and Blaker had been haunting him. Despite the hours now spent in Blaker's company, he had never managed to pose a direct question which was relevant to his investigation, never quite summoned up the nerve. Since Blaker had told him that he was HIV positive, it seemed cruel to do anything other than chat, sit in the sun in Temple Gardens, as if it was really open to the public and they owned it. Very private, better than Embankment Gardens, Blaker said. Donald did not doubt that what Blaker said about being HIV positive was true: people did not announce their own death sentences unless they really wanted attention, and Donald did not think that Blaker wanted that kind. He could check anyway, and it did add another dimension. What did the poor bastard have to lose by issuing threats to a judge, either on his own behalf or someone else's? He was looking at a short life where all the major risks had already been taken and the gamble lost, however long it took the Grim Reaper to call in the debts. He could murder and threaten with impunity; what could punish him now that the worst had happened? And no, he had not asked Blaker if he used internet caffs to send threatening images to a judge; Blaker might tell him, in time. Instead they chatted about Blaker's old friends, and the changing history of Soho. Blaker looked sixty and he was scarcely forty. Donald counted his own luck.

She was a brave lady, Mrs Ivy Schneider, to embrace and befriend an HIV-positive man. Blaker had been diagnosed three years ago, before the last prison stint. Ivy made me check it out, he said. When I found out it was yes, she hugged me. That's as far as we ever got. I reckon she would have shagged me to prove a point, but she knows my preference. Big, dark buggers, who know where to go. The disabled lavatory in Starbucks, more room in there. Donald knew he was not really a citizen of the real world. He belonged in the suburbs, thought he knew about London, but he didn't. He only knew it as it had been, through the pages of history books, which told him it had always been a den of iniquity and delight, not always in equal shares, and not all of those drawn to it survived it.

The different dimension added by Blaker's liability to AIDS was an additional interest in Ivy Schneider or Wiseman, simply because it made her more compassionate. Blaker said she came into Berwick Street once or twice a week, or Embankment Gardens, at no prescribed time, on her way to or from whatever work she was doing. Couldn't stay away, he said, it's my charm. There was something Blaker wanted to tell him about this woman, namely that for all her restored status, he was desperately worried about her and what she might do. It all meant that Donald could not ignore the Ivy connection, or at least it gave him an excuse to protract his useless investigation for a few more days of summer by including her. He could not allow himself to think that such a long-divorced wife who by choice and design maintained no contact with her estranged son could really pose a threat to the good judge, but Blaker had said she hated the man, so he'd better talk to her. Maybe he was barking up the wrong tree with Blaker, and all the threats really came from somewhere else, and she might know about that. She would know about the distant past, not the obvious present.

It was later he remembered the hurried introduction to Rachel Doe, *a good friend of my ex-wife,* and the judge's shifty insistence that this beautiful girl, who looked at him with such undisguised contempt, did not know where said wife lived. Oh yes? What kind of good friend was that? He felt better about the phone call now. A brilliant ploy, an impulse rewarded. Of course he could have hung around Berwick Street waiting for the tall woman to come back, but he was sick of the place. It was dying on its feet. Tesco Metro would bury it. Not that knowing where Ivy Wiseman lodged was an instant answer to making contact, but at least it was a start, as well as a change of scene.

It distracted him from tending to his wilting garden, a domestic task he loathed but that was his by default. Mine's the house, yours is the garden, his dear wife said, and was kind enough not to hold him to that too strictly. Snaresbrook was a nice place to live, convenient for the Central Line, which went straight into the heart of the City, bisecting it from beneath, and from which he emerged, blinking like a mole to breathe the polluted air he preferred, wondering why anyone would be daft enough to imagine Londoners being deterred by bombs. What they did to one another on the street was far more frightening.

Another Sunday task was reading the papers and catching up with the news of what the wider world was up to, as well as what his comrades in arms were doing. Police bulletins, issued daily, including details of the unsolved and the unsolvable. Trying to get better at identifying terrorists made them so much worse at everything else; there were only so many experts to go round. Computer literacy required, far in advance of his own. Good. Leave me alone. Better being an old has-been than being out there with a smoking gun.

He read in the bulletins now e-mailed to him at home about new credit-card scams, exotic thefts and unsolved deaths. No one was any further forward in discovering who had garrotted the injured bloke in the ambulance, except it might have been the product of Albanian gang warfare. Well, maybe; no one wanted to know if it was all home-grown. He read about a man who drank bleach in an office, about another man stabbed in a queue waiting to get an autograph, no progress in any direction, and the only grateful feeling which came to mind was his own huge relief not to be on the night shift which found the bodies.

Night did indeed shift, uncomfortably into day and back

again, like a thief, taking hostages under cover of darkness. It grew cooler as he sat in his untended garden, hoping they would all come back and hoping they wouldn't, grateful for the fact that the afternoon rain meant he did not have to water the plants. It was early yet; they could be hours, those beloved, so often discontented, daughters of his, and their mother who liked to be out of the house.

A woman's rage . . . night shifts. Did anyone notice that the unconnected deaths, two murders and one apparent suicide, all happened around the same time of day? No great force required, two shifty killings, a knife, a garrotte, a woman could have done it. Come on, man; hardly coincidental; homicide usually favours the cover of darkness, unless done in the name of war. How comfortable to reflect upon it in the safety of his own garden. The whole problem in his own little investigation was that the judge was only telling him half of it, and the other half he might not actually know.

The judge, Donald feared, suffered from an unhealthy belief in the essential goodness of human nature, believed everyone deserved a second and third chance. He had that look about him; he was a light sentencer. He had acted upon the threats made against him only for the protection of his son. He did not really believe anyone, apart from a religious fanatic, could nurse purely individual hatred for long, for years if need be, because he could not have done it himself. He would not see the point, any more than his father would dwell on losing the war.

Since meeting Blaker, Donald had reluctantly looked into the matter of Ivy Schneider, née Wiseman, and she had thoroughly taken hold of his imagination. He had the date of the marriage, more than twenty years ago, the date of the death of the child, Cassandra. He knew where Ivy had been born.

He knew she had acquired a minor criminal record in her late twenties, early thirties, drug abuse, clogging up pavements, that kind of thing. No theft, no dishonesty. He knew she had redeemed herself, been rehabilitated, and remained a friend to an HIV-positive loser, and that raised her in his estimation. And what the earlier phone calls of the evening had told him was that the Wisemans owned a farm-cum-guest house in Kent, and apart from the accidental death of the child, nothing was known to their discredit. It was only very recently that they had come to police attention, on the periphery of something else. A young man who had stayed as a paying guest at Midwinter Farm, a Londoner, had disappeared, only to reappear as a drowned corpse on the nearby coast. The last known sighting of him had been in the local pub, getting drunk in the company of Ivy Wiseman and her mother, Grace, before setting off back to his London home. It took three weeks to identify him.

Donald did not know why this stuck in his craw. He was haunted, daily, by the thought that one of his daughters would leave the house one day and never come back. There were plenty of Londoners who thought that with good reason. But not to know what happened and why, that was hell.

Slowly it was coming to him that he might just have to go and find this damn farm, if only because that was where the daughter had died and that provided enough of a link to justify the time in the final report. Donald hated the countryside, but a day out in this weather could be fine.

He heard the phone go from his place in the garden and ambled indoors to answer it without hurrying. Nothing could be terribly urgent on a Sunday evening, except his own business.

'Hello?'

'Rachel Doe. You rang me.'

He was surprised. 'So I did. You told me to get lost.'

She ignored that. 'I want to know why you want to contact Mrs Schneider, and she's called *Wiseman.* You can't just phone up out of the blue and demand to know where someone is . . . why do you want to know?'

She sounded as if she might have been crying. 'I need to know,' she said. Her belligerent voice began to falter. 'And I need to know who gave you this fucking number. It's outrageous, you've no right. Bloody Carl gave you the number, didn't he? *He's* no right.'

Donald drew a deep breath. God save me from wailing women, some king had said.

'As a matter of fact he didn't, Miss Doe. I had your name, and your telephone number's in the directory, if you must know. And I didn't know the lady frequented your establishment until you confirmed it for me.'

There was a pause before her voice resumed with more determination, half belligerent, half pleading.

'I *must* know why you want to contact her. What's she supposed to have done?'

Another deep breath. She was a professional woman, well dressed, well set up, he remembered. He could see a complaint winging in from the side. Something which was not going to improve his already diminished career. Interference with the civil liberty of another, invasion of privacy, blah, blah, blah. He spoke in a conciliatory rush.

'Why, absolutely nothing, madam. Nothing at all. In fact, from what little I know of her, she appears to be a kind woman. It's just that we' – always hide behind 'we' – 'are making enquiries into an unrelated matter which, in which . . .' Now it was he who began to stutter. The jargon failed him. It always did when he was at home.

'Look, Miss Doe, I acted out of turn in phoning you. We are *not* investigating Mrs . . . Wiseman for anything, but we are investigating an acquaintance of hers, from the distant past I believe, and I hoped she could help. That's all.'

'Oh.'

Another pause, then she went on with ever greater certainty.

'So what is it he's supposed to have done? Why should Ivy be able to help?'

'I'm not at liberty to say, madam. Except that it isn't anything particularly serious.'

'Serious enough to be trying to find her on a Sunday evening?'

'Police work knows no set hours, Miss Doe. Sunday evening's a good time to find people at home.'

'This isn't her home. I've no idea where she is. She has stayed here, she doesn't now.'

Too hurried to be truthful, but communicating. It didn't matter. The prospect of a complaint receded. He chanced his arm a little further.

'Could you tell me where she works? I could maybe trace her there. No urgency.'

'Works? Ivy? No one works like Ivy. She works all over the place. West End, City. Night shifts, cleaning, modelling, anything . . .' This, he noted, was said with pride, before another pause. He waited it out.

'Why did you say you thought she *appeared* to be a kind person?'

He thought about that.

'Because she has been conspicuously kind to the person

who is the subject of our enquiries, and believe me, Miss Doe, he's not someone a normal person would want to touch.'

Night shifts.

'Thank you,' she said. She sounded enormously relieved. 'If I see Ivy, I'll think about giving her the message.'

Ivy was the kindest person she had ever met. Rachel told herself she must remember that.

Then why had she done *that*?

Done *what*? The pills must have fallen out of his pocket when the coat was thrown on the bed, but he never kept them in a polythene bag, he wanted them accessible all the time. He always wanted to be able to touch them.

Chapter Fifteen

Rachel could not think of anyone but her father. His coat and his medicines.

She phoned him, simply to hear his voice and to say good night. He was drowsy and did not want to speak. Then she drew his face as best she could remember it on the back of the other drawings, trying to remember the salient details of it, but oddly Carl's face became superimposed on the older one. She was using a pencil stump, which she broke, and the breaking of it made her cry.

She stayed beneath the shower, scrubbing herself pink, trying to wash away the contagions of the day, went to bed.

Nothing had changed over the course of the day, nothing. *There must be some mistake. Dad's pocket was not picked for his drugs on the train; they fell out . . . How?*

She was exhausted and fell into a fitful sleep. Nothing would change what was going to happen on Monday. There was always work, and without it there was no life. She was wishing she had not deviated from that single track and was still the work-devoted, isolated, priggish bore she had been a year ago. Dreams intervened, nudged her awake. This time it was snuffling piglets, nuzzling at the multiple teats of a mother pig who was held by bars so that she could not suffocate them. A rat sneaked in alongside. Someone placed a hand on the back of her neck. The hand was cool and dry, soothing, feeling for a pulse beneath her long hair. Her father had done that once. There was a shuffling in the darkness, a rustling, followed by the sound of the door of her bedroom clicking shut, softly.

She remembered she had left all the windows open at the front. One floor up was all, easily climbed, warnings given all the time about neighbourhood burglary. She might not even have double-locked the door; she never did that now, not with Ivy here. Ivy was far away, Ivy was not here. There was no one here. When Ivy called out in the night, there was always someone there. Rachel repeated her name out loud now, louder and louder, accusing her for her absence. *IVY! Ivy! Ivy!*

The door opened quietly. Ivy, barefoot in a long T-shirt, stood there, framed by the dim light filtering from another room, coming towards her from the light into the dark, her voice a soothing whisper.

'What is it, what's the matter? It's me, only me. Can I come in?'

Yes. Anything, anyone, please. Anyone was better than no one. Rachel lay there stiff with fear. Ivy was matter-of-fact.

'Look,' she said, 'I didn't mean to wake you, but now you are, there's something I've got to tell you. We could leave it until the morning, only it's almost the morning already.'

'I thought you weren't back. I thought . . .'

'That I wouldn't be back until later? I'm here now. Thank God I'm here now. You were dreaming. Can I come in?'

Rachel turned and saw Ivy's profile against the corridor light, her hand with a protective hold on the door, the glint of tears on her face. There was a cool draught from the window. She had been sweatily hot; now she was cold. She buried her head in the pillow, and smelled the scent of fresh soap. The back of her neck itched. She could hear the sound of rain, and shivered. She was naked; the duvet had fallen to the floor. Ivy picked it up and put it back, then peeled off her T-shirt and slid into bed beside Rachel, tucking the duvet round them both. They lay like spoons, Ivy holding her, her body pressed into Rachel's back, her bosom against Rachel's shoulder blades, her chin on Rachel's head. Rachel stiffened, then, slowly, relaxed. The sudden warmth and feeling of safety was utterly seductive. She lay very still, not daring to move. They had never been intimate like this, never unclothed. Hugs and pecking kisses on greeting, easy togetherness, massaging each other's feet at the end of a long day out, but never lying in the same bed, skin against skin. She wondered why. It was nice. She needed it, did not want it, might never want it again, but it was nice.

'This is how Grace used to calm me down,' Ivy said. 'She calls it the human straitjacket.'

'There was somebody else here,' Rachel said. Reality was coming back. Remembrance of the last things she had thought of before going into that awful sleep. She had thought of her father, and of what it would be like to sleep alongside the lovely bulk of Carl. She had imagined his heavy male hand on her neck. Shame on her.

'No, lovely. There was no one. Only me. Unless there was a ghost, escaping the rain. Ghosts don't like rain.'

That was what this was. It was Ivy being mother, acting like Grace, the human straitjacket, making everything right with her warmth, operating on the same instinct to look after someone with the whole of her body.

'What was it you wanted to tell me?'

'I want to tell you what I think happened with your father.'

Rachel stirred, pressed her head further into the pillow. Ivy's weight was light against her. She could move whenever she wanted, waited, breathing hard. Ivy had been crying and her speech was clear and urgent.

'I don't think anyone picked his pocket on the train back. I think he left all his stuff here, in my room. Must have dropped out of his coat pocket. I put his coat in my room, out of the way, remember.'

Rachel was silent. Things did not fall out of pockets, not out of her father's deep pockets, not precious, life-saving objects like that. There was, all the same, a great relief that Ivy was talking about it, not hiding anything, because there was nothing to hide; that Ivy was introducing the subject before she did, and she would not have to admit sneaking around her room and the suspicions which had been the final blow in what felt like a day of treachery. Ivy seemed to sense the slight shift of Rachel's body. She moved her hand and softly eased Rachel's hair away from her face, and stroked it back. That was nice too.

'I found them, I think it was on Friday. You know what a mess my room is. Thought nothing of it. I should have remembered it when you said he'd phoned and he was ill, but I didn't connect, wasn't thinking, so I only remembered halfway through yesterday afternoon, because I was worrying about him. That's why I came back. I thought, supposing Rache finds that medicine, supposing she's looking for something else, what would you think?'

'I don't go into your room,' Rachel lied.

She had a vision of the living room as she had left it. Had she tidied it all away? That would be normal, even when drunk, *especially* then. She had not been drunk on wine, but something else entirely, like the shock of what she had found, and put back, and not being able to remember quite what she had done. Not being able to remember frightened her.

'But if you had,' Ivy continued, still stroking her hair, 'and found your dad's medicines, you might, just *might,* think I had taken them. And I really couldn't bear the thought of you thinking that. I couldn't bear it.'

'Why ever would I think such a thing? I wouldn't.'

She was lying again. That was exactly what she had thought. It was why she was lying here, rigid.

'Why would you think it? Because he was mean to me, because in the past I've done very spiteful things. Because it would be *natural* to suspect me. I'm the loose cannon, remember? I'm the one accused of abusing my own son. God, I was even accused of killing the cat. So it's just what I might do, isn't it? Something spiteful like that. It's what junkies do.'

Ivy began to cry. A large tear fell against Rachel's forehead. The sound of her sobbing was unbearable. Rachel felt ashamed and did not know what to say. Ivy propped her head on her hand, brushed away the tears.

'Sorry. This isn't about self-pity. It's about your dad. He's got to know that he wasn't the victim of a dipper in the train, or he'll never get on a train again. He'll never come back, and he's too insular already. You want him to come back, he's your father. It would be terrible if he thought there were thieves everywhere, even more than he does now. It isn't fair, because it isn't true. He might have been mugged, but not for his pills.'

Her voice was back in control, warm with worry. *She seems to me to be a kind person. Nothing stops her being the most generous person alive.* Things do not spring out of the pockets of a coat left on a bed.

'But on the other hand,' Ivy said. 'I don't know if it's better that he thinks he was stolen from, rather than admit he left the stuff here. He'd hate to admit to being forgetful, wouldn't he? He'd hate to think it was his own fault.'

How observant she was.

'Left them? Not dropped them?'

She could feel Ivy nodding. They were whispering, as if there was someone to hear.

'Yes. Remember when he started getting so cross, and he went to the lavatory?'

No, she did not remember. Only that her father needed a lavatory at any given time. Blamed his age. Ivy's arm crept back round her waist.

'I think he must have gone and found his coat, had a puff, maybe a calming-down pill, and left them out in case he needed another. Then he was mortified by losing his temper, poor thing. It's awful to feel like that. He wanted to go home so much, he forgot. You fetched his coat.'

It made Rachel feel partially to blame. It also rang entirely true. Relief flooded through her like a warm wave. Her breathing had slowed to normal.

'So what will you tell him?' Ivy asked.

'I'll tell him to keep his bloody Ventolin on a chain round his neck.'

They both snuffled with laughter. Rachel relaxed entirely. Ivy's callused hand stroked her hip. Their breathing seemed to have synchronised into one peaceful breath. She wanted this to go on, wanted it to stop. Sleep beckoned, hormones stirred, sleep was winning. She knew with absolute certainty that Ivy would make love to her at the slightest invitation, and was not threatened by the thought. Ivy wanted to strengthen the bond; Ivy wanted to please, and there was no need. The desire for sleep was stronger than anything. One last thing.

'Ivy . . .'

'Yes, love?'

'I do know you, don't I?'

'Better than anyone. But I have lied to you once.'

'Did you?'

'I said I could wait to see my son again. I said it didn't matter. But I think of it all the time.'

'Ivy . . .'

'Don't say it. Go to sleep. I'm here to keep you warm, that's all. I'll always be here for you.'

When she woke, Ivy was gone, the imprint of her left on the side of the bed nearest the wall. The way she had lain meant Rachel could have moved away whenever she wished. She was grateful for that too. Grateful also for the emptiness of the flat she had so loathed. Invigorated, even. Washed and dressed and on the way to work by the time Ivy had been on her morning shift for two hours.

Ivy, in sleep, had the gentlest of touches. She did not hog the bed; she remained still, smelling of cleanliness and soap. Rachel had woken once, watched her for a second. Her face in repose was both hard and vulnerable, giving up to sleep, looking like a picture of the lowest of Victorian household servants, exhausted by hard work, sharing a bed with nothing but honest labour to look forward to, and yet still accused of stealing the family silver. It made Rachel feel an additional bond to her, the simple fact of sharing her bed. Made her realise how much she yearned for skin upon skin, the weight of another body. And a new determination to make things right, not only because she had doubted Ivy's transparent honesty, but because of guilt. The guilt of suspecting her of malice, and the guilt of knowing . . . knowing what? Simply that she wanted to see *him* again. She had dreamed of him, when she slept alongside Ivy, wanted it to be him. The guilty knowledge made her blush in the bathroom mirror, hand poised still with mascara brush, looking at her own dilated eyes.

In the living room it was as tidy as she usually left it, the bag ready with the full sketchbook leaving room for the new one and the new pencils and charcoal she would buy somewhere en route before the last class of term, which would leave the rest of the summer curiously empty. Mid-July now, schools out for summer, that end-of-term feeling. Who had said that? Sam. In all the years since leaving school and university, there had never been a summer when she had not woken, dreaming of taking an examination and not being prepared. Training courses ever since, all culminating in one month of the year. It was what had typified early summer, until now, when the rest of July and August spread forward without punctuation marks. Such small nightmares she had had until now, such small services and mercies she had rendered to anyone else, intolerant, overprivileged, a bit of a shallow bitch, overeducated in everything but real life and the obligations of love.

So thought Rachel, who did not like herself, or much notice how much effect she had on others, getting into gear for Monday morning, dismissing everything irrelevant to the task and only remembering to look as if she mattered. Seeing that in the tidiness of the living room she had left the torn piece of paper which said, *Who is Blaker? DS Cousins? called.* Ivy couldn't have seen that.

She put it into the kitchen bin, tidily. She was back in control. An ache in the heart for Dad, but Dad was all right, and Ivy had not picked his pocket, and everything else she would think of as she went along.

She had dressed for the day in the wrong clothes. It was cool out there. She went back for the older, warmer jacket she had worn to the farm. Clouds filled the sky as she looked up, pacing herself for work, taking the favourite, shortest route, but still looking up and sideways. Looking with pleasure at what she could see. Handsome people, moving with purpose, refreshed by rain in the night and the drop in temperature, like plants in a busy garden.

Grace and Ivy, Ernest and Grace. Bugger the swans, I don't care about swans. And I found my mobile phone after all, back where it belongs, in my bag. She strode along with the bag across her body, one hand in the pocket of her old jacket, felt the tiny piece of bone which was still there from when Ernest had presented her with it as his souvenir. Some of it had fragmented into sharp crumbs which felt like sand. A reminder of time passing, making her feel clear and urgent about what she was going to do. It could not wait. If Ivy had still been beside her when she woke in the morning, she might have changed the plan, told her everything, confident of the response while they lay tucked up and close like that, but now she was glad that Ivy had gone.

Yesterday's plan was still the best. Get Carl to come to the farm, meet Grace and Ernest, take it all from there. Mission for today, suggest this to Grace, as a theory at least. It was the bone that reminded her about the strange sense of running out of time, like summer did in July, before it had scarcely started.

All the same, she would wait and see if Carl phoned her. He had made some kind of commitment, wanted time to think, wanted her to have time to think of the wisdom of her own suggestion. So be it. She would be patient, let things take their course. But by the time Grace phoned in the afternoon, patience was wearing thin.

'How's your father?'

'Better, thank you. How are you?'

'Thank goodness for that. I've been so worried. Tried to phone all day yesterday, but you were out, and I knew Ivy was coming back, so I knew I'd hear one way or another, and I would have heard if the news was bad, because bad news travels fastest. Look, when can you bring him here for a holiday?'

It was a headlong rush of words.

'I know all about asthma. Sam had it when he was little. I'll be able to look after your dad wonderfully.'

'He's not so easy to persuade, Grace. I'll try and talk him into it. He's embarrassed and avoiding me.'

'I can dream. I wish you were here. It's a perfectly glorious day. I want someone to go swimming with. Saturday night turned into a bit of a party. We all need those sometimes. Ernest is in the dumps. Well, something like that. He put his boots in the freezer, God knows why.'

'To cool them down?'

'That'll be it. I almost got them out and roasted them. Are you coming next weekend? Please say yes. Ivy can't, she's got another end-of-run theatre job that lasts all weekend, and pays a fortune, she says, did she tell you? Only I don't want her doing it. I heard on the radio about the man getting stabbed outside.'

'That was last week, Grace. There'll be something else this week.'

'You will come, won't you? I don't want you being in London on your own either.'

It was a little proprietorial. Rachel felt she loved Grace without reservation, but perhaps Grace was taking her role as mother substitute a little too far. Typical Grace, she guessed it.

'Oh Lord, I'm being bossy, aren't I? And talking too much and interrupting your work, just because I've got nothing interesting to do and Ernest is wandering round, lonely as a cloud, somewhere. I'm not your mother, I just wish I was. What's the weather like?'

She was instantly forgiven, the warmth of her lapping round Rachel like a cloak, making her laugh again.

'Cool,' Rachel said, and thought of Sam. 'Listen Grace, I know this is a surprise, but I've found Carl. Carl the younger.'

'Oh my God . . .'

'Now, supposing he could be persuaded to meet up with you and Ernest, just you two, or just you, maybe, at the farm, do you think that would be a good idea?'

Grace choked on a jumble of words, Oh my God, oh dearie me, oh fuck, oh bloody hell, yes. Then stopped abruptly.

'When?'

'I don't know. I'm only supposing. I don't know if it can be done. Soon, perhaps.'

Grace was crying. She made the same crying sounds as Ivy did, recovered quickly.

'Oh my wonderful, darling child. It would make Ernest so happy.' She paused. 'There's no one else here next weekend. Cancellations.'

'I can't promise anything.'

'I know you can't, darling, but I do love you for trying. What have we done to deserve you? Oh, it's all going to be fantastic. I know it in my bones. Just Carl and Ernest and me, working out where it all went wrong. Oh, darling.'

If it made Ernest happy, and that was all it achieved, it was worth doing, Rachel thought. She reminded herself to keep her ambitions small, her excitement under control, because she had no power over anyone or anything, whatever Grace thought. It still felt like progress.

Carl phoned at four thirty. Was she free this evening? He had done enough thinking, he said. Yes, of course she was.

Grace sat in her kitchen, staring at the Rayburn. The domestic machinery hummed, dishwasher and washing machine together making music which was satisfying on a good day, irritating the next. What would she feed him when he came here? What was it he used to like, a dozen years ago? He must come here, he must. Otherwise Ivy would never stop, and Cassie's immortal soul would continue to haunt the lake. He must lay the ghosts to rest, and take his punishment.

Ernest had been busy. He had made the appointment. The lorries would arrive sometime in the next fortnight to take away the cows for sale. Milk did not pay for its own production. The knock-down price of the good cows would pay something towards the debts. The Polish herdsman would go to a bigger herd, saving his salary. It would come to that, unless, unless.

She could hear the sound of Ernest scraping his boots on the mat outside the door before opening it and coming in. He looked clear-eyed and himself today, damp from the rain, sniffing the air for familiar smells, even now always looking round for the old dog he no longer had, or the cat which would spring into his lap as soon as he sat down. Both of them long dead, killed and never replaced.

He washed his hands and sat down expectantly, waiting as he always did for something to be given to him, ever hopeful that something nice would happen, with the optimism which always touched her heart and also made her want to scream. You have to work in the right way for what you want, she had yelled at him once, and work even harder for what you must have. You have to plan for it, and you always left the killing to me until you trained Ivy to do it and made a man of her.

Grace poured the tea. Since this was a good day, he could sense her cautious jubilation. He noticed moods, details, undercurrents only when he chose. He also had ears like a bat, when he chose.

'So you've got him then, have you?'

'Might have,' she said modestly, turning her back on him so that he would not see her face. He drank the damned tea. Grace thought she could have lived for ever without drinking another cup of tea.

'You reckoned that since he couldn't resist our Ivy he'd not be able to resist her friend? You might be right at that.'

'I don't know what you mean, dearest.'

He poured more milk into the mug of tea, and two sugars, for strength.

'There's the difference between you and me,' he said. 'I never could hate anyone for so long. Not like you. Not like Ivy.'

It sounded like an accusation, and she knew it wasn't. It was a sort of wonder.

'No, dearest. But you will do as you're told, won't you?'

He shrugged. He was bent these days, but his shoulders were still broad, even if his belly was soft.

'Don't I always? Don't I know I owe everything to you? I always do what has to be done afterwards? I got rid of that cow, the dog, the cat, how long ago was that?'

'Longer ago than you should be remembering. It doesn't matter now.'

'Why, Grace, why? Why this time?'

It was her turn to shrug. She wanted to brain him with the teapot she carried towards the sink, signalling the interrogation was over.

'Things have to be paid for, darling. In all senses. And I can't have Ivy going on with her practice and getting caught. And because it really is the right time to put everything right. Make a new beginning.'

'Practice makes perfect,' Ernest said.

'Not always,' said Grace. 'Can you think of anything that would put people off going to the lake? I know they're few and far between, but no one at all would be better. A notice, I thought. And something blocking the path. And you could choose a site for the dust.'

'Ding dong bell, pussy's in the well,' Ernest intoned rhythmically. 'What's for tea?'

Chapter Sixteen

It was the funny feeling in the pit of the stomach, the same as it was when she had first encountered Ivy, that there was everything to say and nothing she would be ashamed to admit. Weird in these circumstances, where there was hardly an element of trust, except, self-evidently, his towards her. Could she like a hypocrite, a bully, a multiple offender? But men changed, didn't they?

He was everything she suspected, including his authority, his history and his charm, and yet she approached him with as light a step as if he was real, and as if she had known him for ever. It felt both right and utterly wrong.

They met at St James's Park Underground station, closer to his place of work than hers, an easy passage for her on the Circle Line from the City. A grey day like this was ideal for a walk in the park, he said. Did she like to walk? Yes, she did now, she told him, although she had not always. She had been the one who took the fastest route to the next stop, ignoring the scenery. It was Ivy who encouraged the walking in winter and spring. All the better for feeling free, seeing things, and besides, it's the cheapest way.

On a cooler day, with a troubled, rain-filled sky, the glories of St James's Park became more exclusive to dozens of admirers, rather than thousands. On a hot summer day the grass would be littered with wall-to-wall bodies, sitting on deckchairs, lounging on the ground, clogging the curving pathways which led around the lakes in an inner circle, while on the outer circle people moved purposefully and joggers moved ahead beneath a canopy of trees.

They began at Admiralty Arch, looking down the Mall towards Buckingham Palace in the distance, then walked into the park itself, drawn towards the irregularly shaped lake which meandered the length of the valley, the territory for ducks and swans. Willow trees drooped gracefully from the bank; there was a bridge for standing and dreaming, and halfway down, a mysterious island rising out of the water in a million shades of green, yellow and rust where she somehow imagined all the birds went at night. Seen from the bridge, the ducks were iridescent in shades of turquoise, white, black, brown, comical and ever busy, while the swans moved slowly, pausing as if to acknowledge an audience without any gesture as vulgar as waving.

Carl bought coffees for them both from a stall, and joked as they sat on a bench that it looked as if he certainly knew how to give a girl a good time. A walk in a park, and a cup of coffee. Rachel said that was fine by her, and this was surely the most beautiful park in London, a user-friendly park made for exactly this, sitting on a bench and enjoying. The cool of the evening made her glad of the old jacket, all the same, and she felt for the fragment of bone in the pocket to remind herself of a sense of urgency. They were not addressing the subject matter of their meeting, and yet they were strangely at ease, as if both of them were content to avoid it for a while, and simply *be*. It was a good sensation, and could not last.

'Did we come here to watch the swans?' she asked.

He shook his head. There was energy in all his movements and gestures, but he looked tired. She hoped it was the result of a sleepless night – he deserved that, at the very least – but all the same, she wished he was not tired.

'I come here for all sorts of reasons, I suppose. Principally to see people at peace, enjoying themselves and recuperating. It's an exercise in harmony, isn't it? A walled park, a safe place, mimicking the countryside, but very far away from the rigours of that. Wildness tamed. I wish I could achieve that in my courtroom. I keep saying we should have flowers.'

He waved in the direction of the yellow palace, half hidden through the trees.

'I also come here to admire my inheritance. Palaces, kings and queens, a constitution which still works better than most; it brings out my not so latent patriotism. Makes me proud of what we have. Odd, how unfashionable it is to be patriotic, even at times like these.'

'Part of your own inheritance,' she suggested. 'To have a need for patriotism.' He nodded, and smiled at her, self-conscious and wanting understanding. Rachel did understand. She had taken to counting her own privileges, which included a vote.

'Yes. My father chose to be here. He embraced it. He could take nothing for granted, and nor can I. And I'm so sorry, I forgot to ask, how is *your* father? Better, I hope? When will you see him?'

'When he wants to be seen. Pride, you know.'

She found herself explaining how her father had left his

inhaler and his emergency pills in her flat after he had come for supper and how he had no remedy on the train for an asthma attack. Even as she explained this, as she already had to people at work that day, several times, she wondered if she was repeating it to reassure herself. Embellishing it and adding details to the story to make it ever more true. Such a nice supper too, she added now. Ivy cooked it, she's good at it. She bit her lip; he would know that.

'Did they get on well?' he asked.

'No, not now you mention it, but that's my father for you. He doesn't take to anyone easily.'

He was silent for a minute, nodded in sympathy, then suggested they get up and walk. Finally they were back to Ivy. Rachel noticed how he adapted the pace of his walking to hers, slowing his faster footsteps to match. She wished they could postpone talking about Ivy, Grace and Ernest, and talk about themselves and the colours of the park instead. Sit and people-watch, in shared amazement.

'I liked your Sam,' she said. 'He's outrageous, but he's terrific. He's all flash and fire and no inhibitions. He sort of shines, you know. I wish I could be like that, even for a day.'

Carl raised his eyebrows, grimaced and smiled again. There was pride in his voice.

'Why on earth do you think you aren't? You shine. You shine with beauty and purpose. Sam shines too, but the trouble with him is that he always has to impose. He has to challenge everyone, test their reactions, run the risk of enraging and shocking them, just to see if they're going to accept him. I don't know if that's part of being gay, or just insecure. Or simply mischief, he's got plenty of that. And I like him the way he is. He's acquiring confidence.'

'He can talk for England,' Rachel said. Rounding the last

curve in the lake, facing a bank of vivid flowers, she had a vision of Sam meeting Grace in a flurry of colours and noise. If only it could happen; it would happen; it must happen; it could only enrich them both. Then Ivy would come in, and they would love each other too, and she, Rachel, would slip away, leaving happily ever after.

'Look at the swans,' Carl said. 'I make myself look at the swans.'

'Ivy still likes swans,' Rachel said. 'She has a poster on the wall, of *Leda and the Swan*, Matisse, I think. It's all graceful shapes and curves. The swan is blue and Leda is yellow, all bordered in red. It's a very abstract swan.'

'Leda, wife of a king of Sparta, mother of many famous children, Clytemnestra and Helen, mates with Zeus, who takes the form of a swan and produces a god-like child. Yes, I can see why Ivy would like to have that on the wall. We had it at home.'

Rachel winced at that. It reminded her of everything she did not know. She only knew about the miseries of which she had been told, nothing of the happiness. She felt old, envious and curious.

'Another version of a virginal birth, the god sent from heaven, no choice about it,' Carl murmured. 'Impregnation appears to have happened via the ear, the swan hovering above, but maybe Leda got confused, she had children already. Perhaps Ivy would prefer that as an explanation of conception. Just as she preferred to think that Cassie did not die, but became a swan, like a daughter of Mir, surviving as long as the swan survived. Do you know, I would much rather talk about something else. I didn't bring you here to look at swans. Oh, I wish this was over.'

Obligingly the swans turned a bend on the south of the

island, out of sight. Carl and Rachel got up and moved on. He tucked her arm in his, protectively, shielded her from a boy on skates racing towards them.

'Look,' he said, 'it wasn't so difficult, thinking it over, it's all obvious, isn't it? I have to try and make my peace with Grace and Ernest, for everyone's sake. I have to try and help them financially if they're in trouble, I promised my father that, I made a will when we married . . .'

'Grace never mentioned that.'

'I know that's not the issue. I have to meet them, and from that somehow forge a way not only to persuade my reluctant son to meet his mother, but also to persuade him it was all his own idea. So much is overdue. I can cope with Plan A, so let's do it. I'll go and see them, take it from there.'

He paused. 'But what worries me is you. You're somehow inside the toils of something which has nothing to do with you, and it's going to put you in the awful bind of keeping secrets from a friend, which you must, you know. If I go to Midwinter Farm, say in a day or so, say next weekend, you're the intermediary, which seems bloody unfair to me. I shan't be able to tell my son where I'm going, and you can't tell Ivy. And I want to do this because you were brave enough to suggest it, and at the same time I dearly wish we had met each other in any other context. I want you to know I'm not the devil incarnate, and I should dearly, dearly like to know who hurt you so much that you come out, blinking like a fledgling in sunlight, lovely and shining and determined like you are. I should like to know everything about you, I should like to court you, Miss Doe, I really would, and I am not fit. Yet. And I'd love to meet your father.'

He would like him. Of course he would. The thought of that swam into her consciousness like an injection of something warm. She tried to shut it away, but a feeling of joy persisted.

'I'm not fit to be courted myself, Carl, and what a quaint way to put it. The last man who got close to me was a thief and I sold him down the river. I'm no good at selecting the male of the species, no good at judging, Judge, and I harm the men nearest to me. Are you really saying you would do this, I mean meet Grace and Ernest on their own territory, for the sake of my good opinion? Or is making me blush simply another tactic in your armoury?'

He was serenely unoffended, sat back and considered, smiling.

'The lover-thief might explain a lot about you,' he said.

'I worked with him,' she said. 'He was a . . . colleague.'

Carl stopped smiling and touched her hand.

'Poor you. That must have put you on quite an island. You must have been very lonely. But yes, for the record, I'd go a very long way to secure your good opinion of me. As a preliminary. Anyway, Sam likes you. We do instant liking, Sam and I, instant judgements. Unfortunately for those concerned, they tend to last.'

'So, if he likes me on one meeting, *I* might be in with a chance of persuading him to meet his mother?'

'Play your cards right.'

He was smiling at her, teasing gently, trying to make all this less serious than it was. She could not resist it and smiled back.

'Tell me about the lover-thief.'

Rachel sighed. She wanted to do just that, say what it was like to be a whistle-blower. But it was not the time or the place to describe cynicism and loneliness, unless to say how it was Ivy who had made her change.

'The lover-thief glamorises him rather,' she said. 'I think, in retrospect, his greatest crime was having no sense of humour, and gradually depriving me of mine.'

'But not taking away your ability to do what you thought to be right?'

'No. Not yet.'

'That's my kind of woman. Enough. Now, when shall I go and see these two in the lion's den of Midwinter Farm?'

YES! She took a deep breath.

'Saturday. Ivy won't be there.'

He took a diary out of his back pocket, and then put it back without looking at it, nodded.

'Yes. I know that's good. Free day. Sam's going to Crete on Thursday, so he'll be out of the way, and I'll be able to resist telling him. What about you? Will you be there?'

She hesitated. 'Yes, if you want me . . .'

'Yes, I do.'

'. . . to be there,' she finished.

'Yes,' he said again. 'If I knew you were in the background, it would make it so much easier for me, even though it isn't fair to ask.'

'We've done that bit. I'll be there as a friend of Grace and Ivy and Ernest.'

'And me,' he added.

'Yes,' she said. 'All of you.'

Carl got up, held out his hand, and said, shall we walk and talk of other things?

Of shoes and ships and sealing wax, of cabbages and kings.

It was later, when they parted, with a mutual reluctance they were both trying to hide, that he ruined it all. Ruined the dream that they were two normal people, walking, talking, eating, drinking, enjoying one another.

He insisted on getting a taxi to take her home. It was as quaint as courtship. She didn't want it, but he put his foot down, and while they waited by the side of the road, watching black cabs with orange lights swim by, but quite unable to part, he said, 'There's something else . . . I ought to tell you. Your father and his inhaler. It reminds me of Sam. She used to hide his inhaler, she used to take it away. That was the last straw.'

And then the taxi arrived, and she got in, and he paid, like an old-fashioned gentleman, ignoring protests, making it a courtesy rather than condescension, and leaving her sitting in the back, suspecting him again. He couldn't leave it alone, could he? He had to make an unpleasant suggestion, an implied criticism of Ivy, and leave it lingering, the German bastard. He had to resurrect an image of Ivy as monster mother, to justify himself. Bastard. Rachel was triumphing in what she had achieved, she had been happy, and now she felt limp as she stumbled out of the taxi in front of her house, which no longer felt like home.

Must phone Grace. Must not ever again look in Ivy's room. Must never again betray anyone. Must not divide loyalties, all men were shits, especially charismatic judges, but her eyes in the bathroom mirror where she rushed to wash her face, were shining with hope and doubt.

In the event, as policemen and lawyers are liable to say, Donald Cousins went nowhere that Monday, except to West End Central Police Station, in response to a direction to postpone his hopeless little enquiry into the matters of a lesser judge of German origin, because there were better things to do, even for him, who was so often the last chosen for a team. What was needed, this weekday morning, was old-fashioned skills, of checking and cross-checking, finding and interviewing. They might have remembered he was good at that, but Donald was not kidding himself. He had been hauled back into real work because there was a panic on, the sort of panic started by a tabloid newspaper article the week before, which in turn provoked the sort of activity designed to head off yet more adverse publicity for the police. The subject of the article, copied by other articles on the no-news days which followed the commencement of the holiday season, was inner-city violence, and the disgraceful level of non-detection of apparently casual, apparently alcohol-fuelled murders. Such as the awful death of the man in the ambulance, the death in the autograph-hunters' queue, and one in an office. Some brilliant mind on a computer had come up with the notion of a connection between the latter two. They had both happened at night. The same cleaning company had featured. Not much of a link, and only slightly better than nothing, but it was one of those days when something had to be done.

Donald had been expecting something of the kind, because that was what happened at this time of year. There was a briefing meeting, the necessary flurry of activity. They were like bees, buzzing. He thought of his proposed trip out into the country; he thought of needing to see Blaker, and sighed. It was ever thus. He was never allowed to finish anything, and now, to his own surprise, he needed to finish this little enquiry, even though he had resented it in the first place. He put in his two pennys' worth, his own little mite of observation, which wasn't much. There were all sorts of night shifts, for theatres, offices, shops, bars, pubs, and what did that have to do with anything, he said sagely, and was dismissed as negative. What was this company called? Clean Co. Was it worth pursuing?

We need to find someone who does the theatre shifts, someone said. Can't find a boss, gone on holiday. Donald wanted to say they could never find a needle in a haystack, and thought of haystacks. Then he thought of a way through it. He was skilled in getting what he wanted. Feeling ever so slightly treacherous, he raised his hand and put Blaker in the frame. Said out loud that he knew a parolee, a man with a vicious record and nothing to lose, a man known to work these shifts, could he start with him? Not a suspect, no, but a talker.

It took all day to get that far, to make Blaker officially his. Until he had licence to do what he had wanted to do in the first place. Go and find him, alone. Invite him to assist with enquiries, at least as a general part of rounding up the usual suspects. The day had spread well into the evening before he found him.

Which was why, at nine on a Monday night, he sat with Blaker in the waiting room at Accident and Emergency, with Blaker's mumbling, blood-streaked face in his lap, the grime of mucus making a real mess of his trousers. It was like dealing with a large slobbering dog in someone else's house: some code of manners dictated that you had to let it happen to you. The mumbling had followed the sobbing which followed the other mumbling, and if the body was the temple of the soul, as Donald had been told, this one had been bombed. The injuries were superficial enough, a bang on the head and awful scratches round the neck. It was the damage to the soul that did for him. Donald was rubbing Blaker's back, saying, there, there. Oh, she did, did she? Thinking at the same time that this really was over and above the call of duty, and then thinking maybe not, since Blaker's woeful condition was really his, Donald's fault.

Somewhere along the line he remembered Blaker telling him that a favourite hang-out of his was Victoria Embankment Gardens. The gardens were hidden from view by railings and stretched alongside the Thames by Hungerford Bridge. They were long and narrow and evergreen, good for loitering in any weather because of the shelters. It was too crowded, though, because there was musical entertainment in the summer and too many hobos coming from both sides of the river, too many hot bodies on a hot day, like everywhere. It had not been a hot day; it had been cool and wet when Ivy had found him in the late afternoon, two hours before Donald did.

'She knows I come here most days,' Blaker said. 'I always tell her where I might be. Believe it or not, I try to plan my day.'

'What happened?'

Blaker had been sitting on the ground, recognisable with one swollen eye and only as much ignored by passers-by as the other dozen or so of the walking-wounded homeless who hung around, sleeping off the day's bottle and looking bashed about by falling over. Self-harming, injured people were part of the scenery, to be walked around without eye contact most of the time, pity not something to be wasted on hopeless causes. Nor was anyone likely to interfere in their squabbles, the drunken debates turned sour and the half-hearted spats and blows, the raucous laughter.

'She was angry,' Blaker said. 'I was sitting on a bench by myself, and she just came up behind me, put one hand on my neck, and punched me, then she put both her hands round my neck, and . . . shook me. I didn't see her at first, but I smelt it was her, and I started to choke. I was saying don't, what's the matter, and she just hung on like grim death. Look.' He fingered his own neck, where a line of grazes decorated it like a red and purple necklace. 'I thought she'd kill me. She didn't care who saw. I got my hands on her arms and tried to fight her off, but I was dying there, man, dying, without being able to ask why. And then she stopped. Like all the anger went. She let go. I sort of slumped forward, and . . . and then she came and sat beside me and said she was sorry. And I said, what did you do that for, Ivy? and she said, you know what you did. You've been talking to someone about me.'

Blaker raised bloodshot eyes to Donald's face, the intensity of his gaze shocking in its sorrow.

'I think we'll maybe get to a hospital and get you checked out,' Donald said.

Blaker did not want that, but above all he did not want to be left alone. So they were sitting in the queue, and Blaker, fuelled by burbling sorrow, soreness and the whisky his attacker had left him, began to snore in Donald's lap, and Donald detached him to curl up in the plastic chair next to his own. Then he took out his notebook and started to make notes.

He always wanted to begin, like an old Victorian copper giving evidence, by saying, *As I was proceeding in a westerly direction* . . . he always wanted to write his notes like telling a story, but all notebooks had issue numbers, all had to be accounted for, returned and examined, they were not the place for putting down what you thought. They were for writing a précis of facts and dialogue. He put back the official, date-stamped, serial number 1366197 notebook and took out his own, wrote in that because he could use his own language. He could make up an official record of events later, if ever.

Blaker is a persistent offender, HIV positive, with not a lot to lose. He was attacked today, in the open, by an angry woman he has known for years, simply because she found out I had spoken to him and thus knew of her. She knew this because she stays with Ms Rachel Doe, whom I had phoned because I was idle and in the mood to set a red herring to catch I didn't know what. It follows that Ivy W. has something more than usual to hide about a strange and tragic background. I believe that Blaker (who's a lovely old queen, whatever he's done, including robbing women because he fancied their handbags as much as anything else) is complicit with Ivy, and that Ivy used him to send e-mails, with images, to her ex-husband. I have absolutely no proof of this, but I think it. I also believe that Ivy is violent but not uncontrolled. Blaker bears witness to this. It's a very bold move to attempt to throttle someone in public, very bold indeed. It wasn't her hands she put round his neck . . . looks to me like it was some sort of rope, there are grazes and scratches. A sort of garrotte.

Blaker also bears witness to her kindness. Is this consistent? He says she left in tears and full of apologies after what she had done, giving him a half-bottle of whisky. Kindness, or a short route to oblivion. She left him saying she was very, very sorry, but she had things to do, and he must not talk about her to anyone. Talk about what? What's so bad, that Blaker knows?

Blaker stirred and Donald scribbled.

What is she like? I know this much. She's potentially murderous. She loathes her ex-husband, the judge, so Blaker says. According to the son, she was violent to him. Is either telling the truth? And she's worked endless night shifts. Supposing she has a vendetta? Against men? Or a particular kind of man?

Garrottes. I brought him here because when you've got grazes, however shallow, you risk things getting septic, and I don't know what an HIV bloke should risk. She wasn't trying that hard, not as hard as it looked, she was making a point that she could do far worse, and she could, you know. No one would notice in Victoria Embankment Gardens.

He paused for an irrelevant thought. Queen Victoria had brought the German influence. Through her, the Germans did so much for this particular city. Victorian morality. There was always a down side to the up side of achievement. Poverty, prostitution and monuments went together somehow. Then he shook himself and went on writing.

Ivy W., a girl brought up on a farm. She might know how to kill animals, but not how to kill human beings. Am I missing a trick here?

She's a night-time animal who works and befriends. She is as kind as she is vicious. Blaker keeps talking about practice.

He swapped the private notebook for the one with the serial number, and began again.

I found Mr Blaker, who was poorly and intoxicated. He was unable to tell me anything about Clean Co. because of this. He told me that he had been attacked. I took Mr Blaker to A and E. I am pursuing enquiries into the matter of his alleged assailant . . .

He was full of an unholy sense of glee, yes, yes, yes, because whatever he had seen, he had perfectly legitimate grounds to arrest the ex-Mrs Schneider for assault on Blaker. And he knew where to find her. He could go and haul her in, question her about why she had done that, and about night shifts.

No, he couldn't. The correct course of action would have been to take Blaker to the nearest nick, West End Central, as it happened, and let the locals deal with it, or call someone straight to the scene. Pursue it as just another street crime.

He was perverting some course of justice; he was already hopelessly compromised by what he had done. He was not doing anything like his duty. He was doing what Blaker wanted and shielding him.

Blaker stirred, nuzzling his shoulder, like a child.

'She didn't mean it, you know. Fuck this, can you take me home?'

'You need looking at. Cleaning up. Antibiotics.'

And I need evidence from a doctor.

'You're not going to report her, are you? You're not going to tell anyone what Ivy did to me? I don't want her in trouble. If you do anything like that, I'll just deny it, I'll say it was someone else. I shouldn't have told you. Why the fuck did I tell you? I've been out of it, haven't I? *What else did I tell you?*'

Donald was deliberately silent, for a long time, until Blaker nudged him, hard.

'Promise, fuck you, or I'll get you in trouble.'

Then he began to cry again. 'No, I didn't mean that. Oh please, Don, don't do nothing. I want her to come back. I wish she'd killed me.'

'Why on earth should she do that?'

Blaker shut his eyes.

'Did you e-mail stuff to the judge, Blaker? I thought I heard you say that in your sleep.'

Blaker nodded. The pain was beginning to kick in, along with a dull, defeated, overdue anger, at himself, at everything. This was good, Donald thought, although what the hell he could do with anything Blaker said was another matter. He wished he did not have to react like a policeman and could recover the other instincts of a normal human being and just do something kind, because that was what he wanted to do.

No chance.

'Sending that stuff, pictures from books, is that what she didn't want you to talk about to someone like me?'

Another nod, then a violent shaking of the head, which hurt.

'That's not much to worry about, is it? Or was it something else?'

Blaker was sobbing again, clutching his throat.

'She's going to kill him,' he said at last. 'She's been practising. She boasts about it to me, because no one would believe me. She's going to kill him, one way or another. She says she's got someone to help her.'

Oh, shit. Donald wanted to shout. Here he was in collusion with a fantasist with a death sentence and a horrible knack of telling the truth. Maybe he could restore his reputation with this one. Maybe this was a coup. But Donald had never had a coup in his life, and who would believe Blaker?

What would his wife think if he brought Blaker home? If he turned Blaker in, he'd be bailed by the morning, off and away as soon as he'd retracted everything he'd said, and Donald would look a real Charlie.

A nurse was coming towards them. She looked long-suffering, faced with her twentieth drunk today.

Donald thought it was time he took advice from the judge. Maybe not. The judge would not want Donald going anywhere near his ex-wife, he knew it, otherwise he would have mentioned her in the first place. He nudged Blaker, who was shrinking away from the nurse.

'He's HIV positive,' Donald said to her, wondering if this was information Blaker would have volunteered.

'Oh,' she said. 'I'll just get some gloves.'

Donald settled back.

'Well that's put me to the back of the queue,' Blaker said spitefully, quite cheered by her reaction. 'Thanks.'

No, Donald could not take him home. He wasn't that good a man. He had daughters to consider.

'It'll be all right,' he said. 'Now, my friend. You said this Ivy was a model. When she's not doing something else. Where was it you said she did the modelling?'

Blaker looked up in surprise, confusion coming down again. He could not remember telling Donald that.

'Just up the road. At the art school. She wasn't going to go far away, was she?'

Chapter Seventeen

There was definitely a pattern to Rachel's dealings with the judge, rather like the patterns of a dance. She would be on the one hand appalled by him, or reports of him, then she would see him and feel attracted first, before being repelled again. She had begun by loathing him on the basis of what he would call hearsay evidence, then she admired, then she was hopelessly attracted, then she was repelled, then she was attracted, and then she was confused. She could not believe he was the good man he seemed to her, and the wicked one he seemed to others who had known him so much of his life. Rachel was a novice in the affairs of the body and mind, but she knew that if she had met him without knowing anything about him, ignorance would be bliss, and she would have admired him. But even something as innocent as respect felt like treachery and she could almost have wished she hated him.

She referred to him as 'the judge' in her own mind when she thought of him, which was most of the time during the

Tuesday and the Wednesday, simply to put him at a distance, make him a man without a name, and encourage herself to analyse objectively, instead of saying *Carl.* She tried to put her own feelings in a box marked *Anonymous* and close the lid, instead of spreading the contents out all over some clean floor, like she sometimes did with work documents, to see what caught her eye, to see a sequence, to see what did not fit, to notice what jarred, undistracted by what should have been there. Look at what she saw with her own two eyes, instead of assuming that what she had been told was true. But then she had never felt like this before. She had never felt drawn to the hideously selfish husband of a best friend before. It skewed everything.

I am so insecure, she wrote in the diary at work, *that I fall in love with anyone who pays the slightest bit of positive attention to me. Anyone who takes me seriously. I'm a thirty-two-year-old virgin.* Delete.

She looked out of the window of the office, and watched the people pass, far below. Too much time spent doing this. She kept looking because she was sure, early this morning, that she had seen Grace, stepping out with the rush-hour crowds disgorging themselves from the station, and she had been so sure it was Grace, because of the metallic hair and the way she walked, she had wanted to shout, STOP, and then run downstairs and find her, but waited instead for the figure to pass out of sight. Whenever she thought of Grace, she saw her walking with her own shadow trailing behind, the way she thought about Ivy. A person with a tall and elegant shadow.

It could not have been Grace. Grace was at home, midafternoon, when she rang, full of tales of the weather, until they began to speak in a strange kind of code, as if Ivy was listening.

Saturday OK, Grace? Oh, yes. But you're coming Friday, aren't you? Yes, I think so. Are you sure? If you want . . . Yes, I do want.

Have you *met* him? (This was Grace.) No, not actually, but we've spoken. How did you persuade him, darling, oh you are marvellous.

I didn't persuade him, Grace, I threatened him, and then he volunteered. How easy it was to lie.

I shall have a splendid lunch, Grace said. Ernest is not quite himself. I long to see you. Is Ivy as busy as she says? Yes, thank God. Grace, did you ever meet any of Ivy's friends? No, darling. I don't think she had any other than lowlifes before she met you, I told you. Can you come soon, on Friday, I'm so nervous. And how's your father? Truculent and uncommunicative. Oh my God, aren't they all? Men, bloody men, I love you, dearest. I shall colour my hair scarlet, just to scare him. Take care, talk soon.

Is Ivy as busy as she says?

Two points, which she counted on her fingers. Ivy and Grace clearly chatted like starlings every day, imparted news back and forth in a way she had never guessed and Ivy never said. Ivy had always had friends, but no one Rachel had ever met. Like someone called Blaker.

She took Sam's inhaler . . . it was the last straw.

Ivy had been out when Rachel got home on the Monday night. She was back late and left a note next morning. *See you at drawing class on Wednesday . . . be good.* Where did Ivy go when she did not come home?

Last class of term, and Rachel could not look forward to it

because Ivy would be the model, whereas before it would make the evening. It was the keeping of secrets that made it different, that was all. The spasmodic sightings of Ivy, the communication by note and text which typified their shared existence was only normal flatmate stuff, with one working days and the other, more often, nights, but at the moment it felt as if they were avoiding one another.

Rachel's father remained aloof, as if he too had something he did not want to tell her. He would like her to visit next week, please, when he had finished renovating the bathroom. And how was that friend of hers? Ivy whatsername?

Fine, Dad, fine.

Don't you miss that class of yours.

She took Sam's inhaler . . . it was the last straw. Things don't fall out of pockets. She must focus. The week would go in a flash. She was sure she had seen Grace. No, she was not sure of anything.

She read a newspaper she found lying around, for distraction, and then put it down. Full of the usual crap. *Death in ambulance unsolved.* It was easy to read about London being a dangerous, violent place, and ignore it entirely and effortlessly when you lived in the heart of it. She threw the paper away. That was the London her father feared, not the London she knew.

Towards the end of the long Wednesday afternoon, Rachel was called down to the front desk of her office building, two floors down, with a message that that there was a delivery for her, and the delivery person would like a signed receipt. Unusual, but she went, anything to move.

In the foyer of the building she saw a bright bouquet of flowers on the desk, and beside it, dwarfing it in colour and size, stood Sam Schneider, dressed in white and looking dazzling. She could not help it: his presence created a frisson of shock and a feeling of being intruded upon on her own territory, but he was also instantly familiar, and he made her smile.

'What on earth are you doing here?'

He made an exaggerated bow, scooped the flowers off the desk, handed them to her, and spoke as if he was running in a race.

'Dad sent me. He's got me doing errands, since I'm freed up and he never is. In return for which he may have to pay me back with menial work, such as washing and ironing, at which he excels, did you know that? And basically he trusts me slightly more than Interflora.'

'They're lovely,' she said, burying her nose and her embarrassment in the sweet scent of the flowers. There were jasmine and roses in there. She did not know what to say.

'Or rather,' Sam said, 'he trusts my taste in choosing floral tributes for beautiful women better than his own, done over the phone. Do you really like them?'

'Of course I like them,' she laughed. 'How couldn't I? Can I buy you a drink or a coffee, or would you prefer a more conventional tip?'

Sam doffed an imaginary cap and grinned at her.

'I'm not allowed to take bribes, miss, honest, and I don't usually demean myself with errands either, except when I'm curious. The old meanie hasn't sent flowers to anyone except his clerk in a million years, so please don't send them back.'

'I shan't, I promise, but surely I can give you some reward?'

Sam winked, ludicrously.

'Nope. I'm off on holiday. You could, you know, look after him while I'm away. You're definitely in with a chance.'

Then he waltzed away, leaving her extraordinarily light-headed. She never knew quite what to do with someone who was pleased to see her. There was a note with the flowers, which said, *Thanks for being yourself. See you Saturday at twelve, or before?*

Better not before. When she phoned Carl to thank him, half hoping not to reach him, they talked for an hour, about very little other than the flowers on her desk. What a pity she could not take them home. Ivy would want to know who they were from.

She stayed late at the office and got to the drawing class early, light in heart. The corridor leading to the designated room through the labyrinth of the college was cool and dusty, but the room itself was hotter than an incubator. The flowers would have wilted. Sweaty, bad-tempered, hot-from-malfunctioning heat, left on for the last model with no clothes, still going full blast hours later. Rachel switched it off. She wanted to open the windows, which were set high in the wall, and unable to find a way, left the door open for a faint draught to flow through. In spite of her distractions and the ridiculous heat, Rachel looked at the unkempt, scruffy, paint-smeared place with great affection. In those black old days when she had first sidled in, it was a place she had loved on sight, so much so she liked being early, breathing it in and being the good girl who put out the chairs for the majority who were late, as long as she could avoid the Plonker, who was often early too, on account of not having much more of a life than she did then. It was the last day of term; she did not know if she would ever come back, but she thanked this room for what it had done for her in the dog days of winter and the darkest days of gloom. In this ugly, beautiful space, she had discovered a talent and a whole new world. She began to put out the plastic chairs, looked around for the equally filthy plastic stands on which they would balance the boards, and then she noticed that the room was even more untidy than usual. Chairs had been knocked over by the last class in a stampede to leave; must be the heat. Rachel was back on familiar, if borrowed territory, saying *tut, tut, tut*, under her breath, laughing at herself, looking at the clock, which told her she had ten minutes before the teacher came in, and why was she always such an early bird? It had been nerves, at first.

She heard him before she saw him. A moaning sound, coming from the makeshift little cubicle where the model disrobed behind a limp curtain and came out, into the heat, waiting for instructions. The cubicle was nothing but a corner, conveniently close to the washbasin and its single cold tap, behind the same curtain. The moaning went on. Rachel yanked back the curtain.

The Plonker was behind it, sitting there with his head between his hands and his elbows on his knees, keening to himself. His summer uniform for a hot day was baggy shorts and sandals, exposing large white thighs and hairy calves, and he was a man who should never have worn shorts in public. Winter and summer, he always wore the wrong clothes. Too many, too much, or too few. The wrong clothes, chosen with care in furtherance of a long-dead image taken from a film he had loved featuring a hero with a different figure, and jazzed up by a silly scarf.

'What's the matter?'

'Agghhhhh!'

It was a loud yell in the quiet room. Norman put his hands round his neck and jumped to his feet, then slumped back down heavily on to the stool on which he sat. He wound the silly scarf tightly round his neck with trembling fingers, and coughed loudly. Then he removed one hand from his neck and waggled his fingers. Rachel did not know if this was an apology for the scream, or what it meant. She had a sudden image of what her father might have looked like as a young man. He would have been the sort everyone labelled fusspot or plonker, or something of the kind. It didn't make him bad. It gave him a futile bravery. Norman, the Plonker, looked sad.

'What's the matter?'

He looked up at her beseechingly and made a pathetic attempt to shrug.

'I thought it was Ivy coming back,' he whispered.

'What do you mean, coming back? She'll be here any minute, along with everyone else. What are you doing in there? Come on out.'

He shook his head.

'You don't know, do you? You really don't know. You don't know anything. I'm glad it's you, I thought it was her, coming back. She came ten minutes ago. She told me if I said anything she'd kill me, and she would, I know she would, I . . .'

'What the hell are you talking about?'

'I was with her that night,' he gabbled. 'She ran away from me, she got in the thing, she did it. It had to be her. You've got to tell her I'll never tell anyone, never, ever, ever. She put her hands round my neck and she squeezed.' He fingered the scarf, scratching at it. 'She said . . .'

They could hear footsteps coming towards the open door. He began to stutter. 'You've got to know what she's like. She said if I ever . . .'

Rachel hauled him to his feet and out into the room.

'Don't you mean,' she said, 'that Ivy said she wouldn't go

out with you or sleep with you at the point of a gun? Isn't that what she said when she found you hanging round, waiting for her? Isn't it?'

He looked at her helplessly. He had the expression of a man who was never believed.

'Tell her I won't tell,' he muttered.

Ivy and the teacher swept into the room together, he small and squat, she tall and lithe, an incongruous couple. Ivy knew all the gossip and could talk the teachers' talk. Ivy could talk anyone's talk; she remembered everything they said. She beamed at Rachel and Norman, embracing them both with her smile, stepped across to Rachel and kissed her on the cheek.

'Hello, hello, here we are again, end of term too. Fun time. We've got crisps and wine for the interval. It's a very cheap and refreshingly nasty red. We'll have to make up for it later.'

The Plonker turned away and picked up one of the fallen chairs. He was trembling again. Ivy caught Rachel's eye and raised her own eyebrows, as if to say, what's this about? and Rachel responded with a 'search me' shrug.

'I'll think about that,' Rachel said, grinning back. They had always been conspirators, Ivy and she. It was good to feel that way.

There was a clatter of more footsteps, the main posse arriving with a minute to spare, bringing in a draught of sound and the reassuring presence of the outside world, sorting out easels and stools and boards. Rachel found her familiar place. Out of the corner of her eye she saw Ivy detour on her way to the cubicle, to touch Norman on the arm and smile hello. He flinched away from her, then smiled back. Nothing wrong then. Just besotted.

She tried to will herself back into the state of utter

concentration on the class and the sheer exercise of drawing which had so beguiled her in the first place, and the magic worked, as the still overwarm room fell silent, apart from distant outside noises and the shuffle of bodies and paper. She was sitting opposite the Plonker, who had deliberately placed himself at the far side of the room, not close to anyone else for once. He seemed to have pulled himself together.

'Three-minute poses, please.'

Ivy stepped out of the cubicle, jumped up on to the wooden podium and smiled at them all. She stood stock still with her legs apart, one hand on her hip, the other hanging by her side, head in profile, looking away from Rachel. They had agreed a long time ago that whenever Ivy was the model in this class, she would never look directly at Rachel, because it made them giggle, and when that started it could not be stopped, like laughter in some holy place. Ivy always looked away. Rachel began to draw quickly, get down the outline and place it on the page. It was an easy pose, Ivy knew to begin with easy poses. A quick glance to memorise it, mark the outer dimensions of head and feet and centre body, then go. She glanced up, past Ivy, and saw the Plonker's face, gazing up. His mouth was open; the gaze was one of fear and adoration, like someone imploring a favour from the effigy of a cruel saint. His scarf had slipped; in the harsh light, Rachel could see that his neck was red and his face was pale. She looked away.

'Change pose.'

Ivy moved slightly, changed the angle and let both arms drop by her sides, head flung back. She flexed her fingers but was otherwise still. Rachel could see scratches on her upper arms, red against her tanned skin, shockingly bright scratches which must have bled. The words *road kill* came into her mind, Ivy washing blood from her hands. When and where had she got those? Where had she washed the blood away? Not in their bathroom, surely. Looking at the whole figure, Rachel had a sudden, alternative picture of her, startlingly different from the first. Not an animal, not the hunted running creature she had first seen, but a fighter, curling and uncurling her fingers, ready to do battle, poised and trained. A Boadicea who would cut off her own breast the better to hoist a weapon. A ruthless physical opponent, something merciless. For one brief moment, watching those large hands moving slightly, and the back held taut, Rachel was frightened of her.

The class went on. The image faded in the long poses, when Ivy knelt and leaned forward, exposing her long back, her face concealed, her arms stretched before her, like a supplicant making an obeisance, utterly defenceless. Abused, waiting to be kicked, the scratches on her arms making her victim rather than predator. That was the image Rachel wanted to keep and treasure. The class went on. The interval was spent drinking bad wine; the temperature cooled and Ivy made them laugh. When they resumed their seats for the delayed second half, the Plonker had gone.

'Good,' Ivy said, passing Rachel's seat. 'Are we having a drink? I feel like getting absolutely plastered. Let's.' She held out her arms. 'Look at this. We had to take out some hideous dead plants from the back of an office. Prickly stuff, the bastards. Look what it did.'

The words echoed in Rachel's head. *I don't believe you. I just don't believe you.* You were fighting. You don't get nail scratches at work, not even your work.

She found herself repeating to herself the words *I don't believe you,* to stop herself saying them out loud, and saying instead, 'Honestly, Ivy, if you go round hitting people, you've got to make sure they don't fight back,' and turning away to gather her things, feeling a huge sense of loss because it was such an obvious and glib lie. Ivy grabbed her by the arm. She could feel her hand burning into her bare skin, like being held by hot steel.

'I didn't say anything about hitting people,' she said angrily. 'I said I was moving prickly rubbish.'

'Well I don't think you should be asked to do that on what you get paid,' Rachel said briskly. 'Five pounds an hour doesn't include danger money. Or having fifteen people in a class wondering if you've been snuggling up to a tiger.'

Ivy's eyes lit up with delight at the very idea.

'That's what I hoped they'd think,' she said. 'But they're so polite, aren't they, they didn't even ask, not even Teacher. C'mon, let's go and forget the taste of that red stuff. Drown it in something better. Did I tell you I get ten pounds an hour for the next weekend? Three days solid, they want. I'll be worth a fortune, so I'm paying.'

Go with the flow, it would all be fine. Get down a bottle of wine, wish the week away, stop consulting that little nag in the heart which felt like a stone, the feeling she had seen something she should not have seen, and wished she hadn't. They went out into the light sky and the traffic sound, lulling now at nine at night, with the imprint of Ivy's vice-like fingers still on her arm, and the temperature rising again with the pressure of hundreds of people out there, hunting for a good time.

And there, by the entrance, was DS Cousins, with his droopy moustache and a cigarette in hand, waiting to one side and leaning against the wall like a person waiting to catch a bus from the nearby stop. Rachel recognised him instantly, saw his face and somehow heard again his voice on the phone. He was not looking at her; he was looking across the road. Her response was instinctive. At first she had the absurd desire to barge into him and push him out of the way, and then all the protective urges she had ever felt towards Ivy came in to play and the rest was forgotten; she linked arms, pulled down Ivy's cap, and marched her forward, staring ahead herself, talking hard, until they were well past him. Then she shuffled Ivy along even faster, until the West End pavement crowds swallowed them. Ivy allowed herself to be carried along, laughing that Rachel's enthusiasm for a decent glass of wine was a bit extreme, wasn't it, had the end-of-term class been that bad, and what was the matter with the Plonker, until they detoured left and right and then into the basement bar where Ivy had taken her first.

Ivy pushed through to the front of the crowded room; people made way for Ivy. Rachel grabbed a seat, sat down heavily with the drawing bag banging against her knees, and drew breath. She felt less rage than disappointment. Judge Carl's tame policeman, his sad-looking jackal, had been sent to wait for them. He wanted Ivy; he had been primed, twice, as to where he might find her. And if DS bloody Cousins was to get to Ivy now, whatever innocent thing he wanted to ask, Rachel's underhand dealings with Carl would be revealed. Sure, they would have to come out sometime, but not yet, not until there was a tangible result.

Why hadn't she asked Carl about that damn man? She had simply forgotten. DS Cousins could ruin the plan. Rachel looked towards the door. No one had followed them. DS Cousins in his shirt and tie would stick out a mile in here, and still she felt they were both pursued.

She was so tired, so very tired. Anxiety sapped energy,

but more exhausting still was the solid knowledge of what she had observed in Ivy's naked, speechless body, in Norman's face: that Ivy might be sweet, generous and kind, but she was also a savage; she had never been entirely powerless, and she had done something terribly wrong and was revelling in it.

Ivy was as high as a kite, sailing on nothing but city air and two hours of being admired, pushing her way back to their table with a bottle of wine and two glasses, in party mood, the way she often was after modelling. She sat down and leaned forward confidingly, full of mischief.

'Now, shall I tell you what really happened with the Plonker? What an idiot! Why are we feeling sorry for him?'

'What happened? Why's he so scared of you?'

'Oh, pooh, he's not scared, just embarrassed. I dropped my kit off in the room before class. I was going to go and get a coffee. And he was in the damn cubicle. Waiting for you.'

'For *me*?'

'Yes, darling, for you. Wanted to leap out and say boo and charm you, I expect. You're the only other one who's always early. He was waiting for *you*. A joke. He wanted to play a joke. Fancy him waiting for you. You've got a major fan there.'

Despite herself, Rachel laughed.

'What is it he wants you to know he'll never tell?'

Ivy's expression changed, fleetingly, and then she grinned.

'He knows my dark secret. He hangs around. He saw me,' here Ivy put her hand to her brow in a gesture of profound and dramatic shame, 'pinching the stationery. Yes, I confess it, I also pinched a pen. And do you know *his* sad secret?'

'Nope.'

'He wants to be a . . . model.'

There was a sudden common vision of sad, slack Norman standing on the podium with no clothes and everything pointing down. Cruelly, they both laughed. *I don't believe you* still echoed in Rachel's mind, but she laughed and searched for oblivion via Chardonnay.

Donald watched them go. He nodded to Blaker across the road. Blaker made a thumbs-up signal. ID confirmed. *She's going to kill him, and she has someone to help her.* Well, God help the poor sod, with two furies like that after him. Donald could no more have tried to split up those two than he could have climbed Everest, and it had never been his intention. All he had done was gone in and enquired if a model of that name worked at the college, to be given the information that yes, she did, she would be here later; and then he had gone away, and come back just to get a look at her, and he'd been lucky in that. Rachel Doe being there as well had surprised him. Were they inseparable, as well as living together? She didn't look like a dyke, Miss Doe, but you never could tell. What kind of a bitch was it cosied up to a man and his ex-wife, and pretended to the man she didn't know where the ex-wife lived? For what?

The depth of Donald's wife's friendships with other women never failed to surprise him. Women, it seemed to him, would do anything for one another when push came to shove. It was what made them so radically different to men. Men had limits.

Better get along and keep his appointment with the judge. Sorry about the lateness of the hour, sir, but I've got to be doing this in my own time now. There's another panic on.

Thank you, said the judge, I appreciate it.

But I bet he won't listen to me. I must temper what I say, keep it to facts and questions.

Such as why does your wife want to kill you, and who is it who is going to help?

It looked like Rachel Doe. Shame about the evidence.

Chapter Eighteen

It was a long haul out to the judge's flat on the rail link. He'd said he didn't mind how late it was. Up to him, really.

When he got there, getting himself into the citadel in the darkening light was bad enough, and once through the front door, it was refreshingly untidy. It turned out that Sam was using the living room to spread out his packing for a week's holiday. The severe lines of the place were improved by washing hanging over the balcony. Carl led Donald in, smiling welcome.

'Don't you have a home of your own to go to, Donald, working these hours? Come in, come in, have a drink.'

'Yes, I do have a home, but my wife usually takes the daughters on holiday this time of year. Sun and sand's not for me, so I've got all the time in the world.'

'My good fortune, then. I'm honoured.'

'Maybe not, sir. I'll have a beer please.' He pointed at a pile of shirts on a chair. 'Is your boy expecting his clothes to be ironed by the time he comes home?'

'Probably. The worst of it is, he's probably right.

Donald nodded, understanding. They sat with ice-cold beer, relatively at ease and quite pleased to see each other, apart from the business in hand. Pity it wasn't social, maybe another time. The world would be a better place if judges and coppers drank together.

'I've found the man who sent the e-mail stuff. It *was* Blaker, the man I told you about who knows your ex-wife. I haven't arrested him, there's no official admission, and he's a poor sick creature.'

'Is he the one who got into the office at my chambers?'

The beer was Belgian and delicious, if only he wasn't so tired. Donald had been dreaming strange dreams recently, instead of sleeping. Might be sickening for something. Felt poorly since Sunday night.

'No, I don't think so, or at least if he was, I don't think he was alone. I think that was someone else. Possibly someone with a cleaning crew.'

Donald was making that up, but it sounded plausible, and it was what the other team were working towards. 'I don't know about that, but it's the motive behind the whole thing worries me. Blaker talks to me; he might talk to you if I ask him nicely, and for a reason which might surprise you. He seems to be genuinely worried for your ex-wife . . .'

'Ivy.'

'For reasons beyond my understanding, he's worried about her.'

Carl was silent. Donald took a slug of his beer. The second mouthful was never quite as good as the first.

'Blaker sent the e-mail stuff because Ivy's not so hot on that, although I reckon she was standing over him in the art college where she works, part-time student and model, maybe tore the stuff out of books. Blaker's not fond of you because you sent him down, and Ivy, well, she doesn't like you at all, to put it mildly. Blaker thinks it goes way, way beyond that. Now, sir, could you help me out here and just tell me about your relationship with your ex-wife? Begin at the beginning, it's always easier.'

Carl had left his own beer untouched, listening intently, thinking up an answer which would be both honest and brief.

'Once it was good, in the very beginning, passionate and absolutely hair-raising, then very bad. It would have fallen apart even if my daughter hadn't drowned. I haven't seen Ivy since before we divorced. I settled money on her. She's never asked for anything more.'

'I know about you shooting the swans; your boy Sam told me about that. He also told me his mother mistreated him.'

'He probably thinks I do too. What a trustworthy boy he is. I'm afraid she did. She hated me then, blamed me for the death and especially for the swans. That bit's really too complicated to explain, but she blamed Sam even more for just about everything, for throwing stones, for his very existence. She'd already been experimenting with drugs before the accident . . . making up for stolen youth, poor thing. Ivy's an obsessive personality, she does nothing by halves, and then grief made her go over the edge. I couldn't blame her, or reach her, poor thing, but she was very cruel to Sam, hurt him quite badly.'

He swallowed. 'Poking, pinching, slapping. Took me a while to notice him cowering away. He couldn't say; believe it or not, he was dangerously asthmatic and a deeply introverted boy. I lost count of the times I took him to hospital. Ivy was often out, or out of it. It got to the point where she simply couldn't be left alone with him. She took away his inhaler, she could have killed him. That was the last straw. I got her committed on to a treatment course. She ran away once or twice. Then I couldn't let her come home.'

'So you shut her out.'

'It was her or Sam. He was ten years old. What would you have done?'

Donald got out his cigarettes, and crushed an empty packet.

'I don't know, but if you don't mind my saying so, you could have mentioned some of this at the beginning, because personally, a violent ex-wife is the first person I'd think of when it comes to death threats. I asked you if this could be something personal rather than professional, some woman scorned or whatever, and you said no.'

'Donald, if you haven't seen your ex-wife for nearly a decade, and you know she's turned out all right because you've been in contact with her parents, you don't actually imagine she'll come back out of the blue and send vile messages, especially if she's not exactly literate. She wasn't bad, she was mad, and she surely came to know that. Yes, I know she hated me, and I gave her cause, but she made an alternative life, and hatred dies, doesn't it?'

Donald was patting his pockets, looking for the other packet of cigarettes. He had never been able to stand waiting in a street without smoking a cigarette. The last one had made him light-headed; he really did not need another.

'No, sir. You're way too rational. Hatred doesn't always die. Most of the time, yes, but other times it grows and grows until it becomes all-consuming, people feed off it. Supposing she blames you for everything that happened in her life, the whole mess she made of it was because of you, and the only way out of the mess is revenge. Remember *miasma*. No honour without revenge, the soul rots without revenge. Supposing she thinks you deprived her not only of her daughter, but also her son, and you remain the sole barrier, to what? To him loving her again, to her feeling, how can I put it, *whole*? Back to what she was, with a clean slate?'

Carl walked out of the room and came back with another beer.

'Thanks. It's OK, I'm not driving.'

He felt he had to say that to a judge.

'Sam's the barrier to any reconciliation,' Carl said. 'Not me. As for the rest, with the greatest respect, Donald, what you've said sounds a bit psychobabbly to me. And how does she get her revenge, her *liberation*, by simply making me feel foul with a few futile gestures? What does that show about her feelings for Sam? It certainly doesn't help Sam to hurt me. And why is this man Blaker worried about her?'

Donald wanted to down the beer in one. He deliberated briefly about doing it, and then did it anyway. It was strong stuff.

'Blaker says she wants to wound you. Literally. The e-mails are only to prime you, make you frightened, sort of flush you out into the open. She knows where you are, she knows where you live, even though you've tried to duck and dive for the last few years.'

'*Sam's* tried to hide both of us for the last couple of years. He doesn't want to remember and I don't want him to either.'

'Well, it looks like you. Blaker says he thinks she's enlisted some help, some real muscle apart from him. And she's been practising . . . techniques. Blaker thinks she wants you a dead judge, soon.'

It was Carl's turn to toss back the beer, very quickly. He stood up and paced over to the balcony.

'For God's sake, this is ridiculous. Enlisted help? Ivy can't have much money, unless she's found someone rich. Hitmen don't come cheap. And what could she do on her own? She's a woman. And WHY?'

He stopped short of the balcony and laughed, briefly. 'Maybe she thinks I've still got money, but I sold the house, for God's sake, Ivy got her share, it all went on treatment and whatever. No, they can't think that.'

'Money's the root of all evil, Carl. And who said anything about a hit*man*?'

'Money never meant much to Ivy, and whatever her parlous mental state, I don't believe she could ever carry out a plan to do serious harm to me. She's essentially incredibly kind, and anyway, it would take such *nerve*.'

'Unless she practised,' Donald murmured.

'What did you say?'

'Practice,' Donald said. He was suddenly a bit dizzy and felt awful. 'Dress rehearsals for murder. Have you noticed, everyone gets it in the neck? The man in the office, the man in the ambulance, poor old Blaker. The man off the coast, who'd been staying with them, seaweed all round his neck. A girl bitten by a bloody swan. Always the neck.'

The beer and the earlier drink had finally gone to his head. He realised he was mumbling and incoherent. Bloody Belgian beer, too strong, and himself feeling tearful and stupid. Just as well the judge wasn't listening, because this was a pathetic performance, moving into the realms of conjecture and nightmare he had been hoping to avoid, the same nightmares which ruined his sleep. Carl was still pacing around, making him feel dizzy. Donald sat up straight and tried to control himself. There was another beer in his glass.

'Listen,' he said, 'I agree with you. Bloody women. Fit for

nothing. Murder's a man's job. But what would you do if you were determined to get away with it? Practise. I bloody would. And I wouldn't be worried, Carl, if I hadn't seen already what she might be able to do. I've seen it with Blaker, just like you have with your son. Only he was little then, wasn't he? You've been warned, that's all. Suggest you alter your route to work. And Sam's not your son, is he? He doesn't look like you.'

He still wasn't listening. Donald was looking at the washing hanging around, and it made him feel sad, at the same time as realising his chin was on his chest, and he wanted to blub into his beer, and that he liked this man, very much, he was a good mate and a good dad, which was what counted in the end. It was the washing did it, fucking washing. A man ready to iron clothes for a boy who was not his flesh and blood.

'This is very kind of you,' the judge said, still at the end of his first beer, the bastard. 'If a little extreme. Ivy always fantasised. It's a way of dealing with impotence and frustration when you can't analyse facts. And if she's been fantasising about revenge to a friend, playing with the idea, so be it. As it is, fate's intervened. I think the end may be in sight. There's another way round it. I have been hiding, but I'm not any more. I'm doing the right thing for once. I'm going to meet her parents at their farm on Saturday. Try to bury the bad news of I don't know how many years. See my dad's best friend. My dad was Ivy's father's hero. Difficult to imagine, isn't it, that a German prisoner of war, ten years older, could actually be the soul of glamour. An exotic foreigner, my dad was. Ivy adored her dad. Her dad adored mine. Anyway, I'm digressing. If Ivy's got a bee in her bonnet, I'll find out from them, see what it's all about. If these puerile threats are a plea for help, we'll get the help. Head off trouble. The situation will be defused, and I'm not a humble judge for nothing, diplomacy goes a long way. I'll find out what's up with Ivy, what she wants . . . Why can't she just say what she wants? Rachel was right, approach sideways, via Ernest and Grace, and it's absolutely the right time. Oh shit and damn. If Ivy's really sick, what about Rachel? What have I got her into?'

'You don't want to trust that Rachel, you really don't.'

'What else did you say?'

'Rashell . . . Dow.'

'No, not that. About Sam not being my son.'

Donald felt suddenly faint, the words difficult to articulate, and the judge was looming over him saying, are you all right, are you all right? When did you last eat, for God's sake, I'm so sorry, what an idiot I am, look, what do you think you need? And then Donald leaned over the side of the chair he was in and was gracelessly sick on the laminate floor, immediately better, but weak as a kitten. A long, hot day, and yes, he was hungry. Not much since morning, and far too stressed out and sad to be the inefficient bearer of bad news, even before he got as far as Rachel Doe, and he wasn't going to elaborate on that, and he felt hollow. A hollow man, from his toes to his head. Not good in heat, with only an empty home to go to, and the long-forgotten remnants of a West End doner kebab, still doing damage.

He was left in his chair, drowsing, until a cheese sandwich appeared on a low table by the side of his chair, where a glass of water had materialised minutes earlier, and the sick efficiently removed, so that there was not even a sniff of it. His feet were propped up on a low stool. The judge would make a good wife. Donald wolfed the food. It was like an injection of adrenalin, normality, everything, and left him still awash with the seedy sediments of sentiment. That bloody washing hanging around, that was what did it. Like just before a holiday at home.

'Look, it's late,' Carl was saying. 'You're really welcome to stay here, more than welcome, and I'd rather you did, you look awful, but what will your wife think? Can I phone her and say it's all my fault?'

'I haven't got a wife,' Donald said wearily. 'She died two years ago. Breast cancer. I just go on thinking and acting and pretending as if she's still here. It's the only way.'

'Ah,' Carl said, as if there was nothing wrong or odd about such a statement. 'And the daughters?'

'Oh, they're real all right. Flown the coop, keep coming back. Perhaps makes me understand some of this shit. I wanted to kill the doctors and the nurses when my wife died. As for the kids, if anyone had barred me from one of them when they were small, I'd have killed the bugger and gone to the gallows with a clear conscience.'

'Are you sure you haven't got a nice gay son I could introduce to Sam?'

'No, sorry.'

'They tell me,' Carl said, presenting a snifter of brandy now that the matter of going or staying seemed to have been settled, 'that it's better if your wife dies on you than if she leaves you for someone else. I've always wondered if that was true.'

Donald thought about it and shook his head.

'Don't think so. I think I'd rather she was alive, whoever the hell she was with. Cheers, Judge. Do you want some help with that ironing?'

'No, you're all right there.'

He went into the kitchen and came back with an iron and

board, selected a couple of vibrant shirts. 'The hell with it,' he said. 'You're only an irresponsible, feckless boy once. OK, Don, you talk or sleep or whatever, I'll do his bloody ironing. I quite like it, as it happens.'

'You'd make some woman a lovely husband.'

'I'm thinking of it,' Carl said.

'And you're a Grade A dad. You iron his clothes and spoil him rotten, and he's not even your son.'

'Is that guessing or simple deduction?'

'Guessing. Allowing for appearances to be deceptive, of course.'

Carl was dashing away with the smoothing iron as if he was well in practice. If only his courtroom could see him now, they'd never be scared of His Honour again. His Honour, ironing in a wig, now there was a thought.

'You're quite right. He isn't biologically mine. My fault, and mine by default. Ivy and the horror of motherhood didn't quite gel. She was still a wild child herself. Went straight out of the cage as soon as Cassie was weaned, and as far as I know, shagged everything in sight. Hormonal madness, I think. Hypnotised by living in London. Went to her head.'

He folded shirts with quiet precision.

'Must have taken some explaining.'

'Yes. Evasion, horror, forgiveness, acceptance, and explanation, not necessarily in that order. The most novel explanation was that she'd been impregnated by a swan, all done by magic. I told you she fantasises. She knew I wouldn't walk away and she was more terrified that her parents would find out, especially her father. They never did. They would forgive her anything but that, especially Ernest, who was over the moon about the prospect of a son. Sam was convincingly blond when he was small. He's really quite dark and bleaches it all the colours of the rainbow now. He just got born, somehow.'

'And?'

Carl spread his hands.

'It was love at first sight.'

Donald was now thoroughly drowsy, with sheer, appalled curiosity the only thing keeping him awake.

'I thought it was always the woman who was left holding the baby.'

'Someone has to catch them,' Carl said lightly. 'Every boy deserves a father. And it's been a privilege and a pleasure. Maybe not the next bit, but most of the time.'

'You're a good man, Carl. Does anyone know how good?'

His eyelids drooped. A voice came from a distance.

'First on the left after the kitchen, bathroom on the right. Pyjamas on the bed if you need them.'

Donald hauled himself to his feet.

'Thanks, Dad. I needed that. What are you so fucking cheerful about?'

He was putting away the ironing board.

'It's not been a bad week, Donald. My son's happy, I've met a beautiful woman, we may be on the way to solving a big problem by peaceful means, and I think I've made a good friend. Can't be all bad, can it?'

Donald wanted to cry, smiled slowly instead. If he talked about Rachel Doe now, no one would listen.

'Speaking in my official capacity as a bodyguard, Mr Judge, I shall need to know your movements over the next few days. And I don't think you should go and see your in-laws all by yourself. It's never a good idea.'

'If you don't go to bed,' Carl said, 'I shall give you a good-night kiss.'

Donald hesitated, one last question hovering in his mind.

'Did you really *never* suspect that your wife was behind the threats? She was always artistic, wasn't she?'

Carl shook his head.

'Yes, of course I did. Then someone delivered a rat. A dead rat, remember? I was convinced then it couldn't have been Ivy. Ivy would never go anywhere near a rat. She's terrified of them.'

Chapter Nineteen

What was false and what was true?

Thursday was endless, moving forward in jerking movements, and there was no doubt about Ivy avoiding her. They were avoiding one another. A nice bit of bonhomie engendered through alcohol and cruel laughter, and then to bed, and she had lost her mobile phone again, somewhere in the flat.

A longing for Carl, a conversation with Grace, an avoidance of newspapers and discussions about scratches. Ivy repeating how sorry she was not to be going home that weekend, but perversely excited about the prospect of ten pounds an hour for a whole weekend cleaning out a theatre between productions, if only Clean Co. would confirm, and they had. Never mind how the story slipped and slid a little as they talked in the bar after the class; Rachel was not sure if it was an office or one of the bigger clubs, the Dream Factory, the Lotus, the Shadow Place or whatever. Ivy, briefly seen on the Thursday, first thing in the morning, glittered with unholy happiness, and Rachel could only pity the enthusiasm for earning three hundred pounds cash, which was what she herself earned in far less than a day. Guilt.

Carl phoned. It was becoming a habit, but the phone calls lasted an hour. Grace phoned to discuss the menu for Saturday, sounding sunny and carefree. Her father phoned to say the bathroom was almost complete.

Why should she worry?

Dear Diary, I know he's a good man. I know it.

The flowers glowed on her desk.

It was with huge relief that she drove out of London on Friday afternoon, the car on automatic pilot, Ivy further to the back of her mind, and a box full of goodies in the boot. As if to a family reunion to which she belonged. As if she ever would. Her small family never had any of those. Whatever relatives they had, Dad ignored. Rachel had always felt ignorant of the secrets of family life, always romanticised it.

The further she went from the city, the better she felt. Even the driving held no irritations, because it was a day when everything had worked and looked as if it would continue to do so, from getting up early in the empty flat, to moving unimpeded through the London streets on another fine, clear day which in itself seemed disposed to be helpful, to being able to leave work far sooner than she had hoped, to driving on roads which seemed to make space for her. Since this momentous weekend was arranged, she had suspected something would prevent it, and now it seemed nothing would. She was excited, the way she was the first time she went to the farm, was remembering the associations of pleasure rather than the darker side, determined that Carl and all of them would too. She had planned to use the extra time to detour to the sea, to borrow some of its energy, had left a towel in the back, but the urge to get there was too strong for that.

The countryside had changed subtly in a month; the slender branches which trailed against the side of the car as she turned down the narrow road to the farm seemed thicker and more determined, and the effect of plunging from light into darkness and then into light was more pronounced and exhilarating in this obscure road to a glorious place, making it seem hers and hers alone. She wondered if Carl would remember the way after so many years when he drove down tomorrow, and then thought, of course he would: it was unforgettable and nothing would have changed. Carl, stop thinking of Carl, and knowing full well that part of this excitement was wanting to see him again.

What would Ivy think if she knew was another recurrent thought. Rachel no longer knew what Ivy thought, told herself it was Grace who mattered more at this point. It was Grace who would carry it forward, and Grace was overjoyed with the chance. She would be there, setting the scene, ready to reconcile, smoothing everything, ready to embrace. If Rachel had doubts, and she did, many and various doubts, Grace on the phone dispelled them and treated it all like organising a small party, and it was Grace who said, nothing but good can come of this; there is no bad result, even if it's upsetting. And Ernest is so pleased. You are doing good things, Rachel, you are putting salve on ancient wounds, and I am longing to see you.

Except, when she got there, pulled the car to the side of the road under the shade of a tree about fifty yards from the house and walked towards it, it was all completely quiet. She walked round the house to the ever-open kitchen door and found it shut. The garden was tidy, the yard was swept, and there was no sign of life, not even the rattle of Grace's radio, no yell of welcome, simply an empty house. Rachel knocked on the door and tried the handle; nothing yielded or answered.

She stood back, shielded her eyes and looked up at the windows, which stared back blankly. The house seemed utterly dead, and the only sound which came to her was the humming of bees, busy round a lavender bush nearest the door. The sense of disappointment and mistake was almost overwhelming.

She could imagine the place the way she had never seen it, cold and uncomfortable in winter, with everyone locked inside. She looked up at the crooked chimney, at the mellow brickwork of the walls, which needed repointing, the broken gutter, smelt a faint whiff of rot in the air and remembered the rat, flung into the fire, and for a moment it was as if the whole place was an illusion and had never existed as she remembered it, except in her imagination, and the back door into the magic kitchen had never been open at all. No one lived here really. She shook herself, but could not avoid the feeling of how shabby it was, and how it was a place from which a teenage girl would have wanted to escape.

By now, she wished she had detoured to the sea. She was early, that was all. Perhaps she should drive away and come back, begin all over again, reverse the film. Instead she found herself trying to imagine what Carl would think, and how he would have seen it as a young man. Waiting there, rooted to the spot, she was also trying to reverse the clock on what she now knew about Ivy, what the life drawing class and the evasions so unwittingly revealed, a knowledge so negative and diffuse it amounted to nothing more than a glimpse of something savage which should be ignored, because who would not be so in Ivy's shoes, with Ivy's life, which had never been far from the endless, brutal cycle of life and death, nurture and slaughter which was the real business of life on a farm with animals.

Rachel went back to the car and fished out the towel and T-shirt she had left in the back, and walked in the direction of the lake. The day had grown hotter, the evening would be balmy; she would test the water and try at the same time to see the lake as Carl might see it, and then, when she came back, the slate would be clean, and Grace would be there and the house would take on the warm colours of its owners. Remembering the way as if she had done it a thousand times, already feeling the healing sensation of water on her skin, she halted at the last bend in the path, ready to savour the view, closed her eyes for a minute. When she opened them, she saw a new innovation, a large, hand-painted sign stuck on a stake, reading DANGER. KEEP OUT. POISON WATER. Then she could see Ernest in the near distance, crouching at the edge of the lake. He held out his hand to a swan which floated close to him in the shallows. The swan pecked at whatever he held in his hand and swam away gracefully. Ernest remained as he was, with the breeze off the water ruffling his white hair. It was a pretty sight; Rachel quickened her step and shouted hello. Ernest did not move; he was as unresponsive as the house. She came up behind him and touched him on the shoulder. He turned and smiled sweetly and vacantly, squinting in the sun, as if he did not recognise her at all. There was another stab of disappointment, then of anxiety: was he all right, had his memory gone, was she not important enough to remember, and was it too late for Carl to make any difference?

'Is it safe to swim, today, Ernest? It's me, Rachel.'

'Hello, love, lovely to see you. Do you know, for a minute I thought it was Ivy. Sit yourself down, girl.' He patted the ground next to him.

'Ivy's not coming,' Rachel said, wanting to remind him who she was. 'Not this time.'

'I expect she'll be here later,' he said.

He continued to pat the ground next to him, and she sat. Ernest gazed back over the water to where the swans and their cygnets glided towards the opposite bank of vivid greens. Rachel's desire for immersion in the water faded; she could not share the space with the swans, because of what she knew, and whatever the season of the year, she would always be afraid of them. Nor did she want to undress with Ernest watching, so she sat with him, trying to see the calmness of the lake and not imagine the sound of gunshot, the presence of blood and feathers drifting up to the bank.

'Lot of feathers earlier in the year, when they moult,' Ernest was saying. 'Not so many now.'

'How do you get them to eat out of your hand?'

'Practice.'

'Where's Grace?'

'Oh, she's making ready for the slaughter, or going shopping for knives, or something like that. She keeps leaving me alone just when I need help,' he said, sounding petulant. 'Ivy and her keep arguing about exactly what it is they're going to do. You'd think after all this time they'd know. They want me out of the way, and then she wants me there. Sometimes she talks to me, sometimes she doesn't. Bugger them.'

'Ivy's not coming,' Rachel repeated. 'She's working this weekend.'

'Is she?' he said, suddenly confused. 'Oh, that's all right then. Because Carl's coming, you know. Poor Carl.'

He snorted into a large handkerchief dragged out of his pocket with an effort.

'I loved him, you know. Loved the elder and loved the younger. Should have been my son. He loved me, that Carl, we used to love each other, down here, that Carl, poor lonely sod, never forgot it. We were boys, although he was a big boy, yes, very. Rachel's bringing him. That boy should have been my son all right, though it was only his father knew anything about pigs. And this lake. It's his lake. I want him to see it before they kill him.'

'Kill who, Ernest?'

He looked at her, puzzled, and then back out over the water. The swans had disappeared and half the lake was in shade.

'They want to kill Carl, sweetheart. And the soldiers wanted to kill him. They want to drown him here. Like Cassie drowned. Only the swans won't care, it's the wrong time of year for caring about anything. I told Carl he was wrong for never teaching his boy how to swim.'

He got to his feet, and Rachel did the same. He pointed.

'It never gets much deeper than eight foot. Only in the middle. If he wants to get away, he stays out of that. Goes towards the swans, not away. As long as he remembers he can't swim. When he shot the swans, he waded in, nearly didn't get out.'

He sniggered.

'She doesn't know about the rats. I got Vernon to collect some rats. Lots of rats from the barns, still plenty left.

Couldn't afford that poison, too much money. One got in the house too. There's rats on that bank over there. She'll not go near a rat.'

'Are you feeling ill, Ernest? What the *fuck* are you talking about?'

Rachel did not know if he was talking in the past or the present, listened to his rambling with increasing alarm. She was tempted to feel his forehead in the hope of finding evidence of a raging temperature, but for all Ernest's wholesomeness, she did not want to touch him. He shifted his gaze from the far bank, stared at her as if only just noticing there was anyone there, and then put his head in his arms.

'All this planning and practice,' he muttered. 'Makes me so tired.'

'Planning and practice for what, Ernest?'

He raised his head from his arms and winked at her.

'Doing away with the enemy, my dear. You always have to keep a weapon. You always have to do that. The soldiers are going to do it. Should always have been woman's work, so much better at it than the men, but so much more cruel. I'd just have shot him, more in sorrow than anger, you know, but that's not how they want to play it. They want him to know what it's like to drown. There was never any time for that sort of revenge in the war. My father told me. Better to kill them quick and be done with it. Besides, he'll be harder to burn if he's full of water, heavier to lift, too.'

He plucked a blade of grass, held it between his two thumbs and split it cleanly. Then he did the same with another, and wove the two together.

'Should be using a gun,' he grumbled. 'I've still got that old rifle left. The one Carl learned on with his dad; me too.

World War Two rifle, that; my dad kept three of them. Had to hide that one, so old no one noticed. Grace doesn't know about that.'

He turned to face her. 'When's Ivy coming?' he said.

'She's not coming,' Rachel said for the third time.

'That's a pity. Never mind. I expect she'll get you to help. She's good at that.'

He patted her bare arm. His hand felt cold and left a green mark on her skin.

Rachel scrambled to her feet, left the towel and ran back in the direction of the house. She wanted to run further away than that, back into the womb of the city, anywhere far away from the lake and the sinister ramblings of an old man. Kill who? Who did he mean, was he talking about Carl the elder, Carl the younger, had his addled brain gone back to the war, thinking of death and killing and drowning, not reconciliation, peace or the sight of a once-loved face? She was full of horror for what was in his mind; it couldn't refer to the present, it *couldn't.*

She drew breath near the house, slipped through the gate into the back garden, and there all was normal. Grace's car was parked at a crazy angle to the gate, there were supermarket bags in the yard, the kitchen door was open, and as she drew closer, she could hear Grace singing to the radio. She emerged through the door, bent to pick up her shopping, saw Rachel, dropped the bags and threw her arms open wide in a jangling of bracelets. The shopping seemed to contain a record number of plastic sacks and cleaning stuff, enough for a year.

'Gorgeous! You're here! I saw the car, and I thought what the hell . . . Oh darling, you came to an empty house, I can't bear it . . . how awful.'

Then there was the almighty hug, the sweet smell of her, one hand grabbing Rachel's loose hair, smoothing it, the other hand rubbing her back as if to make something better. Back to normal, the whole world spinning back to normal.

'Good journey, darling? Must have been, to be so early. Where did you go? Are you starving? Is it time for tea, can't be too soon for a drink, come in, come in . . . oh, it's so nice to see you . . . What's the matter, sweetheart? You look like chalk.'

She had to respond to the hug, she could not resist, but then her body went wooden. Grace held her at arm's length, studied her.

'What *is* the matter?'

'I've been down by the lake, listening to Ernest. Has he lost his mind, Grace? Tell me he's lost his mind.'

'What was he saying?'

'About killing . . . someone. He was rambling . . .'

'Oh, my poor darling,' Grace said. 'It was one of those moods, was it? I'm afraid, yes, his mind's been wandering all over the place. Overexcitement. It's because of selling the cows next week. Yes, dear, I'm afraid the decision's been made, sell the cows and keep the pigs. I've been trying to keep him away from the lake, but he keeps on going back. Makes him maudlin. Oh, I wish you hadn't been early and had to face that. It's all very tiresome. What exactly did he say?'

She turned away and bustled into the kitchen, tripping over bags. Moving about automatically, Rachel began to help, picking up bags from the floor and heaving them on to the table.

'None of it was very exact. About drowning someone in

the lake . . . rather than shooting them. He mentioned Carl . . . a rifle.'

Grace nodded understandingly. The kettle on the hob was boiling noisily, the washing machine hummed in the corner. The sinister images began to fade, but not disappear.

'Yes,' Grace said. 'That's the way it usually is, and it's not getting any better. Can you see now how urgent it was to get Carl here sooner rather than later? Before my darling husband slips his moorings completely? Seeing Carl might change all that, of course, I'm hoping it will, because most of the time he's entirely rational and normal. We went to the doctor during the week. Alzheimer's creeping in, but slowly so far. An early stage, still plenty of time for happiness. The mind goes back to the distant past all the time, can't hold on to the present.'

Tea was made in between her hurried but precise words. She cleared a space on the table with her elbow and put down two mugs.

'This really isn't fair on you, darling, when you've been such a complete brick. He's fine as long as he's away from that damn lake. I've got a theory that something horrible happened there when he was a boy, just after the war, when people would kill one another for food and horrible things were happening everywhere, something he'll never say, long, long before Cassie and everything else. It keeps coming up and drowning him.'

'Featuring Carl?'

'Yes. Carl who he always adored. Boy worship. The glamour of being *foreign*, all that shit. And whatever he said, darling, he's not talking about the here and now. I've told him Carl's son is coming to see us, coming home, but I didn't tell him when. He doesn't know it's tomorrow. Oh, bugger this tea, it tastes awful. Let's have a good stiff gin. You deserve it.'

'I thought I saw you in London last week,' Rachel said. 'I must have been thinking of you.'

Relief was washing over her, like a cool shower.

'Fat chance,' Grace snorted. 'I just can't leave him, but I'm telling you, lovey, when this is over, wild horses won't keep me away. Now, tell me all about Carl. What does he sound like? Do you think roast pork is the right thing to give him for lunch? Rather wintry, isn't it?'

There was nothing more comforting, more distracting than domestic detail. It banished anything fantastic. When Ernest came in, he greeted Rachel affectionately, as if she had never seen him by the lake at all. And then she thought, Grace is going to need Ivy and me and a grandson to help her through this. There had to be something good in the future for Grace, and that was all that counted.

And Carl would be free of his past.

Donald Cousins sat with Judge Schneider in his tiny retiring room off Court Seven, arguing quietly. Not quite an argument, but a sort of debate, slightly at cross-purposes, and with the inevitable gaps. Certain fictions had to be maintained between the best of friends or enemies; Donald knew this from having children.

The first fiction was that Donald was not a cunning, underhand bastard who took advantage of hospitality and sneaked around other people's personal documents in the very early hours of the morning, thus knowing the route to the Wiseman place from the road atlas which was open on the desk. He also knew the contents of the judge's last will and testament.

The other fiction hanging round Donald's Friday-afternoon conversation with Carl was that Donald had done nothing in the meantime except become reacquainted with the ordinary day job and its unrelated investigations. Under cover of that convenience he had discovered that Ivy Wiseman was on the books of several cleaning agencies, and her name featured all over the shop. The same researches, conducted by others, had her placed, possibly, at the back of the theatre where the man had been stabbed, as well as, possibly, in the office where the man had drunk bleach. There was no connection with the man in the ambulance in Leicester Square. The Wiseman name came up nowhere else, except as a peripheral part of that dead-end enquiry featuring the young man from London who had drowned in circumstances no longer regarded as suspicious. Donald had found this connection interesting, but did not mention it. Never mention anything to a judge unless you have the evidence for a warrant, and he didn't, even if the same judge had given him a comfortable bed.

The last of the fictions was that he was not worried, and that he did not like Carl Schneider very much indeed. He was not going to tell him what he thought of him, probably ever, but he would have liked the chance. You are naïve, and honourable, and pig-headed, and you know fuck-all about women.

'Two things, Carl, about going to this house in the middle of nowhere. Are you sure your ex isn't going to be there?'

'Yes. Rachel said. That's the whole idea.'

Rachel said, Rachel said . . . Didn't he know Rachel could be part of the problem? *Was* the problem? A cunning bitch, dyke or not. Carl was not going to be told.

'You're absolutely sure?'

'Yes. Ivy's working. Ivy never misses work, Rachel says.'

OK, Rachel says it. Donald believed it because Blaker had said the same. Ivy never missed the chance of work, matter of pride.

'OK, Carl. Good luck. Keep me posted. Families, eh? But what you don't want to do is fall in with what everyone says. Don't be a complete patsy, obeying orders. Be early, be late, be something. Take control.'

'Will you ever stop being a policeman? Are we going out for dinner next week, man to child-free man?'

'That'd be nice, Judge. I'll show you the real world.'

It was only several hours later in his empty Friday evening, when he returned to the police team which had done so much more to so little effect, because all they had unearthed was the fact that there were several people who had been present together at the scene of the theatre and the office, that Donald took advantage of their work after everyone else had gone home. Heads had been knocked together to get agencies and companies to reveal the names of their legal workers, their illegal workers, the lists and shifts of the non-cohesive casual labour they planned to use for the next three days. He studied these with interest.

Ivy featured on two lists as a regular and reliable worker, and on one she was booked to work the whole weekend, as she had done before. But this time her name had been crossed off.

Ms Wiseman, it seemed, had phoned in and cancelled.

Chapter Twenty

Supper was early at the house, just the three of them. It consisted of an assembly of cold foods, hustled together with limp salad, Grace saying it was too hot to do anything else. Ernest was in charge of the wine, the homemade variety with Grace's own label, which tasted as if it was made of acorns. Rachel did not like it much, but Grace was edgy, so she praised it all the same and Ernest filled her glass again. The second glass felt heavy in her hand. By the end of a solid cold pie, all appetite had gone. A scratch meal, without much of the festive feeling which had been present in the other meals eaten here. The effort was being saved for the next day and Rachel thought that perhaps this was what it meant to become a true member of a family. Eating the leftovers, like real family members did, and following instructions to hold back for guests. It could have felt like really being accepted, but it didn't quite. Grace said she felt tired, and blamed the heat; Rachel simply felt dull. There had been talk of maybe going down to the pub, but that faded. Ernest had to milk the cows later, on his own this weekend because the cowman was away. By tacit consent, talk of Carl was left until later.

The only cause for celebration was Ernest being so entirely himself, in full command of his memory, as if everything he had said down by the lake really was part of an ongoing dream he visited in that particular place and nowhere else. Ernest, at least, boded well for tomorrow. He was sweetness and light, talking intelligently of how he would miss the cows when they were gone, but really he was too old for milking at midnight, and he would still have the pigs. They could maybe develop the barn, what did Rachel think? There were grants for such things. They would simply do what the government wanted farmers to do, which was to cease farming. They could develop the lake. He talked of the future, and did not mention the past, as if food restored him to hope. He smiled at them both, looking for approval, particularly from Grace. She patted him on the head, and fetched his boots, and at about ten o'clock he set out to do the milking, as the last of the light finally fled.

Rachel wanted to talk to Grace about Ivy, but the tiredness seemed to mushroom between them into apologetic smiles; there was suddenly little to say, punctuated by awkward silences, without Ernest. Grace did not ask her about Carl, and Rachel did not say what she wanted to say, and it seemed as if Grace wanted her out of the kitchen. Grace was ashamed of being tired, so sorry, love, not like me, it's the stress, you see, and I've been so worried about Ernest. It's sometimes hard to be cheerful. At least I can be tired with you. It's just *this*. You being in the kitchen, like Ivy was, when he came back into the house without Cassie. Him coming here, it's like an anniversary, brings it all back. Makes me stupid and sad. I can't think of anything else. I haven't been sleeping. Let's call it a day, shall we? Tomorrow, well, tomorrow, this time we'll really be celebrating something, won't we, love?

'Tired' varied from flu-type exhaustion, to nice exhilarating tiredness after a long swim, to this kind of tiredness which was like amnesia, and felt like being drunk, although Rachel wasn't. Just tired, from anxiety and relief, punching from different sides and making bruises, tired from the effort of suppressing unease. She was glad to be back in her very own room, with a spray of lavender by her bed. It reminded her of Carl's flowers. She struggled to stay awake; she had a huge desire to phone him and say, It really is nice here, it will all be fine, then she fell asleep. Everything was taken care of, everything.

She was halfway awake, then dozing again, dreaming of voices and closing doors and the sound of an owl. Her eyes opened wide and recognised the clock by the bed, reading three a.m. Grace was shaking her shoulder, jolting her awake, her voice high with anxiety.

'Rachel, love, can you help me? Ernest hasn't come back. Sorry, sweetheart, we've got to put on our boots and go and find him. Sorry, petal, it shouldn't take long, he's probably fallen asleep somewhere. Come on.'

Grace was clad in a floor-length nightie and a very old dressing gown. She held out another one to Rachel. Rachel got out of bed and put it on.

'Boots downstairs,' Grace said. 'What a bugger. Sorry.'

They went down, down, down to the kitchen, which felt as warm as toast. Tired as she was, Grace had cleared it, and it was as clean as a surgery.

'Won't take a minute,' Grace repeated, proffering a pair of boots, which Rachel scooped over her feet. They were too big, her feet slopped around in them, and they were out into the night, the air chill after the kitchen, flapping along with Grace in the lead, talking over her shoulder.

'Wouldn't have bothered you, lovey, but it might be a bit difficult to rouse him by myself.'

'Does this happen often?'

'No. Once or twice.'

It was all different in the darkness; she would not have known the way. The path seemed smooth; Rachel followed, trying to keep up, infected by Grace's urgency. Grace carried a torch which wavered ahead, scarcely piercing the darkness. Rachel remembered the route to the cow barn and milking parlour as being a couple of hundred yards, tried to remember the layout of the place, wishing she had paid more attention, the cow barn first, the pigs and their stench furthest away, the hay barn to the left, and then the buildings looming ahead of her, with the milking parlour first, lit up like a ship floating on a dark sea. They drew close, Rachel stumbling and Grace sure-footed.

The milking parlour was empty. The well of the room, surrounded by the higher railings and stalls, was sluiced down, clean and wet, achingly silent apart from the hum of machinery. It smelled of milk and detergent and the lingering presence of animals, a factory at night, with all the contours stark in the harsh overhead light.

'Ernest!' Grace yelled.

She went through to the anteroom with the milk tanks, from which the humming sound came. Then she came back. She was trembling.

'Come on. Maybe in the shed.'

They went down the ramp into the cows' barn. Semi-lit, it seemed far larger than it had looked in daylight. The sweet smell of hay, silage, molasses caught at Rachel's throat. The standing cows stirred; the place was suddenly full of the subdued noise of shuffling movement, and all she could see was a series of enquiring eyes, resenting disturbance. Her feet moved awkwardly across the hay-strewn floor, clumsy in the boots. Grace shone the torch around the feet of the cows as she walked past slowly. Perhaps she thought Ernest had lain down with his beasts. Rachel kept close. The cows lumbered towards them; Grace shooed them away; they came back. Rachel could feel the presence of tons of flesh and bone ready to walk over them, mash them into the ground with the hay and the shit, and she wanted to scream. She clutched at Grace's sleeve. Grace pulled away.

'Don't be silly,' Grace said angrily. 'They're only curious. Where the hell is he? Come on.'

The cows were so close, Rachel could smell their breath. It made no difference that they meant no harm; it was the crushing weight of them. They reached the far side of the barn, facing open fields and fresher air. Grace paused.

'The daft sod'll have gone to say good night to the damn pigs. That's where he'll be. Come on.'

'I don't want to go there,' Rachel said.

The smell of the pigs was already in her nostrils and her legs were trembling. Grace turned on her and shone the torch in her face.

'Oh *come on,* Rachel love. Don't be so selfish. You really don't know much about the real world, do you? Do you want me to go by myself? If he's in there, we've got to get him out. What kind of daughter are you?'

She moved off, confident that Rachel would follow, and

Rachel did. There was another faint sound of humming as they passed the incinerator of which Ernest was so proud, heating itself at night, for what? The small box of stone radiated heat as they passed. She remembered it was like a safe containing fire, remembered the small particle of bone Ernest had given her. She was ashamed of her cowardice. It was all beginning to feel like a bad dream, and yet she was stung. *You really don't know much about the real world, do you? What kind of daughter are you?*

She stumbled again on the steps leading into the pig barn. Grace pulled at the great wooden bolt of the door, a piece of rustic efficiency Rachel had admired for its simplicity before she had been stunned by the smell. Pig smell, a reeking, penetrating, throat-filling acidic stench which clung to clothes and hair worse than any real filth. Such clean animals to stink like that with their own unforgettable smell and revel in the way they repelled those who did not love them. A pig was a pig was a pig. It knew what it was, and loved no one but its own. Rachel thought of Ernest, talking about pigs. Maybe he *had* come to talk to them.

'Ernest!' Grace yelled. 'Come on out, you daft sod.'

The pigs had none of the silent curiosity of the cows. The sows and the piglets in the ten pens, ranged five each side with the aisle in the middle, reared in their confinement and squealed and snorted. The long, narrow barn was lit by two wavering lights, which moved in the draught from the open door, and the light of Grace's torch, which showed the exit door at the far end and the contours of the metal pens, full of writhing, moving, stinking shapes, pushing snouts through the bars of their cages. They knew no reason for human presence other than food or violence. Someone was there to give food or take the babies away. Rachel felt a snout, protruding through a metal bar, making contact with her bare knee, and heard deafening squeals underlaid with a cacophony of grunting. She swayed on the uneven wooden floor, steadied herself on the nearest rail, and felt another pig nuzzling her hand, and she recoiled as if stung, her scream inaudible above the din, the stench of them making her gag. She crossed her arms and took a tentative step forward, telling herself, they're pigs, where's Grace, where's Ernest, this is hell, and why . . . are they always hungry? What makes them so angry? Why am I here?

She screamed for Grace.

Then it grew quieter.

'If you stay still and do nothing, they'll stop in the end,' Grace said. The voice seemed to come from a distance.

Grace was sitting at the far end of the barn on the step which led to the other door. The light of her torch played on her feet; the light of the building showed the glow of a cigarette. Rachel moved towards the light and the boots, which was all she could see.

'Just stay still, would you?'

The pigs shuffled, disappointed, resigned, grumbling.

'What I really want to know is are you going to help us?' the voice said. 'I thought you would; now I'm not sure. C'mon, darling, give us a hug. Everything's going to be all right.'

Rachel tottered towards the end door. The torchlight swung towards the ceiling. The pigs began to squeal again. She felt a fist connect with her stomach, and all the air went out of her as she stumbled over the boots and fell to her knees and stayed there, clutching herself.

A door slammed, far away. Everything was quiet. Someone was stroking her hair. She was crouched at the foot of the step, still curled. The torchlight played on booted feet. Not the same feet.

'Honestly, Rache, you're such a patsy. Fancy believing a single thing my bloody mother says. Or anyone else for that matter. But you do, don't you? Because it's all true. In a way.'

Ivy.

Rachel raised her head and stared. She could do nothing but stare and saw nothing when she did. She was crouched at Ivy's feet, saying nothing, doing nothing, listening.

Ivy lifted her, effortlessly, so that she sat on the step with her torso grasped between Ivy's knees, Ivy's big hands on her shoulders, pinning her down, and Ivy's hand on the back of her neck. She remembered that. She had a dim memory of when that was *nice*.

'Cat got your tongue?' Ivy said. 'Nothing to say? Well, I bloody have, you bitch. Who's been cosying up to my husband with lots of chummy mobile calls, then? You. Who's the one person I love best in the world? You. Who do my mummy and daddy love so much? Who wants to manage everything and goes in my room when I'm not there? You. Who's sorting everything out where I can't? You. Who's sicked some fucking policeman up on my doorstep, making old Blaker spill his guts, and you don't even tell me except by mistake? You.

'You were supposed to help, you bitch. You were supposed to *stop* me.'

Rachel leant back against her and nodded. The world and the stench of the pigs came back. There was no sound except shuffling, grunting. Ivy's granite knees increased their grip, forcing Rachel's arms to stick out in front from her hunched shoulders. She could see Ivy above her, adopting a pose.

Venus clutching a serpent between her knees. She wondered why she was not so surprised. Ivy the savage, what a nice word that was. She could see her own hands, resting on her own knees; she looked down the alley of the barn. Cows were nothing. Her head could not stop nodding. She was beginning to get the picture she should have got. Bile filled her throat. She hurt all over. Grace loved me. She said I was a daughter.

'So are you going to help us, or what?'

'Do what?'

'What I was always going to do. Kill Carl. Oh, sweetheart, you've been very good. You've got him to come here, do you think I didn't know? I've been practising to kill Carl for months now, ever since I found him. Knew I didn't have the nerve, not without practice. Animals are one thing, humans are another. You're not *supposed* to do it, for a start, can't think why. Killing the thing you loved takes nerve, you know. I've had to learn cold blood. They were all a waste of space, why not? They steadied the hand. But I've got to get away with it, which is all that matters. I'll get away with this now, and bring Sam back. You're my friend, Rache. You should have stopped me.'

Rachel bent her head. There was a *click* as Ivy lit another cigarette.

Rachel heard the sound of her own, controlled, admiring voice.

'You're amazing, Ivy. I love you. Who did you kill for practice?'

'Got in the neck, like Cassie? Oh, one by persuasion, a man who stayed here. He was awful, he had no respect, you know, couldn't swim as well as he thought either. Shit face. Carl can't swim at all. A man in an office who wanted to die, so I helped him swallow it. That one in the ambulance, had to be so quick, I just had to do it, so I'm ready and skilled, Rache, for the main kill. Nerves like steel now. Not quite sure of the method, sure of the nerve. Everything's gotta be learned. So, are you going to help? Are you with us or against us?'

'Does Grace know?'

It was a stupid question.

'Does Grace know what, you silly little thing? It was Grace wanted you here in the first place. Grace suggested it. Grace thinks ahead, see? She said dear Carl would like someone like you. Far less risk if we got him here and killed him than if I killed him somewhere in London. That was the original plan. Flush him out, scare him, kill him, as soon as I knew I could do it. But not good enough, do you see? Not after he sent back Mummy's letters and we knew he would never let me see Sam as long as he was alive. He'd stop Sam coming home to Granny, it would be over his dead body . . .'

'That's not true.'

She could feel the stirrings of anger. She could see more clearly now, wanted to explain, kept her voice low.

'It's Sam who doesn't want to see you. Carl's a good man, he'll do everything reasonable. He must be a good man, because he agreed to this. Oh, Ivy, have you thought . . .'

'So you admit it, you bitch. You've got into bed with him. Yes you have. You've fucked my husband, you've got it out of him. Well, you weren't quite supposed to do that. Christ, you've probably fucked my son as well. I've watched you, Rache, this last week, ever since you snuck out on the Sunday, you've been in some fucking dream. His number on your mobile, messages from coppers you don't tell me about. Quite funny, really. I should kill you now, but I love you, you know, and I thought you loved me. You're a thief.'

'I do love you. If you love me, let me go. Let me tell him not to come. Let me stop you.'

Ivy stroked her hair. She tried not to flinch from the touch, and failed. Ivy noticed.

'Oh no, my darling. Too late for that now. Things have changed, ambitions change, you said that once. I don't just want him dead, I want him to know. I want him throttled and drowned in the lake, and I want him to know, right to the last minute. Like Cassie did.'

'Why? Ivy, why?'

'Because it was all his fault. Because he killed her, and then he killed me. He shut me out and shut me away. He poisoned Sam against me, he made my life hell, he sent me right down to the bottom of hell. And when I got better, when I got to know he was a fucking *judge,* well, that was it. I tell you, Ivy love, it's like having a cancer eating at me, just knowing he's strutting around there, and I can't *live* knowing that. Strutting round in the big wide world, with *my* son. Not *his* son, my son. I can't live with that.'

Not his *son, my son.*

Ivy giggled. It was a horrible sound, worse than the pigs who looked on, quietly now, still hoping for food. Rachel could feel them breathing from the shadows of the pen.

'You'd better not tell anyone else I said that,' Ivy said. 'Ernest only wants Sam because Sam is Carl's. Grace'd go demented. Carl's fucking grandson is all he wants. Now, are you going to help or not? I think I know the answer. Ernest said you wouldn't. Grace said you would. She didn't know you'd fucked him.'

Rachel knew she was damned either way. Ivy was strong and Ivy was mad, and the pigs stank. All she felt in the semi-darkness was an overpowering hurt.

'Didn't I make any difference?' she said. 'Didn't knowing me make any difference? Didn't I make anything better for you, the way you did for me? Did I really not make a difference to that *cancer* of yours?'

The stroking of her hair had stopped. In the silence that followed, she began to hope that Ivy was pausing for thought. Ivy laughed. She laughed like a hyena.

'Of course you made a difference. It was through you that I could see what it would be like to have life without a curse on it. Not a care in the world, a father who loved you instead of wishing you were a son, no real losses, no mistakes, nobody's victim. Lucky you, no scars to speak of, just your pathetic little tragedies and pathetic little morals. I doubt if you've ever made any difference to anyone in your life.'

She laughed again.

'Although you'll certainly have made a difference to Carl's. God, you useless, innocent women make me sick. Besides, you didn't really love me. You don't know what love is.'

She bent forward and whispered in Rachel's ear, her breath on her neck.

'It means being willing to do *anything* for that person, *anything* to make them better. I would have done that for you, Rache, but you're not going to do it for me, are you?'

Rachel jerked her head away. She felt icy cold, but she could speak. She could open her silly big mouth.

'You're mad, Ivy. Madder than you know if you think I'd watch you kill another human being and not try to stop it.'

She could feel Ivy nodding, rocking, still gripping her and holding her still.

'Grace realised that. She said you didn't love us enough. Well, I'm sorry about it.'

She got up to her feet, talking as if to herself. 'Strange, isn't it, I can't actually kill you myself. I can only do it to men. Big mistake, you being here, but Grace didn't think Carl would come unless you were here first. Sorry about that. Shame you don't love us enough.'

Rachel did not move. She wanted to plead, she wanted to spit at Ivy, she wanted to fight, but she did not move. She felt a massive punch to the side of her head and sprawled forwards to the floor. The pigs began squealing again. Rachel was lying with her face against the rough wooden slats of the aisle between the metal pens, facing the curious snout of a huge young pig. They were touching distance.

'It won't hurt much,' Ivy said, almost sorrowfully. 'But the pigs haven't been fed today. Ernest'll come back in a couple of hours and let them out. He just has to press the button outside to release the traps. He said you were scared of them. Don't worry, they won't eat you until they've trampled all over you, you won't be conscious. Don't fight it, but then you never do, do you? You've never had to fight.'

And, as the final valediction, Ivy bent forward and touched her hair one last time.

The door slammed and Rachel heard the heavy wooden bolt slide across. It was the same noise she had scarcely registered from the door she had entered with Grace. Grace had gone out the same way as Ivy came in, her part in it done. Grace might have listened, might have waited behind the heavy door, made to contain an army of giant pigs, which moved about her now, sniffing hungrily. The stench at floor level was overpowering. Her head was thumping; she could feel the imprint of Ivy's fist and she wanted to weep, for everything. For sheer fear, for being hated and loved and betrayed and left to die like this, for what was to follow, until gradually, it was the horror at what she had done that paralysed her most. She had led Carl back to be slaughtered. She rehearsed in her mind all that Ernest had said by the lake, all the lies Ivy had told. How she had ignored what she really knew by instinct, again and again, for the sake of being loved. Ivy had tried to kill her father, Ivy had stolen his pills and inhaler, and she, Rachel, had believed her.

Ivy told lies: that thought comforted her for a moment. It could not be true that hungry pigs would eat a live human being; they ate processed protein, already mashed into pieces. That must be a lie – how could hatred be so extreme? – but she did not know if it was. *You don't know anything. Pigs eat anything.* There was a memory of a woman minced and fed to pigs.

Lying there, it was her own ineffectuality and awful grief which finally angered her into movement. No, she had never had to fight, Ivy was right, but she would fight now. She had to get out before Ernest came and released the pigs to fight over her. She got up and walked unsteadily towards the door, keeping her arms crossed and avoiding touching the railings on either side. As soon as she moved, the pigs squealed; if she stopped, they stopped. She reached the door, pushed it, found it immovable. Then she retraced her steps and went to the other end, accompanied by more racket. It was tempting to stay still, just to stop the noise. She began humming to herself to drown it out. The second door was immovable.

Wearily, Rachel sat down on the step where Ivy had sat, and kept very still.

Silence fell again. Then she was violently sick.

The supper she had eaten in Grace's kitchen spewed forth in volume, hitting her oversized boots and then the planks of the floor. It felt as if she was ejecting poison, and she heaved again and again, feeling the wretchedness of being sick, distant enough to wonder how her own small body could manufacture so much bile and junk from the small amount consumed. It was as if whatever she had eaten and drunk had trebled in volume and gushed forth in a projectile flow. Rachel watched her own emissions with objective distaste. Then she felt slightly better, as if she had at last done something positive. Ejected indecision along with the homemade wine, which had tasted nasty and sent her to sleep, making her biddable and ready for Grace. At least she had got rid of that. There was a glimmer of daylight in the cracks round the far door. It must be cold and bleak here when the wind blew; she supposed pigs made their own insulation. Pigs insulated themselves, pigs were clean, even if they smelt; they would not lie in their own shit. They lay on open slatted wooden boards, cushioned only by straw; the shit and the urine fell through the slats into the cavity beneath to be hosed and swept away, as and when. Not a task for a rainy day, Ernest had said. Dirty straw was swept away, also through the floor.

Rachel lay down and peered through the slats. Dawn was breaking. She could see the dull glimmer of liquid a few feet below. A lake of ordure. That was the way out. She swallowed. The only way out.

Ignoring the piggy protests, grateful for the extra light, which also added to the urgency, Rachel felt for the edges of the boards, looked for the joints. Went back to the other end, worked forward, looking for anything loose, trying to remember where the floor creaked most, trying to recall what Ernest had said about sweeping out the straw: he carried it in, he swept it not out, but down. Not a board in the end, a metal drain in the centre of the aisle. She tried to prise it open, broke her nails on the edge. Worked round, felt for each corner, tried again. Ernest would use a tool; she had no tools. She finally stood on one side of the drain, felt the other side lift slightly, grabbed it and pulled. It fell back, trapping her fingers and she shouted in anger, freed her hands and did it again, held it and danced round, put her boot in the space and heaved. The metal moved with a sticky sound, revealing a hole and intensification of the smell. Rachel paused, then sat on the edge of the hole, her booted feet dangling, her empty stomach heaving.

You've never made a difference to anybody's life. They really are going to kill Carl. Never mind you, you have to warn him. Even if it's the very last thing you do. All this is you own fault.

Rachel dropped through the hole, to the sound of enraged piglets, and sank into liquid manure.

CHAPTER TWENTY-ONE

She landed in a shallow lake of faeces and bodily waste and straw, mercifully upright until she began to wade her way, muck oozing over the boots, and then her feet were stuck as she tried to move and she stumbled into the filth, covering herself with it, trying not to breathe. There was life in the tank below the pig barn; she could feel something running over her arm, kept her mouth closed against the scream and waded to the side, watching the progress of small creatures scuttling ahead, swimming over the top of the slimy debris leading to daylight. Rachel reached for a beam over her head, the floor of the barn where the pigs were inaudible, and, hanging on to it, pulled one foot out of its boot, and then the other. Dense, fetid liquid squelched between her toes, but she could move. She followed the rats towards daylight and the stony surface of the muddy yard. Pure mud was good. There was something reassuring about the rats she had heard scuttling away. They were more frightened of her presence than she was of theirs. They were running away from her.

She stood by the side of the barn, not looking back at it, shaking her filthy, dripping arms, blinking in the light, breathing through her nose, not daring to wipe at her face with her poisonous hands and wanting nothing but water. Shuddering with revulsion, but free. She began to walk back towards the other barns, remembering that Ernest was due back to release the pigs and he might come this way, any time now. Ivy might have lied about that too; Ivy might only have meant to frighten her, but she would not wait to see. Ernest, she hated Ernest, the passive deceiver who let his frailty be used as bait. Grief was giving way to anger. She hated them all.

Rachel did not know a way back except by the main route, short of crawling through the fields on either side. If she saw him, she would simply run. Even barefoot, she could outrun Ernest in his heavy boots, and she thought, I could never outrun Ivy. Supposing it was Ivy who came back and found her gone and the drain open. Rachel stopped and looked around wildly, seeking shelter off the track. Somewhere just for a minute, to stop and think.

She crossed to where the incinerator stood, the hum of its engine only audible from very close, went behind it and crouched down in the nettles which grew at the back. From there she could see the track leading to the cow and hay barns and the house hidden a hundred yards behind. It was a treeless landscape, the hayfields flat after the last mowing, the trees only beginning where the land dipped towards the valley of the lake. Rachel thought longingly of the cows' trough in their barn. She would not be afraid of the bulk of the cows; she would shoo them away with curses to get in their water. Rank as it was, it was better than this.

She had the irrelevant thought that she could now see why

the smell did not matter to those who were accustomed to it. She would never in her life be as repellent as this, if she lived that long. If. If that mattered any longer.

Rachel ducked down. There was an advantage to being covered in ordure. She would merge with the landscape. It took several, itching minutes to be utterly sick of hiding. The filth was drying on her skin.

She had reached the dry stock barn and discovered her second good idea. Sanity was beginning to return, along with a slow-burning fury. She went into the shade of the barn, pulled hay from the nearest unbaled pile and wiped herself with it. Hay and straw kept animals clean. It would do for her. She plucked at more hay, rubbing herself with it. It scratched; she stopped, began more gently. So far she had not bled. Oh for water. The silence of the barn was soothing. A cooling breeze fluttered around it, echoing against the roof. Then, from nearby, she heard the sound of whistling, flattened herself in the shadow of a wall.

Ernest came into sight, plodding along the path, from the direction of the cows. He seemed entirely unperturbed. She watched as he paused in the middle of the barn and scratched his head, as if he had forgotten why he was there, uncertain of his purpose or his direction. Then he nodded to himself, looked at his watch, and plodded away again, not in the direction of the pigs, but towards the milking shed and his cows. Before leaving the barn, he moved to one side and fetched something from behind the drawn-back, roller-driven doors, and then, leaving the place as open as before, moved away out of sight, not whistling this time. He seemed so preoccupied, it seemed safe to follow. He disappeared into the milking shed. Closer, she could hear him calling to the cows. The thought of the cow trough and a depth of water receded into a dim hope. He was too close. Rachel was not afraid of Ernest out in the open because all sorts of dimly remembered lines were coming back into her mind. It would never be Ernest who did the killing. She settled back into the hay with her itching skin which she could no longer smell, and remembered a few things, all coming to connect.

Ernest never killed anything, was Grace's complaint, but Ernest could deal with the result. He could butcher a carcass, he could put it in his precious incinerator and reduce it to fragments of porous bone meal in a matter of hours. It took a long while to get the incinerator up to heat, he did not waste money. It was humming away, ready to receive the human sacrifice of Carl. That was what he had more than hinted at down by the lake, when his mind was not so much fuddled as clear. He knew Carl was coming; he knew his instructions, or if he did not know, he had guessed, he had watched, he had listened as Grace and Ivy planned.

She thought of Grace, dry-eyed, with a cold anger and something like bitter admiration. Grace the consummate actress, so full of love it could be dissembled and turned off, who had such generosity, colour, warmth and utter devotion to no one else on earth except her child. Had Grace meant any of her warmth, ever? Sitting there, feeling the insects in the hay, Rachel wondered if Grace really knew all about Ivy. Or if anyone ever knew all about Ivy. She was coming to conclude that she did. Grace was the diplomat, Ivy the warrior. Grace would use anyone, anything for that child. She could never love anyone else, except useful strangers.

For Ivy, Rachel felt a passionless hatred and primeval fear. She remembered the lines of her naked body, and all she should have known and sensed. She felt bitterly angry for being such a fool, for ignoring what she had surely sensed, again and again. But this was not about her. She rubbed the brown skin on her arms, and saw a bloated insect settle on her bare knee. She was wearing a long T-shirt which had been white when she went to bed. The loaned dressing gown was long gone. Rachel tried to think if she had abandoned it somewhere visible.

This is not about me, or my feelings. If I don't stop them, I may as well die now. I've got time.

There were so many places on a farm to hide and wait, and it was tempting to do that, sit it out. She could not tell the time by the rising sun, or work out how long she had spent in the barn, because it could have been hours. She remembered the clock by the side of her bed saying three a.m., and that was all. So by now it was morning, but not advanced morning, still early. Certainly plenty of places to hide, but none of any use, because Ivy would know them all. Rachel was the stranger here; she had no routes but the obvious, and if Ivy knew she was loose, Ivy would find her, long before Rachel could intercept Carl.

She roused herself. The main thing was to intercept Carl, for which she needed a phone. There was time; her gradually less fuddled mind, beset with images of Ivy, and Ernest, and Grace, and the contempt they felt for her, gave way to him. Carl was the reason for getting out of the pit. A good man, who had raised and saved a child not his own, travelling towards an undetectable murder by a couple of madwomen who blamed him for everything in their lives and wanted to kill him in some insane ritual which would somehow redeem them and bring back the dead. All of it fed by delusions and illusions. That this death would enable them to capture and bring home a beloved grandson for Ernest, resurrect Carl the elder, and snatch back time. They were primitives, nurtured on legends and myths, as if the century in which they lived did not exist. The sheer malice of the enterprise was as breathtaking as the delusion behind it. They did not live in an age where a boy could be suborned against his will. It did not follow from what they planned that Sam would ever love them; exactly the opposite. Would they wait for Sam to grieve for the mysterious disappearance of his father, and then appear with irresistible blandishments and condolences? They were not thinking at all. It was only revenge. They wanted revenge to relieve themselves of the curse of themselves.

And money. What dead Carl would leave, what he had promised, which would only take effect if he died. Money always played a part, but how did they think they would manage the business of getting hold of it? It was with an extra frisson of horror that Rachel realised that in their mad way, Grace and Ivy had come to believe that she might help them in that too, with the professional skills and influence in which they had blind faith, and she wondered, again with horror, what she might have been persuaded to do if their combined seduction of her had been completed, if it had gone on for longer, if her father had died. If she had been absolutely isolated, if she had no one to believe but them. She had taken the initiative too soon and what a terrible disappointment she must be to them, what a mess she had made.

She had a vision of Ivy appearing on Sam's doorstep in all her glory, offering comfort, love, condolences, apologies, a significant part in his future, with sweet-smelling Grace standing beside her. They would be utterly convincing. She could see poor, confused Sam stepping into their arms, dazzled by them and their style, just as she had been. He might not stand a chance.

Rachel was thinking calmly now. Logic came back.

The fact that the Wiseman plan was insane and impossible to fulfil did not mean that they would listen to reason. They were hell-bent on murder; Ivy had dreamt of it, rehearsed it, and Ivy would have her dream. Rachel believed that absolutely. Carl would be held by the neck until he was dead, this very day, unless she stopped it, and if they did not also kill her, they would implicate her.

The Polish cowman was away. There was no one within a mile. It was still early in the morning. Carl was due later; there was still time.

Rachel walked round the cow barn. Ernest had been there for half an hour. After that he would go to the pigs, perhaps, then he would report back, wouldn't he? Then Ivy would come hunting, perhaps. She walked back in the direction of the house, and into the garden. She was trying to think what she had done with her phone. She could see it in her bag, the phone Ivy must have held, looking at Carl's number, working it out, as if she could not already read Rachel better than she could read any book. Get into the house, get the phone and the car keys, get shoes to drive, phone, go. It seemed simple before she was in sight of the back of the house and took shelter behind a tree to watch. Then she could see it was impossible. The back door was open. The sight of that open door made her shake. She imagined the sound of her own footsteps, manoeuvring her way up those stairs, which would creak, barefoot or not, even if she could get past the kitchen or in at the disused front entrance. Even if they did not see or hear her, one of them would smell her. Her own stink would go before her. It would fill the place.

She turned back, and went down the other path which led to the lake. Surely they would not look for her there. She felt she could do nothing, and there was no hiding place from which to strike back as long as she was damned with this smell. There was still time.

The morning was mild, but not warm enough for bare feet and skimpy clothes, and she hugged her arms around herself. The lake looked innocently beautiful in the morning light, although she could not appreciate the loveliness of the water, only the sinister shadows, and the posse of swans, hugging the far bank. Even they held no threat any more. Anything which did not have the shape of Ivy or Grace was nothing. She jogged down the path, and saw by the bank where she had sat with Ernest the shirt and towel she had left the day before. She picked them up: they were damp with dew, but so clean she could have shouted with joy. It was like turning a corner. Rachel peeled off the filthy shirt and waded into the water.

It was icy cold, stinging the grazes on her feet, making her gasp. She waded further out to where the water was deeper, sank down and swam towards the swans, stopping after twenty strokes, which she counted, carefully, to see if she could feel ground beneath her feet. Ernest was right: only the centre was out of her depth, and towards the swans' bank, the ground grew shallow again, and she knelt in clean mud, scrubbed herself with her hands. Then she floated, pushing her hair back, running her fingers against her cold scalp, washing it cleaner. She knelt again, watching the roots of the trees stretching into the water, and kept very still for a moment. What was it Ernest had said, that he had taken rats to the lake? Ernest was the only person who told the truth. Ernest had a rifle.

She could hear and see nothing, swam back, stopped, scrubbed again.

She was not clean, but it would do. Now she could be positive. She was, at the very least, alive and kicking and out in the open. She was revived as she always was by the water, and the shaking with cold and dancing up and down to shake off the moisture and get warm. It did not matter that she would smell for ever.

Wearing the clean shirt and the wet towel tied round her middle, she retraced her steps towards the house, looking for a vantage point from where she could watch. One or other of them would leave it in the course of the morning, especially if Ernest came back with news of her escape. There would be a time in the next hour when she would be able to get in. She looked longingly at Grace's old car, parked near the back door. The keys for that were on a hook in the kitchen. She wished she had the skill to jump-start a car, do anything useful. She wished she had shoes. Even get to the boots in the corner of the kitchen by the washing machine.

Think. Think clearly, think rationally. Ivy and Grace would go nowhere else this morning. They would assume Ernest had done what he was told, and they would cling to one another and get ready. Even if Ernest had not let the pigs out, they would assume that she was safely locked away, to be dealt with later. It was difficult to second-guess their minds, but she had to try. They had everything they needed; soon they would begin to prepare a meal. Then Ivy would hide upstairs; she was not supposed to be there, it was Rachel he would be expecting to see. It was the thought of what he would think once they had got him inside with the wonderful Grace welcome and Ernest's handshake, what he would think when Ivy appeared. Carl would think, Rachel has led me to this. Rachel is Judas. That thought was unbearable. Judas betrayed with a kiss.

She wished she knew what time it was. Think, do what she should have done before, the obvious thing. Skirt round the place, go back in the direction of the lake, take the other track through the woods, cross the field, reconnect with the shady lane which led to the farm, go to the main road, stand in it until someone was forced to stop, get them to call the police. They would have to stop for a deranged woman using a towel to cover herself. Who would believe her, would the police actually come? She would say she'd been raped. Or better still, simply stand and wait at the top of the track, and intercept Carl in his car. Whichever was first. Grab a mobile and call his number, except she could not remember it, it was stored in her phone, not in her memory.

She stumbled back in the direction of the lake, taking a wide detour round the fields, moving slowly on bare feet. She wanted to be as far away from the farm as possible, in case of pursuit, but to get to the road she could see across the field in the distance. She remembered some of the layout of the land she had seen that second time, from the top of the hill. She lost her way, backtracked a bit and started again, hit an insurmountable hedge, then a field of wheat, waded through it and finally reached the road, where she walked back on the grassy verge towards the junction with the track. To call this a main road was an overstatement; it was a lonely country lane where something should come along every five minutes, but nothing did. It would, she was sure someone would. She was hobbling, trying to ignore the cuts and bruises to her feet, panting with effort, but faintly triumphant. She got to where she needed to be, at the point where the only vehicle access to Midwinter Farm met the road, where Carl was bound to pass and see her standing there with the frayed towel wrapped and knotted round her middle.

Then she looked down the narrow green avenue of trees sloping out of sight towards the farm, and there was his car. She walked towards it, staring at it, touching it to be sure. Unmistakably Carl's old car. She knew it from the colour and the unmended dent to the wing. He had parked it carefully on the bank so that it stood at an angle, leaving room for anything else to pass. He must have decided to walk the rest of the way.

Rachel groaned out loud. All that and the judge had outflanked them. Carl Schneider had decided to be early. Yet again, her own stupid manoeuvres had failed. She stood in the road and screamed his name. The hawthorn branches waved back in silence. There was not another vehicle in sight.

Rachel ran back towards the house.

There was nothing else she could do. If they were going to kill Carl, they would have to kill her too. It would not be worth staying alive.

Her feet gave out before her breath, a sharp stone from the recently mended potholes in the road digging deep into her bruised instep, making her wince and lurch to a halt, then go on again with a limping gait until she reached the front of the house, which gazed back innocently, that utterly hateful house which had once seemed heaven. The pain in her feet reminded her of new school shoes. She staggered into the back yard, where the kitchen door was now closed. Windows open, door closed. All quiet, as if no one was there, a faint echo of what it had been like yesterday. Hope sprang: Carl was early, they had gone out, Ivy had gone out hunting her.

Carl had been early, just as she had been; Carl had detoured down to the lake, just as she had done, they were thinking alike, it was all right.

She moved to the side of the house, where the little-used living room was, the windows almost covered in ivy. The room of the rat. *You know what happens to rats. The only thing Ivy's afraid of is rats.*

There was no one in that room. It was as disused as ever, the place for rats.

Rachel crawled through flower beds, round the side of the house towards the back door. Grace's car was where it had been before, ergo, Grace was there. The towel fell off again. She knotted it back, and moved slowly round to the kitchen door, ducking below the window, trying to think. Behind the lavender bush to the left of the door, she saw what looked to her inexperienced eye like an ancient rifle, hidden behind the buzzing of the bees, and then from inside she heard a bellowing scream.

'Where's Rachel? What have you done with Rachel? Where's Rachel?'

Carl's voice, pleading and screaming. For her.

Ivy spoke loudly, with calm precision, as if he was a mistaken child.

'Your lovely Rachel? She should be finished by now. She's *my* friend, you know. She's mine, she was never yours. She was simply there to get you here, have you got that? She hates you like we do, she was only the bait.'

'No,' he said. 'No, no, *no*.'

Rachel launched herself towards the door. If both of them were going to die, the most unbearable thought was that he should go thinking that. She hated Ivy like poison, hated her, hated her, hated her for what she had just said.

Everything that happened in this house happened in the kitchen. She should have known. The towel dropped as she went in.

There was a brief view of the tableau, before Ernest came towards her. Carl, tied to his chair by his feet, looking towards the door, one eye contused into a vivid bruise. The tying-up was improvised, not according to plan. The plan would have involved wire or rope, rather than Grace's old washing line, but Carl had been early. Carl looked at Rachel; Rachel looked at Carl. His eyes travelled from face to groin. She had lost the towel. Grace was on the other side of the table, panic in her eyes. This was not her plan either. She screamed like one of Ernest's pigs and put her hand over her mouth. Only Ivy was calm.

'I didn't know,' Rachel said, looking straight into his eyes. 'I didn't know, honestly.'

He nodded. It was his feet which were tied to the chair. His hands were free, spread palm upwards on the table. There were slashes to both his wrists, which oozed blood, quietly. Ivy had the knife. She seemed to need to explain, as if recounting her symptoms to a doctor. There was no tremor in her voice, no shaking in her hand.

'I wanted him to lose blood,' she explained. 'Make him weak, you see? Could have injected him with the tranqs we use for the cows, but this is better, isn't it? So glad you're on side.'

She seemed to be looking for approval.

Rachel turned to both of the two witches, standing either side of his chair, put her hands on her hips, spoke as if she was managing a financial strategy meeting, where she was supposed to be on the side of everyone. Nodding at them both, laying down the law.

'That's enough. That's more than enough. Let's wrap it up here, shall we? No more time. Strategy failed. This is nonsense. Load of crap. Just get him out of here, he's learned his lesson, he'll do whatever, give me the knife. I'll take him home, sort him out, never a word. OK? I'm on your side. Why did the silly fucker have to be early?'

It almost worked. There was a split second when it might have worked, until Ernest came forward and spoke.

'It's that Rachel,' he said. 'Got no knickers,' he said. 'And she smells. She's been fucking a pig.'

He stood up close to her, his eyes close and confused.

'She was supposed to bring Carl. Little Carl. You get rid of big Carl, that murdering man who killed Nina and Hans, and you leave the little one behind. Where's young Carl, then, where is he? Where's my boy? Where's my little man? You promised.' He wheeled round towards Carl, pinioned in his chair, stabbing his finger towards his face. 'Where's Carl's son, where's my boy?'

'He's somebody's boy, but he isn't Carl's,' Rachel said crisply, full of anger. 'Sam's her bastard. A glorious bastard, but not Carl's. Grandson of you, sweetheart, but not of Carl. You should see him. He's queer as a nine-bob note, with skin darker than a gypsy, and I tell you, to know him is to love him, but he isn't Carl's.'

Grace began to wail.

The kitchen smelled. The prevalent smell was roasting pig. Pork, sizzling in the oven, cooked early, maybe to be eaten cold. A bowl of apples on the table. The clock on the wall said ten.

'Well, time flies when you're having fun,' Rachel said with a gaiety which sounded completely artificial even to her own ears. 'I'll just go upstairs and put on some clothes, take this man away, and then you can get on with lunch. Or I'll take him for a walk and then bring him back if you like.'

The moment really had passed. Ivy shook her head sorrowfully.

'What, go and get your phone, dearest? When I've got it here? Anything else you want to say, you sanctimonious bitch? You BITCH.'

'Wait a minute . . . He's not Carl's boy?' Ernest kept repeating. He looked towards Grace, who was ashen. 'Not Carl's boy? Not my Carl's boy? Where is he?'

'Shut UP, Ernest, SHUT UP. Shut your stupid fucking mouth. Do as you're told,' Grace screamed. 'It isn't true, you silly fool. She's lying.'

'Rachel doesn't tell lies,' Ernest murmured. 'Not . . . Carl's boy. She did it with someone else. Not my boy.'

Rachel moved towards Carl. His eyes were glazed with shock, but he managed a lopsided smile. She put her hands on his shoulders and kissed his cheek. There was a length of rough rope round his neck. She bent down to untie his ankles.

Ernest grabbed her round the middle and dragged her away. Rachel kicked and screamed and over the din of her own screaming heard Carl calling her name. Ernest was stronger than her, even though his hands slipped on her skin. He dragged her out of the open door, and stood, holding her, speaking quietly as she writhed in his grasp.

'They don't need us, dear,' he said. 'They never did.'

From inside, there was another guttural, choking scream.

Chapter Twenty-Two

Ernest held her head down with the massive hand which was Ivy's true inheritance. Strength, without reason.

She could hear Carl's voice, low and pleading and choking.

'Whatever you want,' he was saying. 'Let her go, please,' followed by Grace's voice, saying no, uncertainly. I left her somewhere safe, Grace said. I left her locked in somewhere safe, it's her own fault she left. There were sounds of chairs being moved, and Grace saying, prosaically, I must turn down the oven, or the meat will spoil. Pork never spoils, said Ivy.

Then Carl's voice, saying, 'As a judge, I think I'm entitled to an indictment, at least, before sentence. What exactly have I done?'

'You killed Cassie,' Ivy said. 'You waited until she turned into a swan, and then you killed her. Then you drove me away and buried me alive. You sentenced me to death.'

'Your father made my husband love him more than me,' Grace chanted. 'You stole my grandson.'

'I saved him, Grace. And what about you, what is it you've done? You knew what your daughter was. You couldn't wait to give her away, even to me, Carl's son. You knew what she could do.'

'Shut up, Carl, shut up, shut up, shut up . . .'

Ivy's voice was cold and definite.

'You didn't try to save me, husband. You didn't love me.'

His voice was sad and resigned.

'Oh yes, I did. But not enough. I loved someone else more. I plead guilty to that.'

'Drink up, come on, Mother, give him the drink, hold his head. This is for Cassie, your little anaesthetic. Drink it all.'

There was an unbearable sound of futile struggle, coughing, spluttering, groaning. Then equally unbearable silence.

Beyond the door, Rachel stood trapped in Ernest's sexless embrace, with tears coursing down her face, sick with rage and weakness. After a minute, he seemed impatient with the tears, let her go abruptly and pushed her aside. The freedom was temporary; she staggered, blinded by tears, and then his arm was back round her neck, holding her effortlessly. Something cold prodded into her back. He was old, but a foot taller and still stronger.

'Come away, girl,' he whispered. 'Come away to the lake. They'll come with us. Let them do what they must.'

Grace led the way out of the house. Carl followed with the noose round his neck, tight, loose enough to breathe and swallow without comfort. Liquid dribbled from his slack mouth. Whisky. Ivy was behind him, holding the end of the rope, like walking behind a dog on a leash. Then Grace took Carl's left arm by the elbow and Ivy took the right and they walked away, holding him close to their own bodies. It looked almost affectionate, like a convalescent patient supported by family. His face was purple, his breathing laboured, his wrists were bloody, he looked a sick old drunk and he swayed, but they held him firm and marched him forward. He did not try to resist. Primitive methods of subjugation, no training needed: rope, blood loss, alcohol, enough to make him incoherent, but not enough for the mercy of oblivion. That was the last cruelty. Rachel knew exactly what they were doing, and what they had always intended to do.

They walked and stumbled along in a macabre procession all the way down to the lake, the trio in front, progressing with efficient speed, Ernest and Rachel following behind. She watched Carl sag between them and wanted to believe he was shamming, and that in a minute he would find the strength to break free, cast them off and run back, but they hoisted him straight and on they went. Stop them, Rachel muttered to Ernest as he pushed her forward. He did not reply. Someone will see, she said, someone will come. No they won't, he said, finally, I put up the notice and blocked the path. Rachel looked down at her own feet, and then watched Carl, willing him free. Minutes were the same as hours, but it was only minutes before the two women, by now more urgent in their movements, as if wanting it done, reached the edge of the lake at the shallow bank which was the easiest point of entry. Her own footprints were still upon it. The sun had risen in the sky; she was cold to her bones, yet slippery with sweat, and the gun poked bruises in her side, and she was trying to think and all her effort went into breathing.

They were going to drown him, and he would know what was happening. Ivy would lead him into the lake, push him under the water where it got deep, hold him there. She had the nerve, she had the killing practice, she would not falter now. She had not faltered when she took the vital medicines from Rachel's father's pockets. Again Rachel was full of rage and struggling. Ernest held her back, twenty yards from the lake, close enough to watch.

The movements of the women by the bank were almost graceful, as if the ritual were rehearsed and dignified. Ivy left Carl to Grace and stripped out of her own clothes. Then all three of them, Carl in the centre, waded out into the water, still holding him. At waist height, Grace let go and came back, while Ivy relinquished her grip and twisted the tail of the noose round her arm before wading forward again, yanking it. Carl's whole body jerked; he stood uncertainly; she pulled again and he floundered, bellowing like a wounded calf and coughing. The water was level with Ivy's chest when she yanked the rope again. Her strength was awesome and his weakness awful. Rachel thought of Ivy naked, savage and . . . afraid. It was eerily silent now, only the lapping and splashing of water. It was only deep in the middle, shallow round the edges, a muddy pond for drowning. A little deeper and she would pull or push him under. Or leave him. Ivy pushed him. He sank out of sight.

Ernest took a deep breath. He was whispering something, *Get them apart.*

Rachel tore herself out of his grasp and ran towards Grace, cupping her hands round her mouth and screaming at the top of her voice, 'Ivy! Look out! There's RATS, Ivy! Thousands of rats, LOOK OUT. They're coming for you from the bank, LOOK.'

At the same moment Ivy turned to look, a single swan appeared from the shadow of the far bank, speeding towards the noise. It seemed to bear down upon them fast, wings arched over its back. Carl rose to the surface in its path and sank, choking.

'Rats!' Rachel screamed. 'Rats, rats!'

Ivy was looking towards the swan, listening, reacting. She dropped the rope and half swam half waded back towards Grace. Rachel ran in a straight line through the reeds blocking the nearest edge of the water, well away from them, and splashed in, swam towards the form of Carl thrashing in the deep centre. The strokes felt like slow motion, swimming through treacle with arms like lead, until she reached him.

He struggled as if wanting to pull them both under. She remembered slapping him, stunning him, then holding his head free of the water, kicking back furiously to tow him out of the deep. Not far, she told herself, not far, only a small lake, remember how small, it isn't the sea. Then they were there; she could feel muddy ground beneath her feet. Put your bloody feet down, Carl, yes you can. She looked back and saw Ivy, standing alone in the water, shouting, NO, NO! Then Rachel was holding him up in the reeds, with his body slumped against hers, cursing him, as she heard the sound. That great booming blast of gunshot, echoing away, and then Grace screaming, and Rachel looking back again, and Ivy no longer there.

She would never be able to remember later how she dragged Carl through the obstructive weeds and on to the bank with his heavy body and heavy clothes, or how her nerveless fingers fumbled with the rope which had swollen tighter round his neck, or when it was she realised it was not so much a noose as a simple halter for a bigger beast than he. Or at what point it was, as she began to chew at it with her teeth, listening to his breathing, that someone came to help, or even who that someone was. It could have been Ernest with his knife, sawing through the halter knot; it could have been anyone. It was simply herself and an unknown man who were slapping Carl on the back, making him spew forth pond water and whisky like a fountain. She heard a voice saying, You gotta learn to swim, Judge, and then the same someone told her to sit with her head between her knees, which she did, until she looked up, and wished she had stayed staring at her own muddy groin.

He was strong, old Carl, he got better quick. Donald Cousins rarely acted on instinct unless his sympathies were thoroughly engaged, which they were, and unless it was a bright sunny day, which it was, and unless his conscience really troubled him, which it did. They might even give him something to eat if he got there by noon. Rachel Doe might be a bad girl, and a dangerous combination with Ivy Schneider, but at least she was a professional woman and would exercise caution if he was there. It was the likelihood of the two bitches together in a remote place with the judge which scared him. The old folks didn't count. Two conspiring women did.

He had followed the map and found an empty house, a kitchen smelling of roasting meat, and followed the small spots of blood and his nose. When he came upon the famous lake, he saw from a distance a woman and a clothed man apparently frolicking in the water, moving away from a tall, naked woman, whom he recognised, standing alone with only her feet in the water, shrieking at a swan. A scene of bacchanalia, everyone having fun, no problem at all.

Then he saw an old man raise a heavy rifle and shoot away at Ivy Wiseman from the close range of the bank. He didn't need to have much of an aim to hit a target as near as that, only a few feet, and a helluva blast. The noise was eerie, it bounced about longer than the screams.

Donald ran full tilt towards the old man, and it was as if the old man could hear the vibration of his footsteps as the echo of the murderous sound died away. He turned and pointed the barrel of the gun at Donald's chest.

'Go and help Carl,' he said, gesturing with the gun. 'I can't do this twice.'

Donald would write in his notes later that the old man had a firm grip of the rifle, even though he was weeping and seemed bewildered. At that time, he was only glad that he had brought his mobile and knew the map reference. He was way out of his depth here.

What Rachel remembered later was that they left her alone. That Carl came to his senses far sooner than she, and that he and his friend left her where she was, sitting mostly naked on the bank, and then, not so much later when she stood up, she could see all of them, except for Ernest, pulling the body out of the water. She did not notice the rest of them, except for Carl, sitting on the bank, cradling his dead wife in his arms as if he could not let go, with the crater of a wound in her chest soaking blood into his wet shirt. She was still his wife. The whole posse of swans watched from the centre of the lake.

An ambulance and a police car were rocking down the track. Men appeared, hitting the ground running. Rachel thought, numbly, of being naked from the waist down.

Grace and Ernest stood together as she approached. They, too, were still married. Grace was pale and angry.

'You bitch,' she said to Rachel wearily. 'Why did you tell him it wasn't Carl's son?'

'Not Carl's,' Ernest said. 'Not mine. Bad girl.'

Rachel saw that the rifle lay on the ground where it had been flung. Ernest turned to Grace.

'I forgot to feed the pigs,' he said.

She had eyes only for him now. Eyes only for what was left.

Rachel needed clothes. She did not need recognition. No one noticed as she walked the hateful route back to the house. Ivy was the focus. Passing through the kitchen, she turned off the oven, as Grace would have done. She went upstairs to the room with the lavender by the bed, found her trousers and shirt and car keys. Her feet looked like swollen balloons. She forced them into her sandals, and then, summoning up her last reserves of strength, walked back out of the house for the final time and left.

Driving away was the easiest part. She could drive on automatic pilot. The first hour passed without her noticing. As she got closer to London, instead of going home, she detoured north, following signs for the motorway to Luton.

It was high time she visited her father. She needed him, very much, and that was all he had ever wanted. He was wiser than her after all.

The last image was Carl, holding his wife, trying to coax her awake.

Chapter Twenty-Three

By the end of August, six weeks later, the long, hot summer had finally died.

'Never a good idea to run away,' Donald said to Rachel. 'But I can see why you did.'

'I didn't run, I drove, Don. And I made it easy. I left my phone. I let you know where I was.'

'Very useful it was too. You know what, Rachel? I think you were thinking like a man. It's this awful control and time management thing blokes have. If they've done all that could possibly be done in the circumstances, and nobody needs them at the moment, they tend to fuck off. I used to do it with my wife, before she told me what I was doing. What could I do about her giving birth, for instance? Sweet nothing. I went to the pub. You've lost a bit of weight.'

'Did I ever tell you, Don, that the one thing I loathe and despise is someone telling me they know what I think. Or they think they know what I think.'

He was very cheerful indeed today, at his most irritating.

So he should be, he thought to himself, for being someone who had redeemed a failing career by solving a murder or three by complete accident. On the back of other tragedies, for sure, but never mind that for a minute.

They had advanced, in the first few hours, only as far as her preferring him to anyone else, and how had he done that? Her dad liked him, and he liked her dad. One look at a dad like that, and you knew what she was about. Smashing kitchen he had. Donald became her interrogator of choice, the only one she would talk to, and she had, in police speak, been very helpful.

'My daughter,' Donald said, 'wants to be an accountant. Get rid of the going-nowhere job. Will you talk to her?'

'She's only twenty. Tell her she needs her head examining. Tell her to go and see the world. And tell me what's going on.'

It was he who found her, *not Carl*, and it was he she would rather have round her shambolic, searched-from-top-to-bottom flat. Such a haul, they had, but only from the one room, which was good for her, not so good from the point of view of anyone else who would have preferred the murders to be a conspiracy with two glamorous dykes in the frame rather than a single oddball divorcee who hated her husband so much she went into training to kill him. Donald would have liked to have told her quite how much he had deflected away from her, but he did not have the heart, and besides, she already knew.

'Nice flowers,' he said.

She shuddered. She was good at that. She could shudder from her heels to her head, like a dog fresh out of a pond, sorry, perhaps better not add that to the list of things he admired her for at that point. He and his wife had a dog once. It died. He would get another.

'No charges,' he said.

In Ivy's room there was a bag. In Ivy's bag there was a garrotte and rope, a scalpel fit for an assassin or a barber, and on Ivy's scant supply of clothes an interesting selection of DNA. Then, courtesy of Rachel, there was the Plonker, and what he had seen, namely Ivy, testing her skill and nerve in the back of an ambulance. Then there was Blaker, currently safe and spinning his own story. Not a cat in hell's chance of him being a reliable witness, or a witness at all.

'It's all terrorism now,' Donald said kindly. 'We bury what else we can. So's we can pretend to cope. Things change.'

'No charges?' She looked relieved. 'Really? No charges?'

'Nope. Use your brain. Ernest Wiseman is a bit doolally, but not all the time, prognosis not good. When he's up, he's up, when he's down, he's down. Then when he's halfway up, he falls all the way down. Such as, the pigs wouldn't have eaten you, but then they would, then they wouldn't, that kind of thing. He's never going to be fit to stand trial or give evidence. Grace is a different ball game. She changes her tune all the time. Grace is totting up all the angles, fighting to survive. There's nothing she won't say or do.'

'And?'

He counted on luck as he recited.

'Grace said, at first, that you were implicated. That you set out to get the judge to a place where they could do their business, and you knew all about it. Just as you knew all about the other murders. Stop, don't wave at me like that, I know, I know, I know.'

She was smoking for England. They both were. The smell of nicotine was well absorbed by flowers. Lots of flowers.

'I got sacked, you know,' she said. 'Two weeks off work, whistle-blower to boot, you get sacked. It's pretty easy when you don't fight. And you know? I don't give a shit.'

'That's good. Always another job for someone like you. Sandra . . .' He stopped in confusion. He had just spoken his wife's name. 'Sorry, that just slipped out.'

'You mean, your wife would say it doesn't matter, and she'd be right. And I do understand why you do it.'

'No you don't. And when you say you understand, you should swallow the words. It's as offensive to me as me telling you what you think. Sorry about that. And don't go thinking you understand Carl, either. Not unless you try.'

'Point taken. I understand that my own tragedies in all of this are very small ones in comparison to those of everyone else. I am not related to anyone who was killed on Ivy's practice run. I am not dead or disfigured. My losses are minimal; I must think of others. That's the lucky story of my life. Tell me again why no one will be charged with anything.'

'Because it's better that way, although hardly justice. No charges unless you insist, and if you did, Grace is the only one in the frame, and she will pour shit all over you. And Carl. She'd say you knew all along, and someone will believe her. Beautiful accountant implicated in murder conspiracy. It'll do as much for your career as it will for the judge. Lovely media coverage. And again, there is this little matter of a lack of evidence. It's always the same when the prime mover dies.'

'Ah, I see you've been taking advice from Judge Schneider. An in-house expert on what'll work in front of a jury. How unusual. The victim as expert.'

She knew she sounded bitter. It was the aftermath of two weeks' solid crying. The crying had started as soon as her father had told her how he knew that Ivy had taken his inhaler and his pills, but had not wanted to tell her for fear of causing further offence. That he had known instinctively that Ivy was dangerous, but didn't know how to say. The pathos of that made her cry, and she had not been able to stop. She had grown to appreciate the safety of that little house in Luton, where the floorboards did not creak and the windows stayed closed.

'Grace *not* being charged with conspiracy to murder is, I admit, an absolute disgrace. But where's the evidence? And consider the spin she could put on it. How does it look? She's cunning as a cartload of monkeys, determined not to be parted from her husband. She is, for the sake of the defence argument, completely under the thumb of her psychotic daughter, who began on her homicidal track a long time ago. Ivy killed the pets before she was ten. Ivy's instincts were always there. She killed what she considered to be superfluous, just as Ernest taught her, because he hated to do it. Grace will say there was never any real intention to drown Carl. It was a game. Ivy wanted to make him suffer his daughter's fate, almost, but not quite, and then they would haul him back safely. Ernest, poor soul, got it all wrong. He wasn't told to bring the rifle. He was suddenly, irrationally devastated by the recent news of his daughter's infidelity, and went back into the past. At one point Ernest said he was trying to kill the swan, because it was going for Ivy. At another point he was defending Carl, like he defended him once before. Either way, it was spontaneous. It was a World War Two rifle, carefully preserved, and he hadn't shot a rifle in years. It was an accident he hit her at all, let alone with both barrels.'

'He must have known how to shoot once. He shot Ivy as soon as she was a clear target. As soon as she moved away from Carl.'

'I know,' Donald said. 'I saw. But then again, I might not have seen right.'

'And what about Grace locking me into the pig barn?'

'Ah well, the only witness to that apart from you was Ivy, and Ivy is dead. And you yourself washed away all the traces.'

'I've been scrubbing myself every day, twice a day, ever since. Please tell me there isn't a trace, and I'll make some more tea.'

Tea, the panacea for all ills. Donald liked his with two sugars.

'You were very brave,' he said.

'I don't think so. I did everything wrong. And then Carl was early.'

She liked Donald. He was easy to be with. He never once suggested that she had been a fool; he apologised for suspecting her, but added that it was just as well he had, otherwise he would not have arrived at all, to protect the judge from a pair of harpies. Nor did he say that he thought the end result was all that bad. One way or another, Ivy had to die before she killed anyone else, and it was fitting that she died where she did.

'Ivy told Grace about the other murders, and why. The man in the office, for practice. The man in the ambulance to see if she had the nerve. The man in the theatre queue, ditto. These poor people's families have to know the miserable nature of the motive. Practice.'

Rachel nodded. Another reminder that other people's tragedies made her own seem small.

'And the young man who drowned? The paying guest?'

'I don't know. But it wasn't Ivy who left the pub with him, it was Grace. They were supposed to be going swimming.'

She was crying again.

'You couldn't have prevented any of it,' he said.

'She wanted me to stop her. I didn't stop her. I just wish

you could have seen what she could be like. She was beautiful. She made life *glow.*'

'I know,' Donald said. 'Carl told me.'

There was a pause.

'Without a trial, Sam Schneider is better off. That's Carl's problem at the moment. It's bad enough having to tell your son that his mother was a serial killer; it would be worse if it featured in the news over several weeks. Oh, and yes, your dad isn't your dad.'

'Oh, poor Sam. How on earth do you react to that?'

'Interestingly. He said he's always known about his parentage, he'd known it from looking in the mirror, and anyway, Ivy had told him. After Cassie died, she told him, another sort of punishment. Sam says he knew exactly who his father was, and it was and is Carl in every way that matters, and he doesn't want another. And he doesn't think he's inherited much of his mother, because he hates the countryside and couldn't kill a fly. The irony is that he'll probably inherit a bloody farm some day. That's what's in Ernest's will, anyway.'

It was the first time he had seen her smile.

'And that's where you can help. Sam says talking to you would help. Someone who knew her. Knew the other side of her. Someone who can give the bigger picture, the other side of her. The good things, the life-enhancing things. The reliable worker, the missing bits from the picture. Will you do it?'

'Yes.'

'They're worth a lot, both of them.'

'Grace used to hum this song in the kitchen. I can remember a verse. *She stepped away from me, and she moved through the fair. And fondly I watched her move here and move there, And she made her way homeward with one star awake, As the swan in the evening moves over the lake.*'

'Called "The Bard of Avalon", wherever that is,' Donald said. 'I'd stop humming it, I would if I were you. It's like all those anonymous dirges, they end badly. *Last night I dreamt my lost love came in, So softly she entered, her feet made no din.* Life's a bitch if you don't take your chances. That kind of thing.'

'Donald, I don't know what I'd have done without you. I think you're the nicest man I've ever met, because I can tell you anything. You know what I'm really suffering from?'

'The grief of the abused?'

'Yes, and the conscience of the person who should have seen it all coming. I saw her naked, I saw what she was like. I'll always wonder if she selected me. If she cleaned my office and my desk, and found me that way. Doesn't matter. I know I'll survive, because I can't regret that year of Ivy. I'd like to undo what she did, but I don't want not to have known her. I don't want to go back and forget that. I don't want to forget all she taught me, the world she opened up. I don't want to give back the knowledge and the curiosity, and the way of looking at things. And I don't want to give up trusting people. That, above all. I want to be able to say I'll take that leap of faith, because it's worth it, even if you fail. You have to take the risk, you've got to give. But I'm jealous. She was all charisma to my lack of it. And Carl, well, Carl . . . I can just see him, cradling her in the water. He still loves her. Anyone would. Ivy won in the end, you see. Ivy and Grace, they won. They got him back.'

Donald sat back and lit the last cigarette. He was trying to consider very carefully what to say, and it really was a bit tricky. A test of skills. Ah yes, no doubt the judge had wanted to touch her, one last time. Witnessed by the swans, he had kissed her forehead and murmured he was sorry. Like

Donald had with his wife, without witnesses. Since when did loving one woman stop you loving another? Don't argue with ghosts, live with them. Think of what it was like to clear up after the war. He shook his head. He felt better for shaving off his disguise of a moustache. It made his face even more ordinary and guileless.

'I don't think that had much to do with love, you know. He was on his last legs himself, but I had the distinct impression he was trying to reassure himself that she was really dead. That's what that was about. And I couldn't get her out by myself. And he did come to see you when you were out of it, you know. And there's all these flowers. You're on his mind.'

Her smile widened into a brief laugh.

'How useful to be able to lie,' she said. 'Will I ever learn?'

'Take your chances,' he said. 'Good men are hard to find. I know one when I see one. He really wants to see you. But there's a lot going on there, aside from Sam. Same things as you. Regret, shame, feeling foolish. Failing to see what he should have seen. Worried to death about you. Also that ego thing. Not exactly looking his best when you saw him last, was he? Has to be fucking rescued by a woman, when he's stinking with whisky himself. You know what that does for a man? And at least,' he added, 'you don't get a pig in a poke – sorry I said that, but you know the history – which is more than you usually get. Better watch it, though. He knows fuck-all about women, always the same when the mothers die young. At least my wife stayed the course. And he's seen you in the raw.'

It was not in the best possible taste. He sighed as he left her. That was what being a friend was about. He could have been in with a chance himself. We men, he told his daughter, we're just calculating animals. You want to watch out for us. We need looking after a helluva lot more than you.

They met in St James's Park. The end of summer, recovery time, everything beginning to go back into the ground and change colour. The calm lake mirroring luxurious browns and yellows and greens, the view different and better for the shrinking foliage. Nature tamed beyond danger into harmony, and an early autumn sun, placid, beyond burning the skin. People getting on with it. Everything around them was taking the risk of dying, in order to come back and live again. Ivy had loved beauty as well as ugliness. God rot you and God save you, Ivy. May you not be in hell.

She might never be the first in anyone's life. Second or third would do.

His quiet footsteps came to the bench beside her. He took her cold hand and kissed it.

'I would like it very much,' Carl said, 'if you would teach me how to swim.'

Douglas Petty is a man who enjoys his reputation for too much wine and too many women. Inheriting his father's eccentric estate and dog sanctuary quietened him a little, and marriage to Amy a little more. Even so, it seemed out of character for him a sue a tabloid newspaper for libel when it printed a scurrilous story about him.

His lawyers told him he had a good chance of winning the case, mainly because Amy's testimony would clearly refute the story. But then Amy is involved in a horrendous train crash and while the authorities assume she died in the resulting fire, there is no body to prove it.

In a story of mesmerising suspense, Amy slowly reveals why she cannot return to her beloved home, and why she can never escape from the lies she was told as a child.

*

'A moving tale; wonderfully written and
full of original moments'
The Times

Beautiful, volatile Jessica has long since burned her boats in the village by the sea where she was born. She longs to return, but first she needs to secure the love of the powerful man who has spurned her obsessive adoration.

Sarah Fortune, her older, cynical friend, is keen to distance herself from her usual haunts and welcomes the chance to leave London in the hope that she might she be able to effect a reconciliation between Jessica and her mother. Pennyvale both charms and distracts her with hints of scandal and buried secrets, but it soon begins to disquiet her as cracks of distrust and jealousy show in the polite façades. Sarah is excited when Jessica tells her she is coming home, but she never arrives.

Sarah's instinctive knowledge of Jessica leads her back to the capital, fearful of what she will find. What she discovers reveals a truth more chilling than she could have imagined, but she has to return to Pennyvale to fully understand how Jessica was finally brought home, and why . . .

*

'Her knowledge of the workings of the human mind – or more correctly the soul – is second to none' Ian Rankin